Rafe was still under the ... glowing, glittering sto... since the war he inched a tiny step out of ... darkness and into a world where there was beauty instead of ugliness.

Tiffany, in white lace and white diamonds, appeared at his side. 'Well?' she asked, nodding at the jewels.

He took hold of her hand and held it tightly. 'Congratulations!' he said simply.

His approval, evident in the pressure of his fingers and the sincerity in his voice and eyes, meant more to Tiffany than all the effusions of praise which had been heaped upon her. 'I love them, you know, and not because of their value.'

Also by Carolyn Terry in Sphere Books:

KING OF DIAMONDS

The Fortune Seekers
CAROLYN TERRY

SPHERE BOOKS LIMITED

First published in Great Britain by
Century Publishing Co. Ltd. 1985
Copyright © Carolyn Terry 1985
Published by Sphere Books Ltd 1987
27 Wrights Lane, London W8 5TZ

Set in 10/12 pt Cheltenham

Printed and bound in Great Britain by
Cox & Wyman Ltd, Reading

To the memory of my parents,
Kenneth and Nell Tomlinson

Part One

AMERICA AND ENGLAND
1904–1905

The diamonds lay on the desolate desert shore, shrouded in sand the colour of Miranda's hair and washed by waves as blue as her eyes. They glinted in the fierce sun which burned white-hot like man's lust for the gems, lying beside the bleached skeletons of shipwrecked sailors but with no living thing for company. So the diamonds waited for the day of their discovery: for the feet which would walk along the shore, for the hands which would lift them from their resting place – and for the evil which would surely follow. Because the diamonds were like Tiffany – clear and clean, brilliant and beautiful, with a fire in the heart which dazzled the eyes of men but with a hardness and fascination which could lure those men to their own destruction . . .

CHAPTER ONE

The only sound was the soft swish of antique lace on the thick carpet as the girl moved gracefully to the mirror. She surveyed her reflection with a faintly bored expression, head tilted slightly to one side, but then the corners of her mouth curved up into a smile. At seventeen Tiffany Court would have preferred to be a boy, but if she had to be a girl there was considerable satisfaction in being one of the richest – and certainly the most beautiful – in America.

She glowed like a jewel against the stark white furnishings of the bedroom, her dark hair and gleaming skin in radiant contrast to the white mahogany furniture inlaid with mother-of-pearl. Having been born with a natural talent for making a grand entrance, she was keeping her guests waiting and could visualise exactly the scene below on the terrace of the Newport 'cottage' – the girls muttering spiteful remarks under their breath, the men pacing nervously as they watched for her arrival and watched

3

each other too, wondering who would receive the greatest favour from her today.

The bored expression returned to the lovely face. Tiffany knew she was beautiful in the white lace dress, but what was the point of looking so charming when there was no one downstairs whom she wanted to impress?

Her father had made his fortune on the diamond fields of Kimberley and in the gold mines of Johannesburg, but Tiffany was his greatest treasure. Before her birth, John Court's riches had been barren and useless to him, for he was a man of simple tastes, but now he was glad of every cent of his millions because they could buy his daughter all she could desire. However, fearing that he might be considered *nouveau riche*, he had drawn up a two-part plan to entrench himself in New York society and from the start had geared his entire lifestyle and his every endeavour to providing Tiffany with all the accomplishments and accoutrements necessary for a leading position in the most snobbish society in the world. He sought admission to the 'Four Hundred': the 'Four Hundred' who *were* society and who received the most coveted invitation in America – to Mrs Astor's Ball.

To Court's surprise success came quickly. The first stage of his plan was the establishment of Court Diamonds on Wall Street, although his shareholdings in the international Diamond Company and the gold mines still constituted his major source of income. Prestigious invitations showered on him for two reasons: first, diamonds were not *trade* and second, Court was rich, attractive and unmarried and therefore obviously in need of a wife. The great day arrived: Mrs Astor invited him to her Ball.

As his carriage drew up outside the Astor mansion, which was ablaze with lights, Court was uncomfortably aware that if he made a gaffe tonight it would be a setback from which he – and consequently Tiffany – might never recover. Worse still, if anyone should discover the truth about Tiffany's birth . . . if anyone should find out that he had lied about the death of a wife in childbirth in the

African wild ... With pounding heart Court walked through the hall to where Mrs Astor was receiving her guests. She was distant and dignified, but she smiled and it was with a ridiculous sense of relief that he entered the long art gallery which also served as a ballroom. He paused for a moment to survey the scene, but he did not see particular individuals, not even the matchmakers trying to enmesh him and his fortune. No, Court saw the 'Four Hundred', gathered together in their diamonds and their exclusivity, and in his mind's eye he pictured this same scene when Tiffany made her debut, dominating this magnificent stage with her beauty and his wealth.

Now, in the summer of 1904, that stage was set but John Court had overlooked one vital point – the wishes of Tiffany herself, who was participating in the social round of the American upper class only because there was no alternative. The emptiness and futility of this existence appalled her. The sole aim of the other girls was to catch a husband and then spend that husband's money as quickly, extravagantly and flamboyantly as possible. Tiffany wanted more out of life than that, which was why she wished she were a man. Chafing against the restraints and rebelling against the rules imposed on her, she envied the freedom which the men enjoyed. They could escape the constraints of society by working in their offices, meeting in their clubs, sailing yachts, gambling or drinking. However, if Tiffany could not change her sex, she believed she could change the rules. Her father was malleable and could be cajoled into giving her anything she wanted, but unfortunately Cousin Randolph was proving more difficult to handle.

Tiffany frowned and tapped her foot in the flat-heeled slippers she wore because she was so tall. Cousin Randolph ... How she detested him! Since he had taken up residence at the Court mansion in Fifth Avenue, New York, he was constantly reproving her, chastising her, correcting her – *judging* her. It was Randolph, she reflected bitterly, who was responsible for the presence of his interfering

5

mother and dull sister at Newport this summer. When her governess departed, Randolph had insisted that Tiffany should be chaperoned – 'supervised' was actually the word he had used – and so she had to endure the strictures of Aunt Sarah and the platitudes of Cousin Pauline.

Slowly she settled a wide-brimmed picture hat on her smooth shining blue-black hair from which the childish curl had disappeared many years ago. The estrangement between Tiffany and her own sex stemmed partly from jealousy of her effect on men, but also from the fact that she was not and never would be a woman's woman. Tiffany did not sit down comfortably to gossip, to talk of clothes, parties and the all-important quest for a husband. Indeed she was inclined to treat these vital concerns with contempt – nearly as much contempt as she bestowed on the men themselves. The way the young men fawned upon her, adored her so openly and allowed her the upper hand, only lowered them in Tiffany's estimation. Not one posed a challenge and none was any different from the others. They are all the same, Tiffany said to herself as she pulled on her elegant white gloves – identical in looks, conversation, education, background and prospects. Even the houses they live in are all the same . . . She paused and frowned again. Who had said that? She groped for the elusive memory and a long-forgotten conversation came floating across the years.

'Everyone I know lives in a house like this. They are all the same really.'

'The houses or the people?' Tiffany had asked.

'Both,' replied her faceless companion.

Who was he? Ah yes, she remembered now. The mists cleared, revealing the lake and the swans at that house in England where Papa had visited a grave, and beside her was a boy with shining silver-fair hair and unhappiness in his eyes. But Tiffany could not remember his name.

Now she was ready for the picnic, or the *fête champêtre* as it was called among the élite, only her parasol being needed to complete the picture. Tiffany twirled it saucily and struck a coquettish pose in front of the looking-glass. She never deliberately tried to attract all the men or spoil the chances of the other girls; it happened, effortlessly, as most things did for her. She was more likely to command than to beguile, was acidic rather than sweet and impatient of subterfuge or enticement. Secure, confident and self-assured, Tiffany Court demanded the attention of everyone; love was given to her freely, unearned, yet was an emotion which she rarely considered and certainly never reciprocated.

But perhaps the adoration she received was not completely undeserved, for to look upon her was recompense enough. She was tall – five feet ten inches in her stockinged feet – small-boned and slender, and although her body was graceful she moved with purpose and vitality in her step. Her neck and limbs were long and delicate, her waist and hips narrow, her breasts firm, high and rounded. Unbelievably, however, the eyes of the onlooker did not linger on this exquisite form but returned, hungrily, to her face – hungrily because there was a quality in colour and texture which raised in a man's mind images of edible delights. Indoors, in winter, her skin was magnolia-pale, but outside in the summer its whiteness was the richness of clotted cream; her lips were cherry-red, her hair the blue-black of berries or sloes so that every man longed to devour her with lips and tongue. The delicate heart-shaped face was dominated by enormous violet eyes, fringed with long, silky lashes; they were bold eyes, alert with intelligence, their gaze frank and without finesse.

Tiffany Court would have looked ravishing in rags; dressed in the finest fabrics and jewels the world could provide, the effect was so stunning that she reduced even the sophisticates of New York to speechless wide-eyed wonder. Now, with another twirl of her parasol, she left the room and descended the stairs to meet her guests.

'You are in a jolly good mood today, Tiffany.' She had chosen him to walk beside her through the gardens and

Frank Whitney felt as if he was floating; there was an expression of pure bliss on his honest face.

'Am I not always in a good mood?'

'No, *and* you don't always choose to walk to a picnic instead of riding in a carriage with the others!'

'The exercise will sharpen my appetite.' Her eyes danced, full of mischief and anticipation.

'You,' Frank accused, 'are up to something.'

She did not reply but merely batted her long eyelashes and smiled innocently.

Several young people had opted to walk with them, but the majority of the guests had driven to the picnic place. As the pedestrians approached they could hear a babble of feminine voices, dominated by the shrill tones of Aunt Sarah. The reason for the excitement soon became obvious; instead of tables elegantly laid with linen and silver, the glade was bare of furnishings and the only sign of activity was a pair of chefs basting lamb and sucking-pigs on spits over a pit of glowing charcoal. One of the chefs was bearing the brunt of Aunt Sarah's displeasure.

'There is no need to berate the servants, Aunt,' said Tiffany calmly. 'They are only doing what I told them to do.'

'Tiffany! Where is the food which I ordered? And where are the tables and chairs?'

'I thought it would be fun to have a proper picnic for a change. Most *fêtes champêtres* are exactly the same as ordinary meals, except that the food is eaten out of doors.' Tiffany beamed innocently. 'I intended it as a nice surprise.'

Sarah Court swallowed, forcing herself to overlook the inescapable fact that Tiffany had countermanded her instructions to the servants. 'Most kind of you, dear, but you cannot expect ladies of our age,' and she indicated herself and several other matrons, 'to sit on the ground.'

'Oh dear,' said Tiffany sweetly, 'but I purposely did not invite anyone who was *really* old or infirm.'

There was a noticeable stir among the ladies, several of

whom began to look more kindly and confidently at the ground, while one matron went so far as to demonstrate her youth and agility by sinking to the grass in a flurry of skirts and petticoats. Tiffany hid a smile.

'We will spoil our dresses,' wailed Cousin Pauline, gazing anxiously at the pink muslin which adorned her plump person.

'That can hardly matter in your case,' muttered Tiffany, 'I cannot imagine that you would want to wear *that* dress again anyway.'

'Plates,' said Aunt Sarah dramatically, 'and knives and forks! Or do you expect us to tear at the roast meat with our fingers?'

'Of course not.' Tiffany picked up her skirts and ran towards the dense wood on the far side of the clearing, where she stopped and clapped her hands. Immediately a footman emerged, carrying a large hamper. Tiffany opened it and began handing round a pile of plates – very old, very chipped, very cracked plates. The ladies received them uncertainly, with hesitant but brave smiles, and the sight of this was too much for Tiffany. There was a loud crash as she deliberately dropped the stack of plates and then began to laugh. Their faces! Frozen into masks of politeness and unease, proving that – rich and influential though these women were – they dared not flout *her* wishes. Tiffany did not possess the fortune of an Astor or a Vanderbilt, but her beauty made up the deficit – not even the most formidable dowager challengd her, because to upset Tiffany Court might jeopardise the chances for a favourite son, grandson or nephew to win America's greatest matrimonial prize.

Suddenly bored with the game, she clapped her hands again and this time an army of footmen emerged from the trees, carrying trestle tables ready-laid with shining silver cutlery and plate, sparkling glass and glowing bowls of roses. They brought platters of lobster salad, salmon in claret jelly and cold chicken, together with bottles of fine wine and bowls of fruit. And the servants brought chairs

9

which were greeted with vast relief by both young and middle-aged, who all declared themselves exhausted by the fifteen-minute wait. It was only when the girls were seated that they realised every chair was occupied and all the men still stood – as did Tiffany. They watched furiously as the footmen arranged piles of brightly-coloured cushions in the sunshine on a slope which provided a superb view over the promontory to the sea below. Tiffany subsided gracefully on to the cushions, surrounded by a circle of young men including a contingent from the nearby Naval College. Two or three girls decided that she should not be allowed sole possession of the field and ventured to join her; however, it proved impossible to eat luncheon while holding a parasol in one hand and they retreated in defeat to the shaded table. Tiffany, screened from the sun by the enormous cartwheel of her hat, smiled secretly.

No one watched Tiffany with greater resentment than her cousin Pauline. She was the same age as Tiffany but short and very overweight; folds of fat caused her brown eyes to appear small and dull, while her dark hair was lank and her complexion sallow. She had come to Newport from Boston with such hopes and happiness, but the moment she saw Tiffany those dreams withered and died. How could one possibly compete with *that*! Who would notice Pauline Court when Tiffany Court was present? And then Pauline had fallen in love with Frank Whitney and her misery was complete.

'Tiffany is *fast*,' she hissed, eyes fixed plaintively on Frank's handsome face.

Mrs Whitney smiled, casting a proud glance at her son's place of honour at Tiffany's side. 'You must remember that Tiffany has never known a mother,' she said soothingly. 'Mr Court does his best, but nothing can replace the guidance and influence of a mother. Also, Tiffany was educated at home instead of going to school. All these factors contribute to her ... somewhat unconventional behaviour.'

The girls glowered, aware that the mothers of sons took a more benign view of Tiffany than did the mothers of daughters. Aunt Sarah was sitting next to Mrs Whitney, with whom she had struck up a friendship. The Boston Courts were respectable but not in the same league as the 'Four Hundred' and Aunt Sarah felt more comfortable with Mrs Whitney who, although she bore a famous name, was accepted in society only on account of those prominent relations. A widow, Sarah was devoted to her son Randolph, treating Pauline not as a person but as a daughter whose only destiny was to be a companion for her own old age. She watched Tiffany with pride, secure in her certainty that John Court had selected Randolph for his son-in-law.

'Tiffany is a high-spirited girl,' Sarah said, 'but she will settle down when she is married – and I am quite sure she will marry very soon.' A smug expression settled on her homely features as she contemplated the triumph of her son's match.

'The sooner Tiffany marries, the better,' muttered Pauline vindictively, voicing the opinion of everyone present, 'and her wedding will be the best attended and most popular event of the season!' As long as she does not marry Frank, she thought unhappily. On the other hand, she did not wish Tiffany to marry Randolph either. If that match were to take place, Pauline foresaw a liftetime of moving in Tiffany's shadow.

'Be quiet,' her mother whispered furiously. 'You ought to be grateful to Tiffany for all the advantages she has brought you. Why, Uncle John even paid for that dress you are wearing.'

Still smarting from Tiffany's caustic comment on the frock, Pauline stayed silent.

'Tiffany has yet to make her debut,' sniffed another girl, 'although one would hardly know it from the way she tries to lead society! Why, she has not travelled abroad. *I* bought this dress in Paris from . . .' She was interrupted by a burst of laughter from the bower of cushions and Tiffany chose that moment to saunter towards the table.

'All Tiffany's dresses come from Paris,' said Aunt Sarah loyally. 'The fashion houses make everything to measure for her. However, I feel certain she will travel to Europe next year – on her honeymoon.'

'*Honeymoon!*' The derision in Tiffany's voice made them all start. 'Honeymoons follow weddings, Aunt Sarah, and I will not marry yet!' She ran to a slight rise in the ground, spreading her arms wide to embrace the magnificent vista of the wide blue Atlantic, and her voice rang out clearly. 'There is a whole world out there – a world full of people and places and experiences, waiting for me. And I want to see it and savour it *before* I am married, not afterwards. In fact,' and she tossed her head defiantly, 'I may not marry at all.'

Her face was transfigured. The idea had come to her suddenly, catching her unawares, but now she knew that of course this was the solution to her frustration and boredom. All those new and different experiences waiting for her – and perhaps she would meet a man who was different, too. The men of Newport watched her desolately, sensing her slipping away from them. Then, abruptly, she returned to the present.

'Look!' she said, pointing out to sea. 'I haven't seen that yacht before.'

Seizing the excuse to hurry to her side, her admirers strained their eyes out to sea. The boat was a two-masted schooner, cleaving through the water in a fresh breeze, and it was agreed that she was a newcomer to these waters.

'It is only a very small boat and extremely shabby,' said Tiffany disparagingly, accustomed to the size and luxury of the Astors' *Nourmahal* and J.P. Morgan's *Corsair*.

'She is flying the British flag,' observed a keen-sighted officer from the Naval College.

'Ah, that explains it,' cried Tiffany gleefully. 'The boat is bringing another poverty-stricken English nobleman to seek a rich bride. Well, girls, will he find one or no?'

The girls laughed, but one young lady was heard to observe, 'I wish to God Tiffany would marry an Englishman and then she would be London's problem instead of ours!'

'Far too many American heiresses are marrying into the European aristocracy,' said Aunt Sarah sharply, hoping to appeal to Tiffany's patriotism. 'Such matches drain away our best blood *and* our valuable financial resources. Why, the dowries these girls have taken with them must total more than thirty million dollars. When Consuelo Vanderbilt married the Duke of Marlborough, she took two-and-a-half million dollars; the Duchess of Roxburghe took another two million, Lady Curzon a million – and there was a whole bevy of Countesses. Good American girls should stay here and not be lured away by fancy titles.'

'But, Aunt Sarah,' protested Tiffany wickedly, '*I* am not a "good American" – my mother was English and of noble family, too.' For this was what her father had told her and Tiffany's pulse raced at the prospect of travelling to Europe to try to trace her maternal relatives.

Angry with herself for forgetting this, Sarah said crossly, 'You have been brought up as an American. Anyway, the entire question is hypothetical, because probably there is no nobleman on that wretched boat.'

'No, but the subject of foreign travel is fascinating, isn't it?' Tiffany's mood had changed again and she glanced at Frank. She had shown favour to him today, so now it was time to prick the bubble of his happiness – he could not be allowed to go home under the impression that he had progressed in her affections. And Tiffany knew exactly how to bait him. 'Frank will tell us something about his African journey, won't you, Frank? You are so modest about your adventures in the South African War, yet I am sure you have such exciting stories to tell.'

The sun continued to shine but for Frank the day darkened as he absorbed the impact of Tiffany's mockery, her cruel barb striking deeper than she knew. It was nearly three years since Frank Whitney had returned from South

Africa and no one had succeeded in persuading him to talk about his experiences. His silence aroused suspicions that he must have something to conceal, particularly as he had travelled as a freelance correspondent but did not write his war stories. After an unsuccessful attempt to resume a university education, he had found himself in a dilemma from which he was rescued by John Court who offered him a job with his diamond company. Court was influenced partly by the fact that he had provided Frank with introductions to various people in South Africa and partly because he felt a rapport with the young man, knowing himself what it was to have secrets hidden in the African bush. Frank had accepted joyfully because his only ambition was to be near Tiffany. Most people had forgotten about the South African War, but not Tiffany whose instinct guided her unerringly to a man's weakest spot.

'You don't want to hear about me,' he said now with a weak attempt at a smile. 'I have told you before that wars boil down to politics in the end and are not nearly so exciting as most people think.'

'If you would tell us more about it, we could judge for ourselves,' Tiffany pointed out mercilessly. 'Come on, Frank, I bet you engineered all sorts of daring exploits which you are too modest to tell us about.'

The luminous violet eyes challenged him. Frank would dream about those eyes tonight and they would haunt his waking moments too, for they saw straight through him – Tiffany knew that he was displaying no false modesty because if he had anything to boast about he would boast to her. There was an embarrassed silence and then, having achieved her objective, she shrugged impatiently.

As the picnic party prepared to disperse, Tiffany turned and cast a lazy, casual glance out to sea. The British yacht was rounding the point, heading for harbour, and she paused for a moment to watch the boat disappear from sight before dismissing it from her mind.

CHAPTER TWO

Randolph's personality was expressed even in his walk. He held himself stiffly upright and for a tall man his step was short and precise. It was the walk of a man who took himself seriously and who rarely relaxed, the walk of a careful man, an 'indoors' man. He possessed the gift of sensing the mood of the times but he did not do so by standing in the street to sniff the air – his assessments were made from behind office windows or at his club. By no stretch of the imagination could one envisage Randolph in an open-necked shirt, jacketless, unwinding in the open air.

These characteristics were apparent as he crossed Wall Street and entered the premises of the Court Bank, one of his first decisions having been to move the diamond branch of the business to a brownstone on Lower Fifth Avenue and convert the Wall Street premises into the bank. He walked to his office and sat down behind the desk – it was a large office and an imposing desk, because Randolph believed that appearances were very important to a banker. The New York afternoon was hot and sultry, but his pale face and thin body seemed impervious to the heat; just as one could not visualise him out of doors, so it was impossible to imagine him perspiring or performing any of the other natural – but undignified – bodily functions.

The establishment of the bank had been the second stage of John Court's two-tier plan. His relatives in Boston had maintained a strong banking connection for many years and he had been quick to note the standing this bestowed on them in the community. Perhaps unconsciously trying to compensate for the circumstances surrounding Tiffany's birth, he decided that banking had the solidity and respectability he required for his daughter. However, in what he considered to be a master-stroke of strategy, Court combined this move with his plans for Tiffany's personal future. He intended to give control of the bank to the man he had chosen to be his daughter's husband – Randolph Court, her second cousin. Randolph was endowed with that air of distinction and trustworthiness which a bank, and Court, demanded and in addition was displaying a commendable shrewdness – which was a bonus, because Court believed it was not necessary to be smart to run a bank; he remembered reading somewhere that the business of banking ought to be simple; if it is *hard*, it is *wrong*.

Choosing a member of his own family had other advantages. Court relished the idea of starting his own dynasty to rival the great families of New York, rather than allying himself with existing houses. Also, although he would never admit it, he was planning to maintain his hold and influence over Tiffany even after she was wed. No son-in-law, he reasoned, could refute the authority of his wife's father when that father had given him everything a man could desire: the hand of Tiffany Court in marriage and his own bank. Four years ago Court had summoned Randolph to luncheon in the vast gold and white dining-room of the Fifth Avenue mansion and prepared to enlighten him about the great good fortune which was to be his . . .

Randolph had sat at table, listening to John Court discoursing on the state of the American economy while he waited for his uncle to get to the point. Already he exhibited the traits which were to be the hallmarks of his illustrious career – the ability to listen patiently and to evaluate shrewdly while maintaining a perfect mask over his own conclusions.

He was in his last year at Harvard, but had been born middle-aged. Tall and spare to the point of emaciation, his face managed to be both handsome and unattractive. His features were finely chiselled, the nose patrician and the lips thin and straight, but the paper-white skin was stretched tight over the contours of the bones, its paleness accentuated by his ebony hair and the dull flat humourless pools of his dark brown eyes. There was something sinister about his icy control and withdrawn manner and something repellent about the watchful gaze of those onyx eyes and the long white fingers which toyed with the stem of his brandy glass.

'There are signs that the numbers of banks will increase – indeed it is already increasing, particularly in the farming areas. Mind you,' and Court paused significantly, 'if I were to found a bank I do not think I would base it on agricultural business.'

At last, thought Randolph. Now he knew why he was here.

'No,' he agreed expressionlessly. 'Too much reliance on any one single sector of the economy must be a mistake, but especially agriculture which is subject to such uncontrollable conditions and fluctuations. That being the case, on what type of business would you concentrate?'

'The bond markets. I believe that First National City is on the right lines. Basically it is performing the function of a stockbroker and has become America's biggest underwriter and distributor of government and corporate bonds. This has to be the correct area of operations for big-city banks at the present time.'

'There is an established trend in that direction, notably here in New York and in Chicago and San Francisco.' Randolph was feeling his way with customary caution. 'I assume you would work from a single location at the outset?'

'Yes. As you are aware, Congress allows the State Banking Authorities to license banks and this means, in effect, that a bank can operate only within one state. In 1844 the New York State Legislature dictated that a bank must operate from one location. This "unit rule" no longer applies here, although it has been adopted by other states, but I intend to abide by it for a while.'

'The English economist, Walter Bagehot, was in favour of confining the activities of banks. He wrote: "A banker who lives in the district, who has always lived there, whose whole mind is a history of the district and its changes, is easily able to lend money safely there." There lies the crux of the matter – a good banker makes good loans and the only definition of a good loan is one which is repaid.' Randolph smiled thinly. 'Uncle John, undoubtedly you have the means to found a bank. It is surprising, after all, how little capital such a venture requires – certainly far less than most people imagine. However, running a bank is a very different proposition from mining diamonds. With the greatest respect, you may have the money but do you have the temperament or the expertise?'

'No,' said Court, 'but *you* have.'

There was a small pause, like a soft sigh, as the die was cast.

'Yes,' agreed Randolph, 'and I shall be delighted to join you in the enterprise.'

Court felt a stab of irritation at his kinsman's calm acceptance of such a golden future. There were times when he sensed a lack of affinity and compatibility with the young man, but he did not diverge from his chosen course. A banker needed to be trusted and respected, not to be liked.

'Arrangements are already under way,' said Court, rising to his feet, 'as I wish to be ready by the time you graduate. You will say good-bye to Tiffany before you leave, of course.'

Without waiting for a reply, he led Randolph through a maze of marble corridors to the music room where faltering notes on a piano indicated a lesson was in progress. At their entry Tiffany ceased playing and stood up, greeting them with an unsmiling hauteur which more befitted a queen facing her courtiers than a thirteen-year-old girl welcoming her father and cousin.

'The music sounded lovely, darling,' beamed Court fondly.

Randolph winced. He had a good ear for music, upon

which Tiffany's attempts at Chopin had grated unbearably.

'Are you fond of music, Tiffany?' he asked.

'I hate it.' *And I hate you*, her eyes spat. Tiffany sensed the absence of warmth and spontaneity in her cousin Randolph. He seemed to stand back and look at her from afar; he judged and Tiffany did not like to be judged. She turned to her father. 'And if you think the music sounded "lovely", you are mad,' she said in a tone which her critics would have described as insolent but Court imagined to be candid. 'It was terrible and it is all his fault.' She pointed to the music master, who had withdrawn tactfully to the window.

'Why?' asked Court.

'He is a rotten teacher and I don't want him here any more.'

'Then we shall find you a new teacher,' said Court hastily, motioning the white-faced master outside.

Randolph had listened to the exchange dispassionately. A horrible child, he thought: spoiled, selfish and ill-mannered. Her father is besotted with her and does not see the monster he is raising in his house.

'The man may have dependants, Tiffany. Did you think of that before you had him dismissed so summarily?'

'When they leave, Papa always pays them twice as much as they would earn in a year,' she replied with an indifferent shrug. In truth she had no conception of how people lived outside her mansion and the purpose of her action was not to humiliate or hurt the music master but to illustrate to her cousin that she always got what she wanted. She enjoyed exercising her power; she liked putting her father through hoops.

'When you are older, I think you may have to learn that one has a responsibility towards one's servants,' Randolph observed.

'I don't care what you think.'

'Tiffany!' Court had re-entered the room and his sharp cry was so near correction and criticism that both Tiffany and Randolph looked at him in surprise. 'That remark was abominably rude and completely uncalled-for. Your cousin Randolph is kind to you and fond of you; he is a welcome guest in my house and furthermore we will be seeing a lot more of him in the future. Tell him that you are sorry and that you did not mean it.'

As Randolph watched the mixture of emotions on his uncle's face, he understood that to him was bequeathed the bank and Tiffany was part of the package. John Court dreamed of a dynasty and Randolph was to be its perpetuator. Randolph saw that it was possible: a financial house that could be the biggest bank in America or even the world, a dynasty which could rival the Rothschilds who had sent forth their sons to the great capitals of Europe.

His gaze returned to Tiffany. Spoiled, selfish and ill-mannered – yes, she was all those things but also she showed promise of great beauty. The luxuriant dark hair and those huge violet eyes in that sweet face would be a powerful attraction a few years from now. She was still very young and would change as she grew older; she could be made more malleable, influenced by his example and moulded into a wife suitable for a man of his position. And, reflected Randolph with cool detachment, the first step would be to remove her from the influence of her father.

Tiffany shot a rebellious glance at John Court, but his expression was adamant; this time he really was cross.

'I am sorry, cousin Randolph. I did not mean it.'

'Your apology is accepted, Tiffany,' and Randolph's thin lips stretched into a semblance of a smile.

With a sigh of relief Court moved to the door again. The instant his back was turned, Tiffany made a face at Randolph and stuck out her tongue.

Randolph paid no attention. Unhesitatingly he had accepted the unspoken offer. When Tiffany was eighteen, he would marry her.

* * *

By 1904 Randolph Court was acknowledged to be the perfect banker. He was fond of quoting Bagehot, so maybe he had been moulded by that economist's statement: 'Adventure is the life of commerce but caution, I had almost said timidity, is the life of banking.' In assessing requests for loans Randolph followed the policy of his other idol, John Pierpont Morgan, who based his assessments on a borrower's character. To 'caution' and 'character', Randolph added two more 'Cs' in his judgments of borrowers – capital and capacity. So far, that judgment had been sound.

He had succeeded in building up a well-constituted portfolio of investments to balance the various loans made, some short-term for cash flow and some long-term to earn interest. He had manoeuvred the Court Bank into gaining control of companies in difficulties, had reorganised those companies, reissued their stock and placed himself on the board of directors. Although he was still a very young man, his talent had been recognised and J.P. Morgan himself included the Court Bank in the agreements which controlled the business and political worlds of America. Randolph had made it to the inside track.

He had come on to the scene too late for the massive 'killings' of the 1890s, but could sense the buoyant mood of America as the nation exulted in its growth, wealth and strength at the turn of the century. The national economy was reviving after a long depression; prices were rising and an influx of capital and gold acted as a stimulus to industrial expansion. However, it was the rapid growth of America's cities which particularly interested Randolph. The population of New York, for example, had mushroomed from two million in 1880 to nearly three-and-a-half million in 1900 and he realised that this growth necessitated the provision of an entire infrastructure – everything from transport, water, gas and electricity to the building of sewage systems, docks and roads. When the contracts and franchises for these works were granted, Randolph ensured that the Court Bank was in the forefront of the financiers.

In addition he recognised that the age of consolidation had arrived and was here to stay. Mergers were creating huge corporations which dominated certain industries such as steel, iron, railroads, milling, tobacco, petroleum and electricals, and these combinations were entrenching the position of the men who master-minded them. The richest two per cent of America's population possessed sixty per cent of the nation's wealth – and that two per cent included the Courts. Randolph wanted the wealth, but even more than that he desired the power and influence it bestowed. Banking was the perfect vehicle for his ambition, because by his loans a banker determines who succeeds and who fails.

To Randolph, John Court's dream of a dynasty was natural to the banking sphere: 'The calling is hereditary, the credit of the bank descends from father to son ...' Bagehot again. Most of the top American banks were dominated by the aura of one 'founding father' and it pleased Randolph to think that his influence would stretch into the future, passed from generation to generation.

But the dynasty was dependent on Tiffany and she was the one factor which was not going according to plan.

Sitting at his desk, Randolph paused in his work and frowned, annoyed that thoughts of Tiffany should intrude. Her beauty had fulfilled its promise but she was still wilful, selfish and spoiled. She needed controlling, she needed a firm hand ... Randolph's own hands clenched and a muscle twitched in his cheek as he pictured the physical and mental subjugation of Tiffany. Sometimes when she looked at him with loathing in those lovely eyes, or when she spoke to him so rudely, he was consumed by the desire to hit and whip her into submission. Only a few weeks ago, before her departure for Newport, there had been a case in point.

It had been a Sunday morning, lazy, sunny and hot, but Randolph was no observer of the Sabbath. He had risen early and gone straight to his study in the Court mansion, breaking off from work only to receive two clients who

22

were leaving New York that same day and who had brought documents for his signature. The importance of the transaction was such that Randolph had demeaned himself so far as to personally escort the two men to the front door. After closing the door behind them, he had turned to see Tiffany descending the staircase. And Randolph went rigid – cold with anger but hot with desire.

She was wearing a silk nightgown the colour of pale champagne, and over it had thrown a negligée of the same material but left this unfastened so that it billowed behind her as she walked. The thin material rippled over her flanks and long slim legs, and clung to the shape of full, nearly naked, breasts so that the hallway gleamed with shimmering silk and pearly translucent flesh. She glared at Randolph but did not deign to speak to him, sweeping past to the morning-room where she poured a cup of coffee and yawned sleepily.

Randolph forced his stiff limbs after her and she glanced at him disdainfully as he entered the room.

'You look as though you have been up since dawn,' she remarked scornfully. 'What an eager little beaver you are! Still, I suppose in your position you have to impress Papa with your diligence.'

She treated him like an employee instead of . . . but that factor was not uppermost in Randolph's mind now.

'How dare you come downstairs dressed – or rather *undressed* – in that fashion!'

'*Dare?* I *dare* because this is my house and I will do precisely what I like in it!'

'Tiffany, I have just escorted to the door two male customers of the bank. If you had descended those stairs five seconds earlier, they would have seen you!'

'Am I not worth seeing?'

Randolph moistened his lips, his gaze riveted to that beautiful body. Did she have any perception of her allure or the provocation of her remarks? He knew that John Court had ensured she was kept in ignorance of the facts of life, so perhaps this taunting, tantalising manner was natural to her.

'That is not the point,' he managed to say at last.

'As Papa has frequently come down to breakfast in his dressing-gown, I gather that the point is that there is one rule for boys and another for girls – as usual! Anyway, what's the fuss – no man has seen me.'

'I have seen you.'

'Oh, *you*! You don't count.'

The rage and desire within him were enmeshed, intertwined, indivisible, rising in a red tide of violence . . . Not count? By God, but he would show her . . . He fought to maintain outward control.

'In that assumption you are mistaken, my dear,' he said in an even tone. 'Very mistaken.'

'I repeat that this is my home and I will act in it as I please. If the situation is not to your liking, you can always live elsewhere. In fact nothing would please me more than your permanent departure.'

She had slammed out of the room, leaving him prey to emotions which revolted him; at that moment he hated her for the passions she unleashed and was filled with self-disgust for wanting her. Tiffany disturbed his concentration – but not for much longer. Soon he would speak to her about their marriage and then her wings would be clipped! Her attitude towards him was no barrier to his plans, because Tiffany spoke sharply to every man; besides, if she could not be persuaded, Randolph would find a way of forcing her to submit . . .

'Pardon me, Mr Court, but a Mr Ellenberger wishes to see you.'

Randolph was jerked abruptly back into the present and looked at the clerk irritably, angry at being caught daydreaming. 'Ellenberger? I have never heard of the man. Does he have an appointment?'

'No, sir, but he says it is most important that he speaks to you,'

Randolph looked at the card which the clerk handed to him: Anton Ellenberger of Bright Diamonds, Hatton Garden, London.

'Did you inform Mr Ellenberger that I am not involved in Court Diamonds?'

'He is aware of that, sir, but still insists it is you he wishes to see.'

'Very well. I can give him ten minutes before Mr John Court arrives for our usual meeting.'

Everything about Anton Ellenberger was immaculate – the cut of his suit, the trim of his brown hair and moustache, and his manners – but nothing was remarkable. He was of medium height, his hair was medium brown and his face was pleasant without being handsome. At the first sight of him, Randolph's irritation returned. Why, the man was nothing more than a clerk!

'I really do not see how I can help you, Mr Ellenberger. My uncle, John Court, controls our diamond company while I run the bank.'

'I am aware of that, Mr Court. However, I am not here to transact diamond business. I am here to mend fences and build bridges, metaphorically speaking.' His speech was as precise as his appearance, with a trace of a German accent. 'I refer, of course, to the enmity between my employer and your uncle.'

Randolph had not the remotest idea what the man was talking about, but his interest was well and truly aroused. 'Did Mr Bright tell you about this enmity?' he asked cautiously.

'Sir Matthew,' corrected Ellenberger gently, 'is not a man who confides in anyone. No, it is what he does *not* say, the way he avoids the subject of John Court or reacts angrily when the name is mentioned, which reveals the truth of the situation. Also, although Sir Matthew and Mr Court were partners in Kimberley and both are still closely connected with the Diamond Company, I understand that all their dealings are conducted through third parties.'

Randolph had often thought it strange that his uncle took so little direct interest in the Diamond Company, but had attributed it to a reluctance to travel abroad. Perhaps the real reason was that he did not wish to see Matthew

Bright. 'All this is very enlightening, Mr Ellenberger, but I fail to understand how it affects you or me.'

'As I told you, I am building bridges. One day *you* will control Court Diamonds and then the . . .'

They were interrupted by a knock on the door.

'You can do your fence-mending at the same time,' said Randolph, rising to his feet. 'My uncle always comes to the bank at this hour to sign papers and authorise transactions in his capacity as President.'

'What a happy coincidence,' said Anton smoothly.

As he introduced John Court to the visitor, Randolph's brain clicked into another gear. Like hell it was a coincidence! He was suddenly, absolutely, sure that Ellenberger knew the Court family's routine – had taken the trouble to find it out. He had come to Randolph first because that was where the future lay – and also he might have wished Randolph to perceive his tactics. Watching his uncle's reaction to the name of Bright Diamonds, Randolph saw a third reason – Ellenberger wanted to meet John Court and most assuredly would not have been granted admittance to Court Diamonds. And the more Randolph contemplated the strategy, the more Anton Ellenberger grew in stature and importance.

'How is Sir Matthew?' inquired Court stiffly.

'Extremely well,' replied Anton easily. 'Naturally he is very busy – the death of Cecil Rhodes two and a half years ago left him in charge of the Diamond Company and therefore he has less time to devote to his own business.'

It was obvious that Court was agitated, but he was trying to be polite. 'Ah yes, poor Rhodes! He was still a comparatively young man. Hounded to death, I believe, by some crazy foreign princess.' It was no good; he had to ask. 'Did Matthew send you here?'

'On the contrary, he does not know I have called on you. I was merely anxious to make the acquaintance of one of the foremost diamond magnates of out time.' And Anton bowed courteously to Court.

And to discover if the feud was as intense on this side of

the Atlantic as it is in England, thought Randolph, and the answer to that was very plain. What a shrewd little man this was.

'How do you come to be working for Matthew?'

'I am German by birth, but at an early age went into the diamond business in Amsterdam. It was there that I met Sir Matthew and was fortunate enough to be invited to join his company. His former manager, Reynolds, was retiring and with the death of Lord Nicholas Grafton in the South African War, Sir Matthew needed someone to take charge of his London office.'

Court nodded and was silent for a while, his mind full of memories of Nicholas.

'Are you happy in Sir Matthew's employ?' Randolph inquired, watching Ellenberger's face carefully, certain that this man said nothing unnecessary or unimportant; every word was selected to convey an exact meaning.

Ellenberger turned and looked Randolph straight in the eye. 'Sir Matthew is the most brilliant businessman I have ever known. He possesses a remarkable flair for making advantageous deals, while retaining a sound basic knowledge of the diamond industry. I am fortunate indeed to be in a position to learn from him.' His eyes flickered slightly and he smiled.

Learn from him, but put that knowledge to work for one's own ends; Randolph understood perfectly. When Anton Ellenberger was ready he would leave Bright Diamonds and go into business for himself – and that was when the connection with Court Diamonds and the Court Bank might come in useful. Randolph nodded slowly and returned Ellenberger's smile. It was a tactic worthy of himself and Randolph had no higher praise than that.

'I taught him all I knew about diamonds,' said Court abruptly, 'but the flair is his own, polished and refined by Rhodes and Beit. And now the pupil has surpassed the masters – only Matthew could have acted so swiftly and effectively in the matter of the Premier Mine.'

In 1902 a new diamond discovery had been made near

Pretoria in the Transvaal and when mining began in 1903 the quantity and quality of the stones astonished and alarmed the diamond industry. Not only was the Premier geographically removed from the production centre of Kimberley but Thomas Cullinan, the chairman, refused to be controlled in any way by the Diamond Company which attempted to regulate production and sales throughout the world in order to stabilise prices. The two senior directors of the Diamond Company, Matthew Bright and Alfred Beit, travelled to Pretoria to see the new mine for themselves but their reaction was markedly different: Alfred Beit had a stroke; Matthew purchased an interest in the new venture on behalf of Bright Diamonds and took a seat on the Board.

'The move was masterly,' agreed Anton, 'and I can assure you that Sir Matthew intends to use his influence with Cullinan, the Transvaal government and other shareholders to maintain a sensible policy on sales.'

'I hope he succeeds,' said Court stiffly. 'Not only is Premier's production too high, but they are finding an incredible number of stones larger than 100 carats. However, if any man can solve the problem, Matthew can.' Court's mind went back twenty years and he could hear Matthew's voice saying, 'Diamonds require the most delicate manipulation; they need a hand to hold them back or loose them as the occasion asks. What I intend, John, is that it shall be my hand on the tiller.' Well, Matthew was achieving that aim, even though part of his success was due to the fact that he had simply outlived the other titans of the industry.

'Obviously you have a great respect for Sir Matthew, Mr Court. Next time you are in London, you should put your point of view to him personally.'

Randolph smiled inwardly. Ellenberger was making one final assessment of the relationship between the two men and of the support he could expect to receive from Court Diamonds in the future.

'Nothing,' said Court with quiet intensity, 'could ever make me speak to Matthew Bright again.'

John Court went home to sit in Tiffany's empty bedroom. He would be joining her in Newport within the next few days but while she was separated from him he liked to sit thus, inhaling the faint perfume of her presence which lingered here. However, tonight he had a special reason for wishing to feel close to her . . . Matthew . . .

Of all the diamond magnates, John Court's personality had undergone the most radical change. Of the calm competent geologist who had journeyed to South Africa to seek knowledge rather than wealth, only an empty husk remained, the healthy kernel of his character eroded by the dynamic versatility and ambition of Matthew Bright. But it was not only in business affairs that Court had played second fiddle to his more brilliant partner; he also developed a destructive tendency to fall in love with Matthew's women – something he regretted and despised in himself until a brief afternoon of passion with Anne at the Bright house in Kimberley had brought Tiffany.

All the stories John Court had told about his marriage were untrue. Tiffany was illegitimate; she was the daughter of Lady Anne, the first wife of Matthew Bright.

Knowing full well that Anne's pregnancy was not his doing, Matthew had refused to accept the child and Anne had left Kimberley to give birth secretly in Cape Town. Her maid, Henriette, had brought the baby to John Court and then he had taken Tiffany home to America.

He could not find it in his heart to regret what had happened. He had loved Anne deeply, even sympathising over her neglect at the hands of her handsome golden-haired husband, but above everything John Court loved his daughter who had given meaning to his life. Yet equally he lived in fear that anyone – society, family and especially Tiffany – should discover the truth. Now he glanced fearfully at the table beside her bed, but of course the picture of her 'mother' had gone – Tiffany took it with her everywhere.

As soon as she could talk, Tiffany had started asking questions about her mother and Court had invented a romantic tale to satisfy her curiosity. He told of a well-born English lady, 'almost like a princess', who had suffered much misfortune before he found her in Cape Town, penniless and alone. It was a story of which Tiffany never tired; he had to recount it over and over again and each time he experienced a pang of guilt at the deception and an overwhelming apprehension at the way it had taken root and grown in a way he had never intended. As for the picture, it bore no resemblance to Anne but merely portrayed a dark-haired young woman of unknown origin. However, Tiffany clung to it like a talisman and somehow it had come to represent all that was wrong with their relationship; it was a symbol of Court's over-indulgence of his daughter and his anxiety to please her at all costs – because she had no mother, he was determined she would want for nothing else.

'What would you like for your birthday?' he had asked when she was ten years old. It was not an idle question, because Tiffany already possessed everything money could buy. 'How about some diamonds for America's diamond princess?' he had teased.

At the word 'princess', Tiffany's eyes had flown to the miniature of her supposed mother in its plain gilt frame. 'I want diamonds for Mama – a beautiful diamond frame for her picture.'

Court flinched, but had to continue the deception for it had gone too far to be retracted. 'Very well,' he agreed. 'The frame shall be designed by the best jewellers in New York and when we collect it I will show you the lovely diamond after which you were named.'

Charles Tiffany himself welcomed them to the famous store on Union Square and personally brought her the glowing Tiffany diamond which was the largest yellow-gold diamond in the world, and which had been found by

Court and Matthew in their Kimberley mine. She handled the stone carefully, because for all her faults she respected other people's property and had an instinctive appreciation of the rare and the beautiful, but it was not the right psychological moment for her to admire the smouldering fire of the gem – everything else paled into insignificance beside her mother's picture.

A gold filigree frame had been made for the miniature into which were set exquisite white diamonds in patterns of roses, both buds and full-blown flowers, minute and delicately done. The workmanship was magnificent, but a slight reticence on the part of Mr Tiffany suggested he was not altogether convinced that the item was in good taste.

Tiffany Court cared nothing about taste. She was ten years old and had hallowed her mother's memory in the best way she could devise. And as he watched his daughter's ecstatic face, Court felt panic rising within him – God help him if she ever found out the truth about her birth!

Tonight he experienced that panic again and for the thousandth time went over the list of those who knew the secret. Anne had died ten years ago giving birth to another daughter, so that left Matthew and Henriette – and probably Henriette did not work for the Brights since Anne's death . . . Court's eyes narrowed. There was another man who might suspect the truth: the Boer, Danie Steyn, whom Court had known when Danie was a little boy at the early diamond fields in Kimberley. The had met again in Pretoria in later years and Court still shuddered at the memory.

Once Court had been in love with Danie's sister, Alida, but – as always – she loved Matthew and had died giving birth to Matthew's child. When Tiffany had asked her mother's name, 'Alida' had sprung naturally to his lips; this had given Tiffany an immediate rapport with Danie, who had taken her to his farm to see a portrait of his sister. Frantic with worry over his daughter's disappearance, Court had arrived in time to save her – but save her from what? What had been Danie's intention? All Court knew

31

was that a lovable little boy had turned into a raging fanatic with an overwhelming grudge against Matthew Bright and against the foreigners, or *uitlanders*, who were milking his country of its mineral riches. Danie blamed Matthew for his sister's death, for his father's death, for his foster-mother's death and for the loss of his foster diamond claim and although Court had vowed he would never speak to Matthew again, he had been sufficiently disturbed to pass on a warning of Danie's threats through a third party. There had been a malevolence about Danie which was frightening, and once he had attacked Anne with a knife, yet this was also the man to whom Court had introduced Frank Whitney when the aspiring journalist requested a contact who could supply the Boer point of view about the war.

Court sighed. Even if Danie suspected the identity of Tiffany's mother, it was inconceivable that she would ever meet him again. No, Matthew was the danger. Matthew was the reason why Court held aloof from one aspect of society life: he would not buy a yacht and join the European cruises in which his associates indulged. He could not risk the possibility that Tiffany and Matthew would come face to face.

Moreover, Tiffany had a half-brother and half-sister on the other side of the Atlantic: Philip and Miranda Bright, the children of Matthew and Anne. They constituted only a minor threat since it was unlikely they would be aware of the relationship, but when Court thought about them he was assailed by a sense of danger which he could neither understand nor identify.

He could not see that the peril came from within himself, that he was its architect and builder because he over-indulged his daughter. Tiffany's old nanny was the only one to foresee disaster. She had deprecated strongly the constant capitulation to her charge's whims. 'Miss Tiffany will learn the hard way,' the nanny had said to herself, 'because one day there will be something she wants that she simply cannot have.'

CHAPTER THREE

'But Frank,' said Tiffany in that tone of voice he dreaded hearing, 'I *want* to go!'

'It is out of the question,' he replied with as much conviction as he could muster. Oh God, why did it have to be Tiffany who had overheard the muttered conversation? None of the other girls would have dreamed of making such an outrageous suggestion. 'I keep telling you that girls are not invited.'

Tiffany's eyes gleamed. A party on a yacht to which girls were not invited – it was irresistible. 'I can dress up as a man. You can lend me a suit – you are much the same height as me.'

A vision of Helena rose in Frank's mind – Helena, Danie Steyn's sister-in-law, who had worn men's clothes while riding with Steyn's Commando during the Boer War and who had carried off the disguise perfectly – but then he looked at the provocative swell of Tiffany's bosom and shook his head. 'Don't be ridiculous! You would be unmasked in ten seconds flat.'

'I could just look through the door or the windows for a few moments. I wouldn't speak to anyone.'

'No!'

Much against her will she was forced to wheedle. 'Please, Frank,' she pleaded, laying a coaxing hand on his arm. 'Papa and Randolph are coming on Saturday and you are going back to New York. This is our last chance to have fun together.'

'No.' Frank was feeling desperate. 'Surely you realise what your father would do to me if he found out?'

Tiffany withdrew her hand. 'If you don't take me,' she

said icily, 'I will never speak to you again.'

He stared at her aghast, aware that she was quite capable of carrying out this threat. Losing his job was preferable to such a fate.

'Very well,' he said at last, 'but only to let you look for one minute and then I'm taking you straight home again.'

She laughed triumphantly. Achieving her aims with Frank, as with Papa, always followed the same pattern: she pushed them to an apparent compromise and argued about her ultimate objective later. She had every intention of staying at the party for as long as she liked.

'I do hope you will not be missed,' Frank said nervously at the harbour.

'There is no reason why anyone should come to my room at this time of night.' Tiffany did not really care if her escapade was discovered, having no conception of what the consequences would be for Frank.

In the darkness he could not discern whether or not her disguise was convincing. She was wearing one of his dark suits, a white shirt and dark tie, and her hair was hidden under a straw boater. She walked awkwardly because the shoes were heavy and too large, causing Frank to grin involuntarily at her comical splay-footed gait. However, his amusement died a quick death when he saw the yacht, ablaze with lights, lying at anchor in the bay. He was sure that the ship was anchored far off-shore in order to prevent any observation of the noise and excesses of the entertainment. He had told Tiffany that girls were not invited, but the fact was that *respectable* girls were not invited. The yacht had sailed from New York with a party of America's male aristocrats on board, the intention being that the men should enjoy themselves thoroughly before conforming to the decorum required for a stay in Newport with their families.

To Frank's relief, the boatman took no notice of Tiffany as she boarded the launch and when they reached the yacht the girl negotiated the ladder with ease and agility.

But once they stood on the massive brightly lit deck the danger of discovery returned. Frank pulled Tiffany into the shadows and, walking swiftly and softly, preceded her along the deck until he reached the windows of the main saloon.

'One minute,' he ordered, ' and then I am taking you back. We will tell the boatman you are feeling unwell.'

Tiffany was not listening. Her eyes, wide as saucers, were fixed on the festivities within. She had never seen anything like it before but even at this remove, through a pane of glass, she could sense the atmosphere – the freedom, the camaraderie, the delicious wickedness of it all.

The saloon itself was not unusual, although this boat had been remodelled recently so that the decoration was particularly fine and electricity had been installed. The men were familiar, too – Tiffany recognised several of them – but they were wearing evening dress and were bareheaded so she realised with a pang that she would not be able to go in because her hat would be conspicuous. No, it was the expressions on the men's faces which lay outside Tiffany's experience – their relaxed, confident smiles, the chaffing, the joking and the laughter. And the girls . . . beautiful girls in daring low-cut dresses who were smoking, drinking and pressing themselves against the bodies of their escorts. Card games were in progress and at a table in the centre of the saloon, a roulette wheel was spinning.

Hungrily Tiffany feasted her eyes on the scene, absorbing every detail through the pores of her parched skin, reacting to it with the whole of heart, mind and body. In there was where she belonged, not at stuffy receptions or learning to play bridge! The people in that saloon were living, really *living* – but she was not invited because she was a girl. She knew that those women were not ladies, but as she watched their uninhibited behaviour Tiffany did not blame the men one bit for preferring their company to the stiffness and artificiality of society. Frustration surged within her until she felt she would explode with the restless energy which sought an outlet.

Frank was tugging at her elbow.

'No, not yet,' she said. 'A few more minutes, *please*!'

And then she saw Randolph.

At first she thought she was mistaken. He was due in Newport the next day, supposedly travelling with her father, and surely such a gathering as this was not his milieu. Yet it was Randolph. He was with another man and two girls and his companion slipped a hand inside one girl's dress to caress her breast. Fascinated, indeed hypnotised, Tiffany watched Randolph stretch out an elegant white hand and place it on the second girl's arm, his head inclined towards her. He is going to kiss her, Tiffany thought and felt strangely excited and confused. Randolph jerked the girl roughly towards him and Tiffany flinched when the girl flinched because Randolph did not kiss her – he bit the girl's neck, so hard that his teeth left an angry red mark. She pulled away sharply, her face a mixture of fear and pain, and Tiffany was afraid too – afraid of the taut whiteness of Randolph's face and lips, of bright glitter in his onyx eyes, of the *evil* he seemed to exude. And at that moment he glanced towards the window.

Tiffany turned and ran. She did not know whether Randolph had seen her, she wanted only to put as much distance as possible between herself and that pervading, penetrating aura of viciousness and corruption. She was aware of nothing else, did not even hear Frank's footsteps behind her, but swung herself quickly over the ladder at the side of the ship. She was shaking, her legs felt rubbery and the big heavy shoes were cumbersome but down the ladder she went, half-sliding and occasionally missing her footing in her efforts to escape. Only when she was nearly at the bottom did she realise that the launch was not there, the boatman having returned to shore to make another trip.

She swayed, knees buckling and breath coming in short gasps. Above her she could see Frank's anxious face but, clinging to the ladder, she found that she could not move – for once in her life Tiffany was too confused to know what to do. She turned her head and looked into the darkness of night and sea for inspiration – and her throat went dry. A ship had appeared out of nowhere and seemed to be almost on top of her.

It was the suddenness and silence of its appearance which took her by surprise. Ghosting noiselessly through the waters with its great sails set, the ship seemed an eerie phantom, wraithlike and ethereal, from another time and place. It came whispering by, so close that Tiffany huddled against the ladder and with her lapse of concentration the clumsy shoes slipped on the rungs. With a loud splash she fell into the sea.

The shock of the cold water cleared her mind. As her face broke the surface she managed to shout, 'Frank, I can't swim!' before sinking again. The next time she surfaced, gasping and choking, she could hear loud cries of alarm but to her horror had already drifted some way from the yacht. A lifebelt landed with a splash a few feet away but, try as she would, she could not reach it. She was being dragged down again. These damn shoes, she thought frantically, I must take off these damn shoes and she began wriggling her feet in desperate attempts to kick them away. The water was closing over her face. *Help*, she tried to scream but by now she was submerged and could only think *I do not want to die – and I won't!* Tiffany struggled, fighting the water, lashing out furiously with arms and legs, refusing to be defeated, when suddenly she felt herself being lifted and was aware of a powerful grip as strong arms held her up. With the most wonderful feeling of relief she was conscious of the air on her face and could open her mouth to cough out water and draw in deep shuddering breaths.

The arms were still supporting her, keeping her face above the water, so Tiffany stopped struggling and was content to drift until a deep voice said in her ear, 'Can you climb the ladder without help?' By way of reply she reached for the rungs, thankful she had been able to kick off the shoes, but then paused briefly as she assimilated the fact that this was not the same ladder. Looking up above her head, she saw that indeed it was not the same ship – the billowing sails were flapping free but unquestionably it was the 'ghost ship' which had so startled her and which was now at a standstill facing into the wind.

The climb was more difficult than she had anticipated, weighed down as she was by sodden clothes and with limbs shaky and difficult to control. She gritted her teeth, forcing herself to continue, until a voice said, 'Come on, lad!' and she was pulled to safety. For a moment she sagged to the deck but was determined that no one should think her weak so, wobbling, she hauled herself to her feet. The men around her were staring open-mouthed, and Tiffany remembered that she had lost her hat and that her hair was draped and dripping around her shoulders.

'Well done, Sergeant.' Her rescuer climbed aboard and clapped another man on the back. 'That was as nice an exhibition of seamanship as I have ever seen! I believe you could turn her on a sixpence!' Then he saw Tiffany. 'So,' he said softly, 'someone else has been making an exhibition of themselves but in a less laudable fashion.'

The lamps cast a flickering light over the untidy deck, strewn with ropes and canvas, and Tiffany had an impression of a very tall man, dark-haired, with a lean handsome face and grey eyes which were staring at her sardonically.

'What, in God's name, were you doing?' he demanded. 'Why were you dangling several feet above the bloody ocean on a ladder with no blasted boat at the end of it?'

'There isn't the slightest need to swear!' Tiffany glared at him furiously. It was bad enough being wet through, rocking uncomfortably on this ridiculous boat and feeling foolish, without this uncouth person having the temerity to shout at her. People simply did *not* shout at Tiffany Court. 'And I would have been perfectly all right if you had not sailed this filthy, untidy old tub of yours so close!'

'Ah, so it is my fault, is it?' He laughed and to Tiffany's ever-increasing fury the other sailors laughed too. 'I must confess that we did sail a trifle closer than usual – my helmsman was unable to resist the temptation of taking a peek at the orgy in the saloon. But as you were attending the party I am sure you can understand that.' He placed his hand under her chin and tilted her face up into the light. 'As for the untidiness, we were ship-shape until you launched yourself into the deep. You can be extremely grateful that my crew were able to go about and luff up so quickly in order to stop the boat and pick you up.'

He spoke with an English accent and it dawned on Tiffany that she was aboard the British yacht she had watched a few days ago at the picnic. And she had thought the ship might belong to an English aristocrat! Why, he was not even a gentleman, let alone a duke!

'Why is she dressed like that?' Tiffany heard a sailor ask. 'The strumpets in the saloon were wearing very little, particularly above the waist, and from what I could see the few clothes they had on were being fast removed!'

'Perhaps she is a music-hall girl,' suggested the man who had been addressed as Sergeant. 'You know, like Vesta Tilley, doing a song-and-dance act in man's clothes with a top hat and cane.'

'From what *I* saw of the party, I think it safe to assume that her act goes a lot farther than Vesta Tilley's!' Tiffany's rescuer grinned at her and yanked off Frank's jacket. The wet shirt clung to her body, revealing the outline of her full breasts, and the sight was greeted by a chorus of whistles. 'You wouldn't deny your saviours a song, would you, sweetheart?' he asked softly. 'And I'm sure no man here would object if your gratitude induced you to extend your performance.'

'I am not an actress. I am Tiff . . .' She stopped, unwilling to reveal her identity. Tiffany did not care if society discovered her escapade in attending the party, but she did not want it known that she had fallen in the water, to be rescued by these vulgar foreigners. She revelled in causing gossip, loved to be recognised as being different, but she was damned if she would be laughed at.

'Launch approaching from the yacht, Captain!' sang out one of the crew.

'How many aboard?'

'Boatman and one other.'

The Captain smiled. 'Then the performance depends on whether our visitor is the lady's protector, manager or pimp.'

Frank! Tiffany felt dizzy with relief. Never before had he been as useful or as welcome as he was now.

'What is a pimp?' she asked.

There was a moment's silence, broken by the loud guffaws of the crew, but the Captain gave her a sharp look and suddenly the amusement vanished from his face to be replaced by a doubtful, thoughtful expression.

'Tiffany!' cried Frank, as he rushed on deck. 'Are you all right? Good God . . .' and he stared in disbelief, '. . . Rafe Deverill!'

During their previous acquaintance, this man had not been a ship's captain but an officer in the British cavalry, commanding a troop of irregular horse in the Transvaal. His unit and Steyn's Commando had clashed so many times that it became obvious the meetings were no coincidence. What was it Danie had said? 'Not Deverill's Horse but *Devil's Horse!*' And the last time Frank had set eyes on Rafe Deverill, the handsome Captain had been in a situation which left him stranded, alone except for Helena . . .

'Mr Whitney,' said Rafe coolly, 'I might have known that where there ws a lady in man's clothing you would not be far behind.'

'I don't believe it . . . The last time I saw you . . . Damn it, it's incredible!'

'What you mean, Mr Whitney, is that this is a bloody small world,' said Rafe in bored tones, mocking the well-worn cliché.

'And this is the girl I told you about . . .' Bemused, Frank turned to Tiffany. 'Are you really all right? I've never been so frantic in my life. Captain Deverill, this is Tiffany Court.'

'You bloody fool, Frank! Do you have to tell him who I am?' hissed Tiffany.

'Tiffany! You shouldn't use language like that.' Frank was shocked, genuinely anxious that she should make a good impression after all the things he had said about her to Captain Deverill.

'Well, I don't see why not. Everyone else does.' Safe at last, she glared at him belligerently. 'Why didn't *you* jump in and rescue me?'

Frank hung his head, shamefaced. 'I cannot swim either,' he admitted reluctantly.

And Tiffany tossed her head scornfully.

Rafe beckoned to one of the men. 'You remember Sergeant King from the old days, don't you, Frank? In fact if you look around, you might see a number of familiar faces.'

As the Sergeant stepped forward, Frank raised his head but could not look the man in the eyes. Glancing across the deck he did recognise faces – all of them men from Deverill's Horse – but not a single one of them wore a smile of welcome and the atmosphere was cold with animosity.

'Sergeant, take the lady below and find her a dry shirt and trousers,' Rafe ordered.

'You mean, she is a lady and not a whore?' gasped King in dismay.

'This may sound contradictory, Sergeant, but in my experience it is entirely possible for a woman to be both,' replied Rafe drily.

'We must pay you for the clothes,' said Frank stiffly.

'That will not be necessary. I have gathered that Americans imagine all the British to be paupers, but I think we can just about afford a pair of patched trousers and an old shirt in an emergency.'

As Tiffany went below, she could not decide which man irritated her the most: Frank for making such a naïve remark, or the English Captain for making her feel so small.

41

'She is not the only one who requires dry clothes,' and Rafe led Frank down the companionway to his cabin where he stripped and towelled himself dry.

'Tiffany Court,' Rafe murmured, 'well, well . . .'

This was a pair of eyes whose compelling gaze was inescapable, cold, grey and glittering, boring into Frank's brain. Both were remembering the moment when they had discussed Tiffany . . .

They had been alone briefly on the small plateau in the Eastern Transvaal while Lieutenant Lombard and Japie Malan, the *Khaki Boer*, reconnoitred the path ahead and Charlie, the big Zulu, minded the horses. A waterfall cascaded over the cliff, sending up a delicate misty spray which showered on the clumps of maidenhair fern and flowers fanning over the grey rocks. The droplets sparkled like diamonds, reminding Frank of Tiffany.

'You know, Captain, it's a funny thing but John Court never told me how beautiful Africa is.'

'Didn't he?' Rafe had replied absently. His mind was elsewhere, wondering if Japie had picked up Steyn's trail and whether all was well with Sergeant King and the rest of the troop at base camp.

'Nope. But what is even funnier is that his daughter told me Africa was boring! Isn't that a scream?'

'Absolutely hilarious,' Rafe had agreed sarcastically. 'Evidently she is a young lady possessed either of a well-developed sense of humour or a marked lack of acumen.'

'Tiffany Court,' and Frank's eyes grew dreamy, 'is going to be the most beautiful woman in America and that means she will be the loveliest lady in the whole world.'

'I can think of a few ladies in London who would challenge such patriotic bias.'

'You must visit me at home, Captain, meet Tiffany and judge . . .'

Frank had gone no further because a rifle had cracked

. . .

* * *

Now it was with relief that Frank heard Rafe's next remark – angry though the Captain was, he did not refer to the events of that terrible day during the South African War.

'Did you take the girl to that party?' Rafe demanded.

'She wanted to go.'

'I daresay she did, but that is no reason for acceding to her request. You must have known it was no place for her.'

'You don't know Tiffany,' said Frank miserably and began to explain.

Rafe listened with growing astonishment and exasperation. 'You would have sacrificed your job – and she let you?'

'I don't think she really understood.'

'Then she is stupid or selfish and probably both.'

He finished dressing and walked to the saloon where he poured three glasses of wine, silently handing one glass to Tiffany when she entered. She had tied back the long wet hair from her face and her tall lithe figure showed to advantage even in the shabby clothes. The top buttons of the shirt had been left undone, revealing a glimpse of the bosom beneath. Artifice or innocence? Rafe was not sure.

Tiffany saw his eyes on the opening of the shirt and a flush rose through her, the heat and fire engulfing her body until it flooded her face and stained the ivory skin. He seemed to fill the small saloon, so tall that he had to bend his head slightly under the overhead beams, long-legged in the tight trousers and high boots, broad-shouldered in an open-necked white shirt which bared a wide expanse of the deeply-tanned skin and curling dark hair of his chest. There was something about him – a vitality, an intensity, a magnetism – which made Tiffany think of touching and being touched. The excitement was new and intoxicating, even more stimulating than her emotions when she had watched the party through the pane of glass, but he was not smiling down at her as the stranger had smiled at the girl on the yacht. Instead his grey eyes were cold and full of disdain. He was the first man she had wanted to touch her and the first man she had failed to impress. It was absolutely infuriating and furthermore it was not a situation which could be allowed to continue.

'How do you two come to know each other?' she inquired.

For once Frank did not answer but addressed Rafe. 'I have often wondered what happened to you. Did you reach base camp without difficulty? Did Helena . . .?'

'This is no time for reminiscing,' Rafe interrupted sharply. 'You must take the girl home, particularly as I gather her family believe her to be in bed.'

'We are giving a party at my home tomorrow evening, Captain,' announced Tiffany grandly. 'You are most welcome to attend and talk over old times with Frank. However, my father and cousin will be present, so I regret that the entertainment will not rival the festivities on the yacht this evening.' He has only seen me in trousers and with wet hair, she was thinking, but tomorrow night I will be looking my best and then he will change his tune!

The girl was amazing. Rafe did not know whether to laugh or swear. Not a word of gratitude for being fished out of the sea. Not a word of apology for causing any inconvenience. On the other hand, not a tear nor any display of emotion after a terrifying ordeal. And now a cool invitation to her home, without the slightest hint that she would prefer him not to mention the evening's events to her father. Her bearing and manner, her selfishness, arrogance and pride were everything Rafe disliked, yet one had to admit that Tiffany Court had style.

'We were leaving Newport,' he said reflectively, 'but I do not think my crew would object to a change of plan. I accept your invitation, Miss Court. Thank you.'

'You can wear patched trousers and an old shirt if you have nothing else,' she said, in order to let him know that his earlier sarcasm had not gone unnoticed.

His mouth smiled but no humour reached his eyes. 'Thank you, but I believe I will be able to scrape up something suitable – unless, of course, masquerading is a quaint old American custom and you would care to lend me a dress?'

'We must not keep the launch waiting,' said Frank, concerned at the tone of the conversation.

'Do take care on the journey,' Rafe advised, 'and do learn to swim – both of you!'

The first person Rafe saw at the Court mansion the following evening was Frank, loitering in the hall with eyes fixed wistfully on the stairs.

'As I am too modest to assume that you are waiting for me,' Rafe observed, 'I take it that the fair Tiffany has not yet condescended to put in an appearance.'

'She does like to arrive a little late. I am so glad that you have met her, Captain Deverill – you must agree that I was right and she is the most beautiful girl in the world.'

Rafe shrugged. 'I am in no position to judge. The circumstances of our meeting were neither auspicious nor flattering.'

'You can judge now. She's coming.'

The huge hall was divided into two sections by a row of high archways and decorated columns. Through the arch ahead of him Rafe could see a square of golden Oriental carpet on the marble floor and a toning tapestry on the far wall glowed gold, bronze and red. The white marble staircase, carpeted in gold, curved magnificently to the upper gallery where pictures hung in recessed alcoves. And down this staircase, framed in the archway, floated Tiffany.

She was wearing a gown of white silk chiffon. The bodice was cut wide and low, trimmed with pearls and priceless antique lace, while the full skirt was pleated and flounced, edged with a lace frill which flowed back into a graceful train. Her hair was brushed off her face into a smooth roll and then piled high into bouffant waves on the crown of her head, anchored by a dazzling diamond tiara. More diamonds – the best that John Court could provide – sparkled at her neck, ears and wrists. She walked slowly, head tilted back proudly, the silk and lace of gown and petticoats swishing and rustling as she moved.

'Now do you understand what I mean?' breathed Frank.

Rafe did understand, his pulse racing at the sight of her, and he also comprehended the reason for her arrogance. All this wealth and position, and all this beauty too! Was it any wonder that she was ruled by pride? He glanced compassionately at Frank's ecstatic face. You poor sod, he thought. You have as much chance of possessing her as being elected President of the United States – in fact you have a much better chance of becoming President!

Tiffany was engulfed in a surging tide of admirers, all anxious for a touch of her hand, a smile or a glance from her bright eyes. Rafe, however, leaned against a pillar and watched. She glanced his way, eyes widening at the elegance of his figure, the cut of his clothes and the immaculate grooming of his dark hair. He grinned at her but it was not at all the kind of acknowledgement she was accustomed to receive, being full of impertinence and devoid of adoration. Instead of approaching him as she had intended, Tiffany turned haughtily and swept into the drawing-room.

'Captain Deverill, what a pleasant surprise.'

The man's face was vaguely familiar, but Rafe could not give him a name.

'Anton Ellenberger. We met several years ago at the home of Sir Matthew Bright.'

'Of course.' Theirs was only a casual acquaintance, because Ellenberger did not mix in society, but Rafe was glad of company. With Frank Whitney trailing in Tiffany's wake like a love-lorn spaniel, Rafe was beginning to wonder why he had come. 'Are you still working with Sir Matthew?'

'Indeed yes. Incidentally, I was at Park Lane only a few weeks ago and had the pleasure of meeting Sir Matthew's niece, Lady Julia Fortescue. She was a trifle pale and thin, I thought, but otherwise ravishing ... quite ravishing.' Ellenberger smiled blandly – everyone in London knew that Rafe Deverill was Lady Julia's lover and that she was pining in his absence.

Rafe's face remained impassive. He accepted the offer of a glass of champagne and watched Tiffany talking to a plain dumpy girl dressed in an unfortunate shade of mauve.

'I hope that Sir Matthew's family is well?'

There was a slight emphasis on the word *family* which caught Anton's attention, as if the state of Sir Matthew's own health was of little concern to the inquirer, but it was not his place to comment upon the implications. 'Lady Bright is lovelier than ever – motherhood agrees with her. The only person with whom I have regular contact is Miranda. When she is in London I make a point of calling on her to talk about the business – she is most interested in diamonds and tries so hard to overcome her handicap.' Anton followed the direction of Rafe's gaze. 'The other diamond heiress,' he murmured, 'but what a contrast!'

It was odd, Rafe was thinking, how Tiffany reminded him of someone. He could not recognise the features, but there was something about the way she held herself . . . and the tilt of her head was hauntingly familiar.

Anton was feeling profoundly uncomfortable at being discovered in the company of the Courts, having no desire that news of his presence here should be relayed to Sir Matthew. He must hope that Deverill's taciturnity was typical of the man. A strange fellow, Deverill. What made a man abandon a promising military career, only to go off on these periodic voyages and in between times do nothing in particular? Anton Ellenberger was an excellent judge of character and could have sworn that Rafe Deverill was not the indolent type.

'What brings you to Newport, Captain?' Anton inquired delicately.

'Gun-running,' answered Rafe laconically.

'Good Lord!'

Rafe grinned. 'My description is over-dramatic! In fact I delivered a couple of cannon to Astor for installation on the *Nourmahal*. I met him while he was cruising in the Caribbean and learned that he was worried about pirates.'

'Aren't *you* worried about pirates?'

'Oh, I have a Hotchkiss aboard the *Corsair* for just such a contingency.' Rafe smiled again at Anton's expression. 'I am aware that J.P. Morgan's luxury yacht is named *Corsair*. Unfortunately the resemblance between his vessel and mine ends there.'

Anton laughed politely and Rafe continued, 'Tell me, Ellenberger, are you acquainted with the ladies to whom Miss Court is speaking? I should like to be introduced.'

'Certainly. They are Miss Court's aunt and cousin, and Mrs Whitney.'

Anton introduced him as Captain the Honourable Rafe Deverill in suitably respectful tones and the ladies, already appreciative of his good looks, were now positively overwhelmed.

'Honourable? Does that mean you will be a lord some day?' asked Pauline.

'I fear not. I am a younger son and my elder brother will inherit the title. However, to date the future Lady Ambleside has borne only daughters so I live in hope.' His smile was sardonic and faintly sarcastic.

'Are you inferring that girls don't count?' Tiffany demanded furiously.

'The English upper-class has a system of primogeniture but the titles, and the accompanying fortunes, are passed on through the male line.'

'Disgraceful!' Tiffany declared.

'I daresay you are right, but the system has worked admirably so far. The British nobility has retained its status and wealth, unlike its foreign counterparts who divided the family fortunes among too many siblings. Are you an only child, Miss Court?'

'Yes, thank heavens.' It flashed through Tiffany's mind that having a brother might have been fun – an elder brother who would have taken her to exciting events with his friends. She would have had to share the money, of course, but probably there was enough to go round. But a sister? No, she was glad she did not have a sister. Instinctively Tiffany knew that a sister would mean competition and they would have been bitter rivals. 'I have no brothers or sisters,' she continued slowly, 'but I seem to have a surfeit of cousins.'

Tiffany glanced across the room to where Randolph was standing, but Pauline took the remark personally and flushed. 'We saw your ship and Tiffany thought you might be a duke,' she remarked maliciously.

'Ah, and in her eyes a duke is, *ipso facto*, a dowry-hunter. I am sorry to disappoint you, Miss Court, on both counts.'

'I am not disappointed, because I would not waste my money on a duke anyway,' Tiffany retorted.

'You certainly would not waste it on me,' Rafe replied affably, 'because I am not for sale.'

'My younger son is in England,' observed Mrs Whitney in a desperate attempt to change the subject, 'at Oxford University.'

'At which college?' Ellenberger asked.

'Balliol.'

'Perhaps he has met my employer's son, who is also at Balliol – his name is Philip Bright.'

Tiffany's face grew thoughtful. Where had she heard that name before? And then she remembered. It was the name she had been trying to recall on the day of the picnic – Philip Bright was the boy she had met in England, the boy whose mother was buried in the grave Papa had visited. She had an illogical conviction, loosely based on the misty memory of their conversation, that Philip Bright was different from other boys. This Englishman, this damned Deverill, was different too. Perhaps all Englishmen were different? Tiffany's resolve to travel to Europe hardened.

'My brother has all the brains in the family,' Frank was explaining to Rafe. 'He won a Rhodes scholarship to Oxford – one of the first Americans to be chosen under the terms of Cecil Rhodes' bequest.'

'He may have brains, Frank, but he is not as well travelled as you,' said Rafe politely, out of deference to Mrs Whitney.

TIffany's laugh tinkled as she perceived a cue for one of her favourite games. 'After that remark you have no cause for staying silent about South Africa, Frank. Do you know, Captain Deverill, that he refuses to tell us of his exploits? Such modesty!'

The group of young people around them laughed because they were expected to find Tiffany's baiting of Frank amusing, but Rafe did not smile. He glanced at Frank's white face and then looked at Tiffany with that penetrating stare which seemed to strip the clothes from her body and bare her innermost thoughts – and she knew immediately that she had made a mistake.

'Why, Frank,' Rafe said, in tones of great surprise, 'did you not tell your friends about the time you saved my life?'

The nightmare had closed over Frank, as horrible to him as the waters which had almost engulfed Tiffany. He had learned to live with the teasing of his friends but felt utterly unable to cope in front of Deverill, the one man who knew the facts of his involvement in the war. When he heard Rafe's words, he was totally bewildered.

'My lieutenant and I were captured by a Boer commando with whom Frank had been riding.' Rafe spoke directly to Tiffany. 'Normally the Boers observed the rules regarding prisoners-of-war but on this occasion the guerilla chief, Danie Steyn, decided to arrange a little "accident". Luckily for me, Frank discovered the plot and helped us to escape.'

Rafe's audience, which now included John and Randolph Court, was swelling by the second and listening enthralled. Only Tiffany stood stiff and pale, eyes hard with anger and disbelief, hating every moment of Rafe's revelations.

'We sneaked out of the Boer camp at night,' Rafe went on, 'but our group was forced to separate the next morning when the commando caught up with us. Frank and

Lieutenant Lombard went in one direction and I went in another. Did George Lombard take you through the Lowveld into Natal, Frank?'

Frank nodded. 'Did you ever see the commando again?'

'See it? I annihilated it – except that although Danie's distinctive grey horse lay dead in the valley, he got away.'

'What about Paul?'

'He was taken prisoner,' Rafe replied abruptly.

'That's a relief! He was the nicest guy in the whole outfit.' Frank was beginning to relax and enjoy the admiring glances.

Pauline had been listening intently to the tale of Frank's heroism. 'After the escape, you must have been left all on your own,' she said to Rafe.

'Not quite alone. Three of us did escape from the commando,' and here Rafe's eyes flicked sideways to Frank, 'but unfortunately one of the Boers overheard our plans and had to be persuaded to accompany us. I took him back to my unit. The journey lasted a week – and *he* turned out to be a *she*.'

He smiled straight into Tiffany's eyes and despite her fury she was consumed by a strange excitement. In part she was jealous of the unknown woman who had played the part of a man, but more importantly she tingled at the thought of being alone with this man for a whole week. There was a stir among the other ladies too, even those who were scandalised feeling envious at the same time.

Still smiling, Rafe turned to John Court and smoothly defused the mood. 'To think, Mr Court, that I spent a great deal of my war service in the Transvaal within a few miles of the Premier Mine! If I had been luckier or more astute, I might have been standing here today with a fortune in diamonds instead of possessing only a few yarns to tell.'

'I certainly wish you had been first on the scene at the Premier,' said Court drily. 'I am sure you would have proved more reasonable to deal with than Thomas Cullinan.'

'I had gathered that the last thing the industry wanted was a new diamond discovery.'

The group around them was drifting away to discuss the hidden talents of Frank Whitney, but Tiffany stayed. For one thing she considered she had been made to look a fool and she wished to avoid the spiteful pleasure of the other girls at her downfall; for another, she preferred the company and conversation of men. As a murmur of agreement to Rafe's statement rose, she listened with genuine interest.

'Yet,' Rafe continued, 'surely new discoveries must be made? An enormous proportion of the existing supply is located in South Africa – logically one would expect continents the size of America and Australia to contain valuable deposits.'

'Logic plays a lesser part than luck in diamond prospecting,' said Court ruefully, 'but you are not alone in your reasoning – hundreds of optimistic diggers share your sentiments and are combing the continents for the strike which will make them rich.'

'But basically you are hoping they stay poor?'

'New supplies may be needed but, as Mr Ellenberger and I were discussing the other day, it is a matter of controlling that supply – an undertaking which requires the touch of a firm and astute man.'

'Or a firm and astute woman,' interrupted Tiffany.

Court smiled indulgently and patted her hand. 'You see, Captain Deverill, while America and Australia are obvious places to look, diamonds could be found anywhere – well, *almost* anywhere. The known alluvial deposits show that rivers move the stones from their place of origin and carry them many miles away. Diamonds could be found in a desert if a river runs through the terrain, or if a river had passed that way centuries ago.'

'You remind me of a remark I heard while I was in the Transvaal. A German was talking about the deserts of South-West Africa, saying that surely there must be *something* there.'

'Quite. No land should be completely worthless. The sands of the world's deserts, even the great Sahara itself,

52

may conceal minerals, gems of petroleum beyond our imagining.'

Tiffany's interest was quickening. These men talked about diamonds as if they were . . . *potatoes*! She sensed the romance and glamour of the gems, as well as the wealth they bestowed, and for the first time perceived a new dimension to her inheritance.

'Diamonds were made for woman's pleasure,' she said slowly, in an uncharacteristically serious tone. 'It is women who understand them, appreciate them and treasure them for their beauty instead of treating them as a commodity to be sold for the highest price – as a stepping-stone to another goal.'

The men stared at her in silence. Frank was astonished, Ellenberger and Rafe surprised and suddenly respectful; her father was smiling genially. It was Randolph Court whose reaction was the most marked, his face registering wary displeasure and unease.

'Women should wear diamonds, of course, but I do hope that you are not contemplating a greater involvement in the affairs of the industry,' he said sharply.

'Why not?' Tiffany retorted. 'I am sure I could sell diamonds as well as any man – better, in fact, because I know what women want. When Papa gives me Court Diamonds, I will prove it.'

Court laughed. 'Don't be foolish, darling! Randolph is right; women should wear diamonds and pretty dresses and enjoy themselves having babies – like you will be doing soon. Besides, strictly speaking, Court Diamonds will not be yours.'

'What do you mean?'

'It will be yours, sweetheart, but through Randolph – he will manage the business just as he will manage all your affairs.'

Tiffany frowned with puzzlement but Rafe understood. Randolph was watching Tiffany with an almost feline anticipation, poised like a cat about to pounce on its prey. It should be an interesting contest, Rafe said to himself –

because he did not think for a moment that Tiffany would go quietly – and he almost regretted that he would not be around to see it. Obviously, the import of Court's statement was not clear to Tiffany, but she had stopped trying to fathom the mystery. Her attention was fixed on the girls who hovered on the fringe of their exclusive little group in the hope of attracting the attention of the two war heroes.

'Frank, come for a walk with me.' Tiffany smiled at him winningly. 'Help me choose a site for a swimming-pool. You can come, too, Captain Deverill,' she added graciously.

'Swimming-pool?' inquired Court. 'I was not aware we were installing one!'

'I haven't had a chance to tell you yet, Papa. I only decided this morning.' And she glanced indignantly at Rafe, who had burst out laughing. 'I want to learn to swim. I believe a girl nearly drowned in the harbour last night.'

Again Rafe's white teeth gleamed in acknowledgement of her effrontery, but Frank was alarmed. 'Some of the guys were talking about it,' he explained nervously. 'It seems there was quite a party on one of the yachts.'

'Is that so?' Court frowned disapprovingly. 'I trust it was not the same boat on which you and Ellenberger travelled, Randolph?'

'Indeed not,' lied Randolph glibly. 'By comparison we had an uneventful – in truth, rather dull – voyage, didn't we, Anton?'

Ellenberger made a deprecating 'if-you-say-so' gesture in order to ease his conscience, while Tiffany's fair skin turned from magnolia to fuchsia as she struggled to maintain silence. Frank seized her by the elbow and steered her towards the door leading to the terrace, followed by Rafe. Safely outside, Tiffany exploded.

'He was there! They both were! I saw him with a girl . . .' and she shuddered.

'Well, you would insist on going to the damn party,' said Frank reasonably, 'and you should have expected a few disturbing sights. Anyway, Randolph only kissed her, so I don't see why you should be so upset.'

Tiffany could not explain why she reacted so strongly. 'Oh, fetch me a drink, Frank, and make yourself useful for a change,' she snapped and obediently Frank walked away. As she leaned on the balustrade of the terrace, the sea breeze cooling the angry flush on her cheeks, she became aware of Rafe's tall dark shape beside her.

'You were lying about Frank,' she said suddenly.

'Why should I do that?'

'I don't know,' she admitted, 'but I am sure that if Frank had done those heroic deeds he would have told me.'

'Why?'

These interminable questions were maddening! Tiffany tossed her head and the diamonds gleamed in her hair. 'Frank Whitney would do anything to impress me. Surely it is obvious he is in love with me?'

'And you are a girl who takes love – and most other things – very much for granted?'

'I cannot help it if everyone loves me, can I?'

'And who do you love – apart from yourself?'

'I wish you would answer a question just for once!' she cried.

'I told the truth about Frank.'

'Not the whole truth,' she insisted.

Rafe lit a cigarette and drew on it thoughtfully. She was shrewder than one realised – or was she just a shrew?

'You don't care what happened in South Africa,' he said with that lazy detachment which annoyed her so much. 'You are merely concerned because the story spoiled your act. For myself, I am only sorry that Frank's arrival at my boat last night prevented another performance – your attempt at a song-and-dance act would have been worth seeing.'

Tiffany glared at him. 'You should have known that I was a lady.'

'How was I supposed to tell? In England the voice is helpful in making such assessments, but American women

55

speak the language in such heathenish fashion that I am quite unable to make the necessary distinction.'

'Oh! You are the rudest man I have ever met! The real reason you cannot make the comparison is because you come into contact with gentility so seldom – no *lady* would allow you near her for longer than five minutes.'

'You never did tell me why you were dangling on that ladder,' Rafe reminded her, ignoring her insults, 'or what you intended to do at the party. Were you going to gamble, to dance, or . . . to kiss, like the girl with your cousin? Do tell me, Tiffany. I find the possibilities fascinating.'

His voice had taken on the quality of a caress and Tiffany was bewildered by his changes of mood. Last night it had been exactly the same: anger followed by mockery, enticement followed by indifference. She did not know what to make of Rafe Deverill at all.

'I do not see that it is any of your business, but if you must know I simply wanted to enjoy myself. Take a look through the door at *this* party – cardboard people convincing themselves that this is fun. I know different. The girls on the yacht were really enjoying themselves; they were *alive* and I could be too! I would make an excellent . . .' She stopped, unsure of the correct word for that sort of girl.

It was ridiculous but she was right. The vitality, the passion for living blazed out of her with the force of a hurricane and with that bewitching face and body, how easily she could be misled. But then Rafe thought of Randolph Court and experienced a faint feeling of revulsion at the image of that cold, calculating, cousinly embrace. Tiffany was not fashioned for the boyish Frank, but neither did she deserve the repellent Randolph; she needed a man who would match her, not crush her, a man who would curb her spirit or free it as the occasion demanded – like the control required of the diamonds which were so much a part of her.

'Trollop is probably the word you are seeking,' Rafe remarked, but *trouble* is what you really are, he added silently. 'As for those girls enjoying themselves – well, it is something I have often wondered about. By the way, Frank appears to have been waylaid, so isn't it time you returned to your guests?'

'Yes, but I shall not do so,'

'Even rich girls have responsibilities – and ought to have manners.'

'I don't *want* to go!'

'It is not a matter of what you want and frankly what you *need*, my dear, is a smack across that delectable backside.'

No one had ever spoken to Tiffany in that manner before. She was so thunderstruck that she could only stare at him, speechless with rage.

Rafe sighed. He was being too hard on her, for she was not responsible for her behaviour; as he had observed earlier her pride and conceit were the product of environment, natural gifts and paternal indulgence. It was not Tiffany's fault that she had no conception of the suffering others endured . . . that she had no acquaintance with pain.

He ground out the cigarette with his heel. 'I must leave. We sail for England tomorrow – a resumption of the voyage which you interrupted so spectacularly.' He started to turn away but then paused – for some reason he felt he must warn her. 'By the way, what is the precise relationship between you and Randolph?'

'He is my cousin.

'First cousin?'

'No, second, I think.' Tiffany was puzzled again. His face was serious and she had the oddest feeling that he was trying to tell her something important. 'Our grandfathers were brothers and really that is how I look upon Randolph – as a brother.'

'He does not look at you like a brother,' said Rafe softly and walked away.

No other man had ever departed voluntarily from Tiffany's side, leaving her to stand alone on a terrace. He was the most insufferable man, fumed Tiffany, but her indignation was tempered by the seed of doubt he had sown in her mind concerning Randolph. But no, it was impossible – she simply would not think about it! And anyway no one could force her to ... Tiffany could not bring herself to frame the last two words and she flung out her hands in a gesture as if physically pushing them away. Thank God, she thought, that Papa has never been able to make me do something I do not want to do.

The evening was spoiled. What with Rafe Deverill's imperviousness to her charms and being made to look ridiculous over Frank, the party had not been destined for success, but now her unease about Randolph cast a threatening shadow. Tiffany shivered, yet lingered a moment longer, watching the moonlight on the calm sea. Tomorrow Deverill's ship would sail away on those waters and she was immensely glad he was going. Like so many recipients of bad news, Tiffany blamed the messenger.

CHAPTER FOUR

Against all odds the exclusivity of the 'Four Hundred' had survived into the new century, still representing the pinnacle of achievement and the goal to which all Americans aspired. In this era, when actresses were not respectable, the American public focused its interest on the glamorous lifestyles of the society ladies and of this coterie by far the most renowned was Tiffany Court. The newspapers devoted columns to her beauty, apparel and activities; her face was the most photographed in the entire United States and she was acknowledged to be the most glittering prize in the marriage market. Her attraction went deeper than her face and fortune; Tiffany possessed that indefinable attribute which one day would be called star quality or charisma and her admiring public waited breathlessly for the tragedy which so often strikes at those who ride high on Olympus.

In the autumn Aunt Sarah and Pauline returned temporarily to Boston and although Randolph tried to curb her, Tiffany took full advantage of the extra freedom. She widened her sphere of activities and her choice of partners. Boldly she dined out at Sherry's and at Delmonico's; she paraded along 'Peacock Alley' at the Waldorf-Astoria – her presence never failing to cause a stir among the spectators who lined the long marble corridor – and appeared in the great hotel's Palm Garden. Not only did she change her partners but she permitted them greater liberties: with vivid memories of the girls at the party, Tiffany began to experiment with sex. Her ventures amounted to a kiss or two, nothing more, and were profoundly disappointing. Either the man's mouth was small and tight and she kept bumping into his teeth or else it was wet and slobbery. Whichever it turned out to be, the men were clumsy and the experience was not enjoyable. When they touched her, there were no fireworks and although Tiffany was ignorant of love-making, she was sure there ought to be fireworks.

Out of curiosity she even permitted Frank to kiss her and rather to her surprise he was the best of a bad bunch, although he was too gentle with her, being hesitant and overawed as a dream came true. To Tiffany the embrace, and the others which she occasionally allowed him, meant nothing, but he really thought that he was the only man she kissed and, in the flush of a new-found confidence since the revelations of Rafe Deverill, truly began to believe that she might marry him.

Sometimes Tiffany went out accompanied by her maid – a discreet girl who took pride in her mistress's beauty and style and who could be relied upon to fade tactfully into the background when circumstances required it – but occasionally she was unchaperoned. Eventually Randolph, who had been working too hard to indulge in party-going, could stand the situation no longer; when Tiffany came home late one evening, she was confronted by him and her father.

'Where have you been?' Randolph demanded.

'It is none of your business.'

'It most certainly is my business and I demand that you tell me.'

'And I refuse to tell you!'

'You have been somewhere with a man!' Randolph's face was dead-white and small beads of perspiration glistened on his brow. He was fingering his newly-grown moustache with restless fingers. 'Frank Whitney, I suppose?'

'There is no need to bring him into it. Frank Whitney does not control my actions, nor does he mean anything to me.'

'From the way you have been behaving recently, there

are plenty of other candidates to join you in your promiscuous activities.'

'My what?' Tiffany did not know what the word meant but she did gather the general gist of his tirade. She turned to her father who was listening with obvious distress. 'I concede, Papa, that you have a certain right to question me, so why do you stay silent and allow Randolph to dictate affairs in this house?'

'Randolph speaks for both of us,' answered Court unhappily.

'Does he, Papa?' A chill of foreboding ran through her. 'In everything?'

'Yes.'

Randolph's lips curved in a sneer of triumph. 'My mother will return to New York after Christmas to assist in the preparations for your debut. Until then, either your father or I will escort you to every evening engagement. Furthermore, we will select those engagements which you attend and ensure that you come straight home afterwards.'

Tiffany swept him a contemptuous curtsey and, without favouring her father with another glance, stalked out of the room. In the privacy of her bedroom, she was annoyed to discover that she was trembling and when she lay in bed, sleep eluded her. *Randolph*. The very name had become anathema, evoking that ominous presentiment of menace and sinister evil intent, but what also disturbed Tiffany was the evidence of his increasing influence with her father. Once she had been able to manipulate Court completely – he had been as clay in her hands – and she was desperate to maintain that pre-eminent position. When she finally fell asleep, she had decided what her response to Randolph would be: if she was to be supervised in the evenings, she would go her own way during the day when he was at the bank. She did not know what outlet her need for self-expression would find, but was sure that the path would become clear to her. Tiffany was right – her new diversion manifested itself the very next day and the analogy of 'clay in her hands' proved remarkably apt.

Her luncheon engagement was perfectly proper and therefore rather boring. The hostess being a notorious patroness of the arts, Tiffany supposed she should not have been surprised when a visit to an exhibition at the National Academy of Art was mooted. The lady explained that a young artist whom she had met in Paris was exhibiting there and she was anxious to view his latest work. It was a cold grey November day and, having nothing better to do, Tiffany agreed to go but found the landscapes, still-lifes and copies of Old Masters less than inspiring. Tiffany's drawing classes, like her music lessons, had not been a success and the inspection of other people's art was as undiverting as the production of her own. Her attention strayed and she lagged behind the other members of the party. Then she became aware that she was being watched by a shabbily dressed young man who was loitering on the far side of the gallery. He was moderately good-looking, she thought idly, noticing his thick mane of auburn hair and expressive brown eyes. Her companions moved further away and as she expected the man approached.

'You think they are terrible, too, don't you?' he asked, waving a disgusted hand at the pictures.

'I know nothing whatsoever about art, but if this is anything to go by I don't feel I have missed a thing.'

'I hate myself for having done it! I hate the world for making me do it – for forcing me to bastardise my talent in this way!' He groaned in despair.

'Do you mean that these are your pictures? Then you must know Mrs . . .'

'No, no, they are not *all* mine, thank God!' he cried wildly. 'There are others who are prostituting themselves as well as me.'

'Why do you paint pictures you dislike so much?'

'I have to eat.'

'Oh.' Tiffany stared at him with curiosity. She was not

accustomed to meeting the poor – apart from servants, of course, and they did not count.

'You have the most beautiful head. I would love to sculpt it, but I expect you are too busy to bother and,' his eyes assimilated the import of her expensive clothes, 'too rich.'

'Don't you know who I am?'

'No. I do not exactly mix in society and when one is short of money for food one does not buy newspapers.' His voice was heavy with sarcasm but his eyes glowed with admiration.

Tiffany considered him. Even she was cautious in pursuing this acquaintance, but the artist had one over-whelming attraction for her – he was different from the other young men she had met. And it would be amusing to see how and where real artists worked.

'I might let you sculpt me,' she said. 'I will call on you tomorrow and let you know,'

The artist gaped.

'Give me your address,' she commanded.

'Greenwich Village,' he stuttered. '15 Macdougal Alley. Ask for Gerard.'

Tiffany nodded casually and walked away to rejoin her companions.

The white-painted mews houses of Macdougal Alley were converted from the old stables and servants' accommodation of the mansions on Washington Square. As Tiffany entered the hall of Number 15, she stepped into another world – a Bohemian, gas-lit world of peeling paint, splintered floors and unpaid rents, yet rich in colour, friendships and aspirations. It was a world which was to hold Tiffany briefly, release her and then reclaim her for a lifetime.

A bearded man answered her knock and directed her to the upper floor, his stare boring into her back as she climbed the stairs. Gerard blinked at her in sleepy, bleary-eyed surprise. It was obvious that he had only just got out of bed.

'I didn't think you would come,' he said apologetically.

She glanced at his crumpled, unshaven appearance disparagingly. 'I said I would come,' she pointed out, 'and you won't get much painting or sculpting done if you only rise at noon.'

'It is warmer in bed.'

She had to concede this was true. Gerard's studio was bitterly cold; it was also exceedingly untidy – being littered with paints, easels, completed and half-completed canvases – and it reeked with the smells of artists' materials and cooking which pervaded the entire house. Tiffany wrinkled her nose and looked for something on which to sit; failing to locate a chair, she walked boldly to the bed and sat down on that. Gerard stared at her in utter fascination.

'I take it that the trade in copies of Old Masters has not been too good lately,' Tiffany remarked in her clear bell-like voice, 'as your funds do not stretch to the purchase of fuel.' She shivered and snuggled deeper into her furs. 'You can forget the sculpting – it is far too cold for me to come here again.'

Gerard appraised her carefully. His desire to sculpt her was genuine for she was the most exquisite thing he had ever seen, but if she could be transformed into Lady Bountiful as well so much the better. 'If you paid a good price for the sculpture, I could buy fuel.'

'You wanted to do it,' Tiffany retorted swiftly. 'You should be paying *me!*'

For a moment he was taken aback but then he threw back his head and laughed. 'How did your family make its money?' he asked.

'Diamonds.'

'Most appropriate. The hardest substance known to man – until you came along.'

The riposte appealed to Tiffany far more than the fulsome compliments she was accustomed to receive. 'I will give you money for fuel and some food,' she announced, 'and I might buy the sculpture if it is good enough – but don't rely on it. You see, no one must find out I am coming here.'

Gerard nodded, his guarded expression concealing the cynicism beneath. A bored little rich girl slumming it for a few hours' titillation! Normally the circumstances would not appeal to him, but this girl was so spectacularly gorgeous that he was prepared to make an exception. He would buy the fuel at the first opportunity because he must find out what lay underneath those bulky furs, and Gerard's heart beat faster as he wondered to what lengths she would go to alleviate that boredom.

On this first occasion they were not alone for long. Word of Tiffany's presence had spread and the other artists of the Alley began drifting in. They brought cheap wine, whisky and the smell of unwashed bodies, but also vitality and intelligent conversation. They talked about people and places Tiffany did not know – artists and exhibitions, poets, writers and musicians, Montmartre and London – and of the hardships they endured for the sake of their art. Yet, subtly, Tiffany remained the pivot and focus of the conversation; everything which was said, every expression and emphasis was meant for her. She understood this perfectly and was not surprised – to Tiffany there was not the slightest reason why the inhabitants of Greenwich Village should be any different from the élite of Fifth Avenue.

She came the next day for the first sitting – to a tidier room with coal burning in the stove and a chair for her to sit on, and to a cleaner, more handsome Gerard. His fingers handled the clay sensually and with a deep absorption which had a strangely soothing effect on her – a euphoric, floating feeling, almost as if his fingers were stroking her instead of the clay. He worked in silence but communicated with every movement of his body, drawing her into that peaceful relaxed ambience which yet contained a central pulse of excitement. She was almost sorry when his friends arrived again, breaking the spell.

The intimate dreamlike atmosphere persisted at future

sittings and soon Tiffany was coming to Macdougal Alley as much for this sensation as for the stimulation of new friends and a fresh environment. The stove, fired by Tiffany's dollars, gave out enough heat for her to shed the furs, but she was warmed also by the blaze in Gerard's brown eyes. While she was used to being admired, Gerard's appreciation of her beauty held a special significance; it was as if a favourite and treasured possession had been evaluated by an expert and pronounced to be a rare, genuine and outstanding specimen.

Obviously it was only a matter of time before he kissed her and she waited impatiently and with more anticipation than usual. The moment arrived one afternoon when the clay head achieved some recognisable shape and Gerard stepped back with a sigh of satisfaction, washed his hands and walked towards her, his demeanour suggesting that having reached a certain stage in the project he could permit himself some pleasurable diversion.

Tiffany was not bashful and she stood up to meet him half-way. At first his mouth was hard and bruising but then his lips softened and his tongue was insistently persuasive. She was breathless when he let her go but, yes, definitely there had been a firework or two.

'These damn corsets,' he murmured, his hands caressing her. 'It's like hugging a block of wood or a marble column. Couldn't you leave them off next time you come?'

'No,' said Tiffany decisively. 'My maid would think it extremely odd.'

'Of course. I keep forgetting I am dealing with a rich girl.' His arms tightened around her. 'Take off your clothes, Tiffany. Your head is lovely but I want to model your entire body – your naked body.'

His mouth crushed hers, passionate and demanding, and Tiffany's desire rose to meet his . . . but rose to what? What was it that his body and the response of her own were urging her to do? Tiffany was not afraid of the unknown, but she was confused by an instinctive caution which warred with her equally natural impetuosity.

'No!' she gasped at last.

'Tiffany, I will not hurt you. First and foremost, I am an artist.'

'First and foremost,' she retorted, 'you are a man.'

He did not press her but that night she lay in bed and ran her own hands over her body, imagining that it was Gerard who caressed her through the thin silk of the nightgown, and she quivered with longing. But again the question arose – longing for what? She did not know, except that it had something to do with having babies. Taking off your clothes, Tiffany reasoned in the pale light of dawn, cannot possibly mean you will have a baby.

'Very well,' she told Gerard the next day, 'but you must help me because I have never dressed or undressed myself in my life.'

He stared at her, his eyes glazing. Reverently he spread her fur coat on the grubby floor, pulled her down on to it and with eager, feverish fingers tore off the clothes until her body was exposed in all its perfection.

'A marble column indeed,' he murmured wonderingly, caressing a white rose-tipped breast, 'or alabaster, perhaps. And I was impertinent enough to consider painting or sculpting this! Why, Phidias himself could not do justice to you.'

'Phidias? Does he live in the Alley?'

He laughed, his sensitive artist's fingers sliding over her satin skin. 'Ignorant slut! Don't rich girls receive an education?'

'Of course, though I do admit to being a reluctant pupil. But don't think I am stupid – I can learn quickly enough when I want to.'

'I'll bet you can,' he said huskily and fastened his lips to her nipple while his fingers slid between her legs. The sensation was exquisite – too exquisite. Tiffany jack-knifed away.

'No!'

'Why not?'

'I might have a baby.'

67

'But I'm only . . . Don't you know how babies are made?'

Tiffany averted her face, hating to show her ignorance. 'No.' Then she twisted round and said earnestly, 'I wish you would tell me!'

'I would prefer to show you.' He reached for her again but she shook her head. 'Then I will show you in another way.'

He fetched several sheets of paper and began to sketch, the pencil stabbing the paper in quick bold strokes, and as he drew he talked. Tiffany listened and watched, heart thudding, throat dry, breathing quickening to match his. The pictures were unbelievably erotic and the tingling sensation he had aroused between her legs was developing into a gnawing ache. But at least she now knew why – she would always be grateful to him for that.

He laid down pencil and paper. 'Please,' he whispered, 'please! You cannot know how much I want you and how difficult it is for me to keep away from you!'

'But I might have a baby.'

'I'll pull out of you in time, I promise. *Please.*'

She wanted to give in but the fear of pregnancy was too great. 'Not now.' Suddenly she was aware of her vulnerability, lying naked in the room alone with him, and she pulled the fur protectively around her body.

His face contorted. 'I'll not force you,' he said, his voice brittle, full of frustration and pain. 'Even in the Alley we have some reputation and pride. Do you think I want you running out of here yelling rape? A man – gentleman or artist – would do anything to avoid that!'

Another sleepless night, but now she contemplated her newly acquired knowledge and the series of erotic images which seethed in her mind. Questions were answered, but her curiosity was unsatisfied and her physical longing increased a hundredfold. Did she dare? Could she trust him? . . . It wasn't fair – men had no need to worry about babies! How horrid it was to be a girl! But she would not let an accident of nature spoil her life . . . and he had promised.

Tiffany went to Macdougal Alley earlier than usual the following day because she was impatient and because it could be convenient to find him in bed. The front door was ajar so she ran lightly up the stairs, bursting unannounced into the studio where her greeting died on her lips. Gerard was not in bed; he was lying on the floor or, more precisely, he was lying on a dark-haired girl and after his explicit explanations Tiffany was left in no doubt about what he was doing.

She did not realise that he was fantasising that the girl was her, that he had placed an ancient threadbare rug on the exact spot where he had spread her fur, and that he had chosen the tallest dark-haired prostitute he could find. A hint of the truth reached her when Gerard looked up and, instead of registering horror or surprise, his face was illumined with ecstasy and he kept his eyes fixed on her as he moved within the scrawny body of the girl. However, Tiffany was not concerned with his motives because her feelings were not hurt. She neither loved him nor connected the sexual act with love – to her it was a tactile rather than an emotional experience. What she did feel at that moment was disappointment. She had come here keyed-up and eager for this new experience, this unveiling of the great mystery, and now it would not take place. She was acutely aware of how sordid the act seemed in these squalid surroundings and noted dispassionately that, unlike her, Gerard did not look better without his clothes – quite the contrary: his thin white body in that undignified position was ridiculous and unattractive.

Tiffany walked across the room to where the nearly completed clay head stood on its stand. Calmly she picked it up and dropped it; the nose broke off, but the rest made a most satisfying splodge on the floor. Then she swept out of the room and strode briskly round the corner to Washington Square in search of a cab to take her home. However, the fact that she behaved impeccably for the ensuing few weeks of the Christmas Season betrayed that she was more affected by the incident than she cared to acknowledge.

This was the night John Court had waited for, the culmination of all his work and aspirations, and his happiness was so intense that it hurt. It was January 1905 and Tiffany was the belle of Mrs Astor's ball.

He had attached himself firmly to her side, refusing to miss a moment of her triumph because he was so proud of her and because it was as much his success as hers. She had been prised away from him a few minutes ago, but the reason for this only increased his elation – Tiffany had been summoned to sit beside Mrs Astor on her 'throne' amid the envious eyes of the other guests. It was the ultimate accolade and for Court life had nothing more to offer. Only one thing was missing, he wished that Matthew Bright could have witnessed Tiffany's triumph because no woman in the world, not even little Miranda, could rival the beauty of the daughter *he* had made with Anne.

Randolph was watching Tiffany, too, with a hard discontented expression. Court knew the reason for this and, while he sympathised with the younger man, was glad he had stood up to Randolph in this instance.

'I think, John, that the time has come for me to speak to Tiffany,' Randolph had said a few days ago. He had dropped the 'uncle' recently and the new form of address emphasised the change in the relationship. 'We could announce our engagement at Mrs Astor's ball.'

The marriage with Randolph had been his own idea but now that the plan was reaching fruition, Court found the reality repugnant. Over the years he had grown accustomed to Randolph's ways, but still did not like him. Moreover Court had become aware of the subtle interference in his relationship with his daughter; Randolph directed his attention to Tiffany's faults – the faults to which Court had been blind for years and wished to continue ignoring. However, there was another reason for Court's reluctance to give official sanction to Randolph's

70

suit: he did not wish to give his daughter to any man. She was so beautiful and he loved her so much that he could not bear to part with her. It became abhorrent to him to think of losing even more of his influence – for Court had learned enough from Randolph to know that his earlier dream of maintaining his hold over Tiffany was already shattered – and hideous to visualise her in a man's bed. Court would have liked to freeze her in time, to keep her by him for ever, virginal and exquisite. As this was impossible, it was best she went to Randolph to found the dynasty. He knew his daughter so little that he never dreamed she would object, living as he did in an old-fashioned world where daughters were obedient to the wishes of their elders. Yes, she would go to Randolph – but not on the night of Mrs Astor's ball.

'Afterwards,' he said firmly to Randolph. 'You may speak to her afterwards, but she will go to the ball with me. For that evening she will be mine.'

So Randolph felt cheated, while Court's heart sang as he watched Tiffany talk to Mrs Astor: the old 'Queen', he said to himself, with her rightful successor; and indeed Court was not the only person to whom that thought occurred, because the entertainment was to be remembered as Tiffany Court's début and Caroline Astor's swan song – it was the last ball Mrs Astor gave. The old lady was sprinkled with magnificent jewels as usual, but tonight the 'Marie Antoinette stomacher' was outshone because glowing at Tiffany's throat, perfectly matched by the gold of her dress, was the Tiffany diamond.

The gem had never been worn before and the jewellers had required some persuasion to lend it for the occasion. When it was finally agreed, Court purchased a new diamond necklace and temporarily replaced the huge central pendant with the golden stone. Somehow it added the final touch to Tiffany's perfection, to Court's sense of completeness and to their *cachet* in society. Court was content, with a sense of fulfilment few can achieve, and it never occurred to him that after the pinnacle has been reached, the only way is down.

On the way home Court took hold of Tiffany's hand and

squeezed it. 'You were wonderful, sweetheart.'

In the darkness Tiffany wriggled uncomfortably and extricated her hand. She was not a girl who liked to be touched – except in certain circumstances. Also she was tired and irritable. She had been pleased to wear the famous diamond, but otherwise the evening had been tedious and she could not understand why Papa and so many other people set such store by these occasions. However, in the hall Court grasped her hand again.

'Randolph has something to say to you, darling,' he said. 'I will wait in the library until you are ready for me.' He put both arms around her, held her very tight and then walked slowly away.

For a moment Tiffany stood motionless. She was in no doubt at all about what Randolph would say and was suddenly grateful to that otherwise insufferable Englishman for warning her. With perfect composure she walked into the drawing-room, waited for Randolph to shut the door and then turned to face him. Attack, she had heard, was the best form of defence.

'You intend asking me to marry you,' she said icily, 'but I can save you the trouble because the answer is no.'

Never, in all the delicate negotiations he had conducted, had Randolph been so wrong-footed. He stared at her in genuine astonishment.

'I must ask you to reconsider.'

'No.'

No tantrums, no temper, no histrionics, just an implacable and impenetrable wall. Whatever Randolph had expected – and he had such a high opinion of himself that he had not expected to be rejected – it had not been this. Nonplussed, he tried to be reasonable and persuasive.

'Tiffany, I want to marry you very much so perhaps we could discuss this in a sensible adult way. Please be kind enough to explain your objections.'

'I detest the sight of you and I would not marry you if you were the last man on earth.' She neither shouted nor screamed, but adopted a deliberately matter-of-fact tone.

'But why? What have I done to deserve your dislike? We must sort this out satisfactorily, Tiffany, because your father wants this marriage as much as I do.'

'Have you ever known me to do what my father wants?'

Randolph sighed. 'I must confess that the answer to that is no.' His face hardened. 'In fact your obedience leaves a lot to be desired.'

She smiled sweetly. 'Then there is no reason why I should start now,' and *her* face hardened. 'Particularly *now*!'

Randolph fought against a rising tide of humiliation and fury. To stand here and take these insults from this spoiled child was more than he could bear. But he must endure it because he wanted her – her beauty and her fortune, the Court Bank and Court Diamonds. Resolutely he composed his features into a set smile.

'I am at fault, my dear,' he conceded graciously. 'I have been too preoccupied with business affairs – our *family* affairs – to woo you as you deserve. Also, perhaps you have been accustomed to think of me as a cousin. I do assure you that from now on you will see me in a very different light.' He stepped very close to her, his lips still stretched into a smile, and stroked her cheek. His eyes darkened at this first contact with her and he would have taken the caress further had she not recoiled from him.

'Don't touch me! You loathsome creature, don't ever touch me again!'

Her repugnance was so obvious and so clearly sincere that Randolph's control snapped. Fiercely he fastened his hands round her wrists, holding them to his chest so that she was pinned against him.

'I will marry you, Tiffany,' he hissed, 'and then I will touch you as often as I like!'

'Never! I'll die before I allow your body inside mine in the marriage bed.'

His grip on her wrists tightened so that she winced with pain. 'What do you know of these things?' he asked harshly. 'You are not supposed to know . . . How did you find out? My God, girl, what have you been doing!'

'Why, Randolph, are you wondering if I have been given practical tuition as well as the theory?' Her lovely eyes flashed. 'Well, you can go on wondering because I am not telling you! And let go of me because you are hurting my arms.'

'Hurting you? *Hurting you*? I haven't even started yet!' All pretence had vanished and his face contorted with the intensity of his emotions. 'I will tame you yet and show you who is master. I'll crush you and pin you down, like a butterfly with its wings nailed to a board. I'll . . .' Swiftly he twisted her arms behind her back and jerked her closer, bending his head to press his lips savagely against hers.

Tiffany fought him, twisting and struggling until she succeeded in wrenching her mouth away, but she could not free her hands or arms and his face was still ominously close.

'What are you trying to do? Bite me, like a vampire, like you bit the girl on the boat?'

Again she had surprised him and he relaxed his hold slightly.

'You didn't think I knew about that, did you, Randolph? But I do. I know a lot of things about you – more, apparently, than you know about me! Now, let me go before I start to scream.'

Reason returned and he released her, furious with himself for having lost control. However, his resolve had not weakened. As she went to the door to call Court, he said menacingly, 'You will come to me in the end, Tiffany. I guarantee it.'

'Like hell I will! The devil himself could not devise a set of circumstances which could make it possible – so that is one guarantee on which the Court Bank will default!' At that moment Court entered the room and she rounded on him. 'Whose idea was this? Did Randolph persuade you it was a sound proposition or was the arrangement always in your mind from the time you welcomed him into this house and set him up in business?'

The faces of Tiffany and Randolph clearly told the story

of what had transpired and Court was completely taken aback, not only at Tiffany's recalcitrance but at Randolph's failure.

'You must marry Randolph, darling. It is such a suitable match,' he said helplessly.

'Suitable? *Match*? Am I the subject of business negotiations, of a contract to be signed when all the ends have been neatly tied up? I am not a diamond, Papa,' and her hand went to the golden stone at her neck, 'to be bought or sold or bartered as the occasion asks. I am not a lump of rock which can be disposed of and displayed for the admiration of society.'

'Of course not, sweetheart, but . . .'

'But *nothing*! I will not marry Randolph and there is nothing you can do to force me.' She looked at Court contemptuously. 'Of course you could threaten to turn me out of the house without a cent. Your problem is that I would go and I would make very sure that the whole of America knew why.'

She would, too, thought Randolph, clenching his fists. 'I suggest, John,' he said smoothly, 'that Tiffany needs a little time to consider the matter.'

Court brightened. 'You are absolutely right,' he said eagerly. 'Tiffany, surely that is only fair?'

Tiffany was thinking quickly and divined a way of turning the affair to her own advantage. 'I might think about it,' she remarked with an air of apparent caution, 'but I refuse to live in the same house as Randolph while I do so.'

'But Randolph cannot leave New York at the moment,' cried Court, 'and for him to move to another address in the city would cause gossip.'

'In that case *I* could go away for a time,' Tiffany said, her voice indicating that she was generously fitting in with their arrangments.

'But that would appear even more odd than Randolph's absence,' objected Court.

'Not if I went far away, on vacation – Europe, for instance.'

'Europe!' Court was horrified. It was what he had always dreaded and of course he could not allow her to go. But what was the alternative? Between them Tiffany and Randolph – and now Tiffany's rejection of Randolph – had forced Court out of his dream world into reality. He acknowledged that he could not imprison his daughter for ever – sooner or later she would travel to Europe and surely the chance of her meeting Matthew was very remote. 'Yes,' he said slowly, 'such a trip would seem perfectly normal. Your Aunt Sarah can accompany you.'

'No.' Tiffany's refusal was absolute. 'She would remind me too much of *him*.'

'Then I must go with you myself. Frank and his mother were due to sail to Europe next month, but we cannot both leave the business at the same time. I shall cancel Frank's vacation and . . .'

'Papa,' Tiffany interrupted reproachfully. 'How could you be so unkind? They are going to see Frank's brother, Vincent – he didn't come home for Christmas because he spent the vacation with a friend.' Her mind was analysing the possibilities swiftly. On no account must Papa come with her, because he would never leave her side. 'Why don't I go with Frank and his mother. I quite like Mrs Whitney,' she added graciously.

Court felt that he was being overtaken by events. 'Do you? Then I shall speak to her.' Automatically he glanced at Randolph for approval. The younger man was reflecting carefully on the situation. He disliked Frank Whitney's open devotion to Tiffany, but on the other hand was convinced that Whitney stood no chance of winning Tiffany's affections and that she would be safe with him. All things considered, this was the best short-term solution. Randolph nodded agreement.

Upstairs Pauline sat in her mother's boudoir, trying to prop open weary eyelids. Several times she had suggested it was time for bed, but Sarah Court would not hear of it – she knew Randolph was going to propose to Tiffany after the ball and did not intend to miss the celebrations. So, after being summoned to admire Tiffany in her finery, Pauline had sat here all evening, listening to her mother's praise of Tiffany's beauty, of the success she would be at the ball and how wonderful life would be when she was married to Randolph.

Sarah and her daughter did not warrant an invitation from Mrs Astor, but it was some slight consolation to Pauline that Frank Whitney had not risen that high in the hierarchy either. It was obvious, thought Pauline, her mind wandering from her mother's interminable chatter, that she and Frank were made for each other. If Tiffany married Randolph, perhaps Frank would return from his European vacation with a mended heart and a fresh eye – perhaps he would see *her* in a new light. Her spirits rose a little, but only a little because she was so tired.

They heard Tiffany, Court and Randolph return from the ball. There was a long pause and then Randolph entered the room. He was too proud to go into details; he merely informed them that Tiffany needed a vacation and would travel to Europe with the Whitneys.

Pauline left abruptly. In her bedroom she buried her face in her hands, overcome with despair. It was bad enough to be left at home while Tiffany went to the ball, but this . . . this was too much. She raised her head and gazed at her reflection in the looking-glass. Would anything, *could* anything, ever make her beautiful? And sadly she concluded that nothing – not even all the diamonds in her Uncle John's mines or those which had yet to be discovered in the deserts or the seas – could work that miracle.

Before Tiffany's departure Court spoke to her seriously.

'You may be introduced to English society,' he said, remembering that Vincent Whitney moved in smart circles. 'It is possible, although admittedly unlikely, that you might meet a man called Matthew Bright. If you do, you will be polite but on no account allow yourself to be drawn into conversation with him.'

This was quite the wrong approach because naturally Tiffany was intrigued. 'Why not?'

'He is an old acquaintance of mine, but he is unscrupulous and not to be trusted. In fact we had a difference of opinion over a certain matter many years ago.'

'What did you quarrel about?'

'I cannot tell anyone, not even you,' answered Court, compounding his error. 'Just promise me that you will avoid him.'

'I promise.' Bright, she was thinking, how that name does keep cropping up! The scent of an old family feud was fascinating but Tiffany happily gave her word to Court – after all, the promise had not included Philip.

And indeed it had not. Obsessed with Matthew, Court had forgotten Philip.

The Whitneys and their charge spent the first weeks of their vacation in London, staying at the Savoy where Tiffany's social and financial superiority were advertised by her occupation of a suite at thirty shillings a day, whereas the Whitneys had a single bedroom each at seven shillings and sixpence.

There was too much emphasis on sightseeing for Tiffany's liking but politely, in cold and wet weather, she visited the places on Mrs Whitney's list of cultural centres and historical monuments. She had decided that the wisest policy was to conform at the outset of the trip, but was conscious of holding something in reserve . . . of waiting for something to happen.

Of course, Frank and Mrs Whitney were not aware of the background to Tiffany's sudden desire to travel, but both were delighted that she had honoured them with her presence. The funds provided by John Court eased their own financial burden considerably but, more important, Tiffany's companionship was interpreted as a definite sign of her fondness for Frank. Having dreaded the prospect of the trip because it would part him from her for months, Frank existed in a state of bliss which was only slightly blighted by Tiffany's refusal to grant him more than a brotherly peck on the cheek.

On the last day of March Vincent Whitney arrived. He was a younger version of Frank, but his interest in Tiffany centred on the sensation she would make with the chaps and the resultant prestige for himself rather than on any aspirations to her hand.

'It's the Boat Race tomorrow,' he announced. 'You must come.'

'What sort of boats?' asked Tiffany, with visions of the America's Cup yacht race.

'Rowing boats, of course – eights.'

'Oh.' Tiffany's interest waned. 'It will probably rain,' she said unenthusiastically.

'Do come! It's fearfully thrilling and traditional – Oxford and Cambridge have competed against each other in this race nearly every year since 1829. Mind you, that is positively modern by comparison with my college, Balliol, which was founded in 1263. You wouldn't believe how *old* things are here.'

'Oh yes, I would,' sighed Tiffany with painful memories of her sightseeing trips. 'How long does the race last?'

'Only twenty minutes. Honestly, everyone goes – it's a social occasion. I am looking forward to it immensely because a friend of mine is in the Oxford boat – Philip Bright.'

'I'll come,' she said immediately.

They assembled at Mortlake on a chilly, blustery day, surrounded by a crowd of smart socialites, shabbily-dressed working people and boisterous undergraduates sporting either the light blue colours of Cambridge or the dark blue of Oxford. At last the sound of cheering could be heard up-river and eyes were strained into the distance to see the two boats coming closer. One was well ahead of the other.

'We must win,' Vincent said passionately. 'Cambridge have won for the past three years. By God, it *is* Oxford in the lead. Well done, Philip, well done!'

He began cheering and did not stop until the Oxford Boat shot past the finish three lengths ahead of Cambridge. Tiffany watched as the boats moved to the landing stage and the Oxford crew disembarked. Except for the diminutive cox they were all tall, strongly-built young men, but there was one who topped the others by several inches and whose shoulder muscles rippled beneath his vest. His fair hair glinted, even in the grey of the early Spring day, and as the Oxford supporters cheered again his handsome face lit up with the most beautiful, joyous smile that Tiffany had ever seen.

Please, she prayed silently, *please* let it be him!

CHAPTER FIVE

In . . . out. In . . . out. Although utterly exhausted, Philip's
body still throbbed with the rhythm and he seemed to be
moving in time to the stroke. Every muscle ached but he
grinned triumphantly as he pulled on his flannels and
blazer – how much more leaden would be the limbs of the
defeated Cambridge crew! *He had done it!* Done the impossible – won a seat in the Oxford boat although he had not
rowed for his school, for at Eton Philip had elected to be a
'dry-bob'.

The choice between cricket and rowing had not been
easy and only today could Philip believe he had achieved
the best of both worlds. He knew that at Eton they talked
about him still and that the men of his generation would
continue to relive his innings over their claret and cigars
for as long as cricket was played in England. It was not so
much what he had done – captain of the XI, victor over
Harrow, Winchester and the rest – but *the way* he had
done it. As a tactician he was astute, but as a batsman Philip
was sublime and comparisons were made between the
handsome youth and some of England's greatest players.

However Philip was not only a high-scoring and consist-
ent batsman; there was a refinement in his play, a delicacy
of touch which blended perfectly with the elegance of his
figure. At the crease on a sleepy summer afternoon, tall,
slim-hipped and graceful in white, Philip was a spell-
binder. He was only playing the bowling of schoolboys, of
course, yet a hint of greatness shone through the fluency of
his batting which gave spectators cause to hope for the
future of English cricket.

The only time that Philip regretted the choice between

81

being a cricketer and an oarsman was at Henley when he stood on the towpath to watch the Eton Eight sweep past. Considering his late development as a sportsman, it was astonishing how quickly he had acquired a taste for adulation, how – although he took pains not to show it – he disliked applauding instead of receiving the applause. At Oxford, he decided, he would do both – and so comparisons with C.B. Fry began to grow because Philip, like that gentleman of Edwardian sport, excelled at everything he attempted.

Eton was the cradle of English rowing, supplying a huge majority of Blues for the University crews. In 1897 eight out of nine men in the Oxford boat were Etonians and in 1899 seven rowed for Oxford and five for Cambridge. This year, 1905, the Oxford boat was manned by three men from Eton and Balliol and two from Eton and Merton, while Cambridge included five men from Eton and 3rd Trinity. Philip's pedigree was flawless and the rowing he did in the holidays gave him a sound start. Even so, there were those who asserted that a seat in the Oxford boat simply could not be done. But he *had* done it! And they had won. And now, having walked into the University cricket eleven, he was that rare and glorious being – a Double Blue!

He had not rowed stroke, of course, and therefore a faint regret marred an otherwise perfect day. Stroke controlled the rate and the rhythm like a maestro conducting an orchestra, driving his crew to crescendos of spurts and the limit of their physical endurance. Strokes, it was said, were born and not made, and although Philip was certain he possessed that instinctive quality, Oxford had preferred not to gamble on a comparatively unknown quantity. As he emerged into the throng of cheering Oxford supporters, he knew that the loudest praise would be lavished on the President of the University Boat Club and on Stroke but he knew, too, that he would be mobbed by his own admirers. To many undergraduates Philip Bright of Balliol was the epitome of the University man – a Double Blue who, despite the enormous amount of time he devoted to sporting activities, somehow managed to sail effortlessly through his academic work. Tallest and most handsome of his contemporaries, Philip so represented the perfect undergraduate that no one delved deeper into his character or asked themselves if there was any real substance beneath the veneer.

Chaps were thumping him on the back and wringing his hand, while high-pitched feminine voices in the crowd indicated that the families of crew and supporters were well-represented. No need to look for Sir Matthew Bright, thought Philip cynically; his father must be the only parent in the entire history of the Boat Race who had actually seemed disappointed at his son's prowess on the river. No, Papa would not be here but Laura might . . . My god, there she was, trying to fight her way through the crowd. She must have travelled up from Berkshire especially . . .

Conflicting emotions twisted inside him at the sight of his stepmother, because Laura's marriage to his father had completed Philip's alienation from his family. His own mother, Lady Anne, had died giving birth to Miranda when he was nine years old. But even before her death Philip had been conscious of living a strange and lonely existence on the periphery of the family circle, aware of Anne's lack of interest in him and of Matthew's dislike. His bitterness grew as he observed Matthew's overwhelming love for Miranda.

Then it had seemed that everything might change. He had gone to Brightwell, the family's country home in Berkshire, for the Easter holidays of 1899 to find that his old nanny had been retired but in her place was Miranda's new governess – Laura, with the gleaming chestnut hair, enormous emerald eyes and the sweetest smile in England. She had nursed him and Miranda through a severe bout of scarlet fever and the period of convalecence had been the happiest time of his life. Once she had gathered him into her arms and held him close: he could still smell the perfume of her skin, feel the silkiness of her hair, the sensation of her breasts beneath his cheek . . . but then, as he had begun to love her, she had allied herself with the enemy and gone to South Africa with Miranda and Papa.

He had been consumed with pain when he heard of Laura's marriage to Matthew, filled with a blend of bitterness and rage when he contemplated his goddess's feet of clay and visualised her in his father's bed. Since then he had avoided Laura because her touch revolted him, bringing into sharp relief the caresses she bestowed on his father. Yet that touch fascinated him, too. A deep longing for a family, for motherly love, for sexual love, were mixed up with Philip's hatred of his father – the emotions were suppressed, not fully understood, but extremely potent.

At Mortlake Philip turned away, pretending not to see her. He believed that he was Laura's one failure and took some satisfaction in it – if he could not have her, he could hurt her!

'Philip, well done, well done!' Vincent Whitney pumped his hand enthusiastically after he and Dick Latimer had struggled to Philip's side. 'You must spend the evening with me and my family. There is the most marvellous girl I want you to meet!'

'My dear Vincent, you must be out of your mind,' Philip drawled. 'I have no intention of deviating from the time-honoured traditions of Boat Race night – which means that I shall get roaring drunk and end up at Vine Street police station in the early hours of tomorrow morning. Even as I speak the hostelries of Piccadilly and Leicester Square are preparing for the onslaught I shall unleash upon them, the St James's Restaurant is battening down its hatches, while the police are fingering their truncheons and trying to devise a foolproof method of adhering their helmets to their heads! If a female does feature in my plans, it is not likely to be the sort of girl who would accompany your sainted Mama.' He waited for the laughter to die down and then said slyly, 'An actress is more my mark tonight – my family is famous for its theatrical entrances!'

This time the laughter was more ribald because everyone understood Philip's innuendo. The previous year his cousin Charles, Earl of Highclere, had taken a bride. Pursuant to an affinity for the less well-bred members of society, Highclere had scandalised his peers by marrying a 'Gaiety Girl'. 'If Uncle Matthew can marry the governess,' he had asserted stubbornly to his horrified relatives, 'I can marry whomsoever I please.' What was worse to the diehards among the aristocracy was the fact that the Earl of Highclere had set an example others were prepared to follow – coronets were now the going rate for the favours of the denizens of the West End stage.

'Are you joining us, Vincent?' Philip inquired, 'or will you be spending the evening with your mother and her little friend?'

'I'm coming with you,' Vincent assured him hastily. Much as he admired Tiffany, she would keep until tomorrow while Boat Race night was a transient, ephemeral occasion.

It turned out to be an extremely inebriated occasion and at one stage became argumentative when several of the party took a fancy to the same girl.

'I saw her first,' asserted Dick Latimer stubbornly.

'But she likes me best,' Philip replied.

'Perhaps we should auction her,' suggested Dick, swaying slightly as he staggered to his feet, 'like the barmaids on the diamond fields.'

'To hell with that idea – it sounds expensive! We'll throw for her.' Philip produced a dice from his pocket. 'Everyone call a number, but mine is six.'

They were sitting in a dimly-lit private room at the restaurant and the smoke-filled atmosphere tensed as Philip cleared a space on the table which was littered with the debris of the meal. He drained his glass of champagne, solemnly placed the dice inside the glass and shook it robustly before spilling the dice on to the table.

'Six,' cried Dick in acute disappointment. 'Good God, Philip, don't you ever lose at anything! Here, let me see that dice.'

'By all means.' Philip grinned. 'But surely you know that

there is only one person in the world whom I would cheat?'

'Your father, you mean! Well, the dice appears to be in order. I suppose this is a case of being hoist by my own petard – if it wasn't for me, you would not have been in the bloody Boat Race to start with!'

Good-humouredly Dick beckoned to one of the other girls while the sultry brunette over whom they had been arguing sank down on to Philip's knee. Casually he pulled down the bodice of her dress and began kissing her bare breasts but his mind was far away, recalling the incident to which Dick referred . . .

It had been five years ago when he was summoned from school to London to see Matthew, Laura and Miranda after their return from Kimberley. He had gone straight to his room and, although aware that there was to be some sort of party to celebrate the homecoming, had lain down fully-dressed on the bed and waited. At last the door had burst open to admit Matthew and father and son had stared at each other, the aversion and antipathy between them as strong as it had ever been. Philip looked at the expression in Matthew's blue eyes and wondered what those eyes saw.

In fact Matthew had seen a slender youth who was the image of his first wife, with Anne's pale blonde hair and violet eyes; a boy who was cold, aloof and withdrawn, with an impenetrable reserve – not that Matthew had ever tried to break through the barrier. Matthew's mouth had hardened. He was unable to look at Philip without seeing other images in his mind's eye – memories which still had the power to hurt even after all these years; memories of Anne in another man's arms, reinforcing Matthew's conviction that Philip was not his son.

He was staring at Philip's rumpled suit with distaste. 'You might at least put on a clean collar to meet our guests.'

Philip bowed. 'Sir,' he said in almost mock acquiescence. It was typical of their poor relationship that neither thought it odd that they should talk of Eton collars after a separation of nine months.

'Did Laura tell you what time to be downstairs?'

'I have not seen your wife.' Philip allowed the faintest flick of insolence to flavour his reply. 'However,' he added as Matthew's eyebrows rose in surprise, 'I can relieve your mind of any suspicion of her negligence. I left orders that I should not be disturbed.'

'I shall expect you in the drawing-room at half-past-nine.'

'In a clean collar,' agreed Philip.

Matthew's frown deepened. The long separation appeared to have had an entirely adverse effect upon the boy. 'I gather you have not seen your sister either. She is extremely disappointed.'

'Why? It is May and I have not seen Miranda since last summer. I would not have thought a few more hours made much difference.'

'She has suffered a great deal,' snapped Matthew. 'We all suffered!' He glared at Philip's impassive face and took an impatient step forward. 'God damn it, Philip, aren't you even interested? Don't you care about our ordeal in Kimberley? We were under siege, blast you, in danger of losing our lives. Your Uncle Nicholas *was* killed and Miranda . . . Miranda is hurt. Don't you care at all?'

Philip turned away to the window, choking back the response which rose unbidden to his lips. I cared about being left behind, he wanted to say. I cared that as usual you took Miranda with you while I stayed at school and was passed round the family like an unwanted parcel during the holidays. I mind *desperately* that you, Miranda and Laura had all the fun, the excitement and danger while I declined Latin verbs. And I mind, too, that you married Laura.

'I do not imagine that your progress at school has been startling, or even satisfactory, while I have been away?' Matthew said sarcastically.

Philip seemed to consider the matter, then shook his head. 'No,' he agreed politely.

'Is there anything, anything at all, at which you excel?'

'Oh, no.'

'Or at which you are even passably good?'

'Nothing.' Philip smiled. He knew, and so did his tutors, that he had a fine brain and strong physique and could be brilliant at his studies or on the playing fields if he wished – but Philip did not wish. He did not want to do anything which might please his father.

'Don't think,' said Matthew sharply, 'that just because you are my son you can automatically take your place in my business empire. I do not tolerate fools even if they are my flesh and blood.' Which you are not, he added silently, but even so his words were empty because Matthew was planning his dynasty and perforce Philip was its lynch-pin.

'I quite understand.' This time Philip's lips curved cynically. If only Papa knew! If only he could say that the last thing on earth he wanted was to go into his father's business. Philip knew perfectly well what he wished to do with his life and his ambitions were a world away from gold and diamonds.

Matthew had slammed out of the room and although Philip managed to avoid him at the party, another tense confrontation had taken place at breakfast the next morning, followed by an even more disturbing interview with Laura. Emotionally charged and overexcited, Philip had run upstairs to vent his anger, jealousy and frustration on his sister before rushing out of the house to catch the next train back to school. Eton had been playing Winchester at cricket and that was where Dick Latimer had come in . . .

In the gloom of the restaurant, Philip lifted his head from the girl's breasts and cautiously edged his chair further back from the lighted table and into the shadows, while the girl clung precariously to her perch on his knees. He smiled at her and slid his hands up her stockinged leg . . . garters and then . . . nothing but smooth silken flesh, for she was not wearing any underclothes. She twisted round to kiss him and across her shoulder Philip could just make out Dick Latimer's dark head . . .

*　　*　　*

'What's the score, Dick?' Philip had asked.

'We bowled them out for 120, but now we are 20 for 3.'

'Oh Lord, that isn't so good, is it! Has Maitland come in yet?'

'No, he's batting at Number Six. Anyway, what the hell are you doing here? We weren't expecting you until tomorrow.'

Philip grinned. 'I couldn't miss the match. Damn it, the team need my support – look at the way they collapsed in my absence! They will improve no end now I'm here!'

At that moment a groan echoed round the ground as the Winchester fast bowler lifted the Eton batsman's middle stump.

'Crikey, he's made a ruddy duck,' exclaimed Dick in disgust, turning to Philip. 'Jolly decent of you to come back, old chap, but I reckon we were doing better without you!'

Philip sighed in mock dismay. 'I seem to be as welcome as the flowers in Spring wherever I go,' he said sarcastically.

'Ah, so there's the rub! I gather the advent of the new Lady Bright has not eased the domestic situation. Yet this time last year you were mad about her.'

Philip had no wish to explain his true feelings, even to Dick. 'One does have to accept the unwelcome fact, *mon ami*, that she is not quite *comme il faut*.'

'That doesn't matter,' said Dick thoughtfully. 'Oh look, here comes Maitland – if ever we needed a captain's innings, it's now!' He applauded loudly and then resumed, 'Your father is such a romantic figure that he can get away with it!'

'Romantic! My father!' Philip scoffed. 'It's obvious you don't know him like I do. He's a pain in the neck. He started on again about my going into the business.'

'Most chaps would be quite keen on the idea of mountains of gold and diamonds,' observed Dick drily, 'but of course you have to be different. Why on earth are you so obsessed with motor cars?'

'Lots of reasons.' Philip gazed into the distance, then

focused suddenly on the game and shouted, 'Well played, sir! *That's* a bit more like it,' as Maitland belted a ball for four. 'The machinery fascinates me and I love the speed and the danger of the racing.' He paused again, remembering how his cousin Julia had called him a coward because he had been afraid of horses and how he had sworn that one day he would prove her wrong. 'But there's more to it than that. Motor cars are the coming thing, a symbol of our times, heralding a new, faster, more emancipated age. They shake the foundations of the world our fathers know.'

'Spoken like a true orator,' teased Dick, but he was more impressed than he let on. Richard Latimer, the eldest son of Lord Netherton, was the finest scholar of his generation at Eton, with a clear incisive brain and a maturity beyond his years. Tall and dark-haired, his breeding, good looks and intelligence singled him out as the boy most likely to succeed, who would effortlessly take his predestined place at the forefront of Great Britain's affairs in whatever capacity he chose. His close friendship with Philip Bright surprised many of their fellows, but the two boys were more alike than was at first apparent; people were deceived by Dick's obvious, easy excellence, while Philip concealed his talents under a cloak of indifference.

'You would be an idiot not to take advantage of your father's millions and use them for your own ends,' Dick observed shrewdly.

'I don't want his beastly money!'

'Oh yes, you do! Or put it another way, you *need* it! Motor cars are pretty expensive and I'm sure that racing them eats up the cash like nobody's business.'

'I don't suppose the matter of my entering Bright Diamonds will arise. My father made it very clear that he doesn't suffer fools gladly.'

'You are not a fool! You know it, I know it, everyone knows it.' Dick glared fiercely at his friend. 'You don't try, that's all – and I presume you don't try because Papa wouldn't notice if you did. Have you considered the freedom which academic or sporting excellence would bring?'

'No,' Philip admitted. 'I'm not sure I know what you mean.'

'It would appear that you want as little as possible to do with your family. One way to achieve that independence is to achieve more – show other people how good you are – because if you don't want your father's money, you have to obtain finance elsewhere.'

'I don't see how sport . . .' Philip began but broke off as Maitland's drive shot towards him. He sprang to his feet, scooped up the ball and tossed it to the advancing fielder, all in one fluent graceful movement – '. . . would help.'

'I take it all back! You *are* an idiot after all.' Dick shook his head in exasperation. 'Apart from all the "playing fields of Eton" stuff – with which I agree, incidentally – it stands to reason that driving cars competitively must require a great deal of physical strength, yet you lounge about the place like a languid lily! But you can do it – look how you fielded that ball! Wouldn't you like to play for the First Eleven?'

'Can't say that I'm very bothered one way or the other.'

'Because Papa wouldn't come to watch you play?' Dick sighed. '*I'll* watch, Philip – except that I want to be in the team with you! The other chaps will watch. The *girls* will watch. You are a born cricketer – you have the right build and a natural eye – and you could row, too. Think how the exercise would develop your shoulder and arm muscles, enabling you to hang on to the steering-wheel of a motor car during those gruelling continental races.'

Philip was staring at him, comprehension dawning in his eyes. 'My God, you're right,' he said slowly. His eyes swivelled back to the majestic figure of Maitland at the crease, watching as the Eton captain cut the ball elegantly for another boundary to the cheers of his admirers. It occurred to Philip that there was another advantage to Dick's proposal: if he enhanced his reputation in the eyes of the world, his family would take notice – and then he could show them, in no uncertain terms, that it was too late because *he* would not want *them*!

'Of course I'm right.' Dick grinned, eyes twinkling in a manner which softened the boast. 'I'm available any time you want advice on your future.'

'Dispensing wisdom under the oak tree,' mocked Philip, leaning back to stare at the leafy branches above them, 'like Plato "in the olive grove of Academe".'

'I hope not! "So wise so young, they say, do never live long",' quoted Dick, capping Milton with Shakespeare.

'And we are going to live for ever!'

The two boys smiled at each other and their smile embraced all the boys around them – the beautiful gilded youth of England, bathed in sunshine, poised on the brink of a glorious new century.

'What will you do with your life?' Philip asked.

'Politics.' Dick spoke with calm certainty.

'Is it worth your while? You'll have to trickle along to the House of Lords one day.'

'Not for years and years. Papa is exceptionally hale and hearty and our family is famed for its longevity, I am very glad to say! But come on, old man, tell me about the Siege. I'm dying to hear the gory details.'

'I didn't ask about it.'

'What? Honestly, you are the end!' Dick shook his head in disbelief. 'In that case, tell me the latest about cars. Have you heard from Williams recently?'

'He is still working for Daimler in Coventry.' Philip was always eager to talk about Williams who had once worked as a groom in the stables of Philip's grandfather, and he was off on his favourite hobby-horse. Later, after a glorious victory over Winchester, he contemplated again the door which Dick had opened for him so easily and unexpectedly that afternoon – the door to a whole new attitude, to a positive approach – and a glow of enthusiasm and anticipation spread through him at the prospect of flexing his physical and intellectual muscle . . .

On Boat Race night, however, another muscle was demanding attention. The girl had undone his trousers, her fingers were playing with him and he was acutely aware of that bare bottom beneath her dress. Did he dare? Again he glanced towards the table but no one was taking the least notice. Why not? In an hour he would be too drunk to manage it. He gestured to the girl to sit astride him and she lowered herself on to him, spreading out her full skirts like a crinoline to conceal their activity. For decorum's sake it was necessary to restrict physical movement, but the titillation of making love in public more than compensated. Really, Philip thought, 'making love' was hardly an apt term for this exercise but no matter – as he had decided five years ago at Eton, he was never going to fall in love, never, never, *never*!

At Mortlake Tiffany had watched Philip and his acolytes march away, taking with them all the colour and life of the occasion and leaving behind a drab sense of anti-climax. Fuming at the unaccustomed rebuff, her temper was not improved by the presence of the faithful Frank who, naturally, was not tempted to seek other pleasures.

'I think we should visit Paris,' said Mrs Whitney that evening over dinner. 'Would you like that, Tiffany?'

'*Paris!* But when are we going to Oxford?' cried Tiffany in dismay.

Mrs Whitney was startled by her reaction. Indeed she had been dreading the Oxford visit because her own interest was in Vincent and she was afraid that Tiffany would be bored. 'The University is on vacation, dear. Vincent says we must go to Oxford for something called Eights Week at the end of May.'

'The end of *May!*' It seemed a lifetime away and Tiffany's lips set mutinously. Frank winced; from now on she would be much more difficult to handle.

In fact the weeks passed more quickly than Tiffany anticipated. Paris in the spring had its attractions for even so unromantic a soul as she. Returning to her autocratic ways, she compelled the unwilling Whitney brothers to conspire with her against their mother and escort her to the less

93

desirable parts of the city. On her eighteenth birthday she drank absinthe in a Montmartre cafe, practised her French on the artists and again experienced the lure of Bohemia. So mercurial were her moods that she was almost resentful when she had to leave this free-and-easy atmosphere to return to the stricter confines of society. Her irritation reached its zenith when she heard Mrs Whitney's choice of hotel in Oxford.

'The Randolph,' she said icily to Frank and his mother, 'is completely out of the question.'

'But Vincent says it is the *only* place to stay,' protested Mrs Whitney. 'It has an elevator.'

'As I have a perfectly good pair of legs to carry me up and down the stairs, an elevator is superfluous to my requirements.'

Mrs Whitney began to get fussed. She had suffered from migraines in Paris and kept much to her room while the boys looked after Tiffany; now she could feel another attack coming on. She was falling into the trap of finding it easier to lie in a darkened room than do battle with Tiffany Court. Also, she strongly disapproved of a young unmarried lady mentioning her legs in front of a gentleman. So they stayed at the Mitre on the corner of Turl Street and the High where the food was good, the light was electric and the cellars dated back to the thirteenth century; more to the point, although its advertisements omitted to mention the fact, it received the approval of Tiffany Court.

The weather exerted a powerful influence on England Tiffany decided, as she made her way past Corpus Christi and Merton Colleges and down the avenue of elms across Christ Church meadows. Sightseeing in London in the cold and rain had been dreary and depressing; Oxford in the afternoon sunshine was golden and glorious. The atmosphere was festive: the men in flannels, blazers and straw boaters, the women in colourful summery dresses with huge hats and gay parasols. She was more than usually aware of the heads which turned in her direction and of the buzz of excitement she occasioned. Her gown, hat and parasol were of palest cream lace, the entire ensemble newly-bought in Paris; and remembering the size of a certain oarsman, she had forsaken the customary flat-heeled slippers and purchased a pair of shoes with dainty 'louis' heels which added another inch to her own height. As a result her walk was less impetuous and eager but more swaying and graceful and, holding herself very upright, her air of individuality and presence was even more noticeable than before.

She boarded the Balliol Barge and was ushered to the perfect vantage point from which to view the race. An air of expectancy eddied among the College barges which lined the river-bank like so many festive houseboats with their colourful striped awnings, and among the punts which were ferrying undergraduates to the opposite towpath.

'There is a series of races over six days,' Vincent explained. 'The boats are rowed in single file, with a uniform distance between each, and the objective is to reach, and preferably bump, the boat in front. By the end of the week one boat will have bumped its way to be Head of the River.'

Tiffany nodded impatiently. They were coming: a line of slender skiffs, flashing oars and straining bodies, amid a tumultuous roar of encouragement from the densely-packed crowd on the river-bank.

'We're gaining on BNC! Come on, Balliol, you're *up*,' shouted Vincent, beside himself with excitement, but Tiffany said nothing. Of course Balliol would bump BNC and of course Balliol would be Head of the River – because she was absolutely convinced that Philip Bright never failed at anything he set out to do.

Sure enough, Balliol bumped BNC opposite the barge, arousing a chorus of exultant cheers. The crew in their white red-striped jerseys slumped over their oars, exhausted by their efforts, and several of them looked across to grin at their supporters – and saw Tiffany. Seven oarsmen and the cox gazed at her, but the eighth man did not lift his fair head. Of course not, thought Tiffany; she would not do so either in his place. She was jostled suddenly and unintentionally by the surging Balliol supporters and glanced around her with distaste. She had no wish to meet him here; she wanted to confront him quietly, with space about her, so that nothing should lessen the inevitable impact of so memorable a moment. Mrs Whitney was looking longingly at the buffet and its teapots, but Tiffany had heard the popping of champagne corks.

'Champagne,' she said firmly, 'ashore.'

The towpath and meadows were strewn with picnic parties, the women in their colourful dresses sprinkled like flowers on the green grass. Tiffany paced gravely beside Vincent, Mrs Whitney electing firmly to take some tea and commanding the escort of the reluctant Frank.

'Come and meet Dick Latimer,' invited Vincent, eager to display Tiffany to his friends. 'The Nethertons will have plenty of champagne.'

Tiffany inclined her head graciously during the introductions, but made no effort to distinguish between the people or to remember names and the unfamiliar English titles. She registered the fact that Dick Latimer was a singularly pleasant and good-looking young man, but beyond that remained oddly detached from her surroundings. To anyone who knew her in New York she would not have seemed herself at all and old acquaintances might have concluded she was feeling unwell; only her old nanny would have sensed danger, knowing as she did that Miss Tiffany's quiet items or signs of illness were usually a prelude to mischief – that same nanny who had once muttered that Tiffany would learn the hard way and that one day there would be something she wanted which she simply could not have.

She remained standing, believing that her height enhanced first impressions and that mobility enabled her to control the situation. Sipping her champagne, she waited, pricking up her ears when Vincent asked, 'Have you seen Philip yet, Dick?'

'Not since the race,' Dick Latimer answered. 'He's over there, talking to his family. He'll be along in a moment.'

'Don't tell me that ogre of a father of his has actually come down!'

'No,' Dick laughed. 'But the lovely Laura is here with Philip's little sister, Miranda, his cousin Julia – and friends!'

Dick's mother, Lady Netherton, uttered a distinct snort which she hastily tried to disguise as a cough and Tiffany's sharp ears caught her murmured aside.

'It is disgraceful,' Lady Netherton whispered, 'the way Julia flaunts her lover in public. She is sitting, quite brazenly, with her husband on one side and Rafe Deverill on the other!'

Rafe Deverill! Cautiously Tiffany stole a glance over her shoulder and hurriedly turned her back on what she saw. For some unaccountable reason she did not wish to face Rafe Deverill and his unsettling sarcasm today; neither did she want Philip Bright to see her from a distance.

'Why,' she heard another woman whisper, 'does Rafe Deverill persist with this *affaire* with Julia Fortescue? She is very beautiful, of course, but I really do not see that they are at all suited.'

'The real mystery is why he resigned his commission,' Lady Netherton replied. 'It is such a waste – indeed, the most tragic waste! His mother is in despair.'

'Here comes Philip now,' Vincent observed loudly.

Tiffany set down her champagne glass and drew her parasol a little closer to her head so that she was shrouded from sight. Behind her came a babble of congratulations and laughter, and then: 'Tiffany, I want you to meet Philip Bright,' and she turned very slowly, her lips gently parted, her head tilted slightly to one side and a smile in her eyes. They stared at each other.

They were so exactly alike, although the only facial similarity was two pairs of identical violet eyes – Anne's eyes – which locked together. They were both so confident and carefree, so sure of their attractiveness, so reckless in their pursuit of pleasure. And at the moment pleasure was all they wanted from each other – neither Tiffany nor Philip had any thought of romance. They sensed a bond between them and knew they had found a counterpart; that attraction and recognition were instant, but obvious to no one but themselves.

'Miss Court and her courtiers!' His eyebrows were lifted and his boyish grin illumined his face as he sketched a theatrical bow. 'Is there room for another devotee? I'm a very useful fellow to have around – a regular Jack-of-all-Trades.'

'Jack of diamonds, more like,' laughed Dick.

'Philip, you haven't even said how-do-you-do to Miss Court,' protested Vincent.

'There is no need for such formality,' said Tiffany, 'as Mr Bright and I have met before.'

'Have we?'

'For so unremarkable a man, you have certainly cultivated a way of engraving yourself indelibly on a girl's mind,' mocked Tiffany lightly. 'You have made your mark by being the first man to forget meeting me.'

'My forgetfulness is surpassed only by your modesty, Miss Court.' They smiled at each other with perfect understanding and ease. 'This is my cue to beg your forgiveness, I suppose,' he suggested.

'It is, and I shall grant that forgiveness because our meeting was a long time ago. You were a beastly little boy – you threw a stone at a swan and scowled most horribly.'

'I still do – scowl, I mean. These days the only objects I throw into the water are coxswains after Bumps Races. I say, did you see the splash old Smithers made? For such a little chap, his water displacement was truly astonishing!'

The conversation turned to the river again and attention was momentarily focused on the next race. While all eyes were on the college eights, Philip and Tiffany exchanged a knowing, even intimate, glance and smiled.

'Tiffany's father is in diamonds, too,' informed Vincent, speaking over his shoulder as he watched anxiously to see if Magdalen would bump Merton.

'What a coincidence that we should meet.'

'No coincidence,' Tiffany returned and lowered her voice. 'I sought you out deliberately.'

Again his eyebrows twitched at her boldness but his eyes gleamed with approval; Philip appreciated Tiffany for exactly what she was. 'I am flattered.'

'Don't be,' she replied caustically. 'The reason was not my approval of you but my father's disapproval.'

He laughed. 'How very original – but then you are, aren't you! Have I met your father?'

'No, it seems that John Court and Matthew Bright are old enemies. I had to promise to avoid Sir Matthew at all costs.'

'I see! Well, you are quite safe with me because where I am is the last place he is likely to be!'

'What marvellous freedom you must enjoy,' she said enviously. 'Where is your father now?'

'On his way home from South Africa. Surely you must know why he went there?'

'For heaven's sake,' cried Tiffany, her voice slipping into a twanging American accent in her incredulity, 'I'm not clairvoyant, you know!'

'The diamond – the enormous diamond found by Thomas Cullinan at a mine near Pretoria.'

Tiffany searched her mind for the name. 'At the Premier Mine?'

'Good girl! You see, you're not as stupid as you look,' and he dodged as she essayed to poke him with her parasol. 'It is the biggest gem the world has ever seen, weighing more than three thousand carats, and apparently Papa nearly had a stroke when he heard about it.' Philip sounded faintly regretful that Sir Matthew's health continued to be sound.

'What is it worth?' Tiffany demanded.

'Who knows? Who could possibly place a value on such a stone?'

Tiffany nodded, her face suddenly grave as she considered the implications for the diamond industry. Her reverie was interrupted by Vincent who demanded, 'If you are such a Jack-of-all-trades, Philip, devise some entertainment for us this evening.'

'We could show Tiffany the sights of Oxford,' suggested Dick.

'Not *now*,' she murmured, casting a sideways look at Philip which he interpreted correctly as an invitation for a private tour.

An argument developed over the evening's plans and Philip was able to whisper, 'What time shall we meet?'

'Tomorrow morning – early.'

'Be at Balliol at six.'

She nodded and, raising her voice again, inquired, 'Is that your family over there? Ought you not to join them?'

Philip bestowed a look of complete indifference on the group. 'They are returning to London to meet Papa and will trouble me no more this week. They have been seen to do their duty by me and that is enough.'

Tiffany detected the bitterness in his voice but made no comment. She dared to sneak one more glance in their direction, still hoping that Rafe Deverill had not noticed her. 'Is that your little sister? The one you told me about all those years ago – your father's favourite?'

'The same. And she remains Papa's pet, even though my stepmother is producing babies with a frequency which is positively indecent. Naturally, it does not bother me, but Laura's offspring may resent the competition later on.' He paused and then added offhandedly, 'Miranda is deaf, of course.'

'Deaf!' Tiffany stared at the withdrawn expression and almost motionless body of the young girl. 'She does not look like much competition to me,' she declared disdainfully.

CHAPTER SIX

Miranda was a still small island amid the movement, voices and laughter on the river-bank. Sitting quietly like this, watching the water, she was completely isolated for she could participate in a conversation only if she studied people's faces and read their lips. Usually she concentrated hard upon the task, even though she rarely spoke, but from time to time she withdrew and slid away into her own private world. Now she was unhappy because she was thinking about Philip, wondering why her handsome brother – so much older than herself, so clever and so much to be admired – hated her as he did.

They did not know each other well, the age difference of nine years and family circumstances being such that they spent little time together, but the vital blow to their relationship had been dealt by Philip when he stormed into the nursery before returning to Eton on that crucial day five years ago . . .

Miranda had been nearly six years old at the time and had been so pleased to see her big brother that she had run towards him with arms outstretched, wrapping those arms around his legs, laughing up into his face. But Philip wrenched free and the accidental roughness of his gesture sent the little girl sprawling to the floor where she stayed in a crumpled heap, tears of bewilderment filling her eyes. Philip had not intended to hurt her, but his jealousy surged to the surface in so fierce a flood that it had to be let loose. He began to shout at Miranda, saying the most terrible things he could devise.

He thought she was deaf, thought she could not hear. No

one had explained the extent of her disability and it never occurred to him that she could lip-read. Philip gave full rein to his rage, purging himself of anguish and resentment, spilling out a venomous torrent of words.

At first Miranda did not know what he was saying. He walked round her cowering figure, speaking from behind or from the side so that she could not see his lips. Then he bent down and hissed into her face.

'Always Papa's favourite! Always getting everything you want! Having *all* Papa's love – until now!'

A sob rose in Miranda's throat but Philip had not finished.

'Not any longer! Now Papa has Laura, so there won't be any love left for you. Besides, you are deaf and Papa only likes people who are perfect!'

That threat was too much for Miranda who started to cry, lying on the floor and trying to bury her face in the thin nursery carpet. But even after her tears were dried, the memory remained and the incident affected not only her relationship with Philip but her feelings for Laura and, most important of all, her father. She had adored Laura, but now she believed that the love Papa and Laura felt for each other meant less for her and she began to shut Laura out, retreating more and more within herself. A shuttered look came over her face and she lived in a self-contained isolation which only Matthew could penetrate.

And it was with regard to Matthew that the incident had its greatest effect. Miranda believed that she was no longer worthy of her father's love, yet that love was her whole world and the meaning of her entire existence. From that moment she took nothing for granted, but conscientiously applied herself to the task of earning his love and keeping it.

Papa was coming home tomorrow! She had taken off her hat and was twisting the brim between her hands with excitement at the prospect. Suddenly she was startled by the touch of a hand upon her hair and turning, saw that it had been Captain Deverill who touched her. She smiled at him; she liked Rafe Deverill, because he had given her Richie for her sixth birthday.

'A fly,' Rafe informed her, 'on your hair.' But he did not return her smile and his expression was extremely odd. 'Marianna – Miranda . . . even the names sound the same,' he murmured.

Marianna? Laura had not heard him mention the name before. A girl from his past – or his present? She longed to inquire but did not care to pry. Looking at his taut anguished face, Laura sighed. Oh Rafe, she thought, how you have changed!

The three of them were sitting in a circle of wicker chairs which Rafe had commandeered because Laura was pregnant again. Julia and her husband, Lord Alfred, were talking to friends further down the river-bank, while Laura and Rafe had lapsed into the comfortable silence of old and valued friends. In the peaceful lull, Laura's mind had strayed to another river-bank and to the debt she owed Rafe Deverill . . .

It had not been easy for the former governess to take up the position of Lady Bright in London society. Laura had returned from Kimberley after the Siege to confront an antagonism which erupted from Matthew's family, friends and servants alike. The marriage was considered a disastrous *mésalliance* and Laura had suffered greatly, particularly at the hands of Julia and Henriette, the personal maid of Matthew's first wife who constantly evoked the memory of Lady Anne. When Philip and Miranda had not responded to her sincere efforts to win their affection, Laura had nearly admitted defeat. So far from her normal calm, competent self did she stray that she even began to blame a diamond for her troubles – a pear-shaped pendant which Matthew had given her and which she began to believe was exerting an evil influence over her. She could not turn to Matthew for help because she was terrified he might regret his hasty marriage, therefore she felt compelled to maintain a brave face in front of him. In the event it was Rafe Deverill who rescued her.

In one short afternoon, by the river at Richmond, he had restored her sense of identity and self-esteem with a few words of sympathy . . . and one kiss. He had put everything into perspective, assuring her that Matthew's first marriage had not been happy, that society would accept her eventually and that the only opinion which mattered was Matthew's.

'You have overlooked the most basic component of your marriage. Your husband, Laura, is a most remarkable man. As a boy I admired him tremendously – he was everything I wanted to be: rich, handsome, successful and *different*! Matthew Bright is an original; he is his own man.' Rafe had paused and then said softly, 'Therefore you can be original as well – as long as you do it with *style*.'

She had seen that it was possible but some obstacles remained, not least the diamond.

'You will think me mad, but this diamond is the cause of my troubles.' It blazed on her breast as if branding her with the evil eye, its heaviness pressing into her body and its ice-coldness burning her flesh. 'It was an engagement present from Matthew but it is evil . . . it sticks to me, clings to me, yet I cannot take it off!'

Calmly he leaned towards her and unclasped the pendant from her neck. His face was very close to hers and his eyes had darkened like Matthew's did when he was going to . . . Suddenly Rafe's arms were around her, his mouth on hers . . . Laura had never been kissed by anyone except Matthew but responded naturally, her lips parting to receive him. She was aware of the cool hardness of his mouth, the firm yet gentle searching of his tongue, the latent power of his young body and the warmth of the sun on her head as his hand caressed her back.

'Lucky, lucky Matthew,' he murmured as he pulled away and his voice trembled slightly.

Laura was shaken, too, because she had enjoyed his kiss although she loved Matthew. This was a conundrum she could not unravel and she covered her confusion by adjusting her hair. 'Not as lucky as the girl who will marry you,' she answered with quiet sincerity.

Rafe smiled. 'You must help me to choose a wife – but not yet! In fact I think I will wait until you and Matthew have a daughter of marriageable age. I want a girl exactly like you.'

Laura flushed but retorted, 'I would not want a daughter of mine to marry a man who lies in the long grass on summer afternoons with other men's wives!' She scrambled to her feet, brushing that grass from her dress. 'If ever I can be of help to you,' she said seriously, 'I hope you will not hesitate to ask.'

'Thank you.' Rafe had raised her hand to his lips. 'I will remember.'

That offer of help had seemed ridiculous at the time – but not any more. Obviously something had happened to him during the war and Laura was rather hurt that he had not confided in her, particularly as she was sure Julia knew at least part of the story. A twinge of jealousy touched her at the thought of Julia. Ridiculous . . . she was happily married to Matthew and expecting her third child! Moreover, she was aware that Rafe had begun paying attention to Julia for *her* sake, in order to distract Matthew's niece from a malicious campaign against her. All the same, Laura's breast still constricted at the image of Rafe making love to Julia.

Rafe had been watching Tiffany. For a while he considered approaching her – it would be amusing to have Laura's opinion of her, but on second thoughts Julia's reaction would be the opposite of diverting. He sighed, for Julia was too possessive. He ought to end the liaison, but somehow he remained loyal to a certain bond of shared experience. Besides, he was drifting through such a sea of aimlessness that he could not stir himself sufficiently to make the break. Tiffany seemed to be with the Netherton party. Good chap, Dick Latimer! Now, if Tiffany had been flirting with *him*, Rafe might have intervened, but she was concentrating her efforts on Philip Bright which suited Rafe very well. He disliked Philip, finding the young man's manner towards Laura offensive. No, Rafe decided, those two deserved each other.

He half-closed his eyes, as always finding the presence of Laura infinitely relaxing. She possessed a priceless air of repose and after a few hours in her company he took a less jaundiced view of society in general and the world in which they lived. She was lovely to look at and refreshingly normal, without descending into dullness. Perhaps one day, Rafe thought, he would find another Laura for himself. He looked again at Tiffany Court, reflecting that Laura was beautiful but Tiffany was incomparable. However, living with Tiffany would be akin to wearing a hair-shirt – all irritation, anguish and tension until she deigned for a few seconds to spread balm on your racked body by her caress . . . all the same, it would be quite a caress . . . and if she could attain something of Laura's tranquillity and maturity, Tiffany would be . . . Failing to find an adequate superlative, Rafe's thoughts wandered into a fascinating dream world inhabited by a woman who was a perfect blend of these two.

Then with an effort he forced himself back to reality. 'How is Richie?' he asked Miranda, enunciating the words clearly into her face.

'Fine, thank you.'

Richie was short for Richmond and the dog, a Great Dane, had been named in honour of that other afternoon by the river.

'I hope you don't mind that we gave her a man's name,' Rafe said.

'She can do a man-dog's work,' said Miranda seriously and the words sounded strange coming from the child, almost seeming to foretell Miranda's own future.

'She can indeed – I hope she acts as your ears and protects you from harm. We don't want someone creeping up behind you, do we!'

He heard Laura gasp and as he saw her eyes wide with concern, he felt a chill of premonition grip him.

'But I really intended that she should be your friend,' Rafe continued hurriedly. 'Richie cannot talk, so it does not matter about your ears being bad – you can communicate with her in other ways. Mind you, I made sure I picked the puppy with the loudest bark,' and his charming grin creased the lean brown face.

It was the first time anyone had teased Miranda about her disability and she was such a sensitive child that her reaction could not be predicted. For a moment she stared at Rafe rather blankly but then she smiled, warmly and unselfconsciously.

'Perhaps you could come to Brightwell to see her?' she suggested.

Rafe glanced at Laura inquiringly.

'Matthew is coming home tomorrow,' she reminded him gently.

'Ah!' He gave a short laugh. 'Sorry, Miranda, but I am rather busy at present. Another time!' He looked at Laura again. 'Will you return to Brightwell after your reunion with Matthew or stay for the Season?'

'Go to Brightwell,' she answered unhesitatingly. 'It is by far my favourite place. Brightwell has no . . . memories.' She had nearly said 'ghosts', but remembered Miranda's presence in time. Laura had overcome her sensitivity to Matthew's first marriage, but nonetheless was happiest in the house Anne had never seen.

'Society would wish to see more of you.'

'Do you think so? I cannot agree with you. People single me out for attention only because I spend so much time at Brightwell that I have a rarity value.'

'Here comes a collector now! The Duke of Fontwell is approaching with purpose in every step. Do send the old fossil away, Laura, I beg you!'

'I shall do no such thing,' and she stood up to greet the visitor.

Making polite conversation with the Duke, Laura found

herself facing in the other direction and had a clear view of Philip and his companion. Philip: *how* he hurt her, and she was sure he did so on purpose although she could not imagine why. Then Laura's eyes widened as she saw the girl. What perfection of face, figure and dress! Oh, lucky Philip to be with her and what a handsome couple they made! But who was she? Laura made a mental note to ask Rafe or Julia if they could identify her.

Julia had watched Laura depart and, abandoning her husband, hurried to Rafe's side.

'Thank God, I have you to myself for five minutes,' she announced briskly, ignoring Miranda completely. 'I thought Laura would never move. What you see in that placid cow I cannot imagine – you know that she is breeding again!'

Rafe's eyes had snapped angrily at her discourtesy to Laura, but then the flare of fury died. Poor childless Julia, so envious of Laura's fertility. At least, Rafe thought with cynical humour, some people might consider she was an excellent advertisement for the birth-control leaflets she distributed so assiduously!

'Why did you want to see me alone?' he confined himself to inquiring.

'*Why!*' She stared at him in amazement. 'Because I always want to be alone with you. Because I love you! What other reason could there be?'

'I had hoped for a more constructive purpose,' he replied, deliberately unkind, still smarting for Laura's sake.

'Constructive! How like a man! Why should I be constructive when you are lounging in that chair, looking so damnably attractive that passion is driving all else from my mind?'

'Julia,' he said sharply, 'not in front of the child!'

'Miranda? But she is deaf.'

'She hears more than you think. Don't you, Miranda?'

But Miranda was not to be drawn. She stared at him blankly, face and eyes devoid of expression.

'There are times when that child gives me the shivers,'

said Julia in fluent French. 'Anyway, this language is most expressive when it comes to speaking of love.'

Miranda's French was excellent. The governess and the speech therapist in the Bright household had been joined by a young *mademoiselle* and their pupil's progress was little short of miraculous – even her accent was far better than could have been expected in the circumstances. Obviously languages posed particular difficulties for her, but the obstacles only made Miranda try all the harder. Soon a *fraulein* would be added to the ménage. Therefore she could have listened to her cousin's conversation, but 'love' meant Matthew and so Miranda lapsed once more into contemplation of her father's return.

Julia and Rafe had been lovers for nearly four years, but she never tired of touching him. Careless now of any onlookers, she laid a hand on his thigh and was swamped in a hot fever of sexual anticipation. So obsessed was she by Rafe's physical attraction that she barely remembered the time when Matthew had had precisely the same effect upon her.

Julia was Matthew's niece by blood as well as by marriage, being the daughter of Matthew's brother and Anne's sister, but he had never seemed like an uncle. He had been making his fortune on the diamond fields while she was growing up in the Berkshire countryside, and when he reappeared family circumstances gave him a towering importance in Julia's life. However, it had been Matthew's sexual attraction which gripped her; masculinity emanated from every part of him, flowed from every movement of his body, pulling her helplessly towards him. The situation was impossible, of course. Julia possessed her eccentricities, but incest was not among them. She had married Alfred Fortescue only to discover that he was an extremely ineffectual lover and by 1901, when she was twenty-five, Julia had not yet experienced total fulfilment and still lusted after her attractive uncle.

Then she had danced with Rafe Deverill at a ball. Every remark he made contained an underlying sexual innuendo and he looked at her with an intensity of feeling which Julia had often hoped to see – but hoped to see in Matthew's eyes and in the tautness of Matthew's face. Suddenly Rafe was real, standing out from the crowd with clarity and strength of character, welcome for himself and not merely as a pale means of passing a weary, wasted hour which could not be spent with Matthew. He had steered her expertly through the French windows into the garden where that sensual mouth met hers, sweeping Julia away on a tidal wave of desire which until then had existed only in her imagination, transporting her into a timeless world where nothing and no one else mattered and where love-making was an art.

It had been a long wait for fulfilment . . . weeks of meeting him as often as possible, of living on a knife-edge of excitement, of even welcoming her husband's embrace in the wild hope that for once he might satisfy her, but always Lord Alfred's performance ended prematurely, leaving Julia hot and restless, empty and aching . . . months of frustration after Rafe had returned to the war in South Africa, before she found the means to follow him . . . But in the Transvaal she had gone to bed with him at last and the long wait was worthwhile – my God, was it worthwhile!

She had won him but now was desperate to keep him. Being Julia, she was also trying to mould him into the man she wanted him to be.

'The only thing wrong with you,' she said, speaking in English again as Laura and Alfred rejoined the group, 'is your lack of prospects. Fortunately that shortcoming is entirely your own fault and easily remedied. You must *do* something with your life!'

'And, *fortunately*, you are able to tell me what that something should be,' Rafe said witheringly.

'It stands out a mile! Politics, of course. Rafe, the contribution you could make at Westminster would be enormous.'

'After what we saw in South Africa, Julia, I should have thought you would realise that I want no part of the Establishment.'

'All the more reason to fight them with words instead of

the sword,' she declaimed extravagantly, 'because naturally you must be a Liberal candidate, not a Tory.'

'Now I understand! You are less interested in my prospects than in recruiting me to champion the cause of women's suffrage in Parliament.'

'That would be another advantage, of course. You do support our campaign, don't you?'

'I believe women should have the vote. What I am not so sure about is the type of campaigner with whom you are associating, or your faith in the goodwill of the Liberal Party.'

'The Liberals have been most sympathetic.'

'Maybe,' Rafe agreed, 'but politicians will only support a cause if there is something in it for them.'

'Do you take me for a simpleton? Of course they expect something in return and they will get it – *I* will certainly vote Liberal.'

'But many of your members are radicals – Keir Hardie is one of your most prominent supporters – and so presumably *they* will vote Labour. As for the rest, it is a fact that most women are conservative by nature and by political sympathy – *they* will vote Tory. And the Liberals know it.'

'You are wrong,' Julia asserted vehemently. 'There will be an election next year, the Liberals will win and they will give us the vote.'

'And then everything will be perfect! All the inequalities in society will be ironed out, female "sweated labour" will be eradicated and women will enter upon an ideal world! Julia, Julia, I wish you well with your campaign but do not display such naïvety!'

'Me! Naïve? How dare you! Laura, don't just sit there – tell him how insufferable he is and that you agree with our cause!'

Laura smothered a smile. She loathed Julia's political arguments but could not help being amused at the neat way Rafe had diverted the discussion from himself and his future.

'Julia, I am a suffragist but I do not care for the members

111

of the Women's Social and Political Union who call themselves suffragettes. Too many of those members are not lovers of women's rights but haters of men's liberty, while another faction is fascinated only by the excitement and comradeship the cause – and any cause would do – brings into their drab, unsatisfying lives.'

'That is the most pompous, smug, sickening statement I have ever heard! I defy either of you to place Emmeline Pankhurst, her daughters or myself in any of those categories. Still, I must concede that our plans for action would not appeal to a passive person like you, Laura.' Julia's eyes gleamed. 'I shall be organising a more militant campaign in the autumn, a sort of guerrilla warfare – I learned a few things in South Africa, too!'

'Good heavens, Julia,' Laura cried, 'you are not going to start shooting people, I trust?'

'I don't think we will go quite that far.'

'South Africa is another reason why I would not associate with the Liberals,' remarked Rafe quietly. 'I have it on good authority that they will do a deal with Louis Botha, thus giving away all we fought to keep.'

'Oh, *who cares*!' muttered Julia, meaning that she did not care about the fate of the Transvaal. Suddenly she felt very tired and she was inclined to be irritable when she was tired. In fact she was trying not to take Laura's 'pompous statement' personally; trying not to believe that she was filling a vacuum in her own life with these political and social causes; trying not to believe that deep down she hated men because they always let her down in the end. Rafe won't let me down, she told herself fiercely, he *mustn't* – but suppose he tires of me, or marries, or sails away in that beastly boat again . . . She wanted to take hold of his broad shoulders and shake him out of his lethargy – to do something, anything, to keep him well and happy and by her side. Yet when he was with her, even when he was making love to her, she knew with infinite sadness and awful certainty that his mind was far away.

Rafe was becoming as neutral and characterless as . . . as

Anton Ellenberger, she thought wildly and, lashing out in her hurt and frustration, said so.

'If you are trying to insult me, Julia, you are pretty wide of the mark,' Rafe remarked. 'Ellenberger may not be over-flowing with personality, but he is pleasant, honest and one of the shrewdest men in London. He and Sir Matthew make a formidable pair.'

'I find nothing formidable about so intolerable a bore. On the few occasions I have met him, he mouths pleasantries at me with complete courtesy but total disinterest.'

'But that is precisely his great strength,' Rafe asserted. 'He is absolutely single-minded. Anton Ellenberger is a machine, with a ruthless efficiency and no outside interests to distract him. He has no personal friends, but carefully cultivates his business acquaintances. I don't pretend to know his aim in life, but I am prepared to bet that whatever it is he will achieve it.' He turned to Laura. 'You know him best, Laura. What is your opinion?'

'Actually, I do not know him well at all. He calls at Park Lane from time to time and has been to Brightwell on several occasions to see Matthew on urgent business. But he spends more time with Miranda than with me – doesn't he, Miranda?'

Miranda had not heard. She found it difficult to follow such a general conversation, because she had no means of knowing who would speak next and could not watch the right face at the right time.

Laura leaned closer and repeated the question.

'Yes,' agreed Miranda.

'What does he talk about?' Rafe asked.

'Diamonds, but his stories are not as interesting as Papa's.' Miranda gazed solemnly at Laura. 'I assumed that Papa had asked him to teach me.'

Before Laura could reply, Julia cut in, 'You must be vigilant, Laura. It is obvious that *there* is his aim!'

Laura was shocked. 'You mean Anton would aspire to marrying Miranda? Surely not! Anyway, he is much older than she is – he must be nearly thirty!'

'Coming from a woman who married a man twice her age and old enough to be her father, I find that reasoning distinctly unconvincing,' Julia retorted. 'Just bear in mind that marrying the boss's daughter is a well-trodden rung on the ladder of success. And remember, too, that although Ellenberger lacks the flamboyance and style of the diamond magnates, Miranda is not in a position to pick and choose – a lot of men may consider her disadvantages outweigh her advantages.'

'She will hear you,' said Laura in great distress and she and Rafe both saw the spark of comprehension in the child's eyes, although it was quickly veiled and the shutters came down once more over the little face. Hurriedly Laura began to organise their departure from the riverside. In her anxiety to pass off the awkward moment and to give Miranda something else to think about, she quite forgot to inquire about the identity of the tall, beautiful dark-haired girl.

Laura's efforts were in vain, for Julia's cruel jibe lived on in Miranda's mind together with the memory of Philip's tirade. No one will love me because I am deaf, she thought, but it doesn't matter – as long as Papa loves me, *nothing* matters.

Next day at the Bright mansion in Park Lane, Miranda waited impatiently for her father. She hung about in the hall, backing away as Henriette passed through and climbed the stairs. A chill rang through her: she was rather afraid of Henriette, afraid of the scarred face which had been pitted by smallpox and of a mysterious air of malevolence which surrounded the housekeeper.

But then Papa came home: Papa with his fair hair and suntanned face, the laugh in his bright blue eyes and the strong arms which held her tight, safe, and banished all her fears.

'I do not suppose that you missed me for a single moment,' he teased.

'Oh, I did – terribly,' she assured him seriously, ecstatic because he was home and because his other children were not there, so that she had him to herself – except for Laura, of course. 'Was the Cullinan diamond very big?'

'*Enormous.*' Matthew placed the tips of his fingers and thumbs together and held up his hands to demonstrate the size of the gemstone.

'Will it make a pretty pendant?'

'Pendant?' Matthew laughed. 'Put that rock round your neck and you would tip over frontwards, falling flat on your face! No, it will have to be cut into several smaller stones.'

'What are you going to do with it?'

'I don't know. The Cullinan diamond is literally priceless and no one can decide what value to place upon it.'

'Then we must hope that they do not find any others like it in the Premier Mine.'

'Good girl!' Matthew caressed her blonde hair approvingly. 'Even more important, we must hope that no one discovers another source of diamonds. Do you know why, Miranda?'

'A new discovery would upset the equilibrium of the market,' she replied gravely, 'and supply might exceed demand.'

'Go on.'

Miranda hesitated, frowning, but then her brow cleared. 'Oh yes, I know – Anton was telling me about this the other day. The Syndicate have to buy all the stones from the producers so if output was to become too high, the finances of the Syndicate would be strained.'

Matthew nodded. 'That is the nightmare which haunted Rhodes and which I inherited from him – the spectre of a new source of diamonds which we cannot control, either financially or administratively. Do you realise what the South African production figures were last year?'

It was a genuine inquiry. Miranda was not quite eleven years old but Matthew had been talking to her about diamonds, teaching her about diamonds for years. However, on this occasion she shook her head.

'The Premier produced 750,000 carats and the Kimberley mines produced more than two million carats.

How on earth are we going to sell the bloody things?'

'You will find a way,' Miranda said confidently.

Matthew laughed, the worried expression easing from his face. 'I hope you are right, because an entire industry is depending upon me to solve the problem! Would you like to see Mama's diamonds?'

'Yes, please,' she replied dutifully.

He left the room for a few moments to fetch the gems, leaving Miranda and Laura to sit silently awaiting his return. Laura did not begrudge the attention Matthew was paying to his daughter, knowing that her turn would come later; neither did she envy Miranda possession of the fabulous Bright jewels and she watched serenely as Matthew lifted them from the casket – a tiara, bracelet, ring, earrings and, most magnificent of all, the Bright necklace. Matthew decked his daughter in diamonds and smiled at her.

'Your mother wore them on her wedding day,' he reminded her, 'and on your eighteenth birthday they will be yours.'

'Thank you, Papa.'

She knew that playing with the jewels was intended to be a treat but in truth she did not care for them, finding the stones cold, hard and heavy. Miranda pretended to admire the jewellery for the same reason she displayed an interest in the diamond industry – to please Matthew.

As Miranda smiled at her father, Laura was seized by the first twinge of fear for the child's future. It was not surprising that Matthew meant so much to her. He was so magnificent, so big and golden, shining and splendid. There was something larger than life about him, like a god from ancient mythology or a mediaeval knight, yet he also exuded an all-enveloping security. Matthew kept his women safe. Even during the darkest hours of the Kimberley Siege, Laura had never doubted that he would protect them from harm and that he would always know the right thing to do. But now she realised how the diamonds weighed down on Miranda and foresaw, with uncanny prescience, how Miranda could be burdened by the inheritance of Matthew's diamond empire. Laura also comprehended the other danger which lay ahead: one day Miranda must seek a lover – but could she find a man to equal, let alone outshine, the golden god who was her father?

Matthew was thinking about that future, too. He led Miranda across the drawing-room and helped her climb on to a stool so that she could see herself in a mirror. Side by side they stared at each other in the glass. Briefly Matthew's gaze wandered to the portraits on the wall behind them: his picture in the centre, with Laura to the left and Anne's portrait to the right – Anne in a silver gown and wearing the Bright diamonds. Then he studied Miranda again and his arm went round her to draw her close; she was a replica of him, with his tawny-gold hair and sapphire eyes, his skin and strong, long limbs. There was nothing of Anne in Miranda and there was no doubting her paternity. This was why she must take her place in his kingdom of gold and diamonds. If only she was not deaf . . . and if only it was not his fault.

Matthew believed the story Laura had told him – that Miranda's deafness had been caused by the Boer bombardment during the Siege of Kimberley. In fact the damage had been done by the attack of scarlet fever, but Laura dared not say so: Philip had brought the infection to Brightwell and she had no wish to add to Matthew's peculiar animosity towards his son. Laura could not know that by concealing the true cause of Miranda's disability, for Philip's sake, she passed the burden of guilt to Matthew. He had insisted on staying in Kimberley to defend the city; he, who would have done anything to keep his daughter safe, had exposed her to danger and she had been punished for his obstinacy. Yet guilt was not the only reason why Matthew grieved. He loved Miranda so much that he could not bear to contemplate the suffering and hardship her disability might bring. To a man of his power and means, it was desperately frustrating not to be in full control of the situation, not to be able to wave the magic wand of his enormous fortune to right the wrong.

His mind went back to the medical tests with tuning forks and bells, to the diagnosis of acute otitis media – fluid accumulating in the middle ear – to the operation performed by Sir William Dalby at St George's Hospital and then to the post-operational examination.

'How much can she hear?' Matthew had demanded roughly when the otologist had completed the tests.

'Prior to the operation Miranda had only about twenty per cent of normal hearing. We have increased it to nearly forty per cent.'

'No more than that!' Matthew's voice rasped with disappointment. 'Is there anything else which can be done?'

'Not medically. Doubtless advances will be made in the production of more effective hearing aids, but in the meantime I suggest you continue to encourage the lip-reading.'

Miranda was deaf and she would remain deaf. The agony showed clearly on Matthew's face, while Miranda watched and understood. She had failed. She could not hear properly, therefore she had failed and Papa would not love her any more. As Sir William left the room, the little girl had begun to cry.

'Don't be frightened.' Matthew smoothed back her hair and mouthed the words distinctly into her tear-stained face. 'You can hear better than before and we will get the very best teachers to help you speak properly. It will be difficult sometimes, but I know you will try hard.'

Miranda nodded, slightly comforted. Trying hard, for Papa's sake, was what she had always done.

'It need make no difference,' said Matthew fiercely, as if he was trying to convince himself as much as his daughter. '*No difference* at all!'

But it did make a difference and they all knew it, especially Miranda because to her it meant trying hard for the rest of her life . . .

Now Matthew lifted her off the stool and divested her of the Bright diamonds, replacing them in the casket. He paused before closing the lid, fascinated by the iridescent light of the gems, reluctant to condemn them to darkness again. Light and dark – what was it that the Comtesse had said when she gave him the pear-shaped pendant? 'The story of the diamond is blood and butchery, treachery and evil; diamonds breed jealousy, greed and hate and in their light lurks the darkness of death.' Feminine foolishness, he scoffed silently. Far from harming him, Matthew believed that pendant had brought him luck – it had even been in his pocket when Danie Steyn made that abortive attempt on his life.

All the same he knew a moment's fear for Miranda; during the Siege of Kimberley she had been sent for safety into the depths of the diamond mine and ever since she had been afraid of the dark, for in the dark she could neither see nor hear. But Matthew's anxiety was all for Miranda's deafness. He had forgotten, because he did not take it seriously, the threat which Danie had made at their last meeting – the threat to carry the quarrel into the next generation.

Although it was Matthew's first night at home, they had agreed to attend the Ambleside ball – from Matthew's point of view, Lord and Lady Ambleside were two of his oldest friends, while to Laura they were the parents of Rafe Deverill. At dinner Matthew noted with relief that Charlotte Ambleside had placed Laura and Rafe at opposite ends of the table and had sat a plain but wealthy debutante next to her son. Matthew enjoyed his dinner the better for this arrangement, but after the meal was over and the port had been passed round, he found himself cornered by Rafe alone in the dining-room.

'So, you have just returned from the Transvaal, Sir Matthew. What did you see while you were there?'

'As the whole world is aware, I saw a diamond,' Matthew snapped sarcastically.

'And of course that diamond is *all* you saw.' Rafe leaned back against the dining table and folded his arms. 'It does so happen that there are things in the Transvaal other than diamonds – people, for instance.'

'What the hell are you trying to say?'

'I am asking if the people have recovered from the war. I am asking if they show any sign that they will forgive – or forget.'

'Forgive or forget what?'

'Oh, come on, Sir Matthew! A section of the great British public may be ignorant of the facts, or simply prefer to believe that the stories are not true – after all, who would believe that the British *did* things like that! But you and I know differently – you received an eye-witness account from Julia if from no one else.'

'And naturally *you* are an expert on the conversation and innermost feelings of the female members of my family!'

Rafe ignored the jibe. '*I* know what happened in the South African War because I was there – *I* was one of the men who had to execute the policy,' and at the word 'execute' his grey eyes were cold and bitter.

'You should have been proud to do your duty for your country.'

'Do not misunderstand me, Sir Matthew. I love my country deeply, as I trust all true Englishmen do – but as a soldier I would have been prouder defending the beloved country against the invader instead of feeling that I was the invader myself.' He smiled grimly. 'However, don't imagine for a moment that I allowed my private convictions to interfere with my duty.'

Matthew's dislike of Rafe Deverill, strongly rooted for the past five years, was increasing by the second. He was trying to keep a rein on his temper, reminding himself that this man was the son of his best friends.

'What *I* shall never forget, or forgive, is the way men like you allowed it to happen,' said Rafe softly. 'The Establishment, society, the diamond magnates and the Randlords, sat cosily at home while all hell was being let loose in their name – because say what you will, Sir Matthew, the Boer

War was fought for control of the gold and diamond mines – *your* gold and diamond mines!'

Matthew's face turned a dull purple. 'How dare you!' he roared. 'The war was fought for one reason and one reason only – to protect the rights of the *uitlanders* in the Transvaal who . . .' He broke off. 'For God's sake,' he said violently, 'I don't have to defend myself to you!' And he strode angrily from the room.

In the ballroom Matthew helped himself to a glass of champagne and stood, fuming, watching the other guests. Julia was looking lovely tonight, her pale fair hair gleaming in the light of the chandeliers – she possessed her mother's blonde beauty and that tilt of the head was typical of the Desborough girls. She was glancing round the room, seeking Deverill no doubt. Here came Rafe now and Matthew's hands clenched on his glass as the other man walked straight to Laura's side and raised her hand to his lips. Jealousy tore through Matthew like a physical pain. Here was the basic cause of his dislike of Rafe Deverill: Matthew was fifty-five years old and tormented by the fear that his beautiful young wife might desire a younger man. There were other men, of course, but none posed the same threat as Rafe: none was quite as tall or quite as handsome; none possessed that indefinable *presence* which distinguished the Captain and none paid nearly as much attention to Laura.

Throughout the evening, Matthew continued to watch Rafe Deverill. He saw how the women followed him with their eyes, some wistfully, some boldly, and recognised in Rafe something of himself as he had been thirty years ago. To the quarrel and the jealousy was added envy; Matthew envied Rafe one of the few commodities which not all his millions could buy – youth.

Later, in her bedroom, Laura tried to gauge Matthew's mood. Dare she mention Philip? Well, whatever his reaction, she must do so.

'Miranda and I were at Oxford for the Eights. Balliol bumped BNC and it seems almost certain they will be Head of the River.'

Matthew was silent. He was incapable of voicing, let alone explaining, his complex feelings for Philip. Contrary to the latter's belief, Matthew was well aware that he had reacted boorishly to the news of his son's rowing prowess. Just as Matthew had begun to take some pride in Philip's performance on the cricket field and in the classroom, just as he had begun to hope that he might indeed be his child, the news of Philip's excellence on the water had pricked the bubble of optimism. The needle which pricked that bubble was the old spectre of the Harcourt-Brights' fear of water – and the fact that Philip was not bedevilled by such fear shortened the odds that he was Matthew's son. Such a reaction was irrational – particularly as Matthew himself had not inherited the trait – and Matthew knew this, but could not overcome it. And because he was a man who valued logic and was accustomed to being in control of himself, his antipathy to Philip increased; he resented being placed in this invidious and intolerable position.

The silence stretched.

'Philip is well,' Laura continued with false brightness. 'After the race I saw him talking to the most beautiful girl. Oh, Matthew, I do wish you could have seen her! She was so lovely that every man in the world should have the opportunity of feasting his eyes upon her! You would have appreciated her, I am sure.'

Matthew's good humour was restored. What other wife would express such sentiments or display such open and genuine generosity? 'Who was this paragon?'

'I am afraid I don't know,' Laura confessed. 'I intended to ask, but somehow got distracted. Still, Philip is unlikely to be taking such relationships seriously at his age, so I don't suppose it matters who she was.'

'No,' said Matthew softly, trailing a tender fingertip along the curve of her cheek, 'it cannot possibly matter at all.'

CHAPTER SEVEN

Oxford had been looking its best that morning, mists floating above mellowed walls golden as the May sunshine. Tiffany was early for her appointment and instead of taking the Turl walked to Balliol by way of the High, Carfax and Cornmarket Street, magnificently unselfconscious of the curious stares of others abroad at this hour. She passed the spot where Archbishop Cranmer and Bishops Latimer and Ridley had been burned at the stake in the sixteenth century and then strolled thoughtfully to the gates of Balliol where Philip awaited her. They did not greet each other with excitement or effusion, neither did they suffer an embarrassed silence; Philip and Tiffany joined together in natural companionship as if they had known each other for ever.

She did not even say good morning. 'That Bishop Latimer who was burned to death – was he an ancestor of your friend Dick?'

'I have no idea, but it is quite probable – Dick comes from a frightfully ancient and noble family.'

'And do you?'

'Fairly respectable – my cousin is an earl.'

Tiffany laughed at his casual, understated attitude. 'You could call that *fairly* respectable, I suppose!' They entered the quadrangle at Balliol. 'Is this where you work?'

'Only occasionally – my studying tends to consist mainly of last-minute cramming before examinations. That is the Chapel to the right and the Library on the left. By the way, what message did you leave to explain your absence?'

'Message? I left no message,' Tiffany said scornfully.

'That's right! "Never regret, never explain, never apologise."'

Tiffany stood stockstill in the quadrangle, transported with delight, her spirit in complete accord with the dictum he had expressed. 'Who said that?'

'Benjamin Jowett, the great Master of Balliol.'

'Master of Balliol.' Tiffany savoured the phrase. 'The title has a fine ring to it and so has his philosophy. I like the faces too,' and she pointed, smiling, to the gargoyles on the walls.

But Philip did not wish to linger at Balliol and together they strolled down Broad Street, past Trinity, Blackwell's Bookshop and the Sheldonian and then turned down Catte Street towards the High. The colleges flowed past them: Hertford, All Souls', Queen's and Teddy Hall until they sighted the tower of Magdalen.

'Magdalen Tower,' Philip informed her, 'is where Oxford celebrates May Day. The choristers . . .'

'Don't tell me.' Tiffany held up an admonitory finger. 'Another ancient custom, perpetuated down the centuries! This country is full of them.'

'Have you no respect for tradition?' Philip pretended to be shocked.

'I do not *worship* tradition – unlike Mrs Whitney, who walks on tiptoe and speaks in hushed whispers everywhere we go in England! However, certain aspects of it – for instance, the stones which enshrine and illustrate it,' and here Tiffany gestured to the honeyed haze of towers and spires, 'have made an impression on me. Remember that I am the daughter of a diamond man and accordingly I recognise and value the real thing – and I do concede that England, and Oxford in particular, is the genuine article.'

'I believe Oxford has more appeal for men than women,' Philip observed, 'because its atmosphere is strongly masculine. It is a seductive city but its romance is pure and classical, not passionate and sensual. It is a city of young men whose idea of love is to place a woman on a pedestal and worship her as a goddess.'

'But *you* would not do that!' She did not tell him how much she longed to be a man and so perhaps she was responding to Oxford's male aura.

'Oh, no. I'll pull you down in the gutter with me!'

'Good! Gutters are much more fun than pedestals.'

They had reached Magdalen Bridge and now leaned against the high parapet to look down on the Cherwell below. Weeping willows, chestnuts, elms and oaks transformed the river into a shady bower, its tranquillity disturbed only by swallows and martins which skimmed the surface of the water and by the chattering of sedgewarblers in the dense foliage.

'Why aren't our esteemed parents boon companions?' Philip inquired lazily. 'What happened to tear them asunder?'

'You don't sound very surprised that your father has a mortal enemy.'

'I'm not. On the contrary, it never fails to amaze me that he has any friends. Mind you, those friends are probably only interested in his money.'

'That applies to most friends, not merely your father's,' retorted Tiffany drily. 'And I don't know what happened. Papa would not tell me – and as he tells me most things I want to know, it must have been something really dreadful.'

'They were in Kimberley together, I gather, so it must have happened there. Murder, perhaps? Claim jumping? Illicit Diamond Buying? Or,' and Philip paused dramatically, '*a lady*?'

'Oh, I shouldn't think it was a woman. My father is not a ladies' man. He is a very . . .' she hesitated, '. . . *celibate* person. The atmosphere of Oxford would suit him very well – Papa is a great one for pedestals.'

'So we only know that, like Montague and Capulet, our houses bear an ancient grudge.'

Tiffany laughed. 'I have little sympathy for the sighs and swoons of Romeo and Juliet and no intention of being anyone's lover – star-cross'd or otherwise.'

'Well said! A girl after my own heart! Tiffany Court, you

are the Cullinan diamond among women – unique and beyond price! You know your Shakespeare, too.'

'One of Papa's foibles. He insisted that my governess teach me Shakespeare. Apparently a book of the plays was the first present he gave to my Mama. Stupid – I'm sure she would have preferred a diamond.'

'Perhaps *my* father gave her a diamond,' Philip suggested wickedly. 'Oh, talking about swoons and sighs, look at those two over there!'

A couple had appeared below them, walking through the meadows which bordered on the river-bank, holding hands. They had not seen the watchers on the bridge and paused for a moment, bodies entwining as they exchanged a lingering kiss. Then the lovers strolled on, arms round each other's waist and heads inclined.

'So much for the pure masculine atmosphere,' sniped Tiffany.

'Eights Week,' said Philip dismissively. 'It isn't typical.'

'Ah,' she sighed sarcastically, watching the pair, 'but aren't they *sweet*!'

'Sickeningly sweet,' he agreed and, laughing, caught hold of her hand and clasped it to his chest; then they paraded back across the bridge in exaggerated imitation of the pair below – they were so sure, so confident that they could dictate the terms in any game of love. When they tired of play-acting, Philip retained Tiffany's hand but in no lover-like fashion, swinging it gaily, his boyish smile lighting the morning. And of course it went without saying that their assignation would be their secret, to be shared with no one else.

They met each morning thereafter – only Tiffany's maid being privy to the arrangement – exploring Oxford, punting on the Cherwell and laughing a great deal. So far removed were they from Shakespeare's lovers that they revelled in their fathers' enmity; indeed it was the *raison d'être* for their entire relationship. Both Philip and Tiffany were at odds with their fathers and were enchanted by these stolen meetings which gave them such pleasure and which would arouse in John Court and Matthew Bright such rage and consternation. Yet, unconsciously, they were admitting that the relationship had a deeper significance by the steps they took to conceal it – neither wished it to end.

One morning they strolled in the Botanical Gardens by Magdalen, but were irreverent of their surroundings.

'This is the oldest Botanical Garden in Britain,' announced Philip in his guide-book voice. 'However, and more to the point, the first Englishman to take to the air rose heavenwards from this very spot in 1784.'

'A balloonist? Hm, it may have been a sensation in 1784, but ballooning is old hat since the Wright Brothers flew their machine eighteen months ago. It takes *Americans* to do these things properly.'

'Never! America is way behind in motor cars,' said Philip indignantly. 'All the innovations *and* the major races take place in Europe.'

'They do not – why, I went to the Vanderbilt Cup race myself last fall. I know the Vanderbilts very well,' she added offhandedly in the same tone as Philip had used when he mentioned his cousin was an earl.

Philip burst out laughing. 'And I suppose the Vanderbilts are a *fairly* respectable connection,' he mocked. 'But tell me, did you enjoy the race?'

She launched into a vivid account, describing the cars and drivers and her own sensations, able to tell him who won, what car he was driving and the average speed. Philip was visibly awed.

'I did not think there existed, in the whole wide world, a girl who cared about cars,' he declared, 'but the Vanderbilt Cup is child's play compared with the road races of Europe.'

He began to tell her about the Paris-Vienna race of 1902 and the 'race of death' from Paris to Madrid in 1903, and how its tragic accidents had led to the transfer of competition from roads to closed circuits. 'The Gordon Bennett has been the most interesting race from a British point of view,' he said. 'We won it in 1902 when S.F. Edge drove the Napier to victory.'

'You want to take part, don't you!'

'More than anything.' His customary flippancy was replaced by intense seriousness. 'And I will, as soon as I am free of my studies and have some money of my own.'

'How does one get started?'

'I think the money might help! Also, I have a contact – a man called Williams who used to be a groom at my grandfather's country house. He works for Napier now and I am convinced that is where the future of British racing lies.'

'A groom! You're not exactly a snob, are you?'

'I don't think you are, either.'

Tiffany thought of Gerard and smiled secretly. Then she remembered some of the things Philip had said and looked at him closely. 'That grandfather of yours – was he an earl?'

'No, a duke.'

'Ah.' She paused and then said slowly, 'It's a strange thing, but your eyes are exactly like mine.'

'A sign of our compatibility, my dear!'

'No, you don't understand. Papa told me that my eyes are the same colour as my mother's. Was there anyone in your family called Alida?'

'Not that I know of. Why?'

Tiffany related the story her father had told: the tale of a quarrel in a noble English family, the flight of the couple with their young daughter, the tragic deaths in Cape Town which orphaned beautiful Alida, and her rescue by Court.

'Perhaps she was a member of your family?' she suggested eagerly.

Philip shook his head. 'I do promise you that all my family are accounted for.'

'There might be a cousin of whom you have not heard,' Tiffany persisted.

'We have family skeletons a-plenty in our cupboards, and several black sheep, but no runaways or remittance men in the Cape.'

'Is the name Alida familiar?'

'Never heard of it.'

'I could show you a picture of her.'

'What good would that do?' Philip was impatient and stared at her with a puzzled look. 'And I believed you were not a romantic,' he said slowly.

For the first time Tiffany saw her mother's story through someone else's eyes and as she perceived its shortcomings a tight knot twisted her stomach. The story and the portrait had formed an integral part of her childhood; in her youthful isolation she had allowed the legend to form the basis of her world. Sitting in the sunshine with Philip on this May morning, Tiffany realised that she loved – yes, *loved* – this mother she had never known; or at least, she loved the image of this mother and could not bear it to be taken away from her.

'I am not a romantic,' she replied stiffly. 'Obviously you think the story is . . . exaggerated.'

'Precisely,' he agreed rather too quickly, thankful for an explanation which would not hurt her too much. 'It might be that Alida's family was not as noble as she believed – it would be natural for her parents to over-emphasise their importance.'

Tiffany nodded. 'You are the first person to whom I have mentioned the matter,' she said, 'and I can tell by your reaction that it would be unwise to pursue my investigations. I shall not speak of my mother again, *but*,' and her eyes flashed, 'I shall keep my ears open for any information which will help me to find out exactly who she was. Alida is an unusual name. I met a man in South Africa, Danie Steyn, who had a sister called Alida. I still wonder . . .' She shook herself determinedly and changed the subject. 'It's my last day tomorrow. Shall we go on the river or are you tired of all this rowing and punting?'

'I am giving up rowing.'

'Why, when you are so good at it?'

He shrugged. 'Oxford won the Boat Race and Balliol is Head of the River. What is the incentive to carry on? All that training, all that pain, just for a repeat performance?'

Tiffany did not know what the incentive was, but felt vaguely that there was one and that most people would have responded to it. 'You will never get anywhere in life if you don't stick at things,' she pointed out, only half-seriously.

'I don't need to get anywhere – my father got there before me.' Again that wry curl to his lips and that bitterness in his voice, but it was soon gone and made no lasting impression on Tiffany or the day.

Next morning he took her on the Cherwell in a punt and then they stood on Magdalen Bridge as they had done that first day.

'I shall miss you,' Tiffany said. She wondered what she would miss most and decided that his greatest appeal lay in his wholehearted participation in her schemes. Frank helped her to flout convention but in reluctant fashion; Philip did so eagerly, with no guilty glances over his shoulder.

'We will meet again.' He stated it flatly, as a matter of fact.

'Will you come to New York for the Vanderbilt Cup?'

'Next year perhaps, when I am finished with Oxford.'

'I will come to Europe again before then, preferably unchaperoned.' Tiffany frowned; it would not be easy.

'You have your father in your pocket – you can do anything you want. Use that power, use the diamond business, not for money but for freedom.' Philip smiled as he recalled the advice Dick Latimer had given him.

'Yes,' she said, 'I will.'

'I was surprised, you know, to realise you were unaware of the Cullinan.' He lifted his head from contemplation of the sparkling waters of the Cherwell. 'It would suit your style to be better informed.'

It was like seeing pieces of a jigsaw puzzle sliding into place, hearing her own jumbled thoughts clearly expressed, seeing her future open up before her. Tiffany nodded, her head full of whirling visions and possibilities.

He took hold of her hand. 'I have the most curious feeling,' he said, 'that if you and I were to climb on to the parapet of this bridge and then jump, we would not drop down into the river but would soar into the sky.' He raised their clasped hands aloft and laughed.

Tiffany laughed, too, but when he did not kiss her goodbye she was assailed with a fleeting disappointment, similar to that she had experienced after Rafe Deverill's disappearance from the terrace in Newport. Still, as far as Philip was concerned, this was only *au revoir*.

'Papa, I did miss you very much.' Tiffany smiled seraphically and wound her arms around her father's neck.

They were in Tiffany's bedroom at their New York home because here, she judged, she was safe from Randolph.

John Court wanted to believe her and therefore he did. 'The house has been so empty without you,' he murmured, 'but I hope you enjoyed the vacation. And I hope that . . .'

'I enjoyed it all,' Tiffany cut in quickly and added cleverly, 'particularly Paris, which was preferable to London. I should like to go to Paris again. In fact I should like to travel more often – on business, not pleasure.'

'Business?' Court was bewildered. 'But you are going to be married!'

'Not yet, Papa.' Tiffany sat down gracefully on the edge of the bed and assumed an expression of extreme earnestness. 'I am afraid I need a little longer to consider the matter of marriage with Randolph.' It came hard to her to speak those three words and it was equally difficult to adopt this air of sweet reason instead of screaming her defiance. 'You see, I look upon Randolph as a brother and it takes time to adjust to the idea of accepting him in a different rôle.'

'Randolph will be very upset,' Court said, miserably aware that Randolph's displeasure was a force to be reckoned with.

'What a shame! I mean, upsetting Randolph is the last thing in the world I want to do!' The sarcasm slipped out and Tiffany was forced to make a supreme effort to retain control of her subtle pose. 'I will live in the same house with him while I ponder the problem. I will be polite to him. I will take my place in society and I will cooperate with Aunt Sarah over the arrangements for my official coming-out ball in Newport this summer. *In return . . .*'

Court had brightened visibly at her apparent willingness to compromise and to reconsider her former wild statements. Now he waited in suspense for her ultimatum.

'*In return,*' Tiffany emphasised, in a voice of steel, 'I wish to participate in the affairs of Court Diamonds. No buts,' and she raised a hand in an imperious gesture to silence her father's protest. 'I want to learn how to run that company. You appear to have donated the bank to Randolph, but you will not give him the diamonds as well – the diamonds are mine and I want them!'

Randolph was not going to like this at all, Court thought unhappily, but how could he refuse her? How could he refuse her anything? And it would mean that he could keep her to himself for a little longer . . .

Tiffany was reading his thoughts. 'Just think, Papa,' she said slyly, 'we can go to work together each morning and you can give me an office next door to yours.'

'The move is highly unconventional but . . . very well,' and he was rewarded with a kiss.

'One more thing, Papa. I met no one in England who had heard of Mama. That story is true, isn't it?'

This was Court's last chance. He could seize it, put the record straight – and earn his daughter's contempt. Or he could maintain the status quo. Terrified of losing her affection, he allowed the opportunity to slip away.

'Of course it's true!'

'Thank you, Papa,' and Tiffany smiled radiantly as the doubt was dispelled.

Part Two

AMERICA AND EUROPE
1906–1907

CHAPTER EIGHT

In May of the following year Tiffany sat in her office at Court Diamonds gazing at a desk-top strewn with jewellery – diamond necklaces, sapphire bracelets, ruby rings and emerald ear-drops. She picked up a diamond tiara and examined it closely; the stones were superb, but the setting was heavy and old-fashioned – she had purchased the jewels from a deceased estate and the pieces had been collected during the 1880s. However, if the gems were recut and reset into modern designs . . . Tiffany laid down the tiara on the desk and stared unseeingly out of the far window. Yes, it was a good idea; in fact it was a *very* good idea.

The voice of Charles Tiffany echoed in her head, telling her how antique jewels from Europe had made his reputation and his fortune. The drift of diamonds from the Old World to the New continued until the richest American women were said to possess more jewels than the crowned heads of Europe – except for Queen Victoria and the Czarina of Russia. Perhaps some of these jewels had adorned empresses, queens, countesses or courtesans. Tiffany's fingers touched the stones lightly, lovingly, hovering almost as if she were drawing power from them. Her affinity to the gems was as strong and deep-rooted as the core of magnetism through the earth's crust. Sometimes she felt she had not been born of woman but, like Pallas Athene springing from the head of Zeus, had been catapulted, fully-formed, from the magical heart of a diamond.

Charles Tiffany's store would be an outlet for her restoration work, but New York needed another quality jeweller. Her gaze remained fixed on the magnificent hypnotic fire of the diamonds, seeking inspiration in the iridescent radiance until she was enveloped and immersed in the dazzling blue-white light. Then the thick dark fringe of her eyelashes swept up to reveal an equally beautiful glow in her violet eyes: the diamonds had given Tiffany her answer. 'Cartier,' she murmured aloud.

The House of Cartier had its headquarters in Paris under the management of the founder's son, Alfred, who in turn had brought his three sons Louis, Jacques and Pierre into the business. Jacques had opened a shop in New Bond Street, London, in 1902. If Louis took over from Alfred in Paris, Tiffany reasoned, Pierre could come to New York. She could call at the Rue de la Paix during her forthcoming visit to Europe and sound them out. The Cartiers should not need much convincing that business prospects in America were excellent, and in return for her assistance could be persuaded to place a major proportion of their gem requirements through Court Diamonds.

Idly Tiffany sketched a flower spray on the corner of a sheet of paper in front of her. She possessed no aptitude for drawing yet, although this was little more than a doodle, the design flowed freely from her fingers. To Tiffany it was not a bunch of flowers but a spray of diamonds; in her mind's eye she could envisage the size and cut of each stone. Although only involved directly in the business for a year, she had been exposed to gemstones all her life; from her earliest days Court had shown her the 'pretty stones' which he was accumulating for her personal use, while every society lady she met was loaded with jewellery. She had absorbed her knowledge gradually and unconsciously until now she noticed a woman's jewellery before anything else. Tiffany knew that she was in a unique position to anticipate the market and satisfy its demands.

But what was that market? And who were its customers?

Tiffany rose and walked across the room to the window overlooking Fifth Avenue. The décor of the office was as uncluttered as her simple blue velvet gown. Visitors were surprised at the austerity of the surroundings and of the society-girl-turned-diamond-dealer, but Tiffany possessed impeccable taste. Frills and flounces were wrong for her, overt femininity being alien to her height and personality, but she achieved faultless elegance through cut and fabric. The dark blue velvet she wore today was of the finest quality and as she stood at the window she crossed her arms, running her hands over the sleeves of the dress, enjoying the softness and sheen of the fabric just as she luxuriated in the sensuous touch of silk next to her skin in summer.

The market, she was thinking, is not sound. The price of diamonds was falling, chiefly because the Premier Mine continued to flood the market with stones, and now there was this damned Frenchman who maintained he could *manufacture* diamonds! Tiffany grimaced; she did not believe the Frenchman's claims, but was sufficiently realistic to admit that her scepticism could be born of hope rather than scientific fact. That was another call she must make in Paris! Times were changing and the customers were changing, too. The socialites had been superseded by the self-made millionaires, who in turn had given way to the stage-stars. What group would constitute the next élite? What are needed, Tiffany said to herself, are heroes with whom the public can identify and whose manners and customs they can copy. No, not heroes – *heroines!* It was women who desired diamonds, and for one who could pay $100,000 for a ring there were a hundred who would pay $200 – *if* they began to believe that diamonds were for everyone and not only for the inhabitants of fifth Avenue and Newport, Rhode Island. The mathematics made the kind of sense which appealed to Tiffany's shrewd brain. As Cecil Rhodes had done before her, she envisaged a world where every girl expected to receive a diamond ring when she became engaged; after all, diamonds had been the 'bride's jewel' since the fifteenth century.

Tiffany returned to her desk and for a moment contemplated the ringless state of her own hands. She could appreciate the irony of peddling romance for others while scorning it for herself, but try as she would – and admittedly that was not very hard – she could not imagine wearing a man's ring on her engagement finger. However, perhaps it was not coincidental that her thoughts strayed to Philip Bright and to her third prospective encounter in Paris.

In the meantime she would explore the idea of resetting the jewellery. She needed a goldsmith to fashion the settings for her designs and, because she wanted complete control of the project, the artist must be unknown and willing to take instructions. Meticulously Tiffany locked the jewellery in the safe, partly for security reasons and partly because she did not wish to reveal her plans. Not that anyone would oppose the idea; quite the contrary – John and Randolph Court would have welcomed the plan in the hope that she would sit in a corner and play with the pretty baubles, thereby losing interest in the mainstream of the business. However, nothing could have been further from Tiffany's mind; while she expected to derive personal pleasure from the venture, the jewellery was first and foremost a business proposition, an inseparable arm of the corporate body.

She slipped into the dark furs which looked so well against her magnolia skin and the smooth high cap of her raven hair, picked up her hat and, summoning the driver, swept out of the building to the waiting car. In the car she put on the hat, pulled down the veil to protect her face and eyes and instructed the chauffeur to drive to Macdougal Alley.

From the outside, Number 15 was virtually unchanged – a little shabbier, perhaps, its paint peeling and grimy, but otherwise familiar and oddly welcoming. Tiffany paused before knocking at the door, suddenly aware that she was pleased to be back, that even without the excuse of the jewellery she would have returned here sooner or later.

Naturally Gerard had not expected to see her again and was bemused by her reappearance. However, Tiffany was not a person who carried the past around with her as so much excess baggage. She wanted something. Gerard happened to be able to provide it, therefore she had come. What had taken place between them did not concern her, much less embarrass her. Without preamble she walked across the studio to the easel and inspected the unfinished canvas critically.

'Not bad,' she commented. 'I assume that this is what you paint when the rent has been paid.'

The painting depicted a street scene, presumably in New York but Tiffany did not recognise the locale. However, it was not the backdrop of dingy houses which arrested attention, but the people in the foreground: they were young and old, lounging in shop doorways or hobbling down the street, defiant or resigned – they were The Poor. Tiffany was not possessed of a social conscience, her age, position and upbringing being against such a development; neither was she an art connoisseur; but she could recognise talent when she saw it. A poignancy and an integrity of spirit shone from the canvas with an illumination as strong, true and bright as the beam from a diamond.

Tiffany stared at Gerard silently. She had come to inquire the name of a metal-worker who could execute her designs. Now she was wondering if he could do the work himself, if he could transmute the flair which blazed from paint and canvas to metal and stones.

'You paint and you sculpt,' she said carefully. 'Have you ever tried metal-work?'

'Sure, but the materials come expensive.' He smiled wryly, conscious of an unpleasant sense of inferiority. She was so beautiful, so confident and powerful; it was difficult to realise that once he had held her in his arms, impossible to imagine doing so again. 'Jack-of-all-trades and master of none – that's me!'

The phrase brought back memories of Philip, inducing Tiffany to respond warmly and to incline to an uncharacteristically fatalistic view that her association with

Gerard was preordained. She explained her project to him.

'Will you do it? Do you want to do it?' She rose and stood very close to him, her eyes burning into his. 'Will you give of your very best or will the job merely be a chore to stave off starvation?'

'You care,' he said in surprise. 'You really care about the jewellery yet it is only a strip of gold and a few pebbles.'

'The diamonds are everything to me.'

'I didn't think you could care about anything or anyone, yet now there is an obsession in your eyes which reveals you might sell your very soul to the devil for those diamonds.'

'What do you mean – *might*! I already have!' The reply was glib, she did not really mean it, but as she spoke Tiffany glimpsed a previously unsuspected facet of her nature: were the diamonds all-important to her? If she had to choose between the gems and something – or someone – else she cared for, would the diamonds prevail? Was their hold over her that powerful? Imperceptibly she raised her shoulders in an impatient shrug: why waste time on such a hypothesis? It was inconceivable that such a choice could be laid before her.

'I want to do the job and I will devote every effort to doing it well,' Gerard vowed.

'Swear it!'

'I have no Bible.'

She took his hand and laid it against the surface of the uncompleted canvas. 'Now, swear!'

He did so and Tiffany released his hand. She stared again at the painting. 'I take it that this sort of picture doesn't sell?'

Gerard gave a short laugh. 'You can say that again.'

'Where do you exhibit?'

'Nowhere. There isn't a gallery in New York which will touch the stuff. You see, Tiffany, you and your friends only admire European artists of the old school.'

'In that case,' she said, 'it is high time we opened people's eyes to American art. But not immediately – I will look into it when I return from Europe in the fall. The jewellery must wait until then also, because I shall take the stones to Amsterdam for recutting.' She produced a sheaf of dollar bills and casually handed them to him. 'A mark of my faith and goodwill, Gerard. Also, buy some cheap materials for experimental work – I will drop in a few designs and a handful of poor quality stones before I leave for London. On the basis of what you turn out, I will decide if our partnership is to continue.'

Tiffany arrived in London in June, accompanied only by her faithful and biddable maid. The matter of travelling unchaperoned had raised a storm of protest from John and Randolph Court.

'Every other girl . . .' Court began.

'Surely, Papa, you do not expect your daughter to behave like *every other girl*! I am what you have made me and if you dislike the result of your labour, you must accept that it cannot be undone. You would not foist a chaperone on a son and so you will not do it to me. I go to Europe on business and will not demean myself or undermine my bargaining power by dragging a chaperone to important meetings.'

'But for social engagements . . .'

'There will be no social engagements,' Tiffany informed her father crisply. 'I shall be much too busy during the day to play at night.'

Randolph's mouth tightened angrily at her defiance, but he did not oppose her and Tiffany deduced why: he had decided to give her enough rope with which to hang herself, hoping to step in at the eleventh hour in order to save her from ruin. How little he knew her! As if she would ever lose control of any situation – personal or business – and so place herself within his power!

In London her first priority was business with the Syndicate which, in partnership with the Diamond Company, enjoyed a virtual monopoly on the production from the South African mines. The Syndicate comprised eight companies of which Bright Diamonds was the most prominent, yet the Premier Mine was not marketing through that channel even though Matthew Bright was a director. Tiffany was irresistibly intrigued by him, this man whom everyone seemed to hate and yet who exerted such a powerful influence on all their lives. Curiosity drove her to take a cab to Hatton Garden, where she sat in the vehicle for some twenty minutes watching the entrance to Bright Diamonds. She felt a fundamental, vital need to see him, to put a face to this name which dropped so frequently from the lips of the diamond dealers, to assess her adversary – because she was sure, without knowing why, that one day they would oppose each other. People came and went through the portals of Bright Diamonds, but not one person resembled her image of Sir Matthew. She imagined him to be like her father – old, of course, and grey, but tall and distinguished-looking.

Tiffany was just about to abandon her quest when a car drove up and parked directly outside the entrance. Immediately her hopes revived; it was the new Rolls' Royce 'Silver Ghost' and surely could belong only to someone of Sir Matthew's standing. Then a man strode down the steps of the building, followed by several clerks waving pieces of paper and taking notes – a man in a hurry, firing off last-minute instructions – and Tiffany knew it was him.

He was magnificent, golden hair gleaming in the sun, tanned face alert as he rapped out his orders, grey suit immaculately cut. He was tall and distinguished all right – but old? No, he must be years younger than her father and, my God, he must have been marvellous in his day! Now she knew why men hated him; it was a hatred born of envy because no woman could resist him. Even from across the street, and with the yet-wider gap of the years which separated them, Tiffany could sense his attraction – that rare magnetic pull which flowed from a man whom women would die for. Rafe Deverill had it, too, and at the thought of Rafe an idea came into her mind.

Ordering the cab to move on to her next appointment, Tiffany took stock of what she had learned and in particular assessed the insight the glimpse of Matthew had given into the character of Philip. Small wonder he was bitter. How did one emerge from the shadow of such success and magnificence? Assuredly not through diamonds – Philip must make his mark elsewhere.

That afternoon Tiffany visited the sales office of the Premier Mine and purchased a fine parcel of diamonds. She departed from the office in immensely good spirits, permeated with that particular sense of satisfaction a woman feels when she is holding her own in a man's world. However, the mood was shattered when she bumped into a man in the street – and recognised him.

'Mr Ellenberger!' She had forgotten him – the one person who could divulge her presence in London to Sir Matthew, since the clerks in the sales offices were unlikely to gossip with the great man and she had been at pains to keep her name out of the British newspapers. Tiffany wanted Matthew to receive no hint of her presence here, lest he be put on his guard over Philip. She was intrigued to notice that Ellenberger seemed as disconcerted by the meeting as she. He greeted her politely but glanced around furtively, as if ensuring they were not observed.

'I am somewhat tired, Mr Ellenberger,' she said smoothly, 'and should be grateful if we could talk in the comparative comfort of my cab.' The alacrity with which he accepted this proposal and the privacy it provided confirmed her suspicions, and she settled back in the cab with the smug certainty that she had achieved the upper hand. She had detected Ellenberger's discomfiture without revealing her own weakness. 'You are far from the familiar surroundings of the Syndicate, Mr Ellenberger,' she observed.

'So are you, Miss Court,' he returned, playing for time while he regained his composure.

'Bright Diamonds is a member of the Syndicate, while Court Diamonds is not.'

'But Sir Matthew is a director of the Premier Mine.'

'Of course.' A thought struck her for the first time – if Anton Ellenberger was a loyal servant to Sir Matthew, what had been the reason for his association with Randolph Court? Tiffany was tempted to ask him that question outright but no, subtlety was everything. 'Do you believe the Syndicate's control of the industry will continue?'

Thankfully Ellenberger launched into a detailed analysis of the situation, blissfully unaware that his decorative audience was entirely *au fait* with the position and could have explained it to him with equal succinctness. Meanwhile, Tiffany was putting herself in his place – would she be content to be Sir Matthew's lackey? No, of course not and unless she was very much mistaken, neither was Anton Ellenberger. Like Randolph before her, she pieced together Ellenberger's plans and, with a flash of anger, interpreted the reason for his association with Randolph.

'Very interesting, Mr Ellenberger, but with respect you have not answered my question: will the Syndicate prevail? *And* will the Diamond Company evolve into a worldwide monopoly?'

'Diamonds are a natural monopoly commodity,' he replied and then added softly, 'but whether they will be controlled by *this* Syndicate and *this* Diamond Company is another matter,' and he stared at her out of suddenly penetrating brown eyes, assessing her reaction.

For Tiffany the final piece of the puzzle fell into place. Ellenberger had a strangely neutralising, asexual effect on her, but she experienced a frisson of excitement as she envisaged the battle between him and Matthew Bright for control of the diamond industry. It could be as awesome as the clash of the titans in Kimberley, when Cecil Rhodes defeated Barney Barnato in the fight for Kimberley Central. This contest would be different, of course – more subtle and more patient, a campaign which could span decades *but* . . . and again she felt that surge of anticipation, it was a campaign in which she could participate.

'It is difficult,' she said, 'to see how and when the challenge to the Syndicate could be mounted. Why, Sir Matthew even has a foot inside the Premier.'

'The Premier is not the right vehicle.' Ellenberger dismissed the fabulously rich mine with a wave of his hand. 'But I believe Sir Matthew's tactics with the Premier – working from the inside, as it were – will be worth imitating one day. No, the time will come when another diamond discovery will be made and *that* will provide the basis for the manoeuvre.' Why am I telling her this? Ellenberger thought bemusedly. Am I being manipulated by a beautiful face, or am I merely off-guard because I fear she might blab about my meeting with the Courts all over London? Anyway, she will not talk; she is as intelligent and as close as her cousin Randolph.

Randolph was on Tiffany's mind, too. 'I look forward to our further association, Mr Ellenberger,' she said, extending her hand in a gesture of dismissal. 'I am sure your visit to the United States confirmed that you may rely on the support of the Courts. *However*,' and her tone took on a sharp edge, 'while I appreciate the reasons for cultivating my cousin, in future you will direct your inquiries to me. I am my father's daughter and Court Diamonds is *mine*!'

In her river suite at the Savoy, Tiffany reviewed the information she had acquired and congratulated herself on having given nothing away. Whether Anton Ellenberger was man enough to beat Matthew Bright at his own game remained to be seen; at the moment it was enough that he intended to try. The enmity between the Courts and Brights, plus that premonition of personal rivalry she had sensed when she saw Sir Matthew, left no doubt about which side she would support. But where would that leave Philip?

From the writing desk Tiffany picked up an envelope addressed to Balliol College, Oxford and tapped it thoughtfully with her long white fingers. The bid to wrest power from the Diamond Company and the Syndicate could take years – long enough for Sir Matthew to have died or retired and been succeeded by his son. Philip hated his father, but surely he would fight for his inheritance? On the other hand, would he have the stomach and stamina required for the defence of his interests? Tiffany remembered how quickly he had become bored with rowing and she frowned slightly. The frown deepened as she found it more and more difficult to envisage handsome, fun-loving Philip in this kind of league. There was something insubstantial about his character, some flaw in his make-up which made it impossible to envisage him controlling the cool cut-and-thrust of business dealings. He possessed the intelligence but not the temperament, while *she* had both. Tiffany's fingers rapped a rapid tattoo on the envelope. Life was suddenly becoming more complicated and her assignation with Philip in Paris took on a more serious aspect.

She had contemplated marriage with no one, least of all Philip. He was attractive, good company, a natural friend and, above all, her father had virtually forbidden any contact between them. She believed that she liked him better than any other man, but having not seen him for a year the attraction had become tempered with objectivity. Now she saw that marriage with Philip would bring about the amalgamation of Bright Diamonds and Court Diamonds, to the fury of their fathers and the consternation of the diamond industry. She would be in a position to manipulate Philip – because she was sure she was stronger than he – and bring about the changes in the system inherent in her discussion with Ellenberger: 'working from the inside' indeed, although not in the way he had intended! She might not even need Ellenberger ... Tiffany's thoughts raced ahead, but she made a conscious effort to check these flights of fancy. It was too soon, she did not know Philip well enough, she must be more certain of her strategy ... but the meeting in France definitely assumed a new emphasis. It was typical of her that never for a

146

moment did she contemplate the possibility that Philip might not cooperate, that he might not wish to marry her or that there might be any other obstacle to her ambitions. Neither did it occur to her that she was taking exactly the same calculated approach to Philip as Randolph had taken to her, an attitude she had castigated vehemently.

With her attention once more firmly fixed on the present, Tiffany sat down at the desk to write a short note; the contents were clear and precise, her handwriting large, flowing and emphatic. From the hotel staff she inquired an address and then despatched the note for delivery by hand and the letter for post to Oxford. Then she summoned her maid and spent at least twice as long as usual in dressing for dinner. Eventually her hair was brushed and burnished to her satisfaction, she had chosen a primrose silk dress and was decked in her finest diamond jewellery. She looked stunning – but would he come? Tiffany found herself pacing restlessly in the sitting-room of her suite, angrily telling herself not to be so schoolgirlish and assuring herself that she didn't care if he stayed away because this was purely a business matter. Turning in front of the large mirror on the wall, she received the full impact of the blazing diamonds, while her inner eye conjured up the image of his tall elegant figure, the austerity in his lean face and the glance of his grey eyes.

'You fool,' she said aloud, 'you look like a bloody Christmas tree!' And she ran back into the bedroom where, unaided, she tore off the yellow silk and pulled another dress out of the closet. Black, John Court had opined, was totally unsuitable for a young unmarried girl, but Tiffany knew it was right for tonight. The dress was perfectly plain, of black satin, full-skirted and cut low over her breasts; the dark shining material mirrored her raven hair. Discarding the elaborate extravaganza of the necklace, she substituted a simple pendant of one perfect gem but retained the flashing cascades of diamonds at her ears. A change of shoes and then she resumed her prowl, occasionally seeking reassurance from the looking-glass. Yes, the black was better, *much* better – but would he come? The summons – even Tiffany did not define it as an invitation – had been presented at rather short notice, she thought defensively.

Therefore, when Rafe Deverill did appear, her relief and pleasure were so great that they must be instantly repressed. Instead of greeting him with the warmth which had flooded her at the sight of him, Tiffany swept towards Rafe with one hand outstretched in the manner of the *grande dame*. He bent over the hand in a courteous, graceful gesture, but the glance of his grey eyes was as coolly ironic as ever although Tiffany detected a flicker of approval at her appearance. The touch of his hand on hers was unexpectedly pleasing, light but firm, the skin smooth but hard. She was disappointed when he did not maintain the contact for longer than was strictly necessary. What did he think of her, she wondered suddenly, what did he *really* think?

'May I offer you a drink, Captain?'

'Whisky, thank you.' Rafe watched with a blend of astonishment and amusement as she expertly wielded the decanter and he assimilated the significance of the otherwise empty room. 'Do you always act as barmaid at your own parties?'

'Only when I consider the presence of servants would be intrusive,' she returned boldly.

'Coming from anyone else, that remark would be considered intolerably forward. However, in your case I imagine one must retreat behind the phrase "refreshingly honest".'

'In my case you need retreat behind nothing. I am . . .'

'. . . Tiffany Court,' he supplied, with a sardonic smile. 'I *had* remembered. And Tiffany Court is above the petty rules and regulations which life imposes on the rest of us poor mortals?'

She stared at him defiantly, resentful at the implied criticism. 'Yes, you could put it that way. Incidentally, I decided we would dine in the suite tonight. It is more private.'

'It certainly is,' he agreed lightly. 'Evidently your originality extends to a flagrant disregard for your reputation. However, I'm not sure that *I* should adopt the same attitude, and the Savoy does an excellent supper on the terrace.'

'Perhaps your concern is for *your* reputation?'

He threw back his head and laughed, the first genuine amusement Tiffany could recall seeing him display. 'On the contrary, news of this assignation would only enhance my notoriety and confirm what people have always suspected about me.'

She was not quite sure how to take that; there seemed to be an edge of bitterness, a ring of truth beneath the flippancy. 'We will dine here,' she said with finality. 'No one need know unless you tell someone – certainly I have no intention of broadcasting it.'

'Do you trust the discretion of the Savoy staff?'

'Implicitly – I am a very generous tipper!'

Rafe smiled appreciatively. He was aware, with every moment which passed, of her extraordinary beauty and of the intelligence which blazed from her sharp ripostes and from the deceptively luminous eyes. Tiffany Court was like a diamond, hard, clear and brilliant, a mysterious blend of beauty and evil. She was everything Rafe despised, yet her attraction was magnetic; a man could lose himself in her magical, fathomless beauty, just as he could be drawn into the dazzling blue-white depths of a diamond. She was an enchantress, but Rafe Deverill was on his guard; his prejudice against her remained and he had no intention of becoming another of her victims. He was curious as to why she had summoned him; a business proposition, her note had indicated. He must contain his impatience, however, for it was not polite to mention business until after dinner.

'How long will you stay in London?' he inquired while waiters began serving the meal.

'I leave for Amsterdam the day after tomorrow,' she answered. 'Then I go to Paris before returning to New York.'

'Have you found time to visit Oxford?'

Tiffany nearly choked on her Dover sole and was forced to take a hurried gulp of champagne to wash down the particles of fish which had become lodged in her dry throat. She shook her head.

'Philip will be disappointed,' Rafe remarked wickedly, intrigued by her reaction.

'Philip? Philip who?'

'Come now, you cannot possibly have forgotten so handsome and charming a companion. You were far more interested in him than in the boats.'

'Oh, *that* Philip! Really, I hardly know him, but he was slightly interesting because of his connection with the diamond business.' Tiffany paused, remembering Rafe's position on the river-bank in the company of Philip's relatives. 'Do you know anything about the Bright family?' she asked.

'I know just about everything there is to know – that is to say, everything which is public knowledge.'

'Tell me,' she commanded and he looked at her reflectively. 'Please,' she added hastily with her most winning smile.

'His is not exactly a rags-to-riches story,' Rafe began, 'although at the outset of his career Matthew Bright was virtually penniless. It is a case of that system of primogeniture at work again – Matthew's grandfather was an earl, but he was the younger son of a younger son and consequently no finance was forthcoming from the family. Then there was some sort of scandal, involving a duke's daughter whose papa did not consider Matthew good enough for her, so he rushed off to the diamond fields.'

'Where he met my father.'

'And where the Court-Bright partnership made a fortune. The irony was that Matthew came home and married the youngest daughter of that same Duke – no one has ever forgotten that wedding or the diamonds worn by Lady Anne Bright that day.'

Tiffany's eyes shone. What a superb gesture from that marvellous man! But her mind was centred firmly on business. 'The Court-Bright partnership,' she repeated slowly. 'It turned out to be a very unequal partnership, which left Bright Diamonds with a 30 per cent holding in the Diamond

Company while *I* have only 15 per cent! They quarrelled about something and my father went home, leaving the field wide open to Matthew.'

Her lip curled. Despising her father for his weakness, Tiffany was sure that she would not have given way – in similar circumstances *she* would have stood her ground, forcing her adversary to retreat.

'Do you know what they quarrelled about?' she asked.

Rafe shook his head. 'I hate to tell you this, but the name of John Court means nothing in London.'

'London will know my name one day!'

'Doubtless,' Rafe agreed. 'We must hope that you become famous here in favourable rather than unfavourable circumstances.'

There was a short pause during which Tiffany was gripped by a sharp unease, but then she shrugged it off. 'Matthew Bright came back to London after the formation of the Diamond Company?'

'Yes, and in the nineties he was very much the glamorous diamond magnate and Randlord. After the death of his first wife, he indulged in a liaison with an extremely exotic foreign princess, but in the end he married his daughter's governess.'

'Oh no, he shouldn't have done that!'

'Why not?'

'It smacks of sentimentality. It is too . . . too ordinary, too predictable and . . . oh, you know, too *sugary*, everything neatly parcelled up and tied with a pretty pink bow.'

'Don't you care for happy endings.?'

She hestitated. 'Yes, but that is a *dull* ending. He would have been better off with the princess.' Talk of princesses reminded her of her mother and she was tempted to ask Rafe about Alida, but recollection of Philip's scepticism dissuaded her. 'Tell me about Philip's mother.'

Rafe noticed the wording of her request – in the context of this conversation, an inquiry about 'Lady Anne' or 'Sir Matthew's wife' would have been more usual. After describing Anne's physical attributes, he commented, 'She

151

was gentle but weak, not a bit like her sisters – or her niece,' he added *sotto voce*.

'Julia?'

'Who told you about Julia?' He was angry rather than embarrassed.

But Tiffany just smiled and shook her head, not bothering to explain about Lady Netherton's gossip. The meal had been cleared and they were alone again, Rafe cupping a brandy glass between his hands. Beautiful hands, Tiffany thought, feeling warm and relaxed from the food and wine. She recalled the sensation of their brief contact when he arrived and watched the movement of his long fingers cradling the glass, imagining their touch against her flesh, caressing her body, exploring every inch, every curve, every secret recess ... A tight knot was twisting inside her belly. Hastily she stood up.

'Have a cigar. I like the smell of cigars.'

'Thank you.' He set down the brandy glass and selected a cigar from the box she offered him. To her disappointment he did so without touching her. 'As long as you are quite sure you don't mind?'

'I have often thought of trying one myself'. She replaced the box on the table and replenished her champagne from the bottle in the ice-bucket.

'I would not advise it, but I have the feeling that such discouragement is only likely to increase your determination.'

Rafe was a trifle exasperated with her. In many ways he admired her independent spirit but she carried it too far; if she desired more champagne he would have preferred to pour it for her. There was something about her manner and her actions which emasculated a man. Tiffany was the kind of woman who could render a man impotent – yet watching her in the black dress with that inviting look in her lovely eyes, Rafe felt anything but impotent.

'So, what are you doing with yourself these days, Captain? How do you pass your time – apart from making love to Lady Julia, of course?'

Bitch! Rafe was momentarily stunned into silence. She seemed impossible to comprehend but then, out of nowhere, he found the answer: Tiffany Court was unpredictable because she possessed the body of a beautiful woman, but her mind and manner were those of a man.

'I am a gentleman of leisure,' he replied evenly. 'As you have surmised, I spend a great deal of time in bed.'

'How do you earn a living?'

'I don't – I enjoy the privilege of a small, but at the moment adequate, private income – and just what the hell has it to do with you?'

Tiffany ignored the question. 'You are a typical English gentleman, so doubtless your income derives from the land. Is that your future, Captain? A house in the country, farms and tenants and the annual Season in town?'

His lips were a thin grim line in his white face and he did not reply.

'Perhaps you devote your attention to good causes?' she suggested sweetly.

'No, although I might if someone did not try to push me so hard in that direction.' Rafe replied absently because the reference to Julia, coupled with Tiffany's aggressive approach, had brought a revelation. In Newport Tiffany had reminded him of someone and now he knew who: Julia. The resemblance was there in Tiffany's forceful manner and that tilt of the head.

'As I mentioned in my note, I have a proposition to put to you.' Succinctly Tiffany detailed her scheme for refurbishing antique jewellery.

Rafe listened politely but with noticeable bewilderment. 'Fascinating, my dear. I am sure the project will be an unqualified success and will further increase your already obscene wealth. But I fail to see how the matter can possibly affect me.'

'I can look after the American side of the enterprise, but I need someone to act as my agent in England – to buy up jewellery from deceased estates in particular. I would pay you a retainer plus ten per cent of the profits.'

153

'An *agent* ... *percentages* ... *me!*' Rafe was incredulous.

'Oh dear, have I upset your sensibilities, Captain? Are you too much of an English gentleman to soil your hands with filthy lucre? Do you prefer to deal with that commodity at third hand, through the intermediary of a bailiff or a butler?'

That had been Rafe's reaction exactly, but he was able to appreciate its pomposity. He stood up and bowed.

'My humble apologies, Miss Court. I should have realised that what is good enough for you ought to be good enough for me.'

'Diamonds are not *trade*, Captain Deverill. Dealing in diamonds is a strange and wonderful experience, possessing as many facets as a well-cut gem – excitement, power, romance, the lure of far-away places and beautiful people.' It was the wrong argument to use with Rafe, but her sincerity was compelling. 'You are offended and dislike the idea, but you have the right qualifications for the job and when you were trading in the Caribbean in that ridiculous boat you must have done so for money.'

'That was different.'

'Why? Because you were far from home, where no one recognised you?' Tiffany rose and stood very close to him, laying a cajoling hand on his arm. 'What,' she asked softly, 'can I do to persuade you?'

Rafe looked down into the exquisite face, at the invitation inherent in the violet eyes and gently-parted pink lips, at the creamy skin and the swell of the bosom. He kept his arms firmly at his sides. 'You ought not to entertain men alone in your room and make statements like that. One day someone will take advantage of your apparent ... willingness.'

'Perhaps that is why I asked you here,' Tiffany murmured glibly and was suddenly struck with the appalling possibility that it might be true.

Rafe was angry again, seeing her once more as the spoiled brat, convinced that she was playing a game she did not understand, flirting without any comprehension of the consequences. 'My God, but you need teaching a lesson,' he said roughly and pulled her towards him, crushing his mouth against hers.

He intended to frighten her, expected her to struggle, even to cry out, to resist him at all costs. But Tiffany Court did none of those things. She wrapped her arms round his neck and kissed him back, fervently and hungrily. Instead of a brief, hard, salutary lesson, the gesture evolved into a lingering embrace in which they were only aware of flesh, lips and tongues, drowning in desire. Then they surfaced and, shaken by their mutual longing, drew apart hastily.

'I will leave the offer open, Captain.'

He was tempted to ask 'which offer?' but desisted because he no longer felt invulnerable to her physical attraction. At least, he thought, he knew why she could travel without a chaperone – it was others who needed protection from *her*! 'As you like,' he said offhandedly, 'but it doesn't sound much in my line.'

'Just bear in mind that I have your good at heart as well as mine,' she replied, always coolly in command where business was concerned.

'My difficulty is, Miss Court, that when I try to visualise you as the good fairy you invariably metamorphose into the wicked witch.' He took her hand and brushed it briefly with his lips. 'Thank you for an excellent dinner and a most entertaining evening,' and he strode out of the room.

Tiffany was left standing, eyes wide with indignation, deflated and flat as stale champagne – again! This was the second time the insufferable man had walked out on her! The sense of anti-climax was suffocating, but what had she been expecting? Nothing, she told herself proudly, absolutely nothing. In fact she *wanted* nothing from him. He was the right person to wheedle a few old necklaces from some ancient dowagers, that's all. But in her heart of hearts she knew it was as well he had left because she could not have resisted him and she was still terrified of getting pregnant – yet, contrarily, she seethed that he had not tried to seduce her.

Rafe returned to the Ambleside mansion in Berkeley Square. It was unusual for him to return home at such an early hour and his mother seized the opportunity to way-lay him in the hall. Reluctantly he accompanied her to the drawing-room, dutifully poured two night-caps and sat down to receive the inevitable lecture.

To Charlotte Ambleside Rafe was everything a mother dreamed her son would be – tall, handsome, intelligent, the perfect gentleman and, most important, kind to his mother. He was much admired and Charlotte had been accustomed to being congratulated and envied for her good fortune – or this had been the case while Rafe wore a cavalry uniform. Now gossip and spiteful asides had replaced the compliments. Already upset by Rafe's refusal to explain his departure from the army, Charlotte chan-nelled her hurt into jealousy of Julia Fortescue, on whom she pinned the blame for his deviation from the straight and narrow path – a slur indeed on Julia who, while des-perately trying to keep Rafe in her bed, exerted a great deal of energy in attempting to propel him back on to the lines demanded by society. Charlotte would dearly have liked to be the only woman in Rafe's life. There had been times when she dreaded the prospect of his marriage and having to take second place, but she had decided that the acquisition of a wife would force Rafe to conform. How-ever, it must be a wife of Charlotte's choosing. She was combing the country for the right girl, never ceasing to regret that Miranda Bright was out of the running. The girl was much younger than Rafe, but the age dif-ference was not insurmountable. However, Miranda was deaf and for Charlotte's favourite child only the best would do.

'We are holding a dinner-party on Saturday evening,' she said. 'I should be exceedingly grateful if you could manage to attend.'

'Very well.' Oh Lord, he thought, another prospective bride!

'Miss Palmer will be present.'

'Oh, good.' He failed to keep the sarcasm out of his voice. 'Who *is* Miss Palmer?'

'Really, Rafe, I have mentioned her several times in recent weeks. I do wish you would *listen* occasionally! She is a considerable heiress, an orphan and an only child, in the guardianship of an uncle. The property includes a town house and a magnificent country estate only ten miles from Ambleside – you would be within easy distance of us and . . .'

'. . . you want me to inveigle my way into her heart and into her fortune. You will seat me next to her at dinner, everyone present will be perfectly aware of your intentions and the entire affair will have as much subtlety and refinement as sending a stallion to cover a mare.'

'Rafe!'

'The principle is exactly the same, Mama, so there is no need to look so affronted. Is this renewed campaign prompted by the fact that my brother and his wife are producing only girls? The next Lady Ambleside is pregnant again, I understand, so the future of our family name may not depend on me and my as yet hypothetical heirs.'

'Rafe, I want you to promise me . . .'

'I will attend your dinner-party, Mama,' he said, rising to his feet, 'and I will be polite to Miss Palmer. But I will make *no* promises.'

The coldness of his tone knifed into Charlotte, the pain stripping away the last layer of her defences and jolting her into admission that she loved him more than her other children . . . and more than her husband, too. She felt as though a pane of glass had descended between them, blocking real communication, and her frustration led her to lash out angrily, perhaps in the vain hope that the vibrations would shatter the invisible barrier.

'If you don't marry soon, you will find yourself in real trouble with a woman one of these days,' she shouted.

157

'Julia Fortescue, I suspect, could be very dangerous if crossed and I have no doubt there will be others of the same type. I warn you that if you bring scandal upon our heads you need not look to me for comfort.'

'Under no circumstances, Mama, would I expect you to divide your loyalties,' and he left the room, leaving Charlotte to burst into tears, more distressed at this scene with her son than by any lovers' quarrel.

Upstairs Rafe flung himself on the bed fully-clothed, locked his hands behind his neck and stared at the ceiling. He ought to feel remorse for hurting his mother but could feel no emotion for anyone any more, just as he could find no pleasure in anything he did. The sadness, the *weltschmertz*, weighed him down; he could see only darkness and the tragedies in the world which he was powerless to alleviate. But tonight, he reflected, there had been moments of pleasure in the company of Tiffany Court. He recalled her summing-up of his probable future: a house in the country, farms and tenants and the annual Season in town. Was she right? Was that all that lay beyond Miss Palmer or an endless succession of Miss Palmers? Suddenly Rafe envied his elder brother, who was living just such a life with every appearance of contentment. Perhaps it was easier for the first-born, the heir, whose future was mapped out for him and whose finances were secure. Younger sons had more flexibility and freedom of choice, but the irony was that choice was so limited. Lucky Matthew, Rafe thought again. Diamonds had solved his difficulties, but surely the days of big new finds were past. Besides, Rafe doubted his own ability to exploit people and situations in the way Matthew must have done on his road to success.

Suddenly Rafe was consumed with a longing for the *Corsair* and for the untrammelled, uncharted life of the sea. He ought to sell the boat; while not in debt, his income barely exceeded his expenditure and the *Corsair* cost him money to keep afloat. Only last week the Sergeant had written to request cash for a new sail. Yes, he ought to sell her but could not bring himself to do so, whether from stubbornness, madness or some obscure sentiment he could not say. The *Corsair* was an escape route which must be kept open.

Rafe stood up and walked to the window. Perhaps he should think about marriage. Perhaps this life took on more meaning when a man had duties and responsibilities. He would make a serious attempt to appreciate Miss Palmer's good qualities.

But he would look out for antique jewellery as well – although he was damned if he would accept payment for his services – because it would give him an excuse to meet Tiffany Court again.

CHAPTER NINE

Tiffany spent several days in Amsterdam at Asscher's diamond-cutting works, discussing the size and shape of the gems destined for her jewellery project, listening and learning. She greatly respected these master lapidaries for it was the cutters of the Low Countries who, in the fifteenth century, had begun working to geometrical patterns in order to bring out the fire and brilliance of the diamond.

Then she travelled to Paris, feeling uncharacteristically tense about the rendezvous with Philip, suddenly anxious that their relationship might have suffered through the lengthy, enforced separation.

She chose to meet him in the foyer of the hotel, because it allowed her to make a grand entrance and had the additional advantage of a public rather than a private reunion so that any awkward moments could be passed off more easily. But there were no such awkward moments. He was as handsome, charming and compatible as before. In fact, Tiffany decided, their ease in each other's company was all the more noticeable and welcome after the stress of Rafe Deverill's presence. The moment she looked up into Philip's laughing face the cares of business deals, cousins, fathers and obnoxious English gentlemen melted away; she was light-hearted and happy and the world was filled with sunshine, gaiety and joy.

'I am so pleased that you could come,' and she took his arm to walk out into the Paris afternoon. It occurred to her that, for all her apprehension about this encounter, she had never doubted he would come. 'Was it difficult to get away?'

'Not as difficult as I expected. The examinations are

over, thank God, and I used this diamond-manufacturing affair to persuade Papa. Strange to relate, he was practically civil about the matter – if I didn't know him better, I might have believed he was glad I was taking an interest.' Philip paused in his stride and beamed down at her. 'My God, Tiffany, do you realise that I have finished at Oxford, that education is over, that I am free at last? But no, you haven't been to school – you couldn't possibly understand.'

'If there's one thing I understand, it is personal freedom,' Tiffany retorted sharply. 'But that is excellent news, Philip. It might mean we can meet more often – if you want to, that is,' and her violet eyes laughed into his.

He squeezed her arm. 'You cannot really doubt it!' His white teeth flashed in that charming boyish smile. Life was good that June afternoon in Paris, with the most beautiful girl in the world on his arm and Sir Matthew Bright safely on the other side of La Manche.

'Are you likely to meet anyone you know? Ought we to be frightfully discreet?' Tiffany demanded as they appropriated a table at a pavement café.

Philip shrugged. 'None of *my* friends are in Paris and as far as I know Papa's acquaintances will be in London for the Season. What about you?'

'It is *possible* that I could be recognised.' Tiffany tilted her head impishly. 'I do tend to stand out in a crowd.'

'Your height,' Philip said gravely. 'It is the only remarkable aspect of your appearance.'

Tiffany laughed delightedly, while pretending extreme annoyance. 'It would be best if we stayed away from the smart places – we could go to Montmartre, the cafés and artists are heaps of fun.'

'As you like.'

He seemed curiously apathetic about their plans. Sprawled in his chair, long legs crossed gracefully, he was almost impossibly handsome and thoroughly at home in this environment. Philip was not exactly a *boulevardier* – he was too young for that – but was the eternal undergraduate in blazer and silk scarf, jaunty, pleasure-seeking and ever-youthful.

'I hope you were not offended when I sent you the money for the journey and the hotel,' she said.

'Good Lord, no! I was jolly grateful. Why should I have been offended?'

'I don't know.' And really she did not know, except for some half-formed notion in her head which whispered that a man might feel inferior if offered money by a woman in so blatant a fashion – marrying her for her money was not the same thing at all.

'Why did you send it? Why did you believe I needed it?' His tone was casual enough, but his expression was more alert than before.

'Fragments of our very first conversation keep coming back to me,' she said slowly. 'You remember, when we were children at your country home? You told me that your father never sent you hampers at school, so I assumed he was probably stingy with your allowance.'

'The financial situation has improved a bit over the years. I suspect the influence of my stepmother – she is constantly trying to buy her way into my favour! It was kind of you, dear girl, but actually in this instance your generosity was unnecessary – Papa was so overcome at my mentioning the artificial diamond scare that he forked out in unprecedented fashion.'

'Good.' But in that case it was extremely odd that he did not offer to repay the funds she had sent. It occurred to Tiffany that Philip could be very casual and very extrava-gant with money and that this could be a trait which would need watching. 'So you will be able to come to the race with me?'

'Race?'

'The French Grand Prix, of course,' she said impatiently. 'For heaven's sake, I thought the time and place would be engraved indelibly on your heart.'

'It is. I just did not dare to hope . . .' He leaned across the table, seized her hand and began smothering her palm, fingers and wrist in kisses. 'You are wonderful – beautiful, exciting, intelligent, interested in motors cars and . . .' and he winked, '*rich!*'

'That's settled, then. We will spend three days in Paris before going to Le Mans. Our first priority is this charlatan Lemoine who maintains he can manufacture diamonds.' Tiffany looked at Philip seriously. 'You do believe he is a charlatan, don't you?'

'I haven't the remotest idea,' Philip laughed carelessly. 'Besides, it doesn't matter much, does it?'

'Yes,' Tiffany announced firmly, 'it most certainly does.'

'But just think of the effect on our revered parents! They would both have apoplectic fits!'

'I was thinking,' she said sternly, 'of the effect on the diamond industry and *our* future.'

'Well, there's no hurry,' he answered easily. 'Let's see some of the sights of Paris before we worry about that.'

'No,' and Tiffany rose to her feet. 'Business first. We will go to this Lemoine person tomorrow morning.'

'Don't you want to shop? I thought women made a bee-line for the Paris fashion houses and squandered millions on frocks.'

'Only the women who have nothing better to do. Personally I find shopping a bore and an intolerable intrusion into my busy schedule, added to which I have enough frocks to stock a shop already.'

Philip sighed, but the sight of Tiffany in her violet silk gown soon restored his good-humour. 'Very well, you win! Lemoine it is, *le matin*, but tonight Paris is to be pure pleasure.'

'Claims that artificial diamonds can be manufactured are nothing new, of course,' Tiffany commented the next morning as they drove to the warehouse where Lemoine conducted his experiments. 'And oddly enough, with only one exception the claimants have all been French.'

'What a very knowledgeable little girl you are.'

Tiffany detected a slight inflection in his tone which was

163

not altogether flattering. 'It was you who pointed out that intelligence and information would suit my style,' she reminded him.

'So I did and so it does.'

'Then why . . .' Tiffany stopped, deciding to leave the question unasked. There was a conflict evident in his attitude, a lack of consistency which was puzzling. Perhaps, she reasoned, Philip preferred her business talents to be displayed elsewhere, while with him she should be purely pretty and pleasure-seeking. But to me business is pleasure, she thought, then decided that anyway this was not the reason – the truth was that Philip was simply not interested in diamonds. 'It was Lavoisier who proved that diamonds are merely crystallised carbon,' she continued, 'and experiments were carried out by other French physicists until, in 1880, a Scotsman actually produced diamonds from a charcoal base.'

'James Hannay, but he nearly blew himself up in the process.'

The fact that Philip knew more about the subject than he pretended did not escape her, but she forebore to comment. 'Nevertheless, he manufactured diamonds – microscopic crystals, admittedly, but they were acknowledged to be diamonds. Then a few years ago Henri Moissan announced that he had been successful.'

'Was his claim verified?'

'I believe so. Moissan has been nominated for the Nobel chemistry prize and is a man of the highest repute, but fortunately his process was prohibitively costly – it was cheaper to continue digging out the gems from Kimberley's "diamondiferous blue"! Lemoine was employed by Moissan as an engineer and reckons to have improved on his employer's formula. Well, we shall soon find out – I have requested a full demonstration.'

Lemoine's laboratory was situated in the basement of the warehouse. Tiffany ignored the shabby surroundings and the Frenchman's effusive welcome, concentrating her attention on the electric furnace in which he allegedly produced his gems. She had a shrewd suspicion that she knew the reason for his bonhomie – she and Philip were young, handsome and apparently innocent, merely the children of successful fathers; if the man was a fraud, he could be forgiven for thinking they would be easily fooled. Tiffany said and did nothing to disillusion him. She accepted his statement that the formula was secret, but watched closely as he busied himself at the furnace. Obviously, she reasoned, the essence of the process was to heat powdered carbon at an incredibly high temperature, but presumably there was some sort of secret ingredient. The man had his back to her and she could not see his hands. Her scepticism increased.

It came as no surprise when Lemoine produced a stone from the furnace – fake or genuine, he was bound to produce *something*. She examined the stone closely after it had been cooled in cold water and pronounced it to be a genuine diamond. Philip handled it briefly, nodding his agreement, while Tiffany listened incredulously to Lemoine's smug assertion that he was receiving financial backing for his experiments from Julius Wernher, Alfred Beit's partner, and that he was moving his operation to a factory in the Pyrenees.

Outside, Tiffany caught hold of Philip and waltzed him down the street. 'Thank God,' she exulted. 'He is a fake! I know it but I cannot prove it, not at the moment anyway.'

'How the hell did he fool Julius Wernher?'

'Heaven knows, but that doesn't matter. The important thing is that the industry is safe.'

Philip looked at her curiously. 'Why are you so sure?'

'A gut feeling,' she said slowly. 'The whole set-up was phoney. I was wondering if he had a secret ingredient but I am certain the only secret element was a diamond, slipped into the furnace while his back was turned to us. And I was suspicious of the diamond itself – it looked like a South African stone to me.'

'What on earth do you mean?' Philip asked in astonishment.

'A diamond betrays its origins. An expert can even identify which mine a stone comes from.'

'Good Lord! Could you tell where Lemoine's diamond
originated?'

Tiffany shook her head regretfully. 'I don't possess the
expertise. But I know people who do and I intend to
arrange another demonstration for their benefit.'

'No, don't do that!'

'Why not? We must scotch these rumours once and for
all, expose this fraud for what he is!'

'But Tiffany,' and his tone was cajoling, 'just think of the
anguish our fathers will suffer until they find out the truth!
Surely there is no harm in prolonging their agony, just a
little?'

She had realised that Philip was not interested in the
diamond industry, but had not comprehended his willingness to sacrifice the good of that industry for his own
personal malice. With a supreme effort of will Tiffany prepared to overlook this flaw in him – after all, her plans
centred on his eventual exclusion from the business. But
would she play along? Did she wish to cause *her* father
anguish? Tiffany did not hate her father as Philip detested
Matthew, but she did despise him; she manipulated him
at every turn, but was contemptuous of his constant
capitulation.

'No real harm, I suppose,' she agreed reluctantly, 'as
long as we express grave doubts about Lemoine. I absolutely refuse to pretend to be taken in and look a fool
when he is eventually exposed! *And* I reserve the right to
tell the truth if his activities affect the industry in any way.'
She took hold of Philip's arm, lifted on a wave of lightness
and euphoria as the worry about Lemoine was replaced
with relief. 'Now business is over until after the Grand Prix.
Let us enjoy ourselves!'

They resumed their summer idyll, begun the previous
year in Oxford strolling beside the Seine and in the Bois
de Boulogne. As she had expected, Tiffany was happiest
in Montmartre. She was amused when Philip insisted on

visiting the Café d'Harcourt because, he explained, his full name was really Harcourt-Bright. While they were in the *Café*, a dog approached them, begging for food. Tiffany threw it a few scraps and patted its head, but Philip was less welcoming.

'Are you not fond of dogs?' she inquired.

'I am neither for them nor against them. However, this hound happens to be a Great Dane and I do dislike Great Danes.'

'Why?'

'My sister has one which follows her like a shadow.'

'So you dislike your sister. Why – because she is your father's favourite?'

'Of course not.' This was the real reason and they both knew it, but Philip attempted to justify his attitude. 'It is the way Miranda takes her favouritism so much for granted, with her expression so smug and her demeanour so superior and self-contained.' He smiled suddenly, not wanting Tiffany to suspect he was feeling sorry for himself, and continued, 'It's irritating, that's all. Fortunately I see her only rarely.'

Tiffany of all people should have known that a father's feelings for a favourite daughter are frequently neither justified nor solicited, but on this occasion she was genuinely distressed for Philip, visualising his loneliness on the periphery of the family circle. 'Then I shall dislike Miranda, too. Anything which hurts you, hurts me. After all, we are . . . *friends*.'

She lingered over the word and their eyes met, acknowledging at last that the innocence had faded from their relationship. However, at this juncture they still resisted the fantasy of love. All they were acknowledging was physical attraction and mental compatibility, while in addition Tiffany's astute brain computed the financial and strategic advantages of a merger. Philip took her hand and kissed it, a gesture he had made before but oh, so different in its enactment now, his lips pressing and burning, arousing erotic sensations and images of where the encounter might lead.

Tiffany did not know whether to scream with fury or laugh with relief when the mood was broken by the arrival of the dog's owner. It turned out that the young man was an American and, with a quick glance at Philip, Tiffany invited him to join them. She listened entranced as he described his penniless existence in the attics and cafés of Montmartre.

'The dog eats better than I do,' he said, ruffling the animal's ears. 'I exist on bread, while he begs food from the best restaurants.'

'How do you survive?' Tiffany asked, with memories of Gerard and his imitation Old Masters.

'Portraits – mostly pencil sketches of rich American tourists,' and his grin was lopsided, charming and optimistic.

'Very well, sketch me!'

The result was amazingly good considering the speed of its execution. Tiffany wondered if Philip would buy it, but when he made no move to do so she tossed a generous pile of francs to the artist.

'That should keep you in bread for a year – but mind you share it with the dog!' As the astonished artist began to stammer his thanks, Tiffany inscribed the picture with her name and the date and passed it to Philip. 'To remind you of me.'

Then she whisked away the entire party, including the dog, for a lobster and champagne supper. It was as if she deliberately wanted to avoid being alone with Philip, but that night when he escorted her to her hotel suite, she could postpone the encounter no longer. Instead of leaving her at the door, he stepped quickly into the darkened room and kissed her. He took his time over it and for such a fun-loving and casual fellow, seemed intent on making a serious and thorough job of the matter. It left Tiffany breathless and wanting more but, with an exclamation which might have been an apology, Philip hastily left the room.

It was at that moment, with the imprint of his lips fresh on hers and the sensation of his hands tingling on her body, that Tiffany decided to marry Philip. She had not yet changed her views on romance and still believed she was above the sentimentality and pain of love but, looking to her future, Philip Bright was everything she wanted. He would be friend as well as lover. All she felt for a man like Rafe Deverill, she told herself firmly, was lust – besides, he could not bring a diamond company as a dowry.

Philip hurried out of the hotel to buy himself a girl. Like others before him, he picked the tallest black-haired prostitute he could find and emptied himself into her in a frenzy of longing for Tiffany. He had left her abruptly because he dared not stay – not even Philip ventured to break the iron rule which forbade seduction of an unmarried girl of one's own class.

The girl was good and making love to her was enjoyable, but he had always been fortunate in his sexual encounters, ever since his initiation by his cousin Charles's actress wife. Oh yes, it was wonderful – the softness, the warmth and the wetness – absolutely wonderful, but not once had he confused it with love, although he had thought it was probably the nearest he would ever get. Now, tonight, he was no longer so sure. He was consumed with longing for that exquisite body, aching to release the passion pent-up inside her, but she was so much more than merely beautiful and rich. Philip could have his pick of wealthy lovely ladies, but that night he admitted that Tiffany was special and the faint hope began to burn that his desire for a real family might be granted.

When he returned to his room, he carefully smoothed out the portrait of Tiffany, leaving it where he could see it from his bed and where it would not be overlooked when he packed his valise.

At six o'clock on the morning of 26 June Tiffany and Philip were seated in the grandstand overlooking the La Sarthe circuit just outside Le Mans. Tiffany glanced round a little anxiously, but was relieved to see no familiar faces among the crowd. Nonetheless she kept the veil of her hat pulled down over her face, ostensibly to protect her from sun and dust, but in reality to prevent recognition – it was certainly not beyond the bounds of possibility that some of the Vanderbilts might be here. No such considerations entered Philip's head; he was totally immersed in the race, soaking up the atmosphere and watching the cars lining up at the start of the course.

'I see what you meant when you said that European motor racing was different from the American variety,' Tiffany conceded.

'This is a real test of endurance,' Philip said enthusiastically. 'The cars must complete six laps today and another six laps tomorrow, a distance of about 770 miles. There are no controls – that is, areas where drivers must observe speed restrictions of one sort or another – and only the driver and his riding mechanic may carry out repairs.'

'Who do you think will win?'

'The French,' he replied immediately, 'chiefly because they have entered twenty-six cars, compared with three Germans and six Italians!'

The race began and the might of European automobiles, all with engines over twelve litres, roared into the hazy sunshine of the early morning. Philip was enthralled but Tiffany found the race less exciting than she had expected. She attributed this disappointment to her lack of partisanship: if American or British entrants had been competing she could have taken sides, but could not evince interest in a race between these European countries and drivers she did not know. But her visit to the Grand Prix was worthwhile, because instead of watching the cars she watched Philip. The transformation was unbelievable. The indolence and vacillation vanished and he seemed to grow stronger with every hour that passed; hands clenched as they gripped an imaginary steering-wheel, feet pressed hard on invisible pedals, he participated physically as well as mentally. While obviously wishing that the British were taking part, yet he could identify with the men and machines in a manner which rose above nationality.

Patriotic pride mattered, particularly to the French and the Germans, but the cars – their performance and future development – were all-important. Of consequence to Tiffany, however, was the fact that this was Philip's chosen field, an interest he had selected for himself well outside his father's sphere of influence, well outside his father's shadow. If they should marry, this was where Philip could occupy himself while she managed the diamond business – Randolph could keep his damn bank! Yes, the cars must be encouraged.

'Will you get in touch with Napier when you go home?' she asked the next day as they watched the second session.

'First thing!' He turned towards her, eyes shining. 'There is talk of building a new circuit in England – a proper banked circuit especially designed for racing. By this time next year I intend to be racing cars on that track.'

'And you think you can buy your way into the Napier organisation?' No insult was intended in the question – Tiffany was just very matter-of-fact about money.

'Yes'.

'Do you have the money?'

'Not yet, but I will have as soon as I begin work at Bright Diamonds!'

'On what basis are you working there?' But he only stared at her uncomprehendingly. 'As a partner?' she asked impatiently. 'Or a director? Or as a clerk on a salary? Your father might expect you to start at the bottom and work your way up, in which case the salary won't run to racing cars.'

Philip had not thought about it before. 'As a partner,' he said defensively.

Tiffany doubted it; in fact she doubted it very much indeed. Her information about Sir Matthew, plus her brief glimpse of him, caused her to believe it was unlikely that Philip would win such favourable terms from his father as she had extracted from hers. However, Philip's antipathy to favourite daughters made it unwise to say so.

'Good. All the same, I would be happy to lend you a sum to tide you over.'

His face lit up. 'Would you honestly? Hell, Tiffany, that would be great, simply great!'

'What are friends for?' she said lightly.

'Could I have it now?'

'Well, not *right* now! You will have to wait until I can get to a bank. I don't carry that sort of money in my purse or stuffed up my drawers, you know!'

Philip burst out laughting, delighted by her startling vulgarity. He held her hand tightly, watching the Hungarian Szisz winning the race for France in the big works Renault. 12 hours 14 minutes, he thought, so the speed was about 63 miles per hour. 'Tiffany,' he said, 'you are perfect, absolutely perfect.'

'Yes,' she said, 'I know.'

Still they never spoke of their growing intimacy or of their feelings for each other. To express their love would be to seal it, finalise it, to close the escape routes . . . and they were not ready for that yet. On their last evening together, in Paris, Tiffany again arranged dinner for two in her suite and this time she wore the yellow silk and her best diamonds. She was sad at parting from him so she moved into a higher gear, her wit sharper, her laughter louder, her gaiety more brittle. She was happier with him than with anyone else in the world. He was her other half: her twin, her friend, her lover. She could see the path ahead, clearly signposted, its personal and business branches pointing to success. It was as it should be – the girl who had everything was being provided with the perfect marriage as well.

All evening she waited for him to touch her, deliberately sitting on a sofa after dinner to enable him to sit beside her. Their brightness was becoming dulled and blunted from tiredness and too much champagne. She stared at the floor, but out of the corner of her eye saw his hand move towards her. He began stroking her bare arm, very slowly and thoughtfully, trailing his fingers from shoulder to wrist. He leaned across, brushing his lips against the flesh of her upper arm before kissing the curve of her shoulders and neck. Then he got up from the sofa, walked across the room to lock the door and returned to stand in front of her. He held out both hands.

'Come here.'

She took hold of his hands and was transported – because she had no recollection of actually rising to her feet – into his arms. As he kissed her, he wrenched aside the straps of her dress to release her breasts, baring her nearly to the waist. Then he pulled her down to the floor.

Twenty minutes later her clothing was in worse disarray, her hair had tumbled to her shoulders and her face was flushed. The tingle between her legs had expanded to a screaming ache which begged to be relieved, a void which craved to be filled. But Philip did not fill it. He kissed and caressed her; he panted, groaned and gasped; he lay on top of her and pressed his body against hers so that she could feel its hardness. But he did not take her and eventually they drew apart, trembling and unhappy. Philip stood up and paused a moment, staring down at where Tiffany lay flat on her back, breasts exposed in a swirl of yellow silk, black hair streaming on the carpet.

'Until next year,' she said.

After Philip had gone Tiffany paid her last Parisian call, visiting the House of Cartier in the Rue de la Paix in order to discuss the possibility of their opening a branch in New York. Alfred Cartier listened with interest, commenting that a large number of wealthy Americans patronised the Paris House, and he agreed that his third son Pierre would investigate the matter and visit the United States. Promising to assist Pierre in any way she could, Tiffany took her leave, well-pleased with her negotiations and confident of establishing another outlet for her jewellery.

As she prepared to sail to New York, Tiffany realised that this was the first time a parting had been painful. Not only was it likely to be another year before she saw Philip again, but she was falling under the spell of Europe, enjoying her increasingly cosmopolitan image and the added freedom of these journeys. Perhaps, she mused, it was her English blood which bestowed this affinity with Europe.

Aboard the transatlantic liner, she stared at the diamond-framed miniature of her mother which travelled with her everywhere. As she tried to imagine what kind of woman her mother had been, there came for the first time a discomfiting prickle of guilt that her own birth had robbed her mother of life. Alida had been young, beautiful and presumably happy and she would not have wanted to die. Tiffany was aware of these new emotions, conscious of a warmth, an opening-up, a flowering within her; she had not suspected she was capable of such softness of response, but apparently the seed had only lain dormant within her, awaiting the sunshine of Philip Bright. Philip, Tiffany decided, was good for her.

But New York looked good, too, and there was new and exciting work to be done – and the diamonds wanted to reclaim their favourite daughter. Tiffany possessed the gift of being happiest where she was, a talent for living in the present. Paris and London faded, even if they were not forgotten.

Only Randolph disturbed the pattern, casting a menacing and sinister shadow over her happiness. He was still there, watching and waiting, his courtly air deceiving everyone except herself. Then came the day when he pounced.

'It is time that you and I had a talk, my dear.'

'Is it? About what?' Tiffany prevaricated but knowing that the issue could not be avoided, braced herself for the inevitable confrontation.

'I made you a serious proposal of marriage and I have waited patiently for an answer.'

'I gave you an answer – *no*.'

'After your initial impetuous refusal, you agreed to think it over. Now, unlike your father, I understand you very well. I understand perfectly that you traded your conciliatory offer for additional freedom of movement and involvement in Court Diamonds.' Randolph paused, his pale features set in an expression of bland goodwill. 'I understand that,' he repeated, 'and furthermore, when we are married I would be prepared for you to continue in the same vein.'

'You would be *prepared* . . .' Choking back her indignation at his condescension, Tiffany sat down, leaned back in the chair and considered him. Randolph was a fact of life; this was unfortunate, but no amount of wishing would make him vanish. Whatever happened – if she married Philip, married someone else or stayed single – she must continue to work with Randolph because her father had ensured his position in the family empire. What is more, Tiffany knew that Randolph was a born banker and, even if she could contrive to oust him, it would be virtually an impossible task to replace him without harming the interests of the Court Bank. She must overcome this loathing of him and learn to live with him – as a *cousin*.

'Randolph, I am flattered by your offer but regret that I must still decline to marry you.' The words were stilted and her politeness barely credible to her own ears. The art of compromise came hard to someone who had always spoken her mind. 'I am happy that you have your place in the bank and I have my niche in the diamond company. One day we will both marry and no doubt our families will enjoy a close association. You are more like a brother to me than a cousin, Randolph.'

He smiled stiffly. Tiffany noticed with surprise that he was handsome in a withdrawn, elegant sort of way. His features were regular, refined and aristocratic, his lips well-shaped and his hair thick, dark and shining. She tried to analyse why he so repelled her, but could not attribute it to any individual physical characteristic. It was his manner and his mannerisms, something about the movement of head, body and hands, something in his expression, something about the way he had grabbed hold of that girl on the

175

yacht ... Tiffany grappled with the indefinable and, defeated, returned her attention to what he was saying.

'You are a businesswoman, Tiffany, and an admirable one! However, I wonder if you have considered the difficulties and divisions which may arise if you marry another man and I marry another woman. First, inevitably your husband – who may have married you for your money – would resent my position, causing a strain on your marriage and on our working relationship. Secondly, when our children grow up, who inherits what? Can you imagine the rivalry between our sons – or daughters,' he added hastily. 'Nothing weakens an organisation more than internal division and I do not wish to see the Court empire carved up into small slices in order to give every claimant a share. It must be held together as one great and powerful enterprise: each child making his contribution but *one* – the ablest, not necessarily the eldest – in control. You know I am right, Tiffany, and that this is what we could achieve together.'

Looked at from his point of view, Tiffany could appreciate that it seemed a sensible plan. She could see that the business would flourish and that she could indulge in a few affairs on the side – because that was the bargain he was offering. She could not tell him that the business would also flourish if she achieved control of other diamond interests through Philip; that Philip would not resent Randolph because their aspirations were so diverse; that she would fight tooth and nail to ensure that *her* child controlled the future of the company. And she must not say that – most important of all – she could not bear Randolph to touch her.

'There is another factor to be borne in mind.' He smiled again, with such sincerity that Tiffany was sure he was about to tell her something which was to his advantage rather than hers. 'While you were away, your father informed me of the arrangements made for your welfare in the event of his untimely demise. Put simply, my dear, your financial interests are held in trust until you are twenty-five and I would be your legal guardian.'

Tiffany swore, a stream of unladylike expletives which caused Randolph to raise his eyebrows, but he managed to forbear from chastising her.

'You arranged it! You used your influence with my father while my back was turned,' she accused, her brain whirling. She must demand that her father explain the terms of the trust, but it sounded very much as though she must marry the man of her choice soon or else wait until she was twenty-five, because Randolph would never authorise a match for her. Alternatively, she could pray that John Court lived until she became twenty-five. How old was her father? Sixty-one, she calculated, and in good health. Dear God, let him be in good health!

'Not at all,' Randolph denied smoothly. 'It is an eminently sensible arrangement for a young girl as wealthy as you. As for "influencing your father while your back was turned", it is a charge I deny most strongly, but such behaviour is commonplace in the commercial world. If you leave your post you must always arrange to guard your back. Of course, if you married me you could travel the world with impunity because I would look after your interests for you.'

It was there again, that implied 'arrangement', that offer of personal freedom if she merged her business interests with his. But she conceded that she could trust him – he *would* guard her diamonds and there was no one better able or better placed to do so. But even without Philip, marriage with Randolph would have been impossible. However, at least they were discussing the matter in a mature, reasonable fashion, which was more productive than screaming at each other as they had done on the last occasion.

'I am sorry, Randolph,' and she extended her hand.

'So am I, but I shall continue to wait.' He held her hand lightly, with none of the passion and intensity he had displayed during their previous encounter. 'Yours is a temperament which invites trouble, Tiffany. I should like you to know that you can always rely on my love and assistance if you get into difficulties.'

She laughed incredulously. 'What on earth do you imagine might happen to me?'

'Oh, all sorts of things. You are beautiful but your behaviour is bold and uninhibited – it invites rape, or pregnancy at the very least.'

Randolph succeeded in achieving a certain lightness of tone, but the barb was much too close for comfort.

'You may take me for a whore, Randolph,' Tiffany said sharply, 'but do not insult me by taking me for a fool!'

'I don't, my dear. If you were a fool, I would not wish to marry you.'

'You want my money, not me!'

'That may have been true once, but unfortunately for me I have fallen in love with you. I did not intend to do so; there is something oddly demeaning and *diminishing* in loving someone so much, particularly when the object of one's affections proves so obstinate and unsympathetic. At times I resent being unable to control the emotion and the march of events; at other times I glory in the privilege of loving, even though that love is not returned. Good night, my dear.'

He kissed her hand and withdrew. Tiffany hurried up the stairs to her room and vigorously scrubbed the place where his lips had touched. Then she sat down on the bed to think over the exchange. Did he love her? He had sounded genuine and in this new guise he was almost bearable. At least he had dissolved some of her hate and fear of him. Yet there was a touch of the Machiavelli in Randolph and she could not be sure of his sincerity. Sitting there alone in the gathering dusk, Tiffany had the uncomfortable feeling that she might have been outmanoeuvred.

Randolph also had retreated to his room. He wiped the sweat from his forehead with a hand which trembled from the effort of controlling himself in Tiffany's presence and then unlocked a large cabinet. Inside were rows of books from which he selected a volume, turning the pages slowly and lasciviously with those long white hands, his eyes glittering and breath quickening as he looked at the obscene drawings. The cabinet contained his pornography collection, a rapidly growing library of erotica in which Randolph revelled but which was not enough to satisfy him.

After relocking the cabinet, he left the house and walked swiftly to his mistress's apartment. Wordlessly he gestured towards the bedroom, giving the girl an impatient shove as she moved reluctantly to the door. She was a different girl from the one Tiffany had seen on the yacht, but the look of fear on her face was the same as she gauged from his expression what he wanted of her tonight.

The bedroom was draped in black, from its walls to the bed-covers on which the naked girl lay face down, but the walls were decorated with arrangements of whips. Meticulously Randolph inspected them and selected one which had a thong of knotted cords. Then he too stripped naked, moistening his lips with his tongue as he raised the lash.

The girl was no good, Randolph thought, as he flicked the whip across her back. She was too submissive, too unresponsive, whereas Tiffany would fight and scratch and scream. He enjoyed inflicting pain, but the dumb fear and choked whimpers of this girl were a poor substitute for the fire of the high-spirited thoroughbred whom he sought to subdue. Nevertheless his excitement grew as he unleashed the emotions he had struggled to check in Tiffany's presence. To the girl's relief – the scars had barely healed from the previous assault – he dropped the whip sooner than usual and thrust into her from behind, climaxing quickly with a strange orgasmic cry.

Then he dressed, placed a wad of dollar bills on the table and walked out of the door. He had not addressed one word to the girl. Making his way down the street with that precise step, Randolph reflected that he had handled

Tiffany very well indeed this evening. He would win her in the end, he was quite sure of it.

Before travelling to Brightwell, where Matthew was spending the weekend with Laura and the children, Philip visited the Napier works in order to speak to his old friend Williams. The former groom had grown into a tough, wiry individual in his early thirties, who still seemed to exude the atmosphere of the stables despite his grease-stained overalls. When he saw Philip, William's dirt-smeared face split into a cheerful grin and he walked across, wiping his hands on a filthy rag.

'Master Philip! What a pleasant surprise!'

'Is there any news of the racing circuit?' Philip demanded without preamble.

'Yes, it's on! Mr Locke King is going ahead.'

Philip heaved a sigh of ecstasy and relief. 'Tell me more,' he urged.

'The track is to be built near Weybridge in Surrey at Mr Locke King's home, Brooklands. It will be 100 feet wide and 2¾ miles in circumference, with an extra half-mile inside the circle for a finishing straight. Embankments will ease the bends at each end of the track so that high speeds can be maintained.'

'When will work start?'

'September. Mr Locke King wants it open by next summer.'

'Surely it cannot be ready by then,' Philip exclaimed. 'The embankment alone will be an enormous job.'

Williams shrugged. 'He intends to try. The embankments are not the only obstacle – acres of woodland have to be cleared, swamps drained and bridges built. There is even talk about diverting the River Wey.'

Philip's eyes roved lovingly over the big six-cylinder cars in their distinctive Napier green which had been adopted as the British racing colour. 'I want to help, Williams – more than anything in the world, I want to be involved. Could you put in a word for me with Mr Edge? I'll

180

come and work here for nothing in my spare time – you've taught me everything about engines. And I can drive and I have money . . .' Philip was nearly incoherent with excitement and longing. 'I could buy a car or I could contribute to production expenses if Mr Edge was a bit short.'

'Times have changed, Master Philip,' observed Williams quietly, remembering the wistful and pathetic little boy who once had not enough money for a cab fare.

'I'm about to start work at my father's firm, so I will have plenty of cash. Actually, I have a sample with me,' and Philip casually displayed Tiffany's offering.

'Mr Edge isn't here today but I will mention it, honestly I will.'

Alive with hope, Philip proceeded to Brightwell to give a less than honest account of his trip to Paris.

'Lemoine seemed genuine to me,' he concluded, 'and he told me that his research is being financed by Julius Wernher.' He watched with satisfaction as Matthew's face was suffused with purple.

Indeed Matthew was deeply troubled. Apart from the ghastly implications for the diamond industry, the sensitive man beneath the hard-bitten exterior resented the possiblity that man could manufacture so beautiful and magical a thing as a diamond.

'Continue to keep an eye on Lemoine,' he growled, 'but otherwise your duties at Bright Diamonds will be more mundane. You have a lot to learn and you will learn it like I did – the hard way. There is no substitute for starting at the bottom and working up through the various departments, learning every facet – literally – of the business. I will pay you a purely nominal salary, because you will live at Park Lane and therefore will have few calls upon your pocket.'

Philip went white as his dreams receded, but he was a master at concealing his feelings from his father. He was saved from replying by Laura, who hurried into the room looking agitated. 'The chauffeur has been taken ill suddenly,' she exclaimed, 'and he was to meet Julia off the London train at Reading. I suppose I could send the carriage, but it takes much longer and Julia will be kept waiting.' Her magnificent green eyes seemed to alight on Philip with a look of dawning inspiration. 'Philip! Could you help? Lady Netherton tells me that you and Dick drive regularly at Netherton Park. Do you think you could handle the Rolls?'

Philip hesitated, torn between pride and an aching desire to drive the car. 'Easily,' he said.

'Bless you!' and Laura smiled with relief. Neither Philip nor Matthew ever discovered that the chauffeur's 'indisposition' had been carefully contrived by her in order to overcome Matthew's reluctance to let Philip drive the car.

Philip drove carefully, savouring every second, determined to prove himself worthy of the trust of this beautiful car. If only Tiffany could see him now! Better still, if only she could be sitting beside him! At the wheel, with thoughts of Tiffany, the world seemed a beautiful and a better place where anything was possible. What if Papa was determined to be tight-fisted? There must be lots of ways to make some extra money in a diamond company!

CHAPTER TEN

The day was unusually sunny for the time of year; fluffy white clouds bustled across a sky of robin's-egg blue and the silver birches were tinged with soft green leaf, signalling the start of spring. Therefore nothing would please Miss Palmer but that she spent the afternoon in the open air and that a foursome was formed for croquet. Alice Palmer was very much an outdoor girl, excelling at lawn tennis and croquet, incomparable upon a horse, the type whom Lady Ambleside would describe as the 'backbone of England'. She was utterly fearless when, mounted on her bay hunter, she soared over a five-barred gate; she would be equally undaunted in the Amazon basin, the Himalayas or the Steppes; the only time that naked panic showed in her eyes was when she found herself alone with Rafe Deverill. Then, overwhelmed with shyness, she would blush, stammer and behave with all the gauche ineptness of the schoolgirl she had so recently been. But on the croquet lawn she shone, smacking the ball sweetly with her mallet, exclaiming with pleasure at a good stroke, protesting humorously when a ball went against her, fiercely competitive.

Her partner and opponents enjoyed the game less than she – the sun was without warmth and judging by the nip in the air the fresh breeze had discovered a short cut from the Arctic. But despite the chill Miss Palmer was wearing a thin white dress and a white hat; there was something rather endearingly British about this fortitude – what sons she would bear! Rafe concealed his amusement as he watched his mother's frozen smile and purplish-blue hands; Charlotte Ambleside was suffering but she was suffering graciously – anything, anything to further Rafe's relationship with Alice Palmer!

He had known her for nine months and although other heiresses had been paraded for his approval, he kept coming back to her. The others were prettier but more insipid, or richer but less intelligent; Miss Palmer was no fool and doubtless would learn to relax in his presence. Occasionally Rafe would try to visualise her in his bed but, beyond deciding that he would be able to do his duty and that she would probably whinny when she came, the image remained vague and insubstantial. Impossible to imagine spending a night of unbridled lust with her but, Rafe reminded himself, life consisted of responsibilities rather than passions. Still, it would be pleasant to combine both sides of the coin and, as his eyes endeavoured to strip the white dress from Miss Palmer's sensible body, his mind was filled with an all-pervasive picture of a heart-shaped face, huge violet eyes, a creamy skin and blue-black hair. His hand shook, causing him to mistime his shot and he sent the ball skidding into a flower-bed.

His error caused a commotion which Rafe found ridiculous even though it was feigned and in fun. What on earth was he doing, playing a silly game with a lot of silly people, on such a day and in the full glory of his youth and strength? But they were not silly people: they were his family and – perhaps – his future wife. Rafe grimaced. It was no good, he could fight it no longer, he *must* see Tiffany again. But before he travelled to New York, he would have to speak to Julia.

He called on Julia at her London home, knowing that the acquiescent Lord Alfred was absent. The Fortescues were apart more often than they were together, because Julia found town life essential for organising her suffragette campaigns while Alfred followed traditional country pursuits. Alfred Fortescue and Alice Palmer, reflected Rafe drily, were made for each other.

'I am relieved to find you at home, Julia. These days I approach your door with trepidation, never sure whether you will be here or in Holloway Gaol.'

'I have not succeeded in being arrested – yet!'

'You will! Just keep trying and the martyr's crown will be yours.' He eyed the papers strewn over the writing-desk in Julia's very functional boudoir. 'Ah, devising fresh torture for the Liberals, I see. What is it this time? A raid on the Houses of Parliament or harassment of ministers at public meetings? I . . .'

'If you say "I told you so", I shall scream,' Julia retorted furiously. 'I admit we had high hopes that the new Liberal Government would grant women suffrage, but we were disappointed. Therefore we are adopting more militant tactics in order to achieve our aim. The least you could do is make a donation.' She picked up a collecting-box and rattled it under his nose.

'Sorry, Julia, but I will not finance civil disobedience.'

She snorted her contempt and banged down the box on the desk, its hollow ring betraying its emptiness. 'That is what Uncle Matthew says – and he with all those millions going to waste! Oh well . . .' She sat on the arm of Rafe's chair, stroking his hair. 'I am glad you found me at home. No one will disturb us.' She bent her head to kiss him on the lips while her hand moved to his groin, feeling for him through his trousers.

To his horror Rafe felt his body harden in response to her touch, but he still managed to push her gently away. 'Sit down over there, Julia. I want to talk to you.'

He is going to tell me it's over, she thought dully. He is getting engaged to that ghastly Palmer girl. I cannot bear it – *I simply cannot bear it!* 'No, not today,' she said, her faced fixed in a false bright smile. 'I don't feel like talking today.'

'This moment cannot be put off any longer.' He looked at her compassionately but continued undeterred. 'I must stop seeing you, Julia. Our relationship must end.'

'But you still want me! A moment ago I could *feel* how much you want me!'

'Of course I desire you – you are a very beautiful woman.' It was true: Julia at thirty-two was untouched by

185

time, as slim and glowing as a girl. 'Our affair is common knowledge and a few years ago our indiscretion would have resulted in our being thrown out of polite society. Standards have changed, but not to the extent where our association can avoid hurting others.'

Be reasonable, Julia admonished herself. Do not make a scene – men hate scenes. 'You are intending to marry? Congratulations! I assume the lucky lady is Alice Palmer.'

'I am considering marriage, but not necessarily to her.'

Julia's dull, nagging pain disappeared in a flash, to be replaced with piercing jealousy. Like Charlotte Ambleside, she felt she might be able to become reconciled to Alice Palmer who was plain and could be expected to take a secondary role, but could not abide the possibility that Rafe might marry someone she did not know ... who might be pretty, whom Rafe might actually *love*.

'There is someone else? Who is she?' she asked sharply.

'I'm going away for a short while,' he said, standing up and ignoring her question. 'It is best that we make a clean break of it now.'

'Where are you going?'

'America.'

'Will *she* be there? Is she an American?' Julia was beginning to sound hysterical but could no longer help it.

'I am going to America on business and, at the same time, my journey will allow me to think things over.' Rafe was surprised to find that this was true. He intended to put his life in order and a great deal depended on the reception he received from Tiffany Court.

'Rafe, marry Alice Palmer, *please*! Then we could go on as before – no one need know, we could pretend our affair is over.'

'It *is* over!'

Julia flung herself at him, wrapping her arms round his motionless body, clinging to him with all her strength. 'I cannot let you go, not after all we have shared, all we have been to each other! I will kill myself first!'

Rafe wrenched her away from him and shook her hard. 'Don't be ridiculous! I expected better of you, Julia. Have you no pride?'

'Not where you are concerned.' Tears were streaming down her face, but she made no move to brush them away. 'I thought our relationship was special, founded on those dreadful days in the concentration camps. How could you forget?'

The camps were their bond of shared experience – the refuge centres into which homeless Boer women and children had been herded while the British army pursued a scorched-earth policy in the Transvaal. When rumours of the horrific conditions in these camps reached England, a Ladies' Committee had been appointed to investigate and Julia had succeeded – through her contacts in the women's suffrage movement and her various charitable activities – in joining it. Her basic aim had been simple – to see Rafe Deverill – but it took only one hour in the first camps for her to become genuinely involved in the Committee's mission.

Inadequate accommodation, shortages of food and clothes, contaminated water, open latrines, lack of fuel for cooking food or boiling water and poor hygiene . . . the list went on and on, establishing the camps as breeding grounds for disease. The epidemics raged: measles, enteric, whooping-cough, malaria, jaundice, influenza, pneumonia, bronchitis . . . while unsanitary, unsterilised, understaffed hospitals struggled to cope . . . The death rate among the women and children rose to two thousand a month . . .

Julia knew that administrative difficulties were partly to blame, knew that the population of the camps had grown beyond anyone's imagining, knew also that the Boers were contributing to their own tragedy, but none of these arguments was any comfort when she had to watch, helpless, while another emaciated child died.

She had been crouched over one such deathbed, covered in the child's excrement and vomit, when she had looked up to see Rafe standing beside her. Oh no, she had said, not you, not now! But he had helped her up and told her that she had never looked more beautiful. He had found a place where she could bathe and wash her dress and then he had made love to her with a passion and a sweetness which had driven the torment from her mind . . .

He was watching her now with a haunting sadness in his eyes but inflexibility in the lines of his face.

'Unfortunately,' he said quietly, 'I am never likely to forget the concentration camps.' He took out a handkerchief and gently wiped the tears from her eyes. 'Neither shall I forget you nor the happiness we have known together.'

'Any minute now you will say, "I hope we can always be friends". Well, we can't, not possibly, not now or ever. I can only be your lover or your . . .' She broke off suddenly and looked at him out of frightened eyes.

'. . . enemy?' he asked softly. 'Must it come to that?'

Rafe remembered his mother's warning that Julia might be dangerous if crossed, but was not inclined to take it seriously. Unfortunately he was barely on speaking terms with the one man who could have convinced him that a jilted Julia would go to extraordinary lengths for revenge: Matthew Bright could have spoken from bitter experience.

'This girl,' she said suddenly, 'I suppose she is much younger than me?'

'Age has nothing to do with it.'

It was not the answer Julia had wanted; she sought a denial that there *was* a girl other than Miss Palmer. 'If it is youth you are after,' she snapped spitefully, 'why not wait for Miranda to grow up? She is nearly thirteen and developing into a beauty. Just think of the dowry *she* will bring – and of the cosy relationship you could enjoy with your precious Laura then!'

'I doubt very much whether Sir Matthew would countenance such a match.' Rafe tilted Julia's burning face towards him and pressed cool lips to her hot forehead.

'Good-bye, Julia. Either we can behave in a civilised fashion or we can meet as strangers. The choice is yours.'

Rafe booked into the Waldorf-Astoria and, convincing himself that he needed exercise after the sea voyage, strolled out immediately into the streets of New York. Inevitably, inexorably, he was drawn to the offices of Court Diamonds and, patting the parcel he concealed inside his coat, he thought he might as well see if Tiffany was in. Up to this point his air was admirably casual but when an officious clerk maintained that Miss Court only saw people by appointment his attitude became more typical.

'It is immaterial to me whether or not I see Miss Court,' he said icily, 'but as I have no intention of placing this packet in any hands but hers, you would do well to acquaint her with my presence.'

'Captain Deverill does not need an appointment.' Tiffany's clear voice rang through the room, causing the clerk to spin round in surprise and Rafe's chest to constrict in a most peculiar fashion. He turned slowly to see her standing in the doorway to her office and she motioned Rafe towards her with an imperious wave of her hand. She closed the door behind them and leaned against the dark panelling, a little smile playing round her lips. 'Do you practise cutting people down to size, Captain, or does it just come naturally?' She inquired sweetly. 'However, *I* am extremely pleased to see *you*. Do take a seat.'

Rafe did so feeling thoroughly discomfited but looking aloof and disinterested.

'You should have let me know of your intended visit, Captain, and then I would have arranged a more courteous reception.'

He shrugged. 'I happened to be in New York and thought I would deliver this jewellery personally.'

Tiffany took the parcel he handed to her but did not open it immediately. 'What brought you to America, Captain?'

'A number of things, both business and pleasure,' and

189

some demon prompted him to continue, 'I thought I would get the business over first.'

Other men would cross oceans for her, Tiffany thought furiously, but not this one – oh no, not this one! She made a great show of examining the jewellery contained in the parcel before placing it in the safe and withdrawing a large ledger in which she proceeded to make a series of neat entries. Pen in hand, she paused and considered him. 'Do you still insist on accepting no recompense for your services?' she asked.

Mesmerised by her loveliness in a gown of sapphire blue, a cluster of sapphires and diamonds sparkling on her shoulder, Rafe started visibly as her voice broke into his reverie. However, Tiffany interpreted his lack of attention as indifference and imagined that his mind was elsewhere, focused on his next and more enjoyable appointment. Angrily she thrust the ledger before him and tapped the page with her pen.

'This is what I owe you, Captain, and I would much prefer to pay my debts.'

Rafe studied the page with distaste but was moved to grudging admiration for the meticulous entries detailing each of the parcels he had forwarded to her since their meeting in London the previous summer. 'I do not wish to be paid,' he reiterated, returning the book to her.

'Oh, I never knew anyone who was so ruled by principles and pride,' she cried, irritated by his obstinacy and by the fact that she hated to be in anyone's debt, moral or financial.

'You consider those attributes to be sins, not virtues?'

'I consider them to be *luxuries* which you are fortunate to be able to afford,' she snapped, shutting the large leather-bound ledger with a bang. An awkward silence fell during which Tiffany and Rafe battled with their pride, neither wanting to make the first move but each wishing not to part in anger or in haste.

'If you are free tonight,' Rafe heard himself say, 'I should be grateful if you would allow me to repay the hospitality you extended to me in London.'

'Yes,' Tiffany said eagerly. 'Thank you.'

'Naturally I should be pleased if your father or cousin would join us.'

'Well, I wouldn't,' she replied candidly. 'I would much prefer to come on my own.'

Rafe smiled faintly. 'As you please, but I must warn you that my dining arrangements will be rather more public than yours.'

As soon as they were apart the mood was broken and both of them regretted their weakness, each silently accusing the other of being proud, spoiled and insufferable and furious with themselves for being beguiled so easily. However, the moment they met again the spell wove its magic around them. They dined decorously in the Palm Garden at the Waldorf-Astoria, but afterwards made their way up to the Roof Garden where they found a table sheltered from the cool breeze, away from the blare of the bandstand and the chains of fairy-lights. They sat side by side and close together, ostensibly watching the faces of the other people but in reality aware only of each other. Then, quite suddenly, whether by accident or design they did not know, their hands touched and they were swamped by that overwhelming physical attraction which seemed determined to dominate their bodies while conflict tore at their minds.

Rafe gripped her hand tightly and then lifted it so that their clasped fingers lay on the soft warm folds of her furs. He leaned closer to her and wriggled his free hand under her coat, resting it on the thin silk of her dress. Slowly he began to slide his hand up and down her thigh, feeling the warmth of her flesh beneath the delicate material, lingering over the bump of her suspender and on each upward journey his smooth sensuous caress moved a little closer to the forbidden area which Tiffany was aching for him to touch. All the time he stared straight ahead and, under cover of the table, no one could have remotely guessed what his hands were doing. Tiffany closed her eyes, willing herself to sit motionless although her every instinct was to turn towards him, to press herself against him. Only her hand, which still lay in his, did not remain inert but writhed and twisted, stroking his hand as though it was her body which lay in his grasp. After an eternity, and yet all too soon, Rafe's fingers ceased their erotic wanderings and his hand pressed down firmly, almost violently, on her thigh. She heard him draw a deep shuddering breath.

'Tomorrow,' she said, in a voice which did not sound like her own, 'you must come to see the end result of your jewellery purchases. I am launching the collection at my studio. Seven o'clock. 15 Macdougal Alley ... and do make sure that you stay on after everyone else has gone.'

The address he sought stood out from its neighbours like an orchid in a dandelion patch; its windows blazed with light, its walls and woodwork were freshly painted and the street outside was lined with cars and smart carriages, advertising that society was slumming it in Greenwich Village tonight. Drawing closer to his destination Rafe realised that 15 Macdougal Alley was the largest house in the street, being three residences converted into one and, even though his knowledge of Tiffany tended to the superficial, he had little doubt that the interior would be spectacular.

From the shabby street he walked into a dream, an opulent world of silk and velvet, heady with the fragrance of banked flowers and expensive perfume, brilliant with gems and glowing with colourful canvases on the damask-covered walls. Tiffany had chosen a pale parchment for the furnishings – a clear uncluttered colour which provided an inconspicuous background for the rainbow of jewellery displayed in glass cases in the centre of the room and which brought the paintings on the walls into sharp relief.

There being no sign of Tiffany, Rafe wandered over to

the display cases in order to inspect the jewellery. Lovely pieces, original, well-designed and well-made, and bearing the unmistakable stamp of the twentieth century. For a few moments Rafe was caught up in the magic of the enterprise, ensnared by the romance of the gems. Quite unexpectedly he was gratified at having contributed in some small way to the creation of this shimmering sea of light and colour, and he tried to identify the stones which he had handled even though he knew it to be a hopeless task. Ridiculous, he thought dazedly – they are only bloody pebbles to be worn by empty-headed women who ought to have better things to do with their money. But his happiness persisted and when Tiffany entered the room, Rafe was still under the spell of the winking, glowing, glittering stones and for the first time since the war he inched a tiny step out of the darkness and into a world where there was beauty instead of ugliness.

Tiffany, in white lace and white diamonds, appeared at his side. 'Well?' she asked, nodding at the jewels.

He took hold of her hand and held it tightly. 'Congratulations!' he said simply.

His approval, evident in the pressure of his fingers and the sincerity in his voice and eyes, meant more to Tiffany than all the effusions of praise which had been heaped upon her. 'I love them, you know, and not because of their value.'

Rafe gazed into her glowing eyes, sensing her enslavement, divining that the diamonds were the very essence of her life. He relinquished her hand. 'I can see that. Did you organise the decoration of the house as well?'

'Of course. Unlike some people,' and she shot him that typical acerbic Tiffany glance, 'I am not numbered among the leisured class. I had an extremely busy winter.'

'The houses, and their setting here in Greenwich Village, are ideal for your purposes. You were lucky they were for sale.'

'Lucky, my foot! Opportunities are *made* – they do not come knocking at your door, nor do you trip over them in the street! These houses were not for sale; I expended a great deal of time and money convincing the owners that the sale would definitely be in their best interests.'

'When all the time it was in *your* best interests!'

'In this instance,' said Tiffany demurely, 'all our interests came together in happy conjunction. Now, let me show you round.'

The adjoining room was smaller and contained no jewellery, only an extension of the art exhibition. Beyond that were the workshops where the jewellery was crafted, while the upstairs rooms were let to Gerard and several other artists.

'I have a small studio here myself where I design the pieces,' Tiffany murmured casually, 'but I will show it to you later.'

To take his mind off the possibilities this prospect aroused, Rafe studied the pictures which were painted in vigorous style and depicted a depressing urban environment. He conceded that they were . . . different.

'Your taste in art is somewhat *avant-garde*,' he remarked. 'Who are the artists?'

'You will not know them, but one day their names will be as famous as Rembrandt or Titian,' Tiffany replied fiercely. 'This exhibition includes works by Robert Henri, John Sloan and George Luks. I intend to hold regular showings of their works to which I shall invite these idiots,' and she glowered at the beautifully dressed society people who were wandering through the galleries, staring at the pictures in bewilderment.

'You will teach American society to appreciate American art, whether it wants to or not.' Rafe grinned, but for once his irony was lost on Tiffany.

'Someone must. Just look at these morons – "uptown swillage in the downtown village".' She laughed. 'Not my original turn of phrase, I'm afraid, but extremely apt.'

'You appear to have sold some pictures.'

Tiffany grimaced, partly from dissatisfaction and partly from embarrassment. 'Actually, *I* bought those,' she

194

confessed. She took hold of Rafe's arm and treated him to the full battery of her most beguiling glance and most winning smile. 'Wouldn't you like to buy one? An American painting to remind you of your visit? They are not expensive.'

Rafe stared at the canvases again, striving to imagine these disturbing, violent, *painful* pictures among the pretty charming works of art in his parents' home, and he smiled at the thought of the outraged expression which would settle on his mother's aristocratic features. But then he was struck by another, more alarming, vision: that of Tiffany with her bold bright colours amid the delicate tints and nuances of London society; of Tiffany, with her modern ways and New World bluntness about money matters, in the refined hypocrisy of Lady Ambleside's drawing-room where a girl's dowry was all-important but never, never mentioned. Julia jolted the sensibilities of the duchesses and dowagers, but Tiffany . . .! Tiffany would shock them into stern, unremitting censure, as out of place as a John Sloan amid the Gainsboroughs. But Rafe also knew that such considerations would not weigh with him when it came to making a decision . . . Tiffany was a girl for whom one would dare all, lose all . . . He stared down at her with such a strange intensity in his grey eyes that her knees turned to jelly.

'I must speak to a few more people – give them some sales talk! But don't forget, Captain – I want you to be the last to leave.'

On the opposite side of the room the massive grey-haired figure of John Court was deep in conversation with young Pierre Cartier, who was confirming that the House of Cartier would open on Fifth Avenue the following year. Meanwhile Randolph was watching Rafe and Tiffany. Rafe approached John Court out of courtesy, but he also wanted to speak about the diamond mine which had recently been discovered in Arkansas. He listened politely while Court explained that the blueground pipe resembled those in South Africa to an amazing extent, but that he did not believe the American mine would be a commerical success. Rafe found himself hoping that Court was not as deluded over diamonds as he was over his daughter. He moved away, feeling furtive and guilty about his forthcoming assignation with Tiffany, for in the strange morality of the times sex was acceptable if the lady was married but not if she was young, single and a virgin. But was Tiffany a virgin? Rafe helped himself to another glass of champagne and was about to seek refuge in the workshop until the party was over when he was accosted by Frank Whitney.

Frank had been standing unhappily in a corner of the room with Pauline. He realised, resentfully, that these days he was always relegated to this position. It rankled unbearably that his invitation to the exhibition tonight had not come from Tiffany but had been issued by John Court, asking him to escort Pauline. Gone were the days when Tiffany bestowed on Frank a kiss or an embrace, for now she had no need of him, but as long as she did not banish him completely or marry another man Frank continued to hope.

His feelings for Tiffany were perfectly obvious but, to anyone else, so was Tiffany's attitude towards him. Pauline took encouragement from the fact that evidently Tiffany did not intend to marry him, but was forced to admit that this state of affairs had not advanced her own aspirations. He never seemed to notice her as a woman but always stood thus, gloomily, watching Tiffany. Perhaps if he believed she was popular with other men . . .

'There were lots of men who wanted to come here with me tonight,' she said bravely.

Frank cast her a glance of withering scorn. 'I expect what they really wanted was to see Tiffany.'

'No,' she insisted, 'they wished to be with me.'

'In that case, why did your uncle have to beg *me* to bring you?'

Pauline hesitated, then it occurred to her that one reason for his lack of interest might be ignorance of her feelings for him. 'I wanted to be with you,' she said, stuttering slightly with nervousness.

He laughed a bitter, mocking laugh. There was a cruelty in Frank now, a disregard for other people's feelings, almost a desire to hurt others as he was hurt. He was utterly contemptuous of Pauline, loathing her dullness, her plumpness and plainness and hating, too, her availability while his own dream was unattainable. He escorted her to these functions only because her company allowed him access to Tiffany.

Desperately Pauline made one last effort. 'Uncle John has set up a trust fund for me. Isn't that kind of him! I shall be a wealthy woman when he dies – although I hope that won't be for a long time,' she added hastily.

It was on the tip of Frank's tongue to say that buying a husband was the only way Pauline was likely to acquire one, but instead he merely snorted impatiently and, catching sight of Rafe Deverill, walked away. Pauline was left to fight for composure and wish that it was time to go home.

Frank was delighted to see Rafe again. The Englishman had turned the tide for him, transformed him from a nonentity into somebody, and accordingly had assumed the proportions of a hero in Frank's mind. These days he tended to be pro-British rather than pro-Boer when he talked about the war – which he did with increasing frequency. However, his eyes narrowed when he heard the 'official' reason for Rafe's presence at the party.

'You acquire jewellery for her? You mean that you meet Tiffany when she visits London?' Captain Deverill's tall handsome figure took on a more menacing aspect.

'Why not?'

'Her behaviour is scandalous! I cannot imagine how her father permits her to carry on in this way, travelling without a chaperone at her age . . .' Frank's face twisted with jealousy. 'Each time she goes away we suffer agonies, wondering what might happen to a sweet defenceless girl . . .'

'A *what*? Sweet, defenceless . . . Frank, there are many facets to Tiffany Court's character, but those attributes are not numbered among them!' Rafe shook his head and laughed. 'I thought you might have given up hope by now and married that cousin – what's her name? Pauline.'

'I will only give up hope if she marries someone else. Besides,' Frank added defensively, 'her father likes me – that might help.'

'The only marriage John Court will sanction is with Randolph.'

Frank had heard oblique references to such an eventuality and he could not help but notice Randolph's proprietary air. Even so, he clung stubbornly to his fantasies. 'Maybe,' he said with studied nonchalance, 'but Tiffany doesn't behave as though she wants to marry *him*.'

No, thought Rafe, but Randolph still wants to marry her. Suddenly he felt as though he was tangled in coils of rope or squeezed by the tentacles of an octopus; he could sense the complications of his association with Tiffany closing in, tightening, tying him hand and foot. He had a violent urge to fling his arms wide, to jerk free of these creeping, encroaching coils, to walk out of her and never see her again. But he did not. Rafe was trapped in the spell of the diamonds – the gem which Tiffany so perfectly represented – and the evil side of the stone must also have its day. The devil got into Rafe now. He was unbearably irritated by Frank's naïvety and foolishness – and also, perhaps in a way it was a kindness to tell the truth.

'Even if she doesn't marry Randolph, Tiffany Court is not for you,' he said brutally.

Frank pretended not to hear. 'Have you been back to South Africa since the war?'

'No.'

'I should love to return. I tell you who I would like to see – Paul. He was gentle and kind, quite different from the others. Do you remember Paul?'

'I remember.' Rafe's fingers clenched on the glass. The new devil within him urged him to go on, to tell Frank, to test himself, to find out if there was an explanation or an excuse, to see if at least part of the burden could be lifted from him after all these years.

'He was the only one who tried to defend the *Khaki Boer*, Japie Malan. And when Danie still insisted on killing him, it was Paul who knelt with Japie by the grave and said a prayer with him before tying the blindfold over his eyes.'

'You will not find Paul. He is dead.'

'How do you know? I am positive you said he did not die in the valley when you wiped out the commando.'

'He died afterwards.'

'Are you sure?'

'Quite sure.' Rafe took a gulp of champagne. 'You see, I killed him.'

'*How?*'

'I executed him.' Rafe's flinty grey eyes bored relentlessly into Frank's face and to the young American he seemed like Satan himself. '*Executed* him, Frank. I marched him out on to a bleak hillside and *had him shot.*'

'*Why?*'

'Paul was a Cape Boer. He was a British subject, not a citizen of the Republics of the Transvaal or Orange Free State who were fighting for their so-called freedom. Paul was a traitor.'

Frank's hand was shaking, slopping champagne out of his glass, but he took no notice and simply stared at Rafe in fascinated, mesmerised horror. 'How could you?' he croaked.

'Orders, Frank. For King and Country! That sort of thing.' Calmly Rafe took another gulp of champagne and smiled, a grim feral smile.

'You bastard! In God's name, how *could* you? You should have refused to do something so revolting, so despicable . . . *Paul*, of all people, *Paul* . . .'

'Save the emotional outburst, Frank. After all, Paul would not have officiated at any graveside but for you! Do you grieve equally for Japie Malan? And for Charlie, the Zulu, whose only crime was minding our horses but who was tied to a tree by Danie Steyn and shot? Japie and Charlie might have been alive today *if you had not led us into the trap!*'

Frank flinched and began to back away.

'Just how many times did you change sides during the war, Frank? How many times did you flout your non-combatant status? And how many times did you sully the white flag of surrender – because I remember one instance. I remember it very well indeed!'

'Danie used to call your troop Devil's Horse and he was right! I bet I don't have as much on my conscience as you have on yours!'

Rafe laughed harshly. 'You may be right! Because Paul's execution was not the worst moment of my war . . . and Paul's face is not the only ghost which haunts me!'

Frank blundered off into the crowd in search of another drink – the drink which was becoming more and more his crutch – and Rafe walked through the galleries to the privacy of the deserted workshop. Closing the door, he sat down and raised his glass. 'To King and Country,' he intoned mockingly. For a few moments he succumbed to the pain but then forced it aside, lit a cigarette and smoked quietly, waiting for time to pass. But he had not been in the room for ten minutes before the door opened and Randolph Court stepped inside. Rafe was in no mood for niceties.

'It is the lady you ought to be watching, not me,' he snapped.

'Oh, I do. Believe me, I do!'

They glared at each other with undisguised distaste, yet both at the same time uncomfortably aware of the qualities of the other – Randolph, jealous of Rafe's good looks, that sensual mouth, the air of the maverick which made him irresistible to women and unpredictable to men; Rafe, envious of Randolph's lifestyle and influence, the career running smoothly on well-oiled, approved lines, the control he exerted over his future while Rafe had lost himself in the South African veld.

'I was not aware that your acquaintance with Tiffany had continued beyond your meeting at Newport,' Randolph commented.

'It is comforting to know your intelligence network isn't perfect.'

'I have not chosen to extend it beyond the United States,' Randolph was no whit perturbed by the allegation, 'although it might be time that I did. However, I am aware of the existence of Tiffany's little studio in which she amuses herself upstairs. I take it that you are the latest candidate for seduction?'

'What do you do, Court? Lean a ladder against the wall and peer in through the window?'

'Nothing so crude, Captain. Besides, such drastic measures are hardly necessary. I fear you may be disappointed tonight. For all Tiffany's brazen talk, she is intelligent enough to keep her legs shut even though her mouth may be open.'

Rafe was disgusted at the coarseness of Randolph's speech but knew that his reaction was partly sparked by guilt – Randolph was Tiffany's kin and had the right to defend her virtue against marauding Englishmen. More than ever, Rafe knew he ought to leave but, apart from the fact that he wanted Tiffany so desperately, pride would not permit him to give Randolph victory.

'Another thing, don't dream about marrying her. Tiffany cannot marry without the consent of her father – or guardian – until she is twenty-five. I need hardly add that her father would not consent to a match and neither would I.'

'You being her guardian if her father dies?'

'You catch on quickly, Captain.'

'Not everyone is ruled by money.'

'Maybe not,' said Randolph softly, 'but I would dearly like to meet the man who could divorce Tiffany from her diamond company.' He turned to leave. 'I am sure the Court family can rely on your innate good breeding to ensure that no harm comes to her. You would not wish to jeopardise the reputation of the English gentleman.'

'Don't appeal to my patriotism, Court. I buried it on a hillside in South Africa.'

Randolph raised his eyebrows. 'In that case we must rely on your pride in your own good name and reputation. Good night, Captain.'

After his departure Rafe sat on alone until at last Tiffany beckoned from the doorway. He followed her up the stairs to a large book-lined landing furnished with a desk and chairs. Just as he was thinking that he had misinterpreted her intentions, she pressed a button and the wall swung open, revealing that the shelves of books were only a *trompe l'oeil* – tiny volumes, an inch deep, on minute mahogany shelves. Beyond lay the rich dark ambience of Tiffany's studio; she beckoned again and, rather hesitantly, Rafe walked into the blackness.

When she flicked a switch, the room was suffused with a soft glow of indigo, the dark walls and ceiling studded with bright specks. At first Rafe thought that the décor was intended to represent the night sky, but then he understood that Tiffany's fantasy had led her to create an impression of a diamond mine. She switched on another light, illuminating details in the room: white sofas and thick white carpet, a fireplace flanked by golden statues of a naked woman and a naked man – *sans* fig-leaf – while on the ceiling was a gold and silver sunburst whose rays spiked more naked figures, griffons, dragons and – weirdly after Rafe's earlier sensations – a giant octopus. A narrow frieze ran around the wall and Rafe walked over to inspect it more closely; cherubs disported themselves among the beasts of the field while here and there nude human figures embraced, the males being in an unmistakable and exaggerated state of arousal. It was a frieze worthy of a pagan goddess or the last days of Pompeii, and involuntarily Rafe's own body hardened in response to the erotic display.

Tiffany handed him another glass of champagne. 'I still play barmaid at my own parties.'

'Your so-called studio resembles a brothel rather than a bar.'

'Does it? Never having seen a brothel, I wouldn't know.'

'I cannot believe that you don't recognise pornography when you see it.'

'It's not pornography,' she flashed. 'It's art.'

'An argument as old as time,' he said drily. 'And who, might I ask, is the artist?'

'Gerard. He makes the jewellery, too. He worked on this studio in between the pieces for the collection and his own creations.'

'Lucky Gerard! And were you present during his . . . flashes of inspiration while he was *creating* that frieze?'

'Certainly.' She looked at him haughtily. 'You surely don't think that he and I . . .!'

'The possibility had crossed my mind.' Rafe had placed the champagne glass on the mantleshelf, for he had no wish to advertise the trembling in his limbs. 'If he didn't touch you, he deserves an award for self-control in the face of the utmost provocation – he certainly isn't likely to win one for artistic merit.'

'He did not touch me and, before you ask, I did not pose for him either.'

'That statue,' and Rafe stared accusingly at the naked female figure beside the fireplace, 'looks awfully like you.'

Tiffany's head jerked round and her eyes widened in surprise. Damn it, he was right! She honestly had not noticed the resemblance before. 'I can't help it if I inspire artists to great works,' she said defiantly.

Rafe closed his eyes. Every inch of his body seemed to be throbbing with despair, disappointment and desire. She was so lovely, so infinitely heartrendingly lovely; her beauty and intelligence were as clear, shining and true as the gold and diamonds in which she dealt, so why, *why* did she cheapen herself in this way? Why this apparent obsession with sex? Was she a whore or only a tease? But then, as he tried to come to terms with the sensual side of her nature, he remembered the wild free spirit he had perceived in her during their conversation on the terrace in Newport. She was not being vulgar; probably many women desired sexual freedom, but only the Tiffanys of this world had the courage to reach out and grasp it.

Tiffany was wondering again what he really thought of her and also asking herself why she had invited him here tonight. She had prepared the studio for just such an assignation but, contrary to Randolph's assumptions, Rafe was the first man to receive an invitation. She could not explain it . . . he was always rude to her, yet she continued to seek him out. The only possible reason, she told herself, was this powerful chemistry which existed between them; she constantly wanted to touch him and be touched by him. Normally Tiffany avoided physical contact with other people, but to a small proportion of men she responded passionately and did not consider this was wrong – it would not be considered wrong in a man and therefore ought not to be wrong for her.

She watched the warring emotions in Rafe's face and was unexpectedly hurt by the distaste she detected there. 'Why are you always criticising me? Why do you hate me?' she burst out.

'Hate you?' Rafe looked at her in surprise. 'I don't hate you. I . . .' He stopped, astonished by the words which had sprung uninvited to his lips and which he had nearly voiced. With a sound somewhere between a sigh and a groan he stepped forward and caught her in his arms, gazing into her eyes before bending his head and pressing his mouth to hers. And that perfect fusion occurred again, a blending of bodies which banished the conflict between them and in themselves. Once more they were flesh and nothing but flesh, skin which shivered and yet burned with fire, tongues which probed in imitation of the deeper union they longed to achieve.

Tiffany could feel his hard fingers unhooking the bodice of her dress and then he was pulling aside the brief chemise to cup her breast. He drew her down on to the floor, kissing her breast while he plunged his hand through the layers of lingerie in which an Edwardian lady was enveloped. Swiftly, efficiently, he worked his way under her drawers and at last his fingers touched the wetness between her legs. As Tiffany moaned he stopped her mouth with a kiss while continuing to move his fingers over, around and inside her, both kiss and caress taking on a deeper intensity, a tenderness coupled with insistence.

If Rafe had been naked he could have taken her then, thrust inside her and she would have been his. But he was clothed and he had to release her in order to strip off his jacket. The instant he moved away, Tiffany's reason returned. She could not do it! Much as she longed to be a man and desired the sexual freedom men enjoyed, there was no escaping the fact that she possessed the body of a woman – she could not risk pregnancy. And she must save herself for Philip – the diamonds demanded it.

'No,' she said, pulling down her dress. 'No!'

Rafe paused, hands unbuttoning his shirt, then his arms fell limply to his sides. He smiled crookedly. 'So, Randolph was right!'

'Did you discuss me with Randolph?' Her voice rose in a screech of fury and she scrambled to her feet.

'He discussed you with me, which isn't quite the same thing. It might surprise you to know that he isn't quite as stupid as you think. He will marry you yet.'

'Never! Besides, I am marrying . . .' She broke off.

'Who? *Who* are you marrying?' He jerked her roughly towards him, glaring down at her, consumed with jealousy towards this unknown man who had won her.

'It is none of your business.'

He released her and shrugged on his jacket. 'Well, he's welcome to you and the little games you play. Just tell me one thing: why did you ask me here tonight?'

'I wanted to . . . talk to you.'

Rafe laughed bitterly and gestured to the frieze. 'You have a bloody funny line in conversation pieces, Miss Court. Do you love this man?'

'Of course.'

'I don't believe you. You are not capable of love. You are only for yourself and your damn diamonds. Play with your pieces of carbon, Miss Court, and see if they will satisfy the ache between your legs!'

Tiffany slapped his face but he did not flinch. 'Get out!' she hissed, hating him all the more for being right, hating him for having made her want him so.

For a moment he made no move. His face was very white. 'Some man will rape you one of these days,' he said quietly, 'and up here no one will hear your screams. Don't say that you haven't been warned.'

Rape. Funny how it kept cropping up – now three men had mentioned it. 'Men would never risk being accused of rape,' she replied, remembering Gerard's comment. 'You might at least do up my dress before you go. I can't go home like this.'

'You should have thought of that before,' Rafe said coldly from the doorway. 'I am sure Gerard would be happy to oblige.'

She listened to the sound of his forosteps on the stairs; they grew fainter and then silence hung over the house, heavy and sad. Suppose he was right and she was incapable of love? With an effort she concentrated on Philip; of course she loved Philip and this summer she would prove it. But compelling grey eyes and an in irresistible mouth seemed to mock her wherever she looked.

CHAPTER ELEVEN

The surface of the track was being laid at Brooklands and work on the bridge carrying the Members' Banking over the River Wey had been completed. The circuit would be ready by June, but it was not the grand opening ceremony which occupied Philip's mind; rather, he was engrossed in S.F. Edge's projected twenty-four-hour drive. Edge had announced his intention as soon as the Brooklands course was mooted saying that he wished to book the circuit at the earliest possible date for an attempt to drive a car unassisted for twenty-four hours at an average speed of 60 miles per hour. The challenge posed several interesting problems, not least of which was whether the car would last the pace and whether Edge could stand the strain. This was the first area in which Philip intervened; he suggested that Edge went into athletic training and helped to surpervise that training while participating in it himself. But Philip's ambition was to play a more positive role; to alleviate boredom during the drive, Edge had decided that two other cars would take part and Philip was determined to be one of the drivers.

Gradually he had entered the ranks of the Napier testers, starting with occasional runs when one of the established drivers was not available but, as his skill was recognised, taking an increasing share of the work. Handling the big 60-hp Napiers came easily to Philip, as did all athletic activity; rowing and cricket – those long-discarded pastimes – had developed his muscles and stamina and his natural ability had been noticed by the Napier team who were grooming him for future stardom. Philip would have retained his position in the team without the additional bonus of his financial input, but he did not know that; he believed the money was vital.

Every penny which he could beg, steal or borrow went into car production and gradually he grew more adept at acquiring the funds he needed. At first he merely saved his allowance, fiddled his expenses and filched a few pounds from his father's wallet. When these tactics went undetected, he grew bolder and, as he had anticipated, Bright Diamonds offered the opportunities he sought.

The Syndicate insisted that diamonds were sold in 'parcels', not as individual stones. Therefore, in order to acquire stones of a certain size or shape for which there was a ready sale, a dealer was forced to buy other gems for which he had no immediate use. At the present time the diamond market was in a slump and Bright Diamonds was carrying a stock of surplus stones; moreover, although security arrangements were stringent they were not foolproof. One day Philip found himself alone in the strongroom and made his decision instantly, slipping a packet of small diamonds into his pocket. They would not be missed for quite a while, he reasoned, and even when their disappearance was noticed he would not be suspected since no one would imagine that Philip Bright could possibly be short of money.

Selling the uncut gems posed a problem. Not daring to off-load them in London, he took the diamonds to the Continent where he sold them at knock-down prices, usually to cutters in Amsterdam. Indeed the price was so low that the thefts amounted to petty pilfering and the practice was not particularly profitable. Philip still depended on gifts from Tiffany to finance his investment in the car industry and he did not confide in her the secret of his 'sideline', certain that she would not approve.

But it isn't stealing, he convinced himself, because the diamonds are virtually my own property. At worst I am only stealing from Papa! That aspect of the matter gave him a peculiar satisfaction and Philip smiled as he locked away another batch of diamonds in the bureau in his bedroom at Park Lane. He was due to make another business trip to France soon and would take the stones with him.

He spent nearly all his spare time with the Napier team, but could not avoid the occasional weekend at Brightwell. Just before Tiffany arrived he decided to pay one of these 'duty' visits so that nothing should interfere with the hours he could spend in her company. Matthew was at the racing stables elsewhere on the estate and Laura was alone in the drawing-room.

'Are you enjoying your work at Bright Diamonds?' she asked quietly.

'Of course I am.'

'No, you are not.' She smiled gently as he looked up in surprise. 'You don't fool me, Philip! It isn't there, is it – that fire, that fever, that obsession? That *love affair* with the diamonds which has enthralled your father for years!'

Laura watched his defensive reaction and smiled again. 'Don't worry – I will not tell him! But I will tell *you* something else that Matthew doesn't know. There is a dark side to the diamonds and the influence which the gems exert can be evil and destructive. Oh, not the average stone, of course – just the large and unusual stones and the lure of power in the industry itself.'

'What on earth makes you say that?'

'When your father asked me to marry him, he gave me a diamond – a beautiful pear-shaped pendant. It was the loveliest gem I had ever seen and I was absolutely dazzled by it. But after my return to London, when all the . . .' Laura hesitated, '. . . *trouble* started, it was as if that diamond was casting an evil spell over me. I was aware of it *physically* – it was so cold that it burned, so heavy that it became a burden. Yet at the same time it was sticky, clinging to me so closely that it nearly became a part of me and although I wanted to take it off I seemed powerless to fight it.'

'As I have never seen the diamond, presumably you did manage to remove it.' Philip's tone was sceptical.

'Yes, I did – with a little help. But I have never worn it again.'

'Where is it now?'

'I am ashamed to say that I'm not entirely certain of its whereabouts! My other jewellery is kept under lock and key, but I pushed that diamond into a dressing-table drawer at Park Lane and have not touched it for seven years.'

In Philip's opinion the story was romantic nonsense, but in a way Laura's words and earnestness reminded him of Tiffany's tale about Alida. The thought of Tiffany stayed Philip's tongue, stifling the cynical comment, softening his attitude to his stepmother. Laura wasn't so bad, he thought, and really he had behaved like a stupid child towards her. The acquisition of Tiffany compensated for the losses of the past.

'Doesn't Papa ever ask why you don't wear it?'

'No. Matthew does not have a mind for that kind of detail! He is aware that I am not fond of diamonds and prefer to wear my emeralds. I am sure he has not forgotten the pendant, but sets more store by the Bright diamonds.'

The contentment in Philip ebbed. The Bright diamonds – why should Miranda have them? They ought to be his, to give to his wife. How absolutely stunning Tiffany would look in those jewels! His resentment against Matthew and Miranda remained, but it was not Laura's fault – after all, she had not been offered the Bright diamonds either.

'Philip, I was not intending to relate the story of one stone. I merely wanted to say that if you are not captivated by the diamonds, escape them now while you can. Your father dreams of his dynasty, but you are under no obligation to fulfil his ambitions if they don't coincide with yours. *And* I would like to make it quite clear that I am not saying this in order to advance the claims of my own children!'

Philip looked into her honest face and the clear gaze of those green eyes and he believed her. 'I know ... And thanks,' he said gruffly.

With a flood of thankfulness, Laura sensed the thaw. It must be the cars which had brought about such a glorious change in him, she reflected – or a girl, although he had not mentioned one. Whatever the reason, she did hope nothing would happen to spoil it.

Philip might have dismissed the story of the pear-shaped pendant as romantic rubbish, but when he returned to Park Lane he was consumed with curiosity about the gem. He only wanted to look at it, he thought, just to see what sort of stone could give rise to such flights of fancy. Late one night, almost against his will, he was drawn to Laura's bedroom and rummaged through the drawers in her dressing-table.

But when he found the pendant, his expression changed. Philip did not revere diamonds, but even he was awed by the size and brilliance of this gem. Most of all he was fascinated by the fact that the diamond was utterly right for Tiffany. He must show it to her; it would do no harm if he was to borrow it for a few days. Completely discounting Laura's tale, Philip placed the gem in his bureau along with the others.

The next day Henriette entered Philip's room. Her presence there was not unusual, for in her capacity as house-keeper she was responsible for his comfort at Park Lane. Today, however, she did do something different; she had decided to inspect his clothes in order to ascertain that the valet was carrying out his duties properly. Matthew had decreed that Philip did not need a full-time valet and that his man could look after them both, so it occurred to Henriette that this situation could provide a prime excuse for skimping both jobs. She opened the closet and inspected the clothes, admitting grudgingly that she could find no fault.

It was then that she saw the picture . . .

The simple sketch of the girl's head was tacked inside the door. Beautiful, thought Henriette with a sigh for her

211

own vanished looks. Assuming the girl to be an actress who had caught Philip's fancy, she peered casually at the signature – and froze . . .

How long she stood there she did not know, but eventually her legs began to tremble and she sank down on to the edge of the bed. The signature was scrawled, virtually illegible to anyone who had not heard the name before, certainly indecipherable to valet or maid. But not to Henriette. Her mind flew back to Cape Town in 1887 when she had carried a tiny bundle from Lady Anne's bed and laid it in John Court's arms. It *couldn't* be . . . and yet it was. Coincidence . . . fate . . . destiny . . . whatever it was, the wheel had turned full circle. To Henriette it was heaven-sent; the Lord had delivered the Bright family into her hands. The day she had awaited had come at last.

Thirty years ago she had accompanied Lady Anne to the diamond fields and had remained devoted to her mistress until the day Anne died, never forgetting that Anne had nursed her through the smallpox which left Henriette badly scarred but alive. Her love for Anne was balanced by a deep hatred of Matthew, not only because the marriage had been unhappy but because, to Henriette, Lady Anne had been an angel and Matthew the devil who had destroyed her. Not fond of Philip, she disliked Miranda even more because her birth had killed Anne and because the little girl resembled Matthew so exactly.

She had stayed on in the Bright household because her husband was Matthew's chef, but there had been another reason, too. For years Henriette had brooded, reliving her memories, waiting for the moment when she could avenge the pain Matthew had inflicted upon Anne. She had tried, but failed, to break Laura. Now she had been handed the supreme weapon . . . She knew that she ought to take the picture straight to Sir Matthew, but did not do so. Henriette was content for the drama to unfold for a while longer – she wanted to savour the situation before she ripped it apart.

* * *

Tiffany arrived for her annual visit to Europe and Philip called on her at the Savoy for their first encounter in London. They met secretly a few times and then decided they were tired of skulking and hiding. Deliberately they began to tempt fate, to risk – perhaps seeking – recognition of their relationship, tacitly accepting the consequences such recognition would bring, silently avowing a commitment.

'I have been invited to a Venetian costume party on Saturday,' Philip told her. 'Shall we go?'

'Yes, but there is no time for me to have a dress made.'

'You can wear an ordinary dress. Everyone will be wearing masks, but I can scrounge one for you from the house; there are bound to be old masks of Mama's or Laura's lying around somewhere. I'll ask Henriette.'

'Henriette – you again! You are very assiduous in your concern for my welfare these days.'

'No more than my duty, Master Philip, particularly when Lady Bright is in the country.'

'Thanks awfully for finding the mask.'

'For a special young lady, is it, sir?'

'*Very* special.'

'Do I know her?'

'No, she is an American. Henriette, you were in Kimberley in the early days. Do you remember a man called John Court?'

Remember him? I lived in the same house as him for ten years. 'No.'

'So you wouldn't know the reason why he and Papa quarrelled?'

'I am afraid not.'

'Pity. By the way, I assume Papa is not favouring the Fontwells' party with his presence tonight?'

'Sir Matthew never did care for costume parties, Master Philip, although I remember one . . . No, he isn't going.'

'Thank God for that! Then there is only my dear cousin Julia to be avoided! Good night, Henriette.'

213

I must see Tiffany, she thought, just once, for poor Lady Anne's sake. How fortunate that Pierre is friendly with the Fontwell chefs.

At Fontwell House waiters dressed as gondoliers served the elaborately costumed guests who were seated at clusters of small tables. Julia was with Alfred and a group of friends; Rafe Deverill sat next to Alice Palmer at the Ambleside table with his parents, his brother and sister-in-law – who had borne yet another daughter – and several of his sisters. Rafe was not wearing Venetian costume – despite Lady Ambleside's entreaties he was dressed in the customary severity of his black evening suit, his only mask one of exquisite boredom.

Julia was watching Rafe, trying to attract his attention, but he avoided her eye just as he had avoided her ever since his return from the United States. She drew some small comfort from his evident lack of spirits and his continued companionship with Miss Palmer, until the thought occurred to her that his unhappiness could be caused by separation from the girl she suspected he had seen in America. She watched him closely, covertly, continuously. Therefore she was watching when his expression changed and she saw him come alive, his body movements alert and interested, his face registering in turn incredulity, wild hope, savage despair and brooding pain – the emotions he aroused in Julia but which he had never reciprocated. Slowly, dreading what she might see, she turned to follow the direction of his gaze and saw the two masked figures take their seats. 'But that is Philip,' she thought, puzzled. 'I would know that hair anywhere.' However, another glance at Rafe confirmed that he was staring fixedly at Philip's companion. Oh why, why, Julia cried in silent agony, couldn't he look at me like that!

'I wonder why that woman in black isn't in costume,' remarked one of her friends.

'Perhaps she has just arrived in London,' suggested another, 'from the Continent, maybe.'

'Or from America,' murmured Julia.

Alone at their table for two, Philip showed Tiffany the diamond. It was the most perfect gem she had ever seen and she gazed at it lovingly, handled it reverently, attracted to it by a compelling fascination she had never experienced before. She thought he was giving it to her.

'Thank you,' she said at last. 'I will always treasure it.'

She had misunderstood, but how could he take it away from her? The diamond was so beautiful and so was she. As he had anticipated, they looked right together. Laura would not miss it and if Matthew found out – well, what the hell! Miranda had the Bright diamonds, so why shouldn't he have one pendant! Philip smiled and took her hand.

'And I will treasure you for always,' he said.

Henriette was watching with the other servants, peering down from the gallery above the ballroom. She had manoeuvred herself and Pierre into a place where she could obtain a perfect view of Philip and Tiffany. Although unaware of it, she was watching at the precise moment Philip leaned towards Tiffany and whispered, 'I love you.' But even though Henriette could not hear, their actions told the story clearer than words. Only lovers sat so close, with hands entwined, and only lovers gazed so lingeringly into each other's eyes, lips only inches apart.

At last the moment came when the guests unmasked. Julia, Rafe and Henriette were allowed a brief glimpse of Tiffany's lovely face before she and Philip rose to leave the party.

Henriette knew she ought to follow them, do something, say something, but she could not move. She was frozen into immobility, transfixed with fascinated horror. There was a singing in her head as faces and voices clamoured to be seen and heard; one voice told her that surely they would not go *that* far; another voice was Lady Anne's, pleading with her to stop them. But the dominant face was Matthew's and she could imagine how it would look when he found out – *when she told him!* So Henriette sat on, walled in her hatred and made no attempt to avert disaster.

Afterwards people remarked that the Venetian party was

the only occasion when they could remember Rafe
Deverill being drunk. It made sense later, of course, in the
light of subsequent events; he had been a bit odd ever
since the Boer War, but the night of the party he really
went over the edge. Rafe drank because he knew where
Tiffany and Philip had gone, because he could visualise
– only too vividly – the scene in her hotel suite. To be
rejected for another man was bad enough, but *Philip* . . .
Rafe reached for his glass again as he contemplated that
raw, callow youth with his handsome face, graceful body
and empty selfish head. What twisted the knife was the
fact that the affair must have been going on all these years
– since Oxford – and he had even teased her about it!
Bloody fool that he was, bloody deceitful bitch that *she*
was! How could she . . . And then the light dawned. Of
course. The diamonds – *Bright Diamonds!* Rafe threw
back his head and laughed. Once he had considered that
Tiffany and Philip deserved each other; now he was definitely of the opinion that Randolph and Tiffany were
soul-mates. And his smile grew yet more satanic as he
envisaged Randolph's reaction to Philip.

That night Rafe Deverill proposed marriage to Alice
Palmer and was accepted.

In Tiffany's suite blue Venetian velvet and black satin lay
in discarded heaps while arms and bodies intertwined and
lips kissed or murmured endearments. With his hands
between her legs, his mouth at her breast and his naked
body pressed against hers, Tiffany knew that this time
there was no holding back.

'I don't want to get pregnant,' she managed to say, but
the protest was half-hearted.

'You won't,' Philip assured her. 'It can't happen the first
time.'

Philip knew exactly what he was doing and knew that
he had not told the truth. He wanted her, he did not care
if she became pregnant, in fact he would welcome it if
she did – what better way was there of capturing her

completely, permanently? With a strangled groan he slid inside her.

Afterwards Tiffany, sore but satisfied, lay cradled in his arms.

'You're not sorry, are you?' Philip asked anxiously.

Tiffany remembered their first meeting at Oxford when Philip had introduced her to the wisdom of Benjamin Jowett. 'Never regret, never explain, never apologise,' she whispered.

Nine o'clock on the evening of Friday 28 June and the lamps had been lit at Brooklands – 352 red lanterns, one every ten yards on the 50-foot line, acquired from every road-surveying company in London. Along the top of the bankings smoky Wells flares, screened from the drivers' line of sight, cast an eerie light over the track and on the three cars which were circulating. The night was growing cold and the dark menacing fringe of fir trees added to the unreality of the scene.

Philip, wrapped in warm clothes under his white driving suit, was waiting his turn to drive, waiting with Tiffany by his side. Life, he was thinking, could have little more to offer.

Everything about Brooklands aroused Philip to superlatives. He had watched its development, but his heart still pounded each time he drove through the tunnel under the Members' Banking, emerging into the massive cauldron of the amphitheatre with the awesome steepness of the Banking behind, while in front of him the vast sweep of the Railway Straight stretched towards Byfleet. He had driven on the circuit, touching 70 miles per hour, so high on the banking that he lost all sensation of being on a curve, aware only of the great expanse of the track, of the rushing wind and stinging concrete dust.

The circuit had been officially opened eleven days ago, but today was the day Philip had waited for: Edge's twenty-four-hour drive, trying to beat the record of 1096 miles covered by two Americans at an average speed of

45.6 miles per hour. The three 60-hp Napiers had started at six in the evening to enable the night driving to be accomplished while the team was fresh. Edge, accompanied by his mechanic, was in the car painted British racing green and much modified – its touring body removed and a huge fuel tank attached behind the front seats. The other two cars, painted red and white respectively and also with stripped chassis, were being driven in three-hour spells by the Napier testers. Any moment now Tryon in the white car would be pulling into the pits to hand over to Philip.

'Here he comes.' Philip put his arm round Tiffany, squeezing her tightly. 'A tyre change and then I'll be away. The lanterns are so effective we shall not need the headlights. Are you sure you will be all right? Three hours is a long time.'

'I'll be fine. Good luck!'

'We're well up on the clock.'

A quick kiss and he was running towards the car. Tiffany felt a moment's loneliness and depression; she longed to retreat into the warmth of the tent where food and drink were available but did not wish to speak to anyone. So instead she walked up and down in the shadows, trying to keep warm, trying to keep her mind occupied – because she had other reasons for walking, for taking any exercise she could. She was ten days late.

It's probably nothing to worry about, she tried to convince herself – a false alarm. Perhaps having sex upset one's system. But she could not rid herself of the fear because Tiffany was never late, her menstruation was as regular as the full moon. In her fear she even felt angry with Philip. He had been wrong, because it must have happened that first time. They had made love many times in the three weeks since then, but she had been careful . . . so very careful. Philip had brought a booklet on birth control, apparently acquired from his cousin Julia who distributed such items in the course of her charitable activities. Tiffany learned that the vulcanisation of rubber had resulted in the rubber sheath, which was now preferred to the old-fashioned sheath made of sheep-gut. She became an expert on withdrawal, douching, the 'safe' period and quinine pessaries. So, it could only have been the first time. Now she walked faster and jumped up and down as though the violent exercise would dislodge the unwanted thing inside her. Damn it to hell, how she hated being a woman!

If she was pregnant, had the risk been worth it? Yes, she decided doubtfully. Philip was the most marvellous lover. Besides, she must love him or else she would not be standing out in this goddam field in the freezing cold in the middle of the blasted night!

So far she had not mentioned her fears to him, but perhaps she would tell him tomorrow after the drive. They must make plans. To her surprise John Court's last letter had announced he was sailing for England. She had been furious, but now considered that in the circumstances her father's visit was timed to perfection. Oh, to hell with this, she was frozen! Tiffany walked into the tent, sat down in a corner and pretended to be asleep until Philip returned.

The big Napiers pounded on. Tyres came off rims, the surface of the track began to disintegrate – so badly that gravel had to be shovelled into the holes – water had to be pumped across the circuit to cool the tyres. Edge's windscreen shattered from vibration. But by six o'clock the next evening S.F. Edge had driven continuously for twenty-four hours, covering 1581 miles at an average speed of 65.905 miles per hour, and had established a staggering twenty-six records in various categories. The other two cars were not far behind. The Napier team was ecstatic, none more so than Philip who, although tired, stiff and somewhat bruised, was able to drive back to the White Lion at Chobham where he had reserved rooms. He fell asleep instantly but awoke refreshed a few hours later and reached hungrily for Tiffany. He made love to her slowly, considerately, tenderly . . . and when the passion was spent he lay still, holding her against his heart.

'Give me the perfect end to a perfect day,' he murmured against her hair. 'Say that you will marry me.'

'Of course. In fact I may have to.'

He raised himself on one elbow, gazing eagerly into her face. 'A baby? Already? That's wonderful – but surely it is too soon to tell?'

'Yes to all those points except the wonderful bit. *I* am not pleased! However, as you say, I am not absolutely sure. There is one good thing, though – our dear Papas won't be able to prevent the marriage when they hear about a baby. I could have handled my father, but I have wondered if yours might cut you off without a farthing.'

'We will tell both of them at the same time.'

'That means enticing them into the same room.'

'We will think of something. Oh darling Tiffany, I simply cannot wait to see their faces!'

'When shall we tell them?'

'Let me see ... I have to go to France next week to do another check on the wretched Lemoine – complete waste of time as you well know, but I continue to keep Papa in suspense. By the time I return your father should have arrived. So, as soon as I come back!' He laughed. 'I simply cannot wait,' he repeated.

Tiffany knew a moment's misgiving. A whole lifetime to be planned, yet all Philip seemed to think about was the effect of their marriage on his father. It was important, of course, and Tiffany was relishing it too, but there was so much else to discuss.

And, uncannily, with that perfect accord which illumined their relationship, Philip sensed her disquiet. 'It isn't only that, you know,' he said quietly, 'or the money. I do love you. I really do love you!'

The morning he left London for France Philip, as lovers do, felt the urge to write a letter to his beloved. He had seen Tiffany the previous evening and said his farewells, but still needed to make this last contact with her, to feel closer to her by writing. She had not been to a doctor, but the onset of nausea in the mornings had convinced her that she was pregnant.

'My darling Tiffany,' he wrote, 'I could not leave without

telling you again how much I love you and how much I shall miss you while I am away. Take care of yourself and our baby – I shall insist that you consult a doctor as soon as I return. Then we shall confront John Court and Matthew Bright with our incredible news, in the happy knowledge that your pregnancy means they must accept our marriage without demur. *Au revoir.* I shall love you for ever.'

Philip signed it with a flourish and was closing the envelope when Henriette entered the room.

'Send this to the Savoy, Henriette. I want it to get there no later than this afternoon.'

From an upstairs window she watched him enter the car which would take him to the railway station. As soon as he was out of sight, she walked slowly to her little sitting-room and, with great deliberation, opened the letter . . .

Henriette sat there for a long time. Her body was motionless but her mind was reeling, grappling with horror and revulsion – and with terror for the part she had played in this Aeschylian affair. Utterly appalled, she contemplated this unnatural act, this sin against the laws of nature which to her was none the less terrible for being committed in innocence. She contemplated her own sin and the dreadful certainty that she had failed Lady Anne; her loyalty to her dead mistress had been diverted into the wrong channels by slimy deposits of hate and bitterness – Anne would have wished her to protect the children, not stand by in vicarious fascination while they acted out their tragedy. And, with the scale of the catastrophe and in the light of her own fault, Henriette's hatred of Matthew dissolved. For all these years she had planned revenge and now she could not take it; he must be told, but she could not tell him.

She retraced her steps to Philip's room, removed the sketch of Tiffany from the wardrobe, paused again by the window and saw her deliverance. The chauffeur had delivered Philip to Victoria and collected two passengers from Paddington: Miranda and her governess were ascending the steps to the front door of the house.

In her agitation Henriette had forgotten that Miranda was travelling to London from Brightwell for one of her periodic aural examinations. The appointment was Henriette's salvation, but also meant that she had to endure her agitation throughout the long day. In the afternoon the governess took Miranda to the specialist and brought her home again. Then at last, at long last, Sir Matthew came home from the office. As usual when Laura was in the country, he went straight to the library where Parker had laid the drinks tray and where a fire burned summer or winter. Henriette waited near the library door for Miranda to descend the stairs to see her father.

Here she came now, hair neatly brushed and gleaming tawny gold, sedate steps down the stairs because Miranda never rushed but always took her time, a cautious girl who gave the impression that she knew exactly where she was going and what she was doing. Henriette's dislike of the girl had evaporated along with the hatred of Matthew but she had no pity as she pushed the folded picture and the envelope into the young girl's hand.

'Give these to your father – but do not look at them yourself.'

Miranda nodded. She was not overly curious about papers, assuming them to be connected with household affairs, but anyway had no opportunity to inspect them because she was outside the library door and Henriette watched her go in.

Matthew was standing in front of the fire. For July the weather was cold and grey, but he sought the fire more for the focal point it gave to the room than for the warmth it generated. He missed Laura when she was away.

'Darling!' He held out his arms, hugged Miranda close and kissed her gently on the forehead. 'How lovely to see you. You can stay up and have dinner with me tonight – Philip has gone away.'

Miranda brightened, both at the invitation and the news of Philip's absence. 'I went to see the doctor.'

'What did he say? Is that his report?' Matthew pointed to the papers she was carrying.

'These? No, Henriette asked me to give them to you.' She handed them to him. 'Sir William will send you his report tomorrow,' Miranda continued.

'What did he say?' Matthew asked again. 'Did he find any improvement in your hearing?'

'No change.' She smiled slightly at his disappointed expression. 'Papa, you know that these visits are a waste of time. There isn't likely to be any change. And it doesn't matter. I can manage perfectly well.'

Matthew smiled back. 'You manage wonderfully well. I am proud of you.'

He tapped the papers thoughtfully with his sensitive fingers and then glanced down at them. Turning casually towards the light of the fire, he unrolled the portrait. Beautiful girl, he thought, but why does Henriette imagine she will interest me? She might have done once, mind you! Gorgeous creature . . . Then he read the signature and his heart lurched, twisted, pounded . . . He read the name on the envelope, written in Philip's hand, and with shaking fingers opened it. Finally he read the letter. His face turned a livid purple, he staggered, a ghastly choking sound was forced from his throat and Matthew Bright collapsed. As he fell to the floor the hand holding the papers plunged into the fire, but he was oblivious to pain.

Miranda screamed.

And nothing was ever the same again.

223

CHAPTER TWELVE

The purplish hue had faded, leaving Matthew's face a dull, leaden grey. His right hand was heavily bandaged, but the pain it gave him was infinitesimal compared with the agony in his heart.

'Indefinite rest, Sir Matthew,' prescribed the doctor. 'Undoubtedly you suffered a slight stroke.'

'Nonsense,' said Matthew weakly. 'I tripped over the hearthrug.'

'Your heart is not sound. The slightest exertion may trigger another attack. I really must insist that you stay in bed.'

Matthew jerked the bell-pull with his left hand. 'The doctor is leaving, Henriette. Come back here when you have seen him out.'

When she returned they stared at each other speechlessly, not knowing where to begin.

'I will not ask you how you found out, Henriette,' said Matthew at last. 'I am only grateful that you did. Now I have time to think, to work out what can be done.'

'Isn't it too late to do anything?'

'It is *never* too late! Somehow, something, *someone* can be salvaged . . . Dear God, a baby . . .' Matthew closed his eyes, overwhelmed with the horror of it. 'How did it begin? How did they meet? But there is one thing I have to know, Henriette, and you are one of only two people living who can tell me. How long was Anne sleeping with John Court?'

Henriette was surprised at the question. 'They had plenty of opportunity,' she said slowly, a slight note of reproof for his neglect of Anne creeping into her voice, 'but they took that opportunity only once.'

'Once! Are you absolutely sure?' Matthew was trying to sit up in bed, colour returning to his white cheeks.

'Quite sure,' she answered, 'and the result was Tiffany.' Henriette was beginning to understand his drift. 'I promise you that is the truth – I knew her better than anyone and I was constantly in the house. I would have known if it was otherwise.' She paused. 'Master Philip and Miss Tiffany are *half*-brother and sister,' she said emphatically.

Matthew sank back on to his pillows again and even in the midst of catastrophe, he achieved a measure of inner peace; some good had come out of this ghastly business – he had regained his son. In the wake of the revelation came a feeling of protectiveness. 'Whatever happens, Philip must not find out the truth. Thank God he is away . . . I need time . . .' He reached out his good hand and grasped her arm with all the strength he could muster. 'Henriette, I rely on you to say nothing to anyone, now or ever. Promise me!'

'I promise.'

'You must make light of my *accident* tonight to the other servants and also to Lady Bright. No one must suspect that I was taken ill, no one must know that I was upset. I tripped over the hearthrug and fell into the fire – do you understand?'

'Yes, sir.' Henriette was close to tears. 'But the doctor said you must stay in bed.'

'There is too much to do. I must sort this out . . .' Matthew tried to get out of bed, failed to find the strength and cursed. 'Ask Miranda to come here.' Suddenly his face grew infinitely sad. 'Oh Anne,' he murmured, 'your children . . . your poor, poor children!'

Henriette burst into tears and fled from the room.

Because Henriette needed time to compose herself, it was a while before she summoned Miranda to her father's side. The pause gave Matthew the opportunity for deep regrets – regrets that he had doubted Anne when she affirmed that Philip was his child; regrets that he had turned his back on Tiffany because if he had brought her up as his own daughter, this would never have happened. Briefly he succumbed and railed at the fate which had brought about such a terrible destiny, but when Miranda arrived he was himself again.

Miranda entered hesitantly, her face whiter than his, but when she saw him sitting up in bed she flung herself against his chest.

'I thought you were dead,' she whispered.

'Darling.' Matthew stroked her hair. 'I am sorry to have frightened you. But it's all right. I'm fine and I will be up tomorrow.'

She perched on the edge of the bed. 'Your poor hand,' she said, touching the bandages gently. 'I pulled it out of the fire, but it was terribly burned, all . . .' She shuddered.

'The papers I was holding . . . what happened to the papers?' he asked sharply.

'They were burned. I couldn't save them.'

Thank God. 'You did not read them?'

'I couldn't. I told you they were burned. Were they important?'

'No, not important. Sweetheart, I want you to do something for me. I want you to write to Laura, tell her that I had a little accident and burned my hand. Say that I am well, but my hand is bandaged so I cannot write myself. Will you do that?'

'Of course.'

'Thank you. Bring me the letter when you have finished it and then we will ask Parker to send it to Laura immediately. You see, I don't want her rushing up here to make a fuss.' He smiled at Miranda in conspiratorial fashion. 'I have such a lot of work and she will only try to stop me. What I would like is for you to stay here for a few days, to help me write letters and to run a few errands. Would you?'

'I would love to.' Miranda hugged him. Highly sensitive, she knew something was wrong. She knew that Papa had not tripped over a hearthrug, as Henriette had tried to convince her, and she was perfectly aware that he was hiding something from her. But she was her father's daughter and she could play the same game as he. She even had an inkling that he was using her in some way, that he thought he could fool her while he could not fool Laura, but she did not care; she was too happy to be wanted by him and to be allowed to stay near him, helping him while he was ill.

The next morning Matthew struggled out of bed and insisted on dressing, swearing at the valet for his clumsiness. Patiently the valet cut the shirt-sleeve to permit the passage of the heavily-bandaged hand, adjusted the sling and pinned the empty jacket sleeve so that it did not flap untidily. Matthew made his slightly unsteady way to the library and called for Miranda. He glared at the telephone, cursing the fact that two hands were required to operate it.

'We have a busy day ahead of us,' he informed Miranda gaily. 'I want to get in touch with a Mr John Court.'

By the end of the day Matthew was grey with fatigue and with the pain from his burned hand, but he was also triumphant. To his inestimable relief he had established that John Court would arrive in England three days hence and would be staying at the Savoy with his daughter. Three days ... three days for Matthew to gather his strength and marshall his forces. He had to face his past, the old days in Kimberley, but the fight for the diamond fields was nothing compared with this – the greatest battle of his life.

The days passed with painful slowness. Anton Ellenberger called each morning about business matters and was appalled at Matthew's appearance – the signs of illness were so evident that he could not believe the hearthrug story. The state of Matthew's health was important to Anton for several reasons, not the least being that the time was approaching when he must make his move – break away from Bright Diamonds and start up in business for

227

himself. But, ruthless and efficient though he was in all matters concerning the industry, Anton knew that it would trouble his conscience to leave the company if Matthew was unable to continue running it himself. Philip was useless – uninterested and, Anton felt, untrustworthy – while Miranda was not yet ready . . .

Miranda . . . there lay the real reason for Anton's concern. He called on her as often as propriety would permit, talking to her about diamonds, supplementing the knowledge she was also acquiring from her father. Often they spoke in his native German, which Miranda had added to her knowledge of English and French, and Anton would gently correct her pronunciation and use of idiom, taking infinite pains with the partially-deaf girl until she got the word absolutely right.

However, his interest in his employer's daughter went beyond her linguistic ability and knowledge of diamonds. Julia was right – Anton Ellenberger did dream of marrying Miranda one day. But hand in hand with the obvious commercial advantages to such a union went a genuine fondness and admiration for the girl. He loved her courage and quiet determination, her intelligence and courtesy; and he was awed by the budding beauty of her face and body and the luxuriant golden hair. Yet while Anton possessed complete confidence in business matters, where women were concerned he knew his limitations. With Miranda this innate humility was increased. He was acutely aware of the splendour of her surroundings, the position she occupied in society and, most important of all, her devotion to her brilliant, handsome father. One day, he vowed, he would be able to provide her with the luxuries to which she was accustomed, but as far as the other factors were concerned he must trust in that streak of honesty and integrity within her which would lead her to follow the dictates of her heart. In the meantime, in order to make his own fortune, he must leave London and leave her; but she was only thirteen, so he had time. His immediate concern was that Matthew must recover from this illness, because the battle for control of the diamond industry must be with Matthew himself – the only adversary worthy of Anton's respect.

Therefore, when he called at Park Lane on the fourth day after the alleged accident, Anton was relieved to find Matthew much improved in health and spirits, and pleased to discover Miranda at the writing-desk in the library. After Matthew had left the room, he approached the girl and smiled at her.

'Your father is much better,' he said, speaking in German.

'Do you think so?' She looked at him eagerly. '*I* thought so but sometimes, if one wants something so much, one can imagine it is true.'

'Such an old head on young shoulders,' he murmured. 'Don't worry, Miranda, this time it is true. Have you started the German book I gave you?'

'I have finished it.'

'Already?'

'I have a lot of time for reading because I don't have many friends.' Her glance was frank and without self-pity. Occasionally she thought it might be pleasant to go to school and mix with girls of her own age, but she understood that the special needs of her education made this impossible. She had her books, her dog Richie and Papa – she was content.

'You seem very busy now.'

'I am writing letters for Papa.'

Her eyes glowed and Anton felt again the impossibility of weaning her from Matthew.

'Good. If there is anything I can do to help you, Miranda, you know where to find me.'

'Yes, thank you.'

Anton walked to the door, but paused for a moment. 'It would be beneficial for you to go to school – your speech and lip-reading are quite good enough, you know.'

'I am glad you think so,' and she was, because she

respected his opinion. 'Papa says that I might go to finishing school on the Continent when I'm a bit older. I shall have to choose between French and German but,' and her charming smile flashed briefly, 'I shall choose German.'

He was genuinely pleased and Miranda knew it. After he had gone she briefly analysed their relationship. Anton was more than a servant but less than family, both his relationship with her and his standing in society falling somewhere in between. Perhaps, Miranda reflected, Anton Ellenberger was the nearest she had to a friend.

She looked at the letter she had just finished writing. It was addressed to Mr John Court at the Savoy Hotel and read: 'It is of vital importance that I speak to you and I shall be glad if you will call on me at your earliest convenience. The matter concerns your daughter. Tell no one, including her, where you are going.'

As instructed, Miranda added a sentence to the effect that she was writing on her father's behalf because he had injured his hand – otherwise, Matthew had said, Mr Court would think it odd that the handwriting was not his. Then she sealed the note, asked Parker to send it to the Savoy and began the next letter.

John Court's first reaction to the summons was indignation and an absolute determination not to go. Many times he had insisted that nothing could ever make him speak to Matthew Bright again, nothing could ever be that important. But Tiffany was all-important. What could it be and why must she be kept in ignorance of the meeting? He eyed her across the luncheon table. She seemed in good spirits but was a trifle pale and noticeably off her food – she had hardly touched a scrap of breakfast. The matter Matthew referred to must be connected with diamonds, Court decided, or – and a cold hand clutched his heart – could it be related to earlier events?

When Tiffany announced that she wished to do some shopping during the afternoon, Court accompanied her to Bond Street and then found himself strolling down

Piccadilly to Park Lane. Outside the imposing front of Matthew's home, he hesitated before slowly climbing the steps and being ushered into the library where Matthew was standing in his customary position with his back to the fire. They stared at each other silently. It was twenty years since they had met, yet once they had shared the triumphs and disasters of the diamond fields, lived in the same house, together had built their immense fortunes. All this had been wrecked when Court indulged in one hour's indiscretion with Anne, which Matthew had been unable to forgive. Now both were grateful for Matthew's bandaged right arm which excused them from shaking hands.

'I would not have asked you to come,' said Matthew abruptly, 'if the matter had not been of extreme importance – such importance and so personal that I could not delegate it nor could I convey its import in a letter.'

'And I would not have come if you had not indicated that it concerns Tiffany,' Court replied stiffly. He could sense Matthew's agitation and his own anxiety was rising.

'I assume you are unaware that Tiffany and Philip have been pursuing a close relationship?'

Court went white. 'I expressly forbade her to have anything to do with you!' he cried, the possibilities of the situation beginning to heave in hideous shock waves in his mind.

'You bloody fool! All you succeeded in doing was arousing her curiosity and what is probably a naturally rebellious spirit. It explains everything – she sought out Philip deliberately!'

'It is much more likely that Philip chased after her – she is extremely beautiful,' Court retorted furiously.

'All the more reason why you should have exercised greater control over her,' Matthew shouted. Then he sighed and pressed his sound hand to his forehead. 'There is no use in quarrelling about it, John, and blaming each other. The thing has gone too far for that. They want to get married.'

Court swayed. 'But she is supposed to marry Randolph,'

231

he said piteously, unable to come to grips with this, 'her cousin Randolph.'

'To hell with Randolph! *Tiffany is expecting Philip's baby!*'

Ashen-faced, Court staggered and would have fallen if Matthew had not caught him with his sound arm and helped him to a chair. Court buried his face in his hands and began to sob.

'I am sorry,' he said eventually.

'No need to apologise,' Matthew replied brusquely. 'If it is any comfort to you, your reaction is less drastic than mine. When I found out four days ago, I had a stroke and fell into the fire. How Isobel would have laughed!'

'Isobel!' Court remembered Matthew's early loves – Isobel, Alida, Anne . . . *Anne!* 'This cannot be true,' he said suddenly. 'You are saying it to torment me. You always tormented people and made them suffer for your own ends.' He looked at Matthew, desperately seeking release from the nightmare which had engulfed him, but found no solace in the relentless stare of the other's blue eyes. 'You destroy everyone in the end,' he murmured helplessly.

'Don't say that! Do you not think I realise that if I had not turned my back on the child this ghastly affair would never have happened?'

But such a confession did not comfort Court. 'I wanted her. My life was meaningless until she came. All that money – and no one to spend it on.'

'Why have you never married?' Matthew took up his station before the fire again.

'I could not.' Court glanced at that handsome granite face and looked away again. 'I loved Anne, you know. Really loved her. And then I devoted my whole life to Tiffany.'

'Then you are more of a fool than I took you for! That is the worst mistake a parent can make! A father should love his children but not cling to them, not suffocate them, not live his life through them – he must know when to let the

232

child go!' Perspiration broke out on Matthew's grey face, for he was still far from well and emotion was taking its toll. 'I know how you feel about Tiffany, because I feel the same about Miranda,' he said more quietly. 'I ought not to have favourites but I do. And when the time comes to let her go, I pray that I will remember what I am telling you now.'

Slowly, drop by drop, the truth was permeating Court's consciousness. 'What are we going to do?' he asked helplessly. 'Matthew, in the old days you always knew what to do.'

'One of them has to be told – and it isn't going to be Philip.'

'I cannot possibly tell Tiffany!' Court was absolutely aghast. 'Philip is the man; it is his duty to shoulder the burden.'

'No.' Matthew straightened, squared his shoulders and prepared to fight. 'For twenty years I believed Philip was your son. For twenty years I treated him as though he was your son. There is reparation to be made. He has suffered enough.'

'Everyone has suffered.'

'Everyone *except you*! First me, then Anne, then Philip . . . now Tiffany because she is pregnant with her half-brother's child. Only you escaped – you got off scot-free – you got the child you had always wanted, who gave meaning to your life. Now it is your turn to *pay*!'

'I cannot tell her! I cannot hurt her like that!'

'You must.'

'But what good would it do?' asked Court desperately. 'There is still Philip . . . dear God, there is still the baby!'

'She will tell Philip she made a mistake – that she does not love him and that there is no baby. I will arrange for him to leave London. As soon as he is out of harm's way, we will deal with the rest of the problem. First things first, John – and Philip comes *first*.'

'Only you and I know the truth,' cried Court. 'If we stay silent, they could marry – no one need ever know.'

Matthew's look was so incredulous and appalled that no words were necessary.

'No,' said Court, 'I suppose that would be impossible. But you don't understand, Matthew . . . you aren't aware of the stories, the lovely stories I told her about her mother . . . I cannot tell her!'

'If you do not tell her,' said Matthew, '*I will*.'

John Court returned to the hotel. Offered the use of Matthew's car, he reached his suite long before Tiffany returned from her shopping expedition. From his suitcase he extracted a small revolver. Fastidiously he stepped into the bathroom, where he placed the gun to his head and pulled the trigger.

The maid found the body and most of the blood and brains had been cleared up by the time Tiffany came back.

Why?

The following day Tiffany's head still reeled from shock and confusion, but that question remained uppermost in her mind.

Why?

The police seemed certain it was suicide. There was no sign of a struggle and nothing had been taken from the suite. Possibly it could have been an accident, but it was somewhat bizarre for a man to clean his gun in the bathroom. Suicide. But why? The only clue was the letter from Matthew Bright. By a miraculous stroke of good fortune Tiffany had discovered the letter in her father's bedroom before the police searched the place. Numb with shock, but nonetheless alive to the letter's implications, she had pocketed the note and said nothing. It could have no bearing on the matter, she told herself. Even if Philip's father had unearthed their secret, that could not be a reason for her father to kill himself. No family feud could be *that* bad!

She had taken only two positive steps: she had acquired several sets of black mourning clothes and sent a cable to Randolph. Now she waited for the wretched effects of her early morning sickness to pass off before she made her next move. She was surprised at the depth of grief which she felt for her father, but that grief was tempered with and becoming dominated by anger and fear. Anger because he had deserted her at the time she needed him most. Fear because Randolph was now her legal guardian. Baby or no baby, would Randolph permit her to marry Philip?

At noon Tiffany swept through the foyer of the hotel, ignoring the sympathetic and curious glances, and climbed into a cab.

'Park Lane,' she ordered. 'The home of Sir Matthew Bright.'

She was shown into the drawing-room but remained standing, taking no notice of her surroundings, keeping her eyes fixed on the door. Matthew came in, closed the door behind him and walked towards her. This was the same man she had glimpsed in Hatton Garden but subtly changed – looking older, his face grey and drawn, the vitality gone from his step. He bowed.

'My condolences, Miss Court.'

She had expected him to have heard the news and had no wish to waste time on formalities. Peremptorily she held out the letter. 'Does this throw any light on why he did it?'

'Yes.'

His directness, matching hers, took Tiffany by surprise and she paused. For a brief moment Matthew and Tiffany stood, assessing each other's looks and personality, appreciating one another.

'Then kindly be good enough to tell me.'

'I think you should sit down first.'

'I prefer to stand.'

'As you wish.' Matthew took a deep breath. Shaken by the news of Court's suicide and moved to admiration of the girl's beauty and courage, this was much harder than he had expected. 'Your father and I were partners in Kimberley . . .'

'Get to the point, Sir Matthew.' She was beginning to

hope that in fact Sir Matthew did not know about her relationship with Philip. 'Presumably it has something to do with the quarrel between you and my father. What caused that quarrel?'

'You did.'

'Me?' She was astonished. 'But I was an infant when Papa brought me home to America after my mother died.'

'What did he tell you about your mother?'

'That her name was Alida ...' Tiffany broke off when she saw the expression on Matthew's face. 'What's wrong with that?'

'Alida ... was that the name he chose? Dear God, how old ghosts return to haunt me! No, Tiffany, your mother's name was Anne.' Gently he laid an arm about her shoulders and turned her to face the portraits on the drawing-room wall. He pointed to the picture of the beautiful, fair-haired woman in a silver dress. 'She was your mother. My wife – Anne. And she was Philip's mother, too.'

Tiffany had been pale before Matthew spoke but now the last vestiges of colour drained from her cheeks, leaving her face bloodless and transparent. Her eyes were enormous, widening until they seemed to fill her whole face as she stared at the picture and then at Matthew. But whereas Matthew had fallen at the news and Court had staggered before breaking into tears, Tiffany stood straight and tall, her head held high and her eyes dry.

'I am expecting Philip's child,' she said clearly.

'I know. That is what I told your father yesterday.'

'And he hadn't the guts to tell me!' Anger and contempt burned in her eyes, but otherwise she seemed perfectly in control. 'I think I will sit down now, Sir Matthew, and you can tell me about my father's adulterous relationship with your wife. After that, perhaps we can discuss what Philip and I do about our incestuously conceived child.'

She is incredible, thought Matthew, or she is in a state of shock. Either way she is magnificent! And Matthew's heart began to ache with pity for his son who must lose her.

When Matthew had finished his story, Tiffany nodded. 'I

do see why my father did not tell me the truth, but it does not alter the fact that I shall never forgive him. Right, Sir Matthew, when Philip returns from France the three of us must decide what to do.'

'No, not the *three* of us.'

'The very least you can do is help,' she flashed.

'Oh, I will, but Philip must be left out of it.'

'Like it or not, Philip is *in* it. He must assume equal responsibility.'

'Do you love him?'

'Of course. Very much.'

'If you do love him, you will spare him the agony you are enduring now, the agony of knowing that he made love to his sister.'

Tenaciously Tiffany clung to the facts, concentrating on what she had to *do*, deliberately blotting out how she *felt*. 'I can think of only one way to achieve that – to tell him that I do not love him, there is no baby, the entire affair was a mistake and good-bye for ever.'

Again Matthew was filled with admiration for her cool grasp of the situation. 'My thoughts entirely.'

'He will be devastated,' she said. 'He needs love, for he has had precious little of it in his life,' and she watched coldly as Matthew winced. 'I am not sure which is the lesser of two evils – to tell him the truth or deny him the knowledge that he was – is – loved.'

'He cannot have you, can never marry you, must never see you again – there really is no choice.'

Did she love Philip enough to make this sacrifice and carry the burden alone? In the dark recesses of her mind Tiffany heard the voice of Rafe Deverill taunting her that she was incapable of love, that she loved only herself. 'Very well, I will do it, but in return you must help me to get rid of the baby.'

'Abortion? Are you really prepared to risk it?'

'I thought you must have connections – doctors who would do a proper job.'

Matthew shook his head. 'I can ask my doctor to examine

your health and advise on your pregnancy – in fact I insist on doing so – but no more. It would mean a back-street abortionist and they can kill.'

'I really do not want to die,' she said firmly. 'I have far too much to do.' Her eyes alighted on the portrait again and she remembered how she had gazed at the picture of 'Alida', imagining how that woman would not have wanted to die either. 'So my mother did not die in childbirth after all.'

'As a matter of fact, she did. Anne died giving birth to Miranda.'

Another dimension was added to Tiffany's pain as a fierce surge of jealousy engulfed her. Then she remembered something and glanced again at the letter she was still holding. 'Miranda wrote this letter. Was that wise?'

'She was the only person I could entrust with the task. You see, after Miranda gave me Philip's letter – the one he wrote to you, which . . .'

Tiffany did not listen further – she was too enraged at the revelation that Miranda spied on her brother, not only reading his letters but running with them to Papa. However, resolutely she forced herself to rivet her attention on the most important aspect – the baby.

'Very well, no abortion.' It occurred to her that twice in the course of this conversation Matthew had swayed her judgment and persuaded her to his own point of view. The respect this engendered in her gave her the courage to voice her deepest fear. 'But I am so afraid that a child of incest will be deformed . . . defective . . .' Her voice trailed away.

'An old wives' tale', snapped Matthew roughly, but with such authority that Tiffany obtained some comfort and reassurance from his apparent certainty on the subject. 'No, we have reached the crux of the matter – we must find another father for the child. Your father mentioned Randolph. Would he oblige? Would he do what I did not do – accept another man's bastard as his own?'

'Yes,' replied Tiffany unhesitatingly, 'but it would give him too much *power* over me!'

Matthew nodded, the sentiment arousing an instinctive response.

What a woman and what a fool he had been – how proud he would be to have her for a daughter. 'You couldn't fool him into believing the child was his – sleep with him as soon as possible and then give him a story about a premature birth?'

Tiffany smiled wanly. 'No. He is a man who would be suspicious of such a sudden change of heart.'

'In that case, can you suggest another candidate?'

'Yes,' Tiffany said. 'Yes, I believe I know the very man.'

Matthew listened to the name and smiled. 'Excellent,' he murmured with secret delight. 'Excellent. Then this is what we do . . .'

In the hall Tiffany paused while Matthew summoned the chauffeur to drive her back to the hotel. A movement attracted her attention and she turned her head to watch the young girl descending the stairs.

Miranda. The sister whom Philip detested, his father's favourite, who had taken all the affection for herself and left none for her brother. Miranda who sneaked and spied, whose birth had killed their mother, who was the daughter of that magnificent man. Miranda whose family life was normal, who was legitimate, who had been brought up to know her brother was her brother, who was young and untouched by suffering.

The emotions raged in Tiffany's face, the torture blazed from her eyes. The naked hate, her tall impressive figure, the pallor of her lovely face enhanced by the mourning dress, combined to transmit a message which transfixed Miranda who, having reached the foot of the stairs, shrank back against the newel post.

No word was spoken, but the moment was branded on their memories for ever.

* * *

Tactfully the hotel staff had moved Tiffany to another suite and when she returned her maid had completed the rearrangement of her belongings. Brusquely Tiffany ordered the girl to leave the apartment and not to disturb her during the afternoon. Noticing the maid's concerned expression, Tiffany smiled faintly. 'Do not worry,' she said, 'I am not in the least likely to emulate my father's example.'

Alone, Tiffany let go; she released the control she had exerted so valiantly and sank under the smothering sea of her troubles. Uttering a low animal cry of despair, she cast herself upon the bed and wept.

She wept for her girlhood worship of 'Alida', the mother who had never existed; for Philip, the one thing or person she had wanted but could not possess; for the baby which she did not want but must bear. And, yes, there was an element of self-pity in her sorrow as she came to terms with the hideous reality of her position. But she did not cry for John Court.

Philip was her brother. The brutal fact was sinking in, penetrating the layers of her resistance, exposing raw nerve ends until Tiffany's head seemed to swell nearly to bursting point with pain. Overwhelmed with nausea, she ran to the bathroom and leaned, retching, over the basin. Stomach churning and twisting, she sagged to the floor while the wild hope asserted itself that perhaps the fragile life inside her could not withstand such pressure. But the spasms passed and she did not miscarry.

Tiffany rose to her feet, wiped the beads of perspiration from her chalk-white face and returned to the bedroom. She must dwell no more on the fact that Philip was her brother. He was a past lover, nothing more. That was the only way to preserve her sanity, the only way to cope with the present and face the years which lay ahead. Those hours of weakness and capitulation that afternoon relieved the tension and Tiffany emerged from them even stronger than before. She felt better as she prepared for action. The future was not so bleak; indeed it held exciting possibilities – if she could successfully execute the plan. If she failed, and her face tautened at the prospect, there was no escape from Randolph.

That night, cloaked in black, Tiffany stood alone on Waterloo Bridge, gazing down into the inky waters of the Thames before hurling an object over the parapet. The diamond-encrusted frame surrounding the tiny miniature emitted one final flare of light before it vanished into the darkness, dropping like a stone to the muddy river-bed.

CHAPTER THIRTEEN

'No, I don't believe it! You are upset! You will feel differently when the shock of your father's death has worn off.' Philip, coming to comfort and console, fought frantically against the finality of his dismissal.

'My father's death has influenced me in only one way: it has caused me to reassess my feelings and my future. I am fond of you, Philip, but not fond enough to marry you.'

'You said you *loved* me!' he cried in anguish.

'I was mistaken.'

'The baby . . .'

'There is no baby. I was wrong about that, too.'

'How can you do this? How can you stand there, so calm, so composed in your black dress, while you destroy me?'

'Don't be melodramatic, Philip. I am not destroying you. I am merely telling you that I do not love you. It isn't the end of the world. You will fall in love many times in your life.'

'Never again!' He clutched helplessly at one last straw. 'It's Randolph, isn't it? You're afraid he will not permit you to marry me. I will wait until you are free of his guardianship – I will wait for ever!'

'I do not want to see you again.'

'There is someone else. You have fallen in love with another man.'

'Yes, as a matter of fact I have loved him for a long time.'

Philip stared at her with dull despair. 'Then why did you agree to marry me? Why did you make love with me?'

'You are a very handsome man, Philip – never underestimate your physical attraction – but you have another asset: your diamond company. I believed that a merger of

Court Diamonds and Bright Diamonds could be extremely beneficial. However,' and Tiffany sighed, 'when it came to taking the final step, I found that I could not place the logic in my head before the dictates of my heart.'

Philip swore, richly and blasphemously. 'Diamonds!' he said savagely. 'How I hate the bloody things!' Then a great light dawned in his mind and he stared at Tiffany suspiciously. 'My father is behind this! You have been speaking to my father while I was away and somehow he has persuaded you to change your mind.'

'Nonsense,' said Tiffany sharply. 'Really, Philip, you see your father's influence everywhere.'

'With good reason. He is behind everything which hurts me.'

'You are mistaken. In fact I think you are much mistaken about your father's attitude towards you.' Tiffany possessed sufficient objectivity to appreciate, and envy, Matthew's defence of his son. 'You feel something for your father that I never felt for mine.'

'What's that?'

'Respect.'

Philip laughed bitterly. It was so much easier to blame Matthew than to face up to his own shortcomings or the perfidy of his beloved. 'Like hell I respect him! But I will get my own back for this. Unfortunately I told him Lemoine is a fraud, but there will be another opportunity.'

'I must return this,' and reluctantly Tiffany proffered the pear-shaped pendant.

Now he remembered and reconsidered Laura's story about the evil influence of the gem. Once he had felt that if he could not have Laura, he could hurt her, and now he felt exactly the same about Tiffany. He hoped that the diamond was evil. Let it cast a curse over her!

'Keep it,' he said.

'The mailship leaves Southampton for Cape Town the day after tomorrow.' Matthew placed the ticket on the table beside his son.

Philip was slumped in the chair, face flushed and head lolling from the quantity of whisky he had consumed. He had been drinking steadily since leaving Tiffany and had almost succeeded in reaching a state of blessed numbness and imperviousness to pain. 'I don't want to go to Kimberley,' he mumbled.

'It is an essential part of your training.'

'Why the rush?'

'No particular reason. Perhaps it is rather short notice, but a vacancy has occurred in the Kimberley office of the Company and therefore it is an opportunity not to be missed. I trust the arrangements do not interfere with any commitments you have at home – your motor car interests, for example?'

'To hell with the cars! And you know damn well that I have no other commitments – you have seen to that!'

'I really have not the faintest idea what you are talking about. You will leave tomorrow. I will instruct Henriette to pack your belongings and cable the staff at Kimberley to prepare the house for your arrival.'

'I am not going.'

Matthew sighed. He had hoped this last inducement would not be necessary. 'I think you will,' he said softly, 'unless you want the world to know about these,' and he stretched out his left hand. In the palm glittered a small pile of diamonds.

Philip blundered to his feet and stood, swaying and scarlet-faced, pointing at the diamonds which in his euphoria he had forgotten to take with him to the Continent. 'Those stones are nothing to do with me! Where did you find them?'

'In your desk.'

'How dare you search my room?'

'I dare because you are my son, this is my house and these diamonds are the property of my company.' Matthew had been searching Philip's room for further evidence of the liaison with Tiffany, worried in case valet or maid should find embarrassing information, when he had chanced across the diamonds. He had been horrified at Philip's dishonesty, but had seen how he could turn circumstances to his own advantage.

'Was that when you found, and removed, the picture of Tiffany?'

'Tiffany? Oh, John Court's daughter. Dreadful business! I was not aware you are acquainted with her.'

'Liar!'

Matthew restrained himself with difficulty. 'You will go to Kimberley, Philip, and you will stay for at least a year. And you will refrain from helping yourself to the merchandise – the security arrangements there are excellent.'

'You have it all worked out, haven't you! Very well, it seems I have no option.'

Matthew's breath exhaled in a long sigh of relief. 'When you come home, I hope we can get to know each other better. We have not been as close as I would wish.'

Philip gave him an incredulous look and began to laugh. Still laughing, he picked up the whisky bottle and weaved his unsteady way to his room.

Laura was uneasy. There was something very odd about this weekend house-party, but she could not quite put her finger on what it was. Not so much one glaring anomaly, she decided as she arranged white roses in a silver vase, but a combination of factors which added up to a disturbing total. Perhaps it was only her distress and puzzlement over Philip's precipitate departure for the Cape. Perhaps it was only the heavy overcast weather with the feel of thunder in the air. Perhaps it was only the fact that they did not normally give house-parties in the country in July before the end of the Season. Laura pricked her finger on a thorn, swore a brief but unladylike oath and, losing patience, pushed the remaining blooms in the vase – the effect was decidedly haphazard but, after coping with the formal arrangements of orchids for the dinner-table, she was past caring. It was the guest list, she thought suddenly; it was the combination of *people* which gave her this sensation of impending disaster.

She picked up the list – dictated by Matthew, who was still unable to use his right hand – and perused the names. At first sight all seemed to be well: the Duke and Duchess of Desborough, the Duke and Duchess of Fontwell, the Earl and Countess of Highclere, Lord and Lady Ambleside, Julia and Alfred – normally an inclusion Laura would welcome, because for all their personal differences Julia could be relied upon to be attractive and entertaining – Lady Elizabeth Grafton, Lady Jane and Robert Bruce, and Edward, Julia's younger brother. So far, so good. It was the tail-end of the list which posed the problem: Rafe Deverill, Alice Palmer and Tiffany Court. Apart from the indisputable fact that Matthew detested Rafe, how on earth could he invite him and his fiancée to the same party as Julia? Their affair had been so well publicised for the past five years that Laura was convinced this was the most tactless invitation of the social season and might even be construed as insulting to Miss Palmer. The engagement had not been officially announced but was generally conceded to be imminent.

If the invitation to Rafe was mystifying, that to Tiffany Court was utterly bewildering. The girl was a complete stranger, in mourning for her father and Laura could not imagine how she could possibly be expected to fit in with the other guests. The poor girl was stuck all alone in an hotel while she awaited the arrival of her cousin, Matthew had said – a trifle sanctimoniously, in Laura's opinion – and the least he could do was offer her some hospitality for the sake of his old friend. He assured Laura that Tiffany wanted no special treatment and that the young American wished everyone to laugh and enjoy themselves just as usual. All very well, thought Laura, but *will* people enjoy themselves if she is drooping in a corner like a dying duck in a thunderstorm?

Talking of which . . . Laura strolled to the window and looked out at the sky. The air was more oppressive than ever, very still and heavy, with that deep quiet of the lull before the storm. She shivered suddenly, remembering the last time that thought had crossed her mind; it had been just before the climax of the Siege of Kimberley, just before Nicholas was killed. Don't be silly, Laura told herself sharply, the worst that can transpire is that everyone endures a perfectly miserable, boring weekend and is thoroughly glad when it is over. And on that cheering note for a hostess, she mechanically began to plan the *placement* and the fours for bridge. The allocation of bedrooms – always a delicate decision in Edwardian England – had been decided. Laura could only hope that she had got it right.

In this instance the juggling of people and places had not been too difficult because none of the married couples was carrying on an affair with another, so husbands and wives could be safely stowed in adjacent rooms in the main body of the house. One of the features of Brightwell was its twin towers, each with spiral staircase and rooms of unusual juxtaposition and shape. Accommodation in the towers was eagerly sought after, although Laura tended to allocate it to younger guests. The East Tower and its immediate environs was the preserve of the children, but one room – Philip's – now stood empty. Originally Laura had placed Alice Palmer, Rafe, Julia and Alfred in the West Tower and allocated Philip's room to Miss Court. However Matthew demurred, asserting that it was improper to place Rafe and Miss Palmer close together and that the children might upset Tiffany. Therefore Laura switched Alice Palmer to the East Tower with Edward in the attic room above, while Tiffany, Julia and Alfred occupied the main rooms in the West Tower with Rafe on the upper floor.

Laura sighed and shrugged her shoulders. House-parties were a minefield filled with the unexploded bombs of human relationships, but it did not appear that much could go wrong with these arrangements. At least she no longer lay awake at nights haunted by such matters – thanks to Rafe Deverill. Here a shadow crossed Laura's face. Alice Palmer is not the right woman for him, she thought, but there isn't a thing I can do about it.

Several hours later she was feeling a trifle more optimistic. The party had gathered in the West Gallery for tea, old friends were chatting comfortably together, Julia's feline gaze watched Rafe Deverill's every movement but she was being polite to Miss Palmer, while Matthew was in devastating form. Tiffany Court had not yet arrived. Unaware of her predilection for making an entrance, Laura worried about the girl's welfare and whether there would be any tea left by the time she came. It was really a physical impossibility for those massive piles of sandwiches, cakes, scones, toast, brioches with pots of Tiptree jam, and ginger biscuits from Biarritz to be consumed by eighteen people, but nonetheless Laura worried.

Therefore it was with a mixture of relief and apprehension that she heard the doors of the long gallery open and the butler's voice announce the name of Tiffany Court. Everyone turned their head and silence descended with the finality of a theatre curtain cutting off the first act before the climax of the play.

'It's *her*,' thought Laura as she recognised Philip's companion at Eights Week.

'It's *her*.' Julia, remembering the Venetian party, swiftly swivelled her head to watch Rafe.

Tiffany. Rafe had not known she was coming and for a moment his face betrayed him.

'Tiffany! My dear,' and Matthew took charge, welcoming her, introducing her, holding her arm protectively in fatherly fashion.

The buzz of conversation reverberated round the gallery again, but not so loudly as to prevent Laura hearing Tiffany remark, 'Captain Deverill and I have met,' as they were introduced. Oh my God, she thought, sensing disaster again, seeing clearly how good, how *right* they looked together . . . and seeing this opinion confirmed in Julia's venomous expression and Alice Palmer's drooping air of inferiority.

Tiffany sat down, accepted a cup of tea but politely refused food. Her demeanour was perfect, exhibiting decorum compatible with her bereavement but just enough liveliness to avoid casting a gloom. Her beauty, of course, won the day and the men, especially Edward, were clearly besotted. Again Laura received the impression that she was taking part in a play, a play which she strongly suspected was a tragedy rather than a comedy and of which Tiffany was the undisputed star.

It was typical of Laura that she felt no jealousy of Matthew's attentions to the girl, nor wondered about his ties of friendship with a family of whom she had never before heard, but busied herself in helping others over the crisis.

'Julia, you will be careful, won't you? I know you feel strongly about the suffragettes, but please don't get arrested . . . Alice, what a beautiful dress, such an exquisite shade of blue. When you and Rafe are . . . well, I do hope that we will see you more often *soon*.' And finally: 'Rafe, you are happy, aren't you? Really happy?'

He smiled and, tea over, produced a Faberge cigarette case containing Regie cigarettes from his pocket. 'May I?'

'Of course.'

He lit a cigarette but did not replace the case in his pocket. Instead he turned it over and over in his hands, ostentatiously drawing attention to the item as if it was representative of his position. 'Of course I am happy. How could I be otherwise? Do you like the case? A gift from my fiancée – inscription and all,' and he opened it again to show her the message engraved inside.

'It is lovely – and so is she.' Laura hesitated. 'I'm just not sure about it – your marriage – the case is lovely, but somehow it isn't *you*!'

'Ah, you mean that I am a kept man? That I accept expensive presents from my future wife instead of giving them? Younger sons have to be bought, Laura, it is the only way to survive – unless they make a fortune on the diamond fields!'

'I only want you to be happy.' Laura laid a slender white hand lightly on his arm. 'You, of all people, I want to be happy.'

'I will. Anyway, the die is cast. I have given my word to her and there is no retreat even if I sought it – which I don't.'

'Sometimes,' said Laura slowly, 'I feel I do not know you at all.'

'If you had not been married, and happily married at that, you could have known me very well indeed.'

Heart bumping and stomach knotting from the sensations he always aroused in her, Laura turned thankfully to welcome the children who were brought in to say good night to parents and guests. At Miranda's heels bounded the big Great Dane and Rafe strolled over to stroke the dog's head.

'She has grown somewhat since I saw her last! Was I right! Can you hear her bark?'

Miranda smiled. 'I think the whole of Berkshire can hear her bark!'

'She's seven years old now, isn't she? Has she had any pups?'

Miranda shook her head and Rafe did not miss the wistful look in her eyes. 'Dogs don't live as long as we do,' he said gently, 'and I'm sure you would like Richie's son or daughter for company when she has gone. I have a dog I could send to her.'

The girl's face lit up and Miranda – quiet, undemonstrative Miranda – flung her arms around Rafe and hugged him. He laughed and said teasingly, 'I will do you a few more favours if that is the response I receive! But you must ask your father's permission about the puppies.' He looked round, straight into Matthew's glowering face.

'That's enough, Miranda,' Matthew said sharply. 'Say good night to our other guests.'

But at that moment Miranda saw Tiffany and backed hurriedly out of the room.

Laura was engrossed in the arrangements for the after-tea entertainment. 'Matthew, Tiffany is the girl I told you about – the beautiful girl who was with Philip at the Bumps two years ago. Isn't it a coincidence?'

'Indeed it is. What a pity Philip is not here to renew his acquaintance.'

'I think that's just as well – the existing undercurrents are more than enough! Julia and Alice are beside themselves because Rafe can hardly keep his eyes off her.'

'Deverill wasn't looking at Tiffany a few moments ago. He was giving you his undivided attention before he lavished his charm on Miranda.' The sharpness was noticeable, although he smiled. 'But don't worry your lovely head, my darling. You may leave that quartet to me.'

But Matthew's solution was to escort Alice Palmer to the bridge tables in the Red Drawing-Room and sit down with Elizabeth and Charles. Two other tables were made up while Rafe, Alfred and Edward went to the billiard room, leaving Laura to talk to Tiffany (who did not play bridge), Julia and Charles's vulgar actress wife. Lord, she thought, what a combination of personalities! And was relieved when it was seven-thirty and they could retire to change their gowns for dinner.

They reassembled an hour later in the Blue Salon. Tiffany was last to arrive again, dressed in black lace cut low to reveal the splendour of her alabaster flesh and the proud column of her neck, magnificent diamonds sparkling at throat, ears and wrist – but fortunately not the pear-shaped pendant – and her blue-black hair piled high. At dinner she was seated between Charles, whose suggestive leers she ignored, and Lord Ambleside on whom she turned the full impact of her charm. In addition she was close enough to Matthew to be able to conduct a conversation with him about the diamond industry which ensured she remained at centre-stage amid the admiration of all the men. She was particularly flattering about Matthew's coup in arranging the purchase of the Cullinan diamond for the nominal sum of £125,000 and its imminent presentation to the King for his birthday by the Transvaal Government. She discussed the various aspects of the so-called Chinese 'slave-labour' in the South African mines and the Liberal Government's plans to give self-government to a unified South African state. In short Tiffany Court conversed with the men and was obviously far more at home in their company than with the ladies; so much so that when Laura signalled the women to retire, she was uncomfortably aware that it would be logical to leave Tiffany to drink port. Tiffany sat decorously in the gallery with the women, but conversation flagged and no one was surprised when the men joined them after fifteen minutes instead of the customary half-an-hour and when they showed no great interest in resuming their bridge.

Laura noticed that Tiffany distributed her favours equally. Scrupulously she paid attention to each of them in turn – except Rafe; they had not spoken to each other since that brief initial greeting. Neither had Rafe participated in the conversation at the dinner-table, even though he held strong views on the subjects discussed. Why then, Laura wondered, did she receive the distinct impression that they were constantly aware of each other – that Rafe was the leading male actor in the drama? Oh, do stop it, she admonished herself. Matthew said he would take care of the situation. Leave it to him.

They were late starting the second bridge session and it was after eleven when the women chivvied their partners into the Red Drawing-Room again and Tiffany approached Laura.

'Would you be offended if I went to bed early? I am so very tired.'

'Do forgive me. These interminable bridge games must be terribly boring if you don't play,' exclaimed Laura contritely.

'It isn't that. I don't play card games because I find them so . . . *unproductive*. But at the moment I really am very tired. I have not been sleeping well since . . . since it happened.'

'I am so sorry. Is there something I can do? Is there anything you need?'

Tiffany shook her head, murmured her 'good nights' and glided quietly from the room, leaving behind the overwhelming impression that the evening entertainment was over.

'Two too many for bridge,' Matthew said cheerfully to Rafe. 'Shall you and I take a decanter to the billiard room?'

'But your hand . . .?'

'Oh, it's about time I tried to use the damn thing. Got to start sometime. Let's slip away before Laura notices she is left with a preponderance of females for the fourth table.'

In the billiard room Matthew removed his hand from the sling and struggled to hold the cue. The pain was agonising but he continued to smile and joke about his clumsiness. The game proceeded at a snail's pace and whisky glasses were filled more frequently than balls were struck. After twenty minutes or thereabouts Rafe lined up his next shot, casually asked, 'Why did you want to speak to me?' and expertly struck the cue ball off the red into the centre pocket.

'Let us say it is more a case of not wanting other people to speak to *you*.'

Carefully Rafe laid down the cue, picked up his glass and walked across the room to the fireplace. He leaned one arm on the broad mantelshelf and surveyed Matthew who, in shirt-sleeves, was lounging in a chair a few feet away.

'Anyone in particular?' Rafe asked, his voice deadly quiet.

'Several people but, yes, one in particular.'

'Who?'

'Before I answer that question I would like you, out of deference to my age and present infirmity, to give me some information: are you going to marry Alice Palmer?'

'I fail to see that my marriage plans are any concern of yours.'

'As a husband and father, they are very much my concern.'

'What the hell do you mean by that remark?' Rafe's face was white with anger but Matthew merely smiled.

'Perhaps I should add "as an uncle", too. Your fraternisation, for want of a better word, with the female members of my family has gone on long enough.'

Rafe laughed. 'Exactly what I have been telling Julia for months. I wish you would use your powers of persuasion on *her*, Sir Matthew.' He produced the Faberge case and automatically offered Matthew a cigarette.

'Thank you.' Matthew smiled again as he saw the inscription. 'Well, that is good news and bad news.' When Rafe lifted an inquiring eyebrow, Matthew continued, 'Good news that you are getting married; bad news that the lady is Miss Palmer.'

'I am a guest in your house, Sir Matthew, but don't push me too far!'

'Good news,' Matthew went on, almost dreamily, 'because like most fathers in England I would not wish you to be a bachelor when my daughter reaches maturity. I concede that Julia was no bashful virgin when you took her to your bed, but I should not fancy letting you loose in the same house as Miranda in a few years' time.'

'Miranda would be perfectly safe with me – her resemblance to you is too marked to render her attractive.'

'However, as I say, I could wish that the girl of your choice was not Alice Palmer for she is unlikely to hold your attention for long. I do appreciate, of course, that her money is the lure. Quite understandable.' Matthew smiled disarmingly. 'I was a younger son, too, but I went out into the world and made money from diamonds – by the sweat of my brow, digging the stones out of the earth with my bare hands.' He stared at his hands, one large and strong, one under its bandages. 'You ought to try doing the same thing.'

'The only thing I feel like doing with my hands is punching you in the face,' said Rafe pleasantly.

Matthew ignored the remark, rose to refill his glass and stood on the other side of the fireplace. 'If you want to marry money, Tiffany Court would be the ideal match. What is more, I have the distinct impression that she would be agreeable to the idea; I noticed her making eyes at you all evening.'

'Then you noticed more than I did. You surprise me, Sir Matthew, because I would have thought it obvious that I have given my word to Alice and am not free to make promises to anyone else.'

'Oh, you haven't made an official announcement and Alice is not the sort of girl to make trouble. Your father was, if I may say so, particularly enchanted with Miss Court. As for public opinion, I will guarantee all the husbands and fathers will feel as I do – only too glad to smooth your path to the other side of the Atlantic.'

'I have been aware of your dislike of me for some years,' said Rafe carefully, 'and accordingly I was surprised by your invitation here this weekend. I do not understand why you are being so deliberately offensive, but I shall not give you the opportunity for further insults.' He bowed stiffly and started towards the door.

'One moment, Deverill – I have not answered the first question you asked. I have not named that one particular person whom I wanted to keep out of your way. It is Laura.' Matthew paused and looked levelly at Rafe, all mockery and humour gone from his eyes. '*Laura*, Deverill,' he repeated. '*Keep your hands off my wife!*'

The door slammed and Matthew sank back into his chair. 'I have done my bit, Tiffany,' he murmured, 'now the rest is up to you.'

The door to Tiffany's bedroom was slightly ajar. She had dismissed her maid and, clad in her flimsiest and most beguiling nightgown, she strained her ears to catch the sound of a footstep on the stairs. If Matthew had played his part successfully it should be any time now . . . Ah, there it was! Cautiously Tiffany peered round the door and caught a glimpse of Rafe as he climbed the next spiral of the staircase to his room on the upper floor. Matthew had been right – Rafe had come direct to his room from the billiard table, too agitated to face his fellow guests.

She sighed with relief. So far the plan was working perfectly. Matthew had said that Laura always allocated the

Tower rooms to young people and had promised to ensure that she and Rafe were placed in the same wing. All she had to do now was wait for him to descend the stairs again to the bathroom on her floor. The waiting was the worst part . . . the temptation to climb the stairs was nearly too great . . . but no, he must come to her room, not she to his – particularly if she had to implement the emergency plan.

A last look in the mirror at cascading raven hair and the beautiful body which gleamed through the almost transparent silk, but showed no sign of the baby within her . . . And then footsteps descending the stairs again, the click of the bathroom door closing . . . nearly time . . .

'Rafe, I must speak to you, please!'

He was surprised, angry and embarrassed. Dressed only in a blue silk dressing-gown and with bare feet, obviously he had not anticipated meeting anyone.

'We have nothing to say to each other,' he said coldly, 'particularly here, particularly *now*.' And he tried to walk past her to the stairs, but she blocked his path.

'*Please* – I need your help!'

That appeal made him waver, as she had known it would.

'Very well,' he agreed, 'but only for five minutes,' and he entered the room.

Tiffany closed the door and walked towards him, standing very close, but he averted his eyes from the delicious mounds of her breasts, barely covered by the nightgown, and moved a few steps away.

'Actually, I wanted to apologise.'

'*You* wanted to apologise! I didn't think you knew the word or the sentiment existed.'

'I have been so miserable since we parted on such bad terms in New York.'

'Didn't your lover take your mind off that unpleasantness? Didn't Philip make amends?'

Tiffany was disconcerted; she did not realise he had known about Philip. 'No, and for a very good reason.

256

When I reached London I realised that I had made a terrible mistake and I did not love him after all.' She paused. 'It is you I love.'

'Then that is your second mistake,' he answered coolly.

He was standing very still, hands thrust into the pockets of the blue silk robe, and Tiffany was certain he was wearing nothing underneath. Her stomach began to knot and the ache started to spread as the fire grew inside her. The plan was paramount but she desired him, too. With a jolt she admitted that she had always desired him.

'Why? Surely your feelings for me have not changed? Please tell me your feelings haven't changed!' She stood in front of him, her hands unfastening the belt of his robe, running those hands over the firmness of his naked body, caressing the tight buttocks before moving to clasp his erect penis. She heard the breath catch in his throat and thought triumphantly that she had won – he would believe the child was his and he of all people could force Randolph to allow the marriage.

'My feelings have nothing to do with it. In the high-flown phrase suitable for a melodrama such as this, "I am promised to another".' But he did not move away.

'Oh, *her*! You don't love her! Come to New York with me.'

'Strange that you should possess such an excellent grasp of business affairs and yet know so little about honour.'

'My honour is one of the things I have been looking forward to losing.' She transferred her hands to his bare back, pressing her breasts against his chest and her groin against his.

'What would Randolph have to say about that?'

'He would not be able to say anything,' she whispered, nuzzling his neck, 'if you had made love to me.'

Slowly he withdrew his hands from his pockets and wrapped his arms around her, pulling her even tighter against his body. As he kissed her, he caressed her breast, stroking her nipple until it hardened and stiffened under his touch and then he lifted her and carried her to the bed.

With his mouth welded to hers, his fingers probed the wetness between her legs, arousing her to a frenzy of longing for the magic moment when he would thrust into her. Tonight there need be no holding back, because now there were no fears or inhibitions and while Philip had been a satisfactory lover, he had never aroused her to such a pitch of desire as this.

'Now,' she whispered urgently, 'now!'

But with a superhuman effort Rafe Deverill rolled off the bed and stood up, wrapping the robe around him and tying the belt with a decisive jerk.

'I don't know what your game is, Tiffany,' he said, 'but I am not playing.'

'You cannot leave me like . . . like *this*,' she pleaded.

'You left me like *that*,' he reminded her. He stared at her, grey eyes boring into her brain. 'There is something very odd going on in this house. First, Philip disappears suddenly from the scene and I receive an unexpected invitation, only to be grossly insulted by my host. Then you arrive, to the evident surprise of everyone except Sir Matthew, and now you pretend to have undergone a change of heart.' He paused, shaking his head sardonically. 'Tiffany Court does not apologise, neither does she tell a man she loves him before he has made a similar declaration to her – Tiffany Court is too proud to do those things. You don't love me, Tiffany, you are *using* me. And I am not a man to be used.'

The sexual frustration was passing, the heat dying in the coldness of his words, to be replaced by despair. For once Tiffany had nothing to say; she had failed and could not bring herself to plead for a lost cause.

'Added to which, I will not renege on my word to Alice Palmer. She does not possess your beauty or your millions, but neither is she a calculating, unprincipled slut!'

Tiffany rose from the bed and placed herself between Rafe and the door. She had failed. She had wanted to marry him so much, but perforce must implement the emergency plan. The agony in her eyes came straight from the heart, because now nothing could save her from Randolph. Strange, she thought with peculiar detachment, how inevitably it had to end this way; how the remarks made by Gerard, by Randolph and by Rafe himself had all pointed to this inescapable conclusion. She glanced at her wristwatch: half-past midnight. And Tiffany opened her mouth and began to scream.

Matthew was taken aback when the bridge parties began yawning over their sandwiches and drinks at midnight, half an hour earlier than was customary at Brightwell. Tiffany's departure had taken the zest from the evening and this feeling had been enhanced by the absence in the billiard room of the two most attractive men.

'Where is Rafe?' Charlotte Ambleside inquired.

'Gone for a walk. I'm afraid my showing at billiards tonight was enough to drive any man out of the house in disgust,' Matthew replied easily.

The guests were drifting away to bed. Thank God it was Julia and Alfred who shared the lodgings in the West Tower and he could detain them for a while.

'Laura, I shall be upstairs shortly . . . Julia, Alfred, don't go – join your old uncle for a last nightcap.'

Julia yawned widely. 'Very flattering of you to ask, Uncle Matthew, but not tonight. I am out on my feet.'

He grinned. 'As you like but it is a pity, just as I was in the mood for hearing a list of your most deserving causes *and* for discovering whether this damn hand is capable of signing cheques!'

'Oh well, in that case I will have a whisky. So will Alfred. Sit down over there, Alfred, like a good chap . . . Now . . .'

Twenty minutes and several promises later, Matthew looked at his watch and manoeuvred the conversation to a close. Alfred was fast asleep in his chair.

'Shall we leave him there?' Matthew asked.

'Oh God, yes, he'll wander up eventually.' Julia bestowed a look of affectionate contempt on her husband

and slipped her arm through Matthew's. 'I've enjoyed our chat, Matthew.'

He smiled, knowing that Julia only called him 'Matthew' when she was feeling happy and looking on him in distinctly unavuncular terms. It was pleasant to be reassured that the charm still worked. He glanced again at his watch. Twenty-five minutes past twelve. 'I will see you to your room.'

'Good God! How extremely gallant of you. It isn't necessary, no one is in the least likely to rape me on the stairs – unfortunately!'

'I would not wish to take the risk.' Their arms still intertwined, he clasped her hand warmly. 'My mother did a poor job of my upbringing – she concentrated most of her efforts on your father who was, as we know, even stonier ground for her endeavours – but it has stuck in my mind that a gentleman always sees a lady right to her door.'

'I don't know what has got into you tonight, but it's so pleasant that I am not arguing. I know, it's that American girl. She has gone to your head – I do hope that is the only part of your anatomy she has infiltrated.'

'My dear Julia, what a shocking suggestion.' They had reached the foot of the spiral staircase and began the ascent.

'Hm. You don't fool me. If you were a few years younger . . .'

'Age has nothing to do with it,' Matthew interrupted, 'but Laura has plenty to do with it.'

'I still find it impossible to place you in the role of faithful family man.'

'If I was not your uncle, Julia, I would ensure that you found it even more difficult.' He squeezed her hand and gave her a flash of that wicked grin. 'As it is, you must find someone else to scratch that itch.'

'Bastard!' She paused a few steps from the landing and glared at him. Then she laughed. 'You always were a bastard, Matthew. I suppose that is one of the reasons I like you so much. I always fall for bastards.' Her expression changed to sadness mixed with fury, frustration and jealousy. 'But you don't top the list. The biggest bastard in England is . . .'

The scream split the air like a rifle shot and Matthew and Julia froze, glancing at each other in apparent bewilderment and shock; but when the screams persisted, he released her hand and sprinted up the remaining stairs. He flung open Tiffany's door, with Julia right behind him.

Tiffany was beating her fists on Rafe's chest. When Matthew burst into the room, she turned and threw herself into his arms, clinging to him and sobbing bitterly. Matthew tugged his bandaged hand free of the sling, tenderly placed both arms around her and hugged her protectively.

'Dear girl, tell me what happened. Did he . . .'

Tiffany nodded. 'I was in bed . . . he came into the room . . . put his hand over my mouth to stop me screaming and then . . . ' She shuddered. 'I wouldn't have come if I had known he was here,' she cried incoherently. 'He tried once before; in New York.'

Matthew patted her shoulder, but it was unnecessary for him to speak because Julia flew at Rafe like a wildcat.

'Rape!' she screamed. 'Not content with what you can get legally or willingly, you force yourself on a guest in my uncle's house! Bed – that's all you ever think about. A new body, a new way to refine your techniques. Your overweening vanity convinces you that every woman alive is crying out for your lovemaking.' A sob rose in Julia's throat at the memories of his embrace, of his touch which could turn her to fire. '*Rape*,' she spat again, 'but don't think you can get away with it. I will shout it from the rooftops. I will personally ensure that *everyone* knows!'

Yes, Julia, thought Matthew, somehow I thought you would. He squeezed Tiffany's shoulder encouragingly. 'Enough, Julia. I think Tiffany is more in need of your attention than he is.'

'We must wake the household. Everyone must know!'

'In the morning. Allow Lord and Lady Ambleside one last good night's sleep.'

Rafe had neither moved nor spoken. He saw only too clearly that denial would be futile – his word against that of the beautiful innocent girl in mourning for her father! Somehow he galvanised his frozen limbs into action and moved to the door. There he paused and stared into Matthew's blue eyes.

'You have not heard the last of me, Sir Matthew,' he said clearly, 'and although I do not understand your contribution to this night's work, I shall not forget it. *And*, as I shall not now be marrying Alice Palmer, perhaps you had best lock up your daughter!'

He leaped up the stairs to his room and slammed the door. With an oath Matthew followed and turned the key in the lock. Brandishing the key, he returned to the weeping Julia and the stony-faced Tiffany. 'I will fetch Laura,' he said.

Much later, Laura eased herself up on her pillows, checked that Matthew was fast asleep and then slid out of bed. Silently she padded across the thick carpet to the dressing-table, picked up the key, extracted something from a drawer and crept out of the room. Then she ran through the long corridors, down stairs, up stairs, to the attic room in the West Wing. With trembling fingers she inserted the key in the lock and opened the door.

Rafe was standing by the open window, fully dressed, peering into the darkness in search of footholds and handholds on the steep uncompromising walls.

'Laura – I should have known you would not desert me!'

'It's crazy. The whole thing is crazy. I know you didn't do it but . . .'

'My word against hers,' he supplied, smiling. 'I know.'

'We could wait for the "inquest" tomorrow morning. Your mother might be able to persuade Tiffany to change her story.'

'My mother made her position clear not so very long ago. She is quite prepared to hear the worst about me. My mother,' Rafe prophesied correctly, 'will disown me first thing in the morning.'

'Then you must get away, because the scandal will ruin you. Unless,' and Laura looked at him seriously, 'you appeal to Alice. She loves you very much and would still marry you, I think.'

'No.' He shook his head emphatically. 'I seem to have spent the whole day declaring my fidelity to her but you, Matthew and Tiffany were right – I don't love her and our marriage would never work. No, the kindest thing I can do for Alice is to disappear and give her the opportunity to find someone else.'

'I can let you out of the house, but how else can I help you? My dearest Rafe, you have done so much for me. Allow me, now, to help you.'

He hesitated, fighting with his pride, but then the tension eased as he gazed into her loving face. 'Money. I hate to ask, but could you let me have a little cash? Apart from a recurring shortage of funds, I cannot present myself at my bank on Monday.'

'I had thought of that.' Laura held out a bundle of banknotes.

'Thank you.' He pushed them into his pocket as the storm broke and thunder clapped overhead. 'Will you do me another favour?'

'Of course.'

Rapidly he penned a few lines on a sheet of paper. 'Send this note to Sergeant King at that address. It asks him to muster a crew and meet me at the *Corsair*.'

'And when you are aboard the boat, where will you go?' Laura could not hide her desolation.

'Anywhere. Anywhere that the winds and tides do take me.' Rafe placed his hands on her shoulders. 'But wherever I go,' he said softly, 'I shall be thinking of you.' His grip tightened and his kiss was that same sweet blend of tenderness and passion. Then, after Laura had locked the door behind them, they crept to the front porch and he disappeared into the raging storm and the awakening light of the summer dawn.

CHAPTER FOURTEEN

'Did he really force himself on you – all the way?' Randolph's expression was carefully non-committal.

'Yes.'

'Then you will marry me, of course.'

'Not necessarily, Randolph. I have no cause yet to fear that there may be . . . consequences.'

'Everyone is talking about it. We must close ranks or the business will suffer.'

Tiffany steeled herself. Once she had said that the devil himself could not devise circumstances which would make her marry Randolph, but she had reckoned without Matthew Bright. 'I will marry you, Randolph, *but* under one condition. You can keep your bank, but the diamond company is mine.'

'Agreed.'

Randolph's answer was prompt, for he had anticipated the stand she would take. Also, he was well aware of the peculiar circumstances of the alleged rape; he was sure that it was no coincidence that the attack had taken place in the house of John Court's oldest enemy, so soon after the former's suicide. Despite shrewd questioning, Randolph had never succeeded in persuading John Court to tell him more about that old feud, but quite obviously these latest tragedies were linked to it. However, he did not press Tiffany for explanations – he had got what he wanted and, for the time being anyway, was content to leave it at that.

They sailed for New York with John Court's coffin in the hold, arriving to clicking cameras and crowd hysteria. After the funeral, Tiffany travelled to Newport to prepare for her wedding. An elaborate ceremony was out of the question in the circumstances, but she was shrewd enough not to cheat her adoring public – she dressed superbly in white and posed for photographs on the terrace wearing an expression which was exactly the right blend of happiness and grief. The pictures showed Randolph smiling at her tenderly, while his right hand rested on a silver-topped cane.

That night Tiffany retired to her beautiful white bedroom, where her maid brushed the shining blue-black hair and shook out the shimmering folds of the silk nightgown. Left alone, Tiffany prowled restlessly round the room, her stomach in tight knots of apprehension, her face drawn and pale. When Randolph walked in she tensed but faced him proudly, her eyes holding a challenge. His appearance was slightly incongruous – he was wearing a dressing-gown but carrying his cane. Please, Tiffany prayed silently, please let him be quick about it.

His mouth twisted. 'Take off that nightgown!' he commanded brusquely.

She glared at him. How dare he speak to her like that! But then she interpreted his remark as impatience and, in the hope that it heralded a perfunctory performance, complied.

Randolph's dark eyes glittered as he gazed upon the perfection of that white body. It was all he had expected it to be, but equally pleasing to him was the wariness of her face. He laid down the cane and removed his dressing-gown, revealing a body as white and slim as hers but with broad strong shoulders and well-muscled arms. He grabbed hold of her, straining her against him, his mouth bruising hers and nearly asphyxiating her with the roughness of his kiss. Holding her by the arms, he gradually increased the pressure of his hands until Tiffany tore her mouth free and let out a gasp of pain.

'You are hurting me. For God's sake, let's get this over with, shall we!'

'Why, Tiffany, you surprise me! I thought you were a passionate woman.'

His hands were locked hard on her arms and Tiffany

winced. 'Your bedroom manner leaves a great deal to be desired, Randolph. I would hardly describe you as a Casanova – you don't exactly go out of your way to woo and win!'

'No,' he replied softly, 'my tastes are more nearly based on those of a contemporary of his. Did you prefer Rafe Deverill's bedroom manner, Tiffany? Describe it to me.'

'Don't be ridiculous.'

'*Tell me!*' With a swift, easy movement he tipped her over on to the bed so that she lay on her back, his hands on her upper arms pinning her down, luxuriating in the power of his physical strength over her.

'No!' Her violet eyes blazed in her white face and her body was rigid with disgust and fear. The smell of his cologne was making her feel sick. 'What are you – some sort of pervert or *voyeur* who gets a kick out of hearing about such things?'

'You could say that, I suppose.'

Suddenly he released her and she went limp with relief, crossing her arms to rub her hands against the tender flesh and scarlet marks left by his grip. She turned on to her side so that she could press her face into the silken coolness of the sheets, gratefully aware that he had moved away from her. Then she felt the searing pain as a vicious blow struck her buttocks.

Tiffany screamed and jack-knifed off the bed, turning to face him as he stood, poised, with the cane in his right hand.

'Merely a little foreplay, Tiffany. I do hope you will cooperate.'

'Foreplay! You call flagellation *foreplay*!' but she was frightened and it showed in her eyes. Tiffany saw not only the horror of this night, but of all the other nights which were to come.

'You should not have been so proud, Tiffany. You should not have made it so necessary for me to crush that wilful spirit.'

He raised the silver-topped cane again and Tiffany tried

to dodge out of reach, but the cane caught her a glancing blow and she staggered and nearly fell. He came after her again and desperately she tried to evade him and reach for the bell which would summon her maid; but just as her hand stretched out to the bell-pull the cane cracked across her knuckles. Hugging her injured hand, Tiffany shrank into a corner of the room, but she was not finished yet.

'I will divorce you! I'll charge you with assault!'

Perspiration was shining on his face and he was breathing hard, physically aroused as never before. 'Do that and you lose your diamond company. Surely the diamonds are worth the sacrifice?'

She stared at him with utter loathing, knowing he was right, that she would endure anything for the sake of the gems. 'You cannot hit me. Other people will notice the marks. I'm not some lower-class whore to be beaten so that you can satisfy your perverted cravings!'

He had known she would fight back, had wanted her to resist because then the ultimate submission would be all the more satisfying. But she was right about the marks on her body. It would never do for the maid to see them and to guess what had taken place. He would not hit her again tonight. However, he still threatened her with the cane.

'Get back on the bed.'

Silently, her eyes never leaving his face, Tiffany dragged herself to the bed, watching as Randolph dropped the cane and drew several pieces of cloth from his dressing-gown pocket.

'What are you doing?'

In answer he grabbed her right ankle, wound the cloth around it and began tying it to the foot of the bed. Momentarily Tiffany was transfixed but then she began to struggle, trying to free her ankle, to kick him with her free leg, to scratch his face and tear at his hair. Randolph was laughing, coping easily with her onslaught, catching hold of her other ankle when he had secured the first until Tiffany lay spreadeagled before him, her legs spread wide, helpless.

Randolph knelt between her legs, pinning her wrists to the bed. 'Nailed like a butterfly,' he said softly, 'just as I promised,' and then he thrust into her, so savagely that she cried out. Ecstatically he watched the emotions raging on her face – hate, fear and pain – as he savoured every second of his triumph.

Afterwards he untied her legs, lay down beside her and was soon asleep but Tiffany's eyes stayed open. For the sake of the diamonds she must live with Randolph, but how could she endure it? What could she *do*?

Any decision was taken out of her hands temporarily because the next day Tiffany miscarried Philip's child – whether or not as a result of Randolph's violence, she did not know. Passing off the miscarriage as a particularly heavy period, for a few wonderful days she was able to sink back into some kind of peace and try to allow her mind and body to heal. But with the return of her health came the return of Randolph to her room and in sheer disbelief and horror she saw that he had brought a whip.

'You are crazy,' she burst out and in a fit of fury jerked the whip out of his hand and lashed him with it. Only later did she remember that he had made no attempt to retain his hold on the weapon. Now, in her total rage, she simply hit him as hard as she could . . . until she saw his face and realised that he was enjoying it.

Randolph was a true sadist whose pleasure was in inflicting pain, not receiving it. However, with Tiffany his perversion was refined; he desired to dominate her and there were a variety of ways by which he could achieve this end. The poet Swinburne was a devotee of flagellation and described its attraction as lying in the fact that 'the floggee is the powerless victim of the furious rage of a beautiful woman'. This was not Randolph's style at all, but his devious mind had divined a variation on the theme.

Tiffany dropped the whip and buried her face in her hands, feeling utterly degraded in the knowledge that her struggle against him provided him with such perverted pleasure. She understood the bargain – that if she flogged him, he would refrain from hitting her. Tiffany was not afraid of pain, but she could not bear to contemplate the scarring and spoiling of her beautiful body. Slowly she picked up the whip and struck him, learning only gradually that Randolph's satisfaction was not in the pain she inflicted but in the self-disgust she felt when she performed these obscene rites – that the fact that she had to battle with herself on each occasion, that she detested doing it but was forced to comply, proved Randolph's dominance over her.

Three months later she was pregnant and Tiffany – who hated being a woman and dreaded babies – was happy beyond words. Not that she welcomed motherhood as such. No, she merely guessed – correctly – that Randolph would leave her alone until after the baby arrived.

'We must call him John after your father,' observed Randolph when their son was born.

'Under no circumstances will I ever call *anything* after my father, least of all my child.'

'Randolph, then, after me.'

'His name is Benjamin.'

'*Benjamin!* For God's sake, why Benjamin?'

Tiffany did not answer. She picked up the baby and held him tight, willing him to be her child and not Randolph's; transmitting to him her spirit, her beliefs and aspirations, transporting them both to a sunny quadrangle in Oxford – *never regret, never explain, never apologise.*

Part Three

GERMAN SOUTH-WEST AFRICA
1908

CHAPTER FIFTEEN

Viewed from the sea the shore appeared utterly desolate. Grey granite rocks, worn smooth and sculpted into weird abstract shapes by sandstorms, reared up in tiers of barren ridges amid the soft shifting dunes of the Namib Desert. Nowhere could a tree or living shrub or even a blade of grass be seen. A lashing wind disturbed the pitiless heat, an east wind off the land which the Hottentots call the 'soo-oop-wa', but instead of cooling the air it brought gusts of hot, stinging sand. Bleak, harsh, uncompromising ... Philip had thought Kimberley parched and hostile, but the Diamond City was an oasis compared with this – Luderitzbucht in German South-West Africa.

He leaned on the rail of the coaster which had brought him from Cape Town, his hands unsteady but not from the effects of the voyage – for more than a year he had sought oblivion in a steady obliterating stream of beer, wine and whisky. Emotional strain, alcohol, lack of appetite and the Kimberley climate had affected his health, leaving him gaunt and thin with shaking limbs and bloodshot eyes which were dull in his deeply-tanned face. He had expected to be en route for England by this time – August 1908 – but instead his father had ordered him here. Stay about two weeks, Matthew had commanded, and carry out a thorough investigation; then you can come home. Philip didn't care one way or the other ... whether he went home or stayed here or travelled elsewhere . . . since losing Tiffany he didn't care about anything.

He might have recovered faster if he had remained in familiar surroundings, with his friends and his motor cars, immersing himself in activity which Tiffany had touched

273

only briefly. In Kimberley he was bored, so he brooded and drank. He had not heard or read Tiffany's name since leaving England, for although he constantly tortured himself by imagining her life and loves, he dared not pick up a newspaper lest it reveal a reality which was worse than his wildest nightmares, and all personal letters were tossed away – unopened, unread and unanswered.

Philip had not forgotten Tiffany, neither had he forgiven Matthew for the part he was sure his father had played in the affair. Kimberley had offered no opportunity for revenge, but Luderitzbucht might be more promising. Diamonds had been found here and Matthew wanted information about the quantity and quality of the stones. In fact Matthew's agitation about the new discovery had positively pulsated from every cable and letter he had sent on the subject. As Philip stared out across the deep blue waters of the South Atlantic, he felt the first quickening of interest in fourteen months.

Ashore he was surprised at the amount of activity in the tiny settlement. The Germans were putting up substantial buildings of stone and brick – houses, shops and offices, hotels and beer-halls, a picturesque kaleidoscope of turrets and spires, high roofs and gables, timber- and iron-work, painted in charming colours which glowed against the stark backdrop of the Namib. Labourers were levelling the sandy tracks into passable roads and laying rails for horse-drawn trolleys, while the presence of the Deutsche Afrika Bank in newly-opened offices added to the air of prosperity and permanence. Luderitzbucht was a mining camp, but with typical Teutonic thoroughness the Germans were demonstrating their faith in the future of the diamond discoveries by transforming it into a neat and attractive town.

But there was a long way to go. Today it was still a desert outpost and Philip, trudging through deep heavy sand, was glad to reach the refuge of Kapps Hotel. He pushed his way into the dark mahogany bar which gleamed with polished brass and sat down at a table beneath portraits of Crown Prince Frederick William and Crown Princess Victoria, parents of the present Kaiser. He downed a beer and ordered another – one shilling and sixpence per bottle and the mineral water was nearly as expensive, but Philip was not counting the cost – not while Papa and the Company were paying. He ordered a third beer and began to feel almost human again. Glancing round the bar he saw a man watching him from the doorway and then the stranger walked briskly towards him.

'It is a pleasure to meet you, Mr Bright.' The young man sat down. 'We have been expecting you.'

'I had no idea that my movements were of such compelling interest.'

'Sir Matthew and the Diamond Company were bound to send someone to inspect our enterprise.'

Philip smiled crookedly. 'Of course. It is my father who is famous, not I. Unfortunately you share obscurity with me – I have not the remotest idea who you are.'

'Hugo Werth.' The German extended a hand which Philip shook laconically. 'I am the Bezirksamtmann – the District Officer, you would say – of Keetmanshoop but have been seconded to Luderitzbucht to control developments here. In all probability I shall be appointed the official Government representative in charge of diamond production.'

'Bully for you!'

Werth shot him a sharp glance but decided that no offence was intended. 'Are you familiar with details of the diamond discovery?'

'Oh, I have been informed of the bare facts, but I don't mind hearing the saga again.' Philip's tone was light, faintly bored, that of a man who would listen because he had nothing better to do.

'The diamonds were found by a railway worker called August Stauch. He was stationed at Grasplatz where he worked with a foreman and a staff of about one hundred Cape Coloureds, keeping the Keetmanshoop-Luderitzbucht railway-line clear of sand which encroaches from the shifting dunes. He had requested a transfer from Germany to South-West because he believed the climate would be beneficial to his asthma. Personally I would not have imagined that the dust and sandstorms of the Namib helped his health, but it certainly proved good for his pocket!'

'You sound as if you think he came specifically to look for diamonds?'

'I think it is possible. He lost no time in obtaining a prospecting licence from the Deutsche Kolonial-gesellschaft für Südwest-Afrika which holds the concessions here, and he promptly ordered his Coloured labourers to look out for diamonds. Undoubtedly they thought he was crazy – some had been in Kimberley, working the blueground so very different from this terrain – but in April this year one of them brought Stauch a small stone and when he scratched it across the glass face of his watch he found that it was a diamond.'

'But it was only in June that the news reached the outside world,' Philip commented lazily.

'Stauch played his cards perfectly, consolidating his own position before publicising the find. Diamond fever erupted in Luderitzbucht when the claim was verified and the usual riff-raff, plus some genuine prospectors, descended on the town. I was despatched from Keetmanshoop to ensure that law and order prevailed and the Secretary for the Colonies travelled out from Berlin. Soon we will place the industry on a proper footing – we are already refusing to issue further prospecting licences.'

Hugo Werth paused. He was completely puzzled by Philip's lack of real interest, wondering why the obvious questions went unasked. He had expected a vigorous cross-examination on the quantity of stones discovered, their colour, size and quality; most important, he had expected the Diamond Company representative to broach the vital matter of marketing the stones and to try to reach an agreement whereby the German diamonds would be sold through the Syndicate. Philip Bright's silence on these subjects was deafening, yet he could be no fool or his father would not have sent him.

'Of course,' Hugo said slowly, 'you are unlikely to be impressed by our infant diamond industry, having been brought up on your father's experiences in Kimberley.'

'Oh yes, my entire childhood was spent at my father's knee, listening to his fascinating stories of diamonds and derring-do.'

Hugo perceived the sarcasm but not its cause. He rose. 'Doubtless you wish to see the diggings for yourself. I shall be pleased to escort you there tomorrow.'

'Why do I need a chaperone?'

'For security reasons we do not encourage stray visitors. But also it is unwise for a man to venture into the desert alone, even though the diggings are only a few miles from the town. Till tomorrow, then.'

Next day Philip's spirits were not improved by the fact that he had to ride from Luderitzbucht to the diggings at Kolmanskop. He had overcome his childhood fear of horses, but continued to dislike riding and so was surly and taciturn during the hour-long journey. Hugo Werth tried to make polite conversation by relating the history of Luderitzbucht which had been settled by the Germans in 1883, but gave up after a while in the face of his companion's moody silence.

However, Philip's sullen expression lightened when he saw the bustle and activity of the mining camp at Kolmanskop. Originally the labourers had crawled on their hands and knees, picking up diamonds from the surface of the sand. Now they were digging for the stones, but after the sophistication of the Kimberley operation the proceedings were primitive to Philip's experienced eye. Surface sand was passed through a swinging sieve, about five feet long; the residue was poured into a circular hand-sieve and shaken under water, so that the heavier stones gravitated to the centre of the sieve and were then tipped on to a sorting table. Philip watched one table for about five minutes, during which time six diamonds aggregating two-and-a-half carats were picked out. Then he was shown the results of two days' digging – a collection of gems totalling about nine hundred carats. The stones were small but of exceptional quality, and Philip calculated that as there would be little waste in cutting, they would fetch high prices.

'Other exploration is being undertaken, I suppose?' he asked.

Hugo spread his hands in a gesture which embraced the vastness of the desert. 'The average width of the Namib is about sixty miles and it extends for approximately one thousand miles north from the Orange River into Angola. It would be strange indeed if the worthy *oberbahnmeister* chanced across the only source of diamonds in that immense expanse of desert.'

Philip nodded. 'They are alluvial diamonds, of course,' he said slowly, 'deposited here by some great river or even by the sea. I wonder where the original pipe is ... fascinating ...' He began to smile happily – *alluvial* diamonds! Of course, there was his excuse ...

Suddenly Hugo waved at one of the overseers. 'Danie! I have a message for you.'

The man approached, his eyes fixed on Philip. He was short and stocky, with thick black hair and beard, a dark deeply tanned skin, but it was those eyes which arrested attention: grey-green and glittering.

'Danie, Helena has come down from Keetmanshoop and wants to see you.'

Wrenching his gaze from Philip, the man looked sharply at Hugo. 'Is all well at the farm? No trouble with Susannah and the children, I hope?'

'No, no, nothing like that! I gathered that the matter is personal to Helena herself. Is she getting married at last?'

Danie shrugged, frowning.

'This man,' and Hugo turned to Philip, 'has the loveliest sister-in-law in the whole of South-West Africa, but she is driving the male population – who heavily outnumber the females – wild because she obstinately refuses to take a husband! By the way, let me introduce you: Philip Bright, Danie Steyn.'

278

'Yes,' said Danie slowly, 'I heard it was him.'

Still smiling at the plans which were forming in his mind, Philip held out his hand and, after a moment's hesitation, Danie touched it – but briefly, as if the contact burned.

'I knew your father in Kimberley, before you were born.'

'Ah, so you watched the great man on his path to fame and fortune! Evidently you are not so fortunate in the scramble for success on *those* diamond fields.' Philip looked pointedly at Danie's dirty, shabby clothes, making an obvious reference to the man's subservient salaried position.

'No. I left Kimberley twenty-five years ago when I was eighteen.'

'Then you were lucky, after all! The less fortunate stayed in Kimberley and were forced to pursue their acquaintance with my father.'

Danie's frown deepened and he gazed at Philip reflectively. 'Did Matthew ever mention me?'

'No. Sorry, old chap, but I've never heard of you before.'

Danie seemed to struggle with himself for a moment and then abruptly turned on his heel and walked away.

'What an odd fellow,' Philip remarked casually. 'Who is he?'

'Danie Steyn is one of the malcontent Boers who came to this country in 1902 after the South African War. He farms at Keetmanshoop but times have been hard and, knowing he needed money, I suggested he took a job here. He was a natural choice for an overseer because he lived on the Kimberley fields for thirteen years and, although only a boy at the time, acquired much useful experience.'

'Who looks after the farm in his absence?'

'His wife, Susannah.' Hugo laughed at Philip's raised eyebrows. 'You would not be so surprised if you had met Frau Steyn – she is a very tough lady! Mind you, her sister Helena is tough too – she rode with Danie on commando during the war.'

'How exceedingly unfeminine.'

But Hugo Werth just smiled.

Back at the hotel Philip sat down to write a letter. He began by giving a fairly accurate description of the diggings, the diamonds he had seen and current production.

'However,' he concluded, 'there is little chance of the fields developing into a viable industry. The few diamonds found are small and insignificant compared with the fine gems mined in Kimberley. The difficulty of the terrain, together with the expense of exploration and mining here, make further discoveries extremely unlikely. Undoubtedly German optimism is coloured by their desire to attract immigration and investment to this God-forsaken barren land.

'Most important of all, the diamonds are alluvial. Indications are that the stones are scattered thinly over the surface of the sand and that the supply will soon be exhausted.

'Kolmanskop is a freak – after all, who ever heard of diamonds in the desert? It is not a worthwhile investment and certainly poses no threat to the future of the Company.'

Philip signed the letter with a flourish, addressed it to his father and consigned it to the post-bag. If his father believed him – and there was no reason why he shouldn't – Philip had just ensured that Matthew Bright would play no part in the development of the South-West African diamond industry. But that was not all – Philip smiled as he envisaged the difficulties Matthew would face when the sparkling stream of South-West African diamonds poured on to a market which was already over-supplied.

'I came to tell you that I am leaving South-West. I am going home.'

Already disturbed by the meeting with Philip, Danie

rounded on Helena furiously. 'Do you mean to say that you would swear allegiance to the British crown? Because that is what you must do if you return to South Africa!'

'What is the difference between doing that and living here as a subject of the Kaiser?' Helena demanded.

'You can ask such a question after what you witnessed during the war? After the death of Marianna?'

'The war ended six years ago, Danie! Plans are being made to unify the four provinces and it is certain that an Afrikaner will be Prime Minister – probably it will be Louis Botha.'

'Botha! I don't trust him. It was Botha and Jan Smuts who made peace with the British.'

'They are trying to build a new South Africa in which Boer and Briton can live together in peace and harmony, without one dominating the other. It is the way forward for our country, Danie. I believe that and I believe it passionately!'

'*Our* country,' Danie repeated and his grey-green eyes glowed. 'It belongs to us, not to the British, and there is no reason why we should share it with them or anyone else!'

'Oh no, you are going to start raving about the *uitlanders* again, the Randlords who stole our gold and diamonds!' Helena closed her eyes in despair. 'You must stop living in the past! Can't you see that your old grudges are destroying you?'

'We fought that war for freedom, but Louis Botha must continue dancing to the British tune when he is Prime Minister. South Africa must be independent – and one day it will be free, because there are plenty of Afrikaners who feel as I do.'

'And there are plenty who agree with me,' Helena retorted. 'The irony is, Danie, that one of the reasons you fought that war was the unification of the Afrikaner people. At that time we were divided – half belonging in the self-governing Republics of the Transvaal and Orange Free State, while the other half lived under British rule in Natal and the Cape Colony. All you succeeded in doing was dividing our people along different lines: *hensoppers* – "handsuppers" – who realised the cause was lost, and *bittereinders* who were as fanatical as you!'

'No one would think that you and Susannah were of the same blood.'

'I know she agrees with you and I can see that you are educating your children along the same lines. That is why I cannot stay. I can't live in that atmosphere of festering hate and resentment any longer.' Helena paused, staring at him helplessly. 'You must stop living in the past,' she repeated. 'If it isn't the war or the *uitlanders*, it's Matthew Bright. You talk of nothing else.'

'I met his son today.'

Oh God, no! 'Philip Bright? *Here?*'

'Someone was bound to come to see the diamonds. I was rather hoping that it would be Matthew himself.'

Her trepidation was growing into a gnawing fear. 'Leave it alone, Danie! You tried to kill Matthew after the Siege – isn't that enough?'

'No, it is not enough – because I *failed* to kill him!'

'I know all about your grudges against him, but it is your sister's death that hurts most, isn't it! Alida died bearing Matthew's child, but it doesn't ever occur to you that she may have loved him!' Helena hesitated. 'It is possible for a Boer girl to love an Englishman,' she said softly, her brown eyes dreamy with memories.

Danie's face contorted. He could not bring himself to contemplate such a possibility, would not discuss it! 'He robbed me of the diamonds, too, by stealing my foster-father's diamond claims in Kimberley. He follows me everywhere – first to Kimberley, then to the gold mines of the Transvaal and now here. But he will not stay here – Matthew Bright must not ruin South-West Africa for me as he has ruined everything else!'

'It is *Philip* Bright who is here, not Matthew, and you have no quarrel with him.'

Danie was silent, remembering Philip's tall figure and handsome face, but the anger was rising within him again

282

at the recollection that Matthew's son had denied all knowledge of him. So trapped was Danie in his bitterness that he could not bear to think that his enemy had escaped the same fate – that Matthew was happy and free of the past.

'I told Matthew that I would carry the fight into the next generation,' he said, half to himself, 'and that is precisely what I intend to do.'

'You are mad,' Helena gasped. 'You really are mad!'

He took no notice, hardly realising that he had spoken aloud. 'You are boarding the next steamer for Cape Town?'

'Yes.'

Danie glanced round the sitting-room of the tiny house which comprised his home in Luderitzbucht. 'It is due the day after tomorrow. You can stay here while you wait; I will sleep on the sofa while you take the bed. I shall return to the mine tomorrow morning but,' and he smiled, 'I will be back before the steamer sails.'

Helena went into the bedroom and sat down on the bed. He would be back – to see Philip Bright? Oh, how weary she was of Danie and his old feuds and how she longed to be back with her brothers in the Transvaal! She must have been insane to stay in South-West for so long – come to think of it, why had she stayed? Helena rose and crossed the room to her meagre pile of possessions. Slowly she pulled out a pair of faded khaki trousers, a khaki shirt and a battered, flattened slouch hat. She fingered the garments, the conversation with Danie having aroused her memories of the war. It had begun with the *hensopper* – she had stayed with Danie because of Japie Malan.

When the Khakis came, Helena had been about her duties on the farm with her pony and rifle, tending the stock in the absence of her brothers on commando. She had crouched on a kopje and watched in dumb horror as the Khakis set light to the farmhouse and watched, too, the forlorn procession which took her mother, her sister Susannah (who was pregnant) and her sister-in-law and three children to the concentration camp. She realised that Danie and Frank, who had been visiting the farm in order to obtain food supplies for the commando, had escaped capture and resolutely Helena determined to do likewise. Knowing the approximate location of the commando base, she followed Danie and persuaded him to let her stay.

With her slim figure concealed beneath the shapeless jacket, shirt and trousers, with her long dark hair hidden under a hat, she was indistinguishable from the young boys. She could ride and shoot as well as any man, and in the months which followed she learned the ways of the veld and the ways of war.

'Guerrilla warfare', the British were calling it – where instead of fighting old-fashioned pitched battles, the commandos operated in small groups in hit-and-run attacks on enemy communications and columns. It was a life of hunger and thirst, of perpetual danger and narrow escapes, of struggling on without sleep and coaxing another mile out of weary horses. In summer conditions were easier, even though it rained, but in winter the commandos battled against dust and cruel winds, lying at night under threadbare blankets or grain-bags, shivering with cold. In the morning the blankets would be stiff and covered in a white rime of frost, while nearby pools crackled with ice. But summer or winter, too many dawns broke to the shout of '*Opsaal! Opsaal!* Khakis coming!' forcing tired men and horses on the move again.

When supplies could not be stolen from the enemy and the men wearied of biltong and mealie-meal or pumpkin and potato, the commando plundered local farms. But then Danie had raided the orchard of Japie Malan. A furious argument had erupted between them, Danie accusing the *hensopper* of cowardice and appeasement, of living safely at home while the commandos fought the enemy. Japie had shown no sign of being ashamed but stood his ground and made his reply firmly.

'I fought at the beginning of the war, for love of my

country and out of duty to my country, even though it was obvious our cause was doomed. But now you confuse courage with obstinacy. You will not admit that the bitter end *has* come and that the admission takes more courage than prolonging the futile fight.'

Malan's reply infuriated Danie, who sprang to where his horse was tethered and from under the flap of his saddle-bag pulled out a sjambok, its lethal leather thong uncoiling in a sinister ribbon on the ground. He raised the whip and with an expert flick of the wrist curled the rawhide lash across Malan's back, ripping through the man's shirt to the flesh beneath. No one else moved – not Helena, not Frank Whitney, not a commando, not even Malan; there was no attempt to hold the man or bind him, yet he did not try to run away. Helena could remember vividly the eerie silence which settled over the orchard in the heat of the midday sun, a stillness stiff with tension, broken only by the whistle of the whip as it cracked through the air to bite again into human flesh. The third stroke pushed Malan to his knees, blood pouring from gaping weals, the tatters of his shirt barely distinguishable from the tatters of skin. Twice more Danie wielded the sjambok but although Malan sagged to the ground, he resolutely dragged himself back into a kneeling position, eyes staring defiantly at the watching Boers, mouth clenched tight so that no cry of pain escaped him.

'That is what we do to cowards,' Danie had snarled. 'I would force you to come with us on commando but, like General de Wet says, we cannot chase a hare with unwilling dogs! But let me warn you, Japie Malan, that this is *nothing* compared with what we do to traitors who give active aid to the Khakis.'

Despite such incidents, the days had a charm about them; the easy camaraderie, the open air, nights round a camp-fire under the stars, with a saddle for a pillow. In a world which extended no further than the blue hills on the horizon, Helena could understand why the commandos could not bring themselves back to reality. Then the tempo quickened. Danie knew that it had been Deverill's Horse who burned the farm; he was constantly watching for Deverill and, when the commando's train-wrecking activities, their raids on British camps and blockhouses began to go awry, it became obvious that Deverill was watching them. Danie soon discovered the reason: Deverill's Horse possessed the services of a *hensopper* turned *Khaki Boer*, or National Scout, a Transvaaler who knew every kopje and fold in the landscape – and that man was Japie Malan. With the help of Frank Whitney, Danie had laid the trap to capture the two men he wanted most – the trap which led to the execution of Malan and of the Zulu, executions carried out summarily without trial.

While attention was focused on the burial parties, Helena had hurried out of the camp to find refuge on a lonely hillside where the gathering darkness cloaked her anguish and her shame.

She respected Danie, trusted in him and it shook the foundations of Helena's world to doubt him, let alone to disagree with him as violently as she did now. But Danie was wrong . . . the executions were wrong . . . or was she being a mere weak-willed woman, unworthy to serve with the commando? She tried to think it through calmly, devoid of emotion, and always she came back to the same opinion: that any man, white or black, had the right to a fair trial and that no man, even Danie Steyn, had the right to take the law into his own hands.

At that time Helena, too, had hated Japie Malan as an example of the *Khaki Boere* who were traitors to their people, but his murder – for surely that was what she had witnessed – prompted a reappraisal. Malan was a brother-Boer and the Transvaal was as much his country as that of the Steyns or Groblers – he was entitled to his point of view. And Helena had stared into the distance, into the deepening shadows of the valley and into the darkness of the future, seeing with terrible foreboding that, whatever the outcome of the war, the *Khaki Boere*, the *hensoppers* and the *bittereinders* could never live in perfect peace and brotherhood again.

What would the British officers be thinking of them? She saw again the grief of the young Lieutenant at the death of his loyal servant and winced at the memory of the expression on Deverill's face. All Danie had achieved today was to prove the arrogant British right in their belief that the Boers were uncivilised and unable to govern a country for themselves. Danie had shamed the Afrikaner people before the eyes of their enemy.

To Helena this was the most disturbing revelation of all. On that wild hillside she gained her first insight into the mind of Danie Steyn and saw that he was not quite ... normal. She began to understand that his obsession was extreme, that her hero was a dangerous and violent fanatic instead of a true Afrikaner devoted to the cause of his country. He used to quote the Bible frequently and she remembered the passage from Leviticus which he would proclaim when anyone raised the matter of how greatly the British soldiers outnumbered the Boers: 'If ye walk in my statutes and keep my commandments, ye shall chase your enemies and they shall fall before you by the sword. And five of you shall chase an hundred, and an hundred of you shall put ten thousand to flight, and your enemies shall fall before you.'

Now Helena realised that Danie had no god but the god of hate.

Even so, she might not have changed her own point of view quite so markedly but for that week with Rafe Deverill. The memories swamped her, soaked her – a series of blurred images of the veld, blackened farmhouses mocking the beauty of pink and white blossom in the orchards; cotton-frocked, sun-bonneted women and children at farms which had been reprieved, grinding mealies at handmills, kneading dough with sleeves rolled up above the elbows, roasting acorns in three-legged pots to make a coffee substitute with wheat and dried peaches. She remembered his horse, a 'toll-free' chestnut – so-called by

287

the Boers because in olden times a chestnut horse which had a white face and four white socks was allowed to pass through a toll-gate without charge.

For thirty-six hours she kept up the pretence of being a boy, but then his patience with his unwelcome guest had snapped.

'For God's sake, *say* something, even if it is only to tell me to go to hell. And look me in the face while you are saying it – I swear you even bathe in that hat, if you ever do wash which is doubtful.'

He jerked the hat off her head and Helena's hair tumbled to her shoulders. They stared at each other for a long time and it began then – that mysterious, all-pervading eroticism.

'Who are you?'

She replied, but as stiffly as a prisoner-of-war giving name, rank and number.

'Why did you join the commando?'

'It was that or the concentration camp.' She stared him straight in the face now, her features finely etched in the firelight and the resentment in her eyes no more than he expected. 'But you will send me there anyway, I suppose?'

'I will try to find some other solution,' he said quietly and stretched out a reassuring hand, but she recoiled violently. 'You are quite safe with me,' he said harshly, 'particularly until you have had a wash.'

They had lain down to sleep, stretched out several feet apart, but tired as they were oblivion eluded them. Helena had been tense, guessing at his emotions – a man enduring celibacy through the exigencies of war – waiting for him to rape her. But he had not touched her. Eventually she conceded defeat to her weariness and fell asleep.

The sensual mood persisted the next day as they continued their ride south. This part of the Transvaal was exceptionally fertile and that day it had seemed almost voluptuous in its abundance of flowers and the heavy fragrance of fruit-blossom. The gardens of the abandoned homesteads were laden with the promise of a fruitful

288

season – figs, quince, mulberries, grapes, pomegranate and prickly-pear. Clumps of oaks and weeping willows gave way to rows of blue-gums, stretches of suikerbos and thorn trees thick with fluffy yellow flowers.

To Helena the sensation was like sleeping in the saddle; only he was real and everything else was hazy and out of focus. She was aware of every movement of his body and of her own so that even the hills took on phallic shapes or the appearance of a woman's breast. During the heat of the day the feelings were bearable, controllable, but when the soft warm darkness enveloped them in its velvet folds, Rafe and Helena seemed to be cut off completely from the outside world and surely it was inevitable that he would come to her. But he did not.

When she saw that he was asleep, she had risen quietly and crept through the trees down the slope to a small stream. Leaving her clothes on the bank, she had stepped into the water to bathe, a pale sliver of moon casting so little light that she was only a dark shape against the silvery water. He was waiting when she emerged and although she started with surprise she did not run away. He had taken off his shirt and gently began rubbing it over her body to dry her. Slowly and sensuously he drew it across her back and buttocks, his hands caressing her through the thin, rapidly dampening material and then, with mounting excitement, she felt him dry her breasts – small, tip-tilted, conical breasts which had aided her disguise as a man. With a groan Rafe had dropped the shirt and clasped the ice-cold breasts in eager tender fingers, but although Helena had stood motionless while the material was between them, she fled as soon as flesh touched flesh, running like a gazelle up the hillside.

He had not touched her again and she knew that he understood. Her expressionless face had transmitted the message: 'I am here – yet I am not here. I am your prisoner in body, but my spirit is my own.' Rafe comprehended that her reluctance to make love with him was not a physical aversion to his touch or a laudable desire to retain her virginity, but a refusal to allow a British officer that ultimate conquest. He was the enemy of her people. And while Rafe was willing to woo her and persuade her to respond, he would not force her to submit. Helena Grobler remained in his mind as a symbol of the indomitable spirit of the Afrikaner women – the British were beating the Boer men in the war game but they had not conquered the women.

Helena was conscious of the symbolism, too. The British were raping her country, but this man had not raped her. She would not forget that – or him. And Rafe never knew how Helena had struggled against her feelings; never knew how much she wished Rafe was the friend of her people instead of the foe.

After the defeat of Steyn's Commando he had let her go. He was supposed to be escorting her to the Middelburg Camp but on a low hill, overlooking the sprawling tents, he had reined in the toll-free chestnut.

'Do you know where Danie would have gone after the battle?'

Helena thought of the bivouac to which she had made her way after the burning of the farm. 'Yes, but nothing you can do will make me tell you.'

'I am not asking you to tell me.' Rafe turned in the saddle and stared at her. 'Your non-arrival in the camp is unlikely to be noticed – the administration of these places is notoriously lax. If you were to ride away from here now, only I would know. And I promise not to tell.'

He untied a spare rifle from his saddle and handed it to her. 'And six bullets,' he said. 'I must trust you not to waste one on me.'

Helena took the gun and ammunition and cantered off without a word. However, after she had gone a little way she paused and turned again, raising one arm in a dignified gesture of farewell while Rafe lifted a hand in acknowledgement.

She and Danie had ended the war with Smuts in the North-West Cape and then she had accompanied him to

South-West Africa. She felt instinctively that he must be watched and that only she was in a position to understand the threat he posed – a threat which grew more ominous with each year of exile. Danie Steyn was like a rogue elephant, roaming at the edge of the herd, dangerous and unpredictable. Helena tried to suppress the nagging conviction that rogue elephants have to be shot.

CHAPTER SIXTEEN

The next morning Helena went shopping. She bought meat and fresh vegetables to make a stew, wincing at the price of food on the diamond fields, but found that she could not dismiss Philip Bright from her mind. She was drawn to Kapps Hotel, but why? Curiosity? Did Philip Bright have horns, cloven feet and a forked tail as Danie would assert? Helena only knew that she must see him and could not explain why she asked for him at the hotel.

'Mr Bright?' Her heart beat faster when she was confronted by his tall handsome figure and she quailed at her impertinence at approaching him. 'I am Helena Grobler, Danie Steyn's sister-in-law. He told me that you were here. I just wanted to . . .' Her voice trailed away. What *did* she want?

'How kind of you to call.' Philip grinned at her charmingly. She was so much more attractive than he had imagined and he was bored, waiting for the steamer in this desert outpost. 'Why don't you put down that basket? Better still, why don't I carry it for you?'

'Thank you. It's only food . . . but you could share it with me if you liked . . . if you have nothing else to do.' Helena managed a smile, drawing courage from the attention she had received from the men of Keetmanshoop.

'My day was a yawning void – until now,' Philip assured her, taking the basket.

Danie's tiny shack was only ten minutes away but the walk seemed endless as Helena tried to overcome her shyness. However, on the way Philip bought several bottles of wine and he sprawled in a kitchen chair with a glass in his hand, watching her prepare the food with every indication of enjoyment and perfectly at his ease.

She was twenty-five years old, tall and slim, her luxuriant dark hair pinned into a plain coil at the nape of her neck, her deep brown eyes velvety and lustrous. Her body had ripened, her breasts were now full and inviting, and her complexion too betrayed the passing of the years, her skin being weathered to a rich bronze and prematurely aged by the dry heat, dust and wind of South-West Africa. To Philip, she possessed an earthy quality; hers was a simple unsentimental carnality which sprang straight from the soil. He gained pleasure from watching the unhurried movements of her shapely body, of the strong brown arms and hands as they prepared the vegetables, and of the steady gaze of those fathomless but essentially honest eyes. It occurred to him that no woman had ever prepared a meal for him before – servants, yes, but not a woman . . . not like this.

But he might have dismissed his feelings as merely those of aristocrat for peasant girl if it had not been for a remark Helena made when she was talking about South-West Africa.

'I dislike this country, but there are many Germans who love it. They say that, after South-West, Europe seems claustrophobic in its softness, cloying in its lush fertility. South-West is a land of fierce extremes and contrasts, hard, bold, clearly-defined – *elemental*. Here one is close to life – and to death.'

Elemental. Yes, and so was Helena. She was the earth-mother who could bring a man to rebirth or to death. Philip's hand trembled slightly from the odd foreboding – which was it to be? He shook his head in an attempt to clear it of such nonsense, yet surely the analogy was not wholly fantastic? Surely that was motherly anxiety in her eyes as if she was trying to penetrate the sadness behind his own, and surely it was a feeling of motherly responsibility which caused her to heap his plate with generous helpings of food? Something inside him reached out to her, to be healed, to be touched by her maternal compassion in a way that Anne, Laura and Tiffany had failed to achieve.

Helena stood beside him, about to lift the coffee cup, but Philip intercepted her hand and laid it softly against his cheek. She flushed, disconcerted because she felt that she knew her limitations. In her simple cotton dress, with her sunburned skin and what she believed was a coarsening body, she bore little resemblance to the beautiful, rich and sophisticated women with whom a man like Philip would mix. It cannot be love-making he wants, she thought, not really . . . Yet he wants something, *needs* something . . .

'That was the best meal I have ever eaten.'

Her colour deepened and pain flared in her eyes as she imagined he was being sarcastic.

'I mean it.' Philip sprang to his feet and seized hold of her hands. 'Don't be upset – I really do mean it.'

'In that case you can help me with the washing-up.'

'Are you certain that you wish to entrust me with the task – I have never washed a cup or a plate in my life!'

She smiled and handed him a cloth. 'Afterwards we will go for a walk – I think you probably need to clear your head,' and she glanced meaningfully at the empty wine bottles.

Oddly Philip did not take offence at this gentle reprimand. In fact he was inclined to feel guilty about his excessive drinking, even a little ashamed. There was an integrity in Helena which enabled him to take things in the spirit in which they were meant, and he understood that her observation was not criticism but a genuine concern for his welfare.

Leaving the house, they strolled to the quiet empty spaces beyond the settlement where the giant shifting dunes encroached on to grey sandstone rock. The heat was intense, the breeze was stirring puffs of sand, but by unspoken consent Philip and Helena walked on until they were sure they could not be seen or disturbed. To the west was the Bay of Luderitz, sparkling sapphire under the cobalt sky, guarded by three islands whose rocks glared

294

white with guano, while to the east were only grey boulders, the white sand of the beach and the pale gold of the dunes. But, magically, there was a touch of green, for by some happy chance Helena wore a green dress ... leaf green, grass green, Nature's green ... fresh, fertile, earth-mother's green ... and when Philip reached out for her it seemed the most natural thing in the world.

The sand burned; it was too hot for them to undress but not too hot to deter them from lying down in its soft embrace. He unbuttoned her dress to bare her breasts, smiling at their whiteness compared with the brown of her face, throat and arms, and then burrowed beneath her skirt – no complicated underclothes, not in the heat of South-West Africa, but swift and easy access. He slid inside her and as he moved kept his eyes fixed on her face. Helena was as he had known she would be – wholesome, ripe and clean; he had never made love in the open air before, but with her it was right and good. And as he had hoped, he felt her healing touch, the generosity of her spirit. With Helena, inside Helena, Philip was close to the womb, wrapped in a protective peace and warmth which he had always sought but never found, not even in his mother, Anne. He watched with pleasure as Helena arched her back, shuddered and came; and as Philip released himself into her the thought came with him: *life or death, earth-mother, which shall it be?*

Helena was engulfed in the glow of her first orgasm, amazed by the flood of tenderness she felt for this man. At the outset she had not been aroused to any pitch of sexual desire, but had given herself to him because she sensed he needed her – needed *something* from her and that her body was its source and vessel. But when he had begun to touch her, quite unexpectedly the passion had ignited. Far from feeling humiliated or deprived of her dignity by his casual use of her, Helena was glad to have given and grateful for what she had received. But had she given as much as she had received? Anxiously she looked at him and was reassured by the deep peace and repose in his face. As she gently stroked his cheek, she knew that this was only one brief encounter in the desert, nothing more, but she would feed off the memory for ever.

In light-hearted mood Philip entered the hotel bar that evening and ordered a beer. Outside fog was rolling in from the sea as it did so many nights on this coast, rising from the cold currents in the South Atlantic and sweeping in dense clouds over the desert to dispense drops of life-giving moisture to the few succulents, insects and reptiles which survived in the harsh environment of the Namib. But in the cheerful warmth and light of the brass and mahogany bar of Kapps Hotel, the eeriness of the fog-enshrouded desert seemed far away. Helena's influence receded and the recollection of the letter he had written to Matthew returned. Philip's bonhomie increased with each beer and he conversed jovially with several strangers, but when Danie joined him he was still far from being drunk. Danie seemed fascinated by Matthew, asking all manner of questions about him, and Philip noted with some amusement that his companion was annoyed by the answers.

'Will you give him a good report of our diamonds when you return to London?' Danie inquired.

'I have written my report already,' replied Philip cheerfully.

'Already?' Danie stiffened. 'What did you tell him?'

'You don't like my father, do you?'

With an oath, Danie launched into a tirade of all the wrongs he had suffered at Matthew's hands. Philip listened with peculiar detachment because his own grievances were so intense and all-absorbing that he had little interest in other people's problems.

'I will not allow Matthew Bright to interfere in my affairs again *or* in the affairs of South-West Africa,' Danie hissed in conclusion.

'Oh, if that's all that's worrying you, old son, you can relax.' Philip was a little drunk now but *happily* drunk. 'I have made sure that Papa won't come anywhere near

South-West Africa.' And he told Danie about the letter.

Danie had been keeping a steady supply of beer at Philip's elbow, but was drinking very little himself. He was more alert than he had been for a long time as the possibilities of this situation penetrated his half-crazed mind.

'I do not believe a son would cheat his father in this way,' he said at last. 'Show me the letter.'

'I have posted it. Hold on a minute. I think I may have a copy – the rough draft I wrote first.' Philip fumbled in his pocket and produced the copy, then watched, smiling, as Danie read it – that letter was giving Philip real pleasure.

'Very well, I believe you.' Danie returned the letter and fixed his grey-green eyes on Philip's face. 'Why did you do it?'

But Philip was not ready to confide the whole story. 'He broke up a love affair of mine,' he said curtly.

It was an answer which delighted Danie. He wanted to kill Philip, because surely this was the ultimate revenge on Matthew – to take the life of the handsome son on whom doubtless Matthew doted, and who was heir to Matthew's ill-gotten fortune. But in some strange way Danie needed a sound reason for doing so and now Philip himself had supplied that reason, for Danie genuinely did not trust him to keep up the pretence over the diamond discoveries when he returned to London. The young man would soon find another girl and the grudge would be forgotten, Danie thought, but if Philip died he could never tell his father the truth.

Danie glanced out of the bar window. Dare he venture into the desert at night in the fog? It was risky, tempting fate and flirting with death, but he must try. Quickly he thought it through: most of the equipment he would need remained in his saddle-bag after the ride from Kolmanskop and the rest was easily acquired from the stables. Afterwards he could return to the mine and no one would be any the wiser. Helena might wonder why he had not returned to the house, but she would be boarding the steamer for Cape Town tomorrow. Fingering his revolver lovingly, Danie ordered another beer for his companion and waited for him to become yet more drunk.

'It's a funny thing,' said Philip unsteadily, 'but your name is sort of familiar. I've heard it somewhere before – not from Papa but from someone else.'

'Is that so? Now I wonder who that someone could be – Rafe Deverill, perhaps?'

'Do you know Deverill? Good Lord ... but no, I don't think it was him. Oh, now I remember . . .' and Philip's face tautened. 'It was Tiffany. She was talking about her mother.'

'Tiffany Court? So you have met your sister?'

'No,' Philip insisted. 'You have got it wrong. Not my sister – Tiffany.'

'But,' said Danie softly, 'Tiffany is your sister – your half-sister.'

Philip stared at him wordlessly, white-faced.

'Didn't you know? Did Matthew and John Court keep you in ignorance? But if you met, you must have known – you both have Lady Anne's eyes.'

The room was tilting and heaving and Philip, swaying in his seat, clutched at the table for support. From a very long way off he heard Danie describing how he had worked out the relationship. 'It was the name John Court ascribed to her mother – Alida, my sister's name . . . there could not have been two Alidas in John Court's life . . .'

'I think I'm going to be sick.' Philip stood up and groped his way to the door, stumbling out into the cold foggy street where he sagged to the ground, vomiting.

Danie glanced round the crowded bar. Philip's precipitate departure had passed unnoticed and although some men might recall them talking, he was not the only person with whom Philip had conversed and no one would see them leave together. He followed Philip into the deserted street where the thick fog swirled up the sandy track, cloaking them in obscurity. He eyed the hunched figure with satisfaction but distaste, ascribing his collapse merely to drunkenness. Taking the revolver from his belt, he hit Philip hard on the back of the head and dragged the unconscious body round to the back of the building before hurrying to the stables. He returned ten minutes later with two horses, several water bottles and a small bucket, some biltong, rope and a compass. Bracing himself, for Philip was by far the taller of the two, he heaved Philip over the horse's back and after mounting the second horse led the pack-animal and its burden through the empty streets, hooves muffled in the soft sand, figures blanketed in fog. Lights shone dimly from a few windows and the sound of raucous voices floated from the bars and beer-halls, but once Danie had groped his way to the outskirts of the little town all was darkness and silence. The eeriness of the drifting fog was uncanny and momentarily he hesitated, but his hatred spurred him on. He edged towards the beach, calculating that he could move south along the sand by keeping within sound of the sea before heading inland to the dunes where, after abandoning his victim, he could circle back to Kolmanskop.

Behind him Philip moaned so Danie dismounted, took the rope and bound his captive's ankles and wrists before setting off again along the beach. Now that he was clear of the town he wished the fog would lift; he found the mist claustrophobic and would have been more confident in his navigation if he could see the stars. His progress was slow but he was fortunate because the fog lifted early, allowing the sun to gild the gold and red of the dunes and light the way to the interior. Danie turned to the east, searching for a navigable route through the towering cliffs of sand. Finding a promising slope, he began the ascent, carefully checking his compass course and the position of the sun because this was the most dangerous part of the journey – here there were no landmarks and the shifting dunes constantly changed position and shape; here men who lost their bearings died.

As soon as he was over the first crest, Danie halted, pulled Philip off the horse and watched as he tried to sit up and to open dazed eyes. Deliberately Danie squatted on his haunches in front of his victim, drinking slowly and with exaggerated enjoyment from one of the water bottles. He laughed as Philip gazed longingly at the liquid, but shook his head and instead poured a measure of water into the bucket, first for one horse and then the other.

'Your father's money cannot help you now. Not all the diamonds in the world can buy water in the desert.'

The ache in Philip's head was excruciating, a white-hot searing pain which threatened to blind him with its intensity – the result of a hangover, a blow from a revolver butt and the blazing desert sun. But despite the agony, memory was returning . . . Tiffany . . . the man could be lying, but somehow Philip was certain it was true . . . and it explained so much. The mental and physical burdens he was enduring were so great that he could not fight them, could not even open his parched mouth to ask his tormentor why he was doing this to him. Anyway, Philip did not need to ask – he understood that he was Matthew Bright's son and to Danie Steyn that was enough.

Danie untied Philip's ankles, attached the rope to the pack-horse's bridle and rode on. Philip's legs and feet were numb and he stumbled continually in the deep soft sand, falling, being dragged along face-down until he managed to lurch to his feet again for a few brief steps, hands still tied behind his back. Thirst was becoming his dominant sensation, superseding even the pain in his head.

Eventually Danie halted again and for the second time went through the ritual with the water, rationing his supplies, gauging how much he and the horses required to reach safety. He dared go no further, for he must reach the diamond fields before the day wore on. Their tracks stretched back to the shore, but Danie did not consider them a threat to his plan – by the time the alarm was raised in Luderitzbucht, the wind and constant movement of the sand would have obliterated the spoor. Roughly untying Philip's hands, Danie mounted his horse and, leading the other animal which he intended to set loose nearer to Kolmanskop, rode off. Not once did he look back.

Philip was lying in an exhausted, crumpled heap, his shirt and trousers torn, his skin burned and lacerated by the sun and gritty sand. He was half-mad with thirst, desperately trying to clear his mind of this enveloping haze of pain and confusion. A long time elapsed before he opened his eyes, but then he saw to his surprise that he was not alone. A beetle emerged from the sand only inches from his face and scuttled away with a curious swimming, skimming movement. After a few minutes he noticed a lizard with a shovel-shaped snout which suddenly dived head-first into the sand. Slowly, painfully, Philip manoeuvred himself into a sitting position. Nearby the sand was disturbed again; a snake emerged, moving sideways up the slope of the dune with a side-winding, jerking motion of its looped body. Some faint, instinctive desire to live began to penetrate Philip's heat- and thirst-crazed brain. Water, he must find water! Damn it, if these creatures could survive in the desert, so could he. Staggering to his feet, he began to stumble through the sand, following the horses' spoor.

His lips were cracked and his tongue enormously swollen. Water was the driving force which urged him on, step by agonising step, towards the beach where help might be found. But his physical condition, already weakened by a year of heavy drinking, had deteriorated too much in this ordeal and he had to stop frequently, gazing despairingly at the seemingly limitless humps of red and gold dunes – desolate, empty and lonely. He was reduced to crawling on hands and knees now, his grotesque tongue hanging from his parched mouth like a ghastly lump of leather. He had no idea how far he had travelled or the distance he still must go. Water, he must find water, and somehow he dragged his failing body forwards.

But the breeze was rising, stirring the surface of the desert, gradually obliterating the spoor. Frantically Philip tried to go faster, scrabbling at the sand with sore bleeding fingers, but to no avail; there came the moment when the surface ahead was smooth and unbroken. He was lost.

So little moisture was left in him that he could not even cry. He lay for a moment on the hot sand, staring up at the pitiless sun which scorched his head and body, his brain too confused to take directions. The wind was strengthening, blowing stinging sand into his face, forcing him to close his eyes and so struggle on blindly – but he moved only in circles, choking ... choking ... The pauses between his movements grew longer until at last his outstretched hands, straining for a purchase on the sand, lay still. No images of Matthew or Tiffany entered his crazed head, only water ... *Life or death, earth-mother?* – now he knew which it was to be ...

Part Four

*SOUTHERN AFRICA
1914*

CHAPTER SEVENTEEN

Miranda loved ragtime. Her body swayed, her face glowed, her foot tapped to the insistent frenzied beat. It was an enthusiasm which her partner found puzzling. Being ten years older, he was less captivated by the syncopated rhythms and brazen brashness of American folk art and also he found the craze at odds with Miranda's quiet, withdrawn personality. The fashion for Russian culture should have been more to her taste, he felt, but while Miranda had appreciated Diaghilev's Russian ballet, particularly the movements and colourful silks of *Sheherazade*, she had remained immune to the current passion for Chaliapin and *Boris Godunov*. Yet from the moment *Hullo Ragtime!* opened at the London Hippodrome, no number of renderings of 'Alexander's Ragtime Band' or 'Waiting for the Robert E. Lee' would satisfy her.

The tapping foot was the clue. Ragtime was *loud*. Ragtime was music which Miranda could hear, or at least she could *feel* the vibrations of the beat. Ragtime was full of freshness and zest and for the first time she could participate, if only partially, in an excitement and atmosphere others took for granted. Oh yes, Miranda loved ragtime.

It was a compliment to her that people were inclined to forget her deafness and this was partly because she never looked upon it as a handicap, never expected any special treatment nor made it an excuse to avoid unwelcome responsibilities. If Miranda was invited to the opera, she went even though she could gain little enjoyment from the experience. The theatre was better – her eyes were exceptionally sharp, as if compensating for the imperfection of her ears, and she could lip-read from a considerable distance. In conversation only the faintly monotonous tone of her voice, the way she sometimes spoke too loudly and her habit of watching the speaker's face betrayed her disability. Like so many upper-class girls of her generation Miranda spoke fluent French and German, together with a smattering of Italian, but for her the struggle and the achievement had been greater. However, to boast of her success was not Miranda's style; all her efforts were made for Matthew and as long as he appreciated her endeavours she had no need for self-advertisement.

The only activity she declined was dancing. She was tall – the same height as Tiffany – and this, coupled with her inability to hear the music properly, convinced her that she would look ungainly and ridiculous. So she would only watch, calmly and with no expression of envy, as her contemporaries executed the tango, the 'Turkey Trot' and the 'Bunny Hug'. In deference to her wishes, her escort tended to take her to dinner instead and now they were sitting in the Savoy after a visit to the theatre.

'I hope those shadows under your eyes are not an indication that you are working too hard,' Dick Latimer remarked gently.

She had been close to Dick for more than a year, but it continued to surprise Miranda that Philip's friend should take such obvious interest in her. Her self-esteem had been seriously undermined by her brother's dislike and she could not imagine why this man of Philip's age, who had shared his company for so many years, should react differently. She supposed that in some way he sought her out because she was Philip's sister and so provided a link with the past – or, of course, he could be attracted by her fortune. Julia's jibe, made all those years ago, that her deafness limited her marriage prospects, was engraved indelibly on Miranda's heart and mind. Other people might disregard her handicap but never, not for one waking moment, did Miranda herself forget. It simply did not occur to her that her lovely face, tumbling tawny-gold hair and eyes of cornflower blue, her tall slim figure and charming personality could be an attraction in themselves. Her natural modesty was strengthened by the fact that her composure, her air of being complete in herself, discouraged confidences and compliments.

'I do work hard but only by choice.' Miranda spoke defensively because instead of appreciating his concern for her health, she interpreted his remark as criticism of her appearance.

Dick sighed. Just how did one get *through* to this girl! Her reserve seemed impenetrable, yet he was sure that warmth and fire trembled just beneath the surface, awaiting only some magic touch to bring them blazing into life. Whatever the mysteries and problems posed by her personality, there was no doubt that she was her father's daughter. And no one, man or woman, young or old, could be unaware of Matthew's vibrant vitality and sexuality . . .

With difficulty Dick forced himself to concentrate on the actual moment rather than his hopes and fantasies. 'Isn't it possible that you permit the diamonds to dominate you too totally,' he suggested delicately. 'Is it not time to allow something, or *someone*, else into your life?'

For 'diamonds' Dick meant 'Matthew', although he did not resent her close relationship with her father. He wanted her – physically and for her own lovely self but, yes, he wanted her fortune too, because even the heir to an ancient title had need of the wealth and power bestowed by the Diamond Company and the Syndicate. If winning her entailed sharing her with Matthew, then so be it. All he was trying to do now was hint at his interest in her future.

However, the change in Miranda was immediate. 'The diamonds *are* my life,' she replied crisply. 'I was born for the diamond business, trained to it by the best teacher in the world and I am good at it.'

'It isn't like you to admit to being good at something!'

'I only say so because it is my father's opinion, not mine. I trust his judgment and have confidence in the training he has given me. And yet there is more to it even than that . . .' She paused, trying to find the words with which to explain. 'The business world has a finite quality. It possesses clearly-defined yardsticks of success and failure against which one can measure one's own ability. It is clean and clear – and profit-and-loss accounts are much easier to understand than people! Also, in our business being a woman is not a disadvantage. Neither,' and this with studied deliberation and candour, 'is being deaf.'

It was the longest statement he had ever heard her make. Was she reminding him of her deafness because the conversation had suddenly become too personal? To Dick it was more interesting that Miranda was aware that she was better at business than at personal relationships, a theme which he might develop later.

'I am worried that you are taking on too much.' Dick hesitated, wondering if he dared voice his next thought, but decided that, as Philip's friend, he had the right. 'You cannot be expected to fulfil Philip's role as well as your own.'

'Oh, but I can. What is more, I *must* and want to do so. Someone must be ready to take over if Papa . . . retires.'

'Philip's death changed everything for you, didn't it?'

'Philip's death changed everything for a lot of people.'

'You must miss him dreadfully. I know that I do.'

Miranda hesitated, truthfulness in conflict with tact. It was true that Philip's death had made a deep and permanent impact on the family but, on a personal level, for her the loss was difficult to define. She grieved less for her brother than for her father's heir and rightful successor.

'Of course we miss him, although,' because Miranda's innate honesty could not be subdued, 'we did not see him often.'

'I don't suppose we shall ever know what happened.'

'No.'

In silence they reviewed the few known facts about Philip's disappearance – details gleaned by Anton Ellenberger who had travelled to South-West Africa, Matthew having suffered another heart attack when he heard the news.

308

'No trace of his body was ever found,' Miranda said quietly, 'although his horse returned safely and diligent searches were made of the surrounding area. There were no suspicious circumstances. The conclusion was that he went out into the desert alone and lost his way. No one survives long in that environment without water.'

'But why would he go into the desert alone?'

Miranda shook her head. 'Heaven knows. He had been drinking heavily – reports from Kimberley said the same. Perhaps he wanted to take another look at the diamond fields. Perhaps he wanted some fresh air! The general opinion was that his drunken state caused him to fall off his horse and also further reduced his chances of survival.'

'It does not sound much like Philip to me.'

'Funny you should say that. My cousin Julia became quite hysterical when she heard Anton's report. She said, "I don't care how drunk Philip was – *nothing* would make him get on a horse if he did not *have* to!"'

Mention of the report shifted Miranda's mind to other aspects of the matter. In retrospect she found it strange that Philip should have been so mistaken in his assessment of the rich German diamond fields and that his views had not been contradicted by Anton. Indeed Anton's only action after his return from South-West Africa had been to resign his position at Bright Diamonds and form his own company in Kimberley.

'I should like to visit South-West myself,' Miranda continued. 'It is too late to gather any additional information, but I feel that in some way such a gesture might help Papa. He seems to blame himself for Philip's death, yet I cannot see why because all the trouble really began the year before . . .' Miranda's voice trailed away and to her mortification her eyes filled with tears. Her memories of that time were as confused as her emotions; she felt guilty, partly because she did not grieve for her brother as she believed she should and partly because she felt she had played some part, albeit unwittingly, in those dreadful events – when she closed her eyes she could still see the tall black-robed figure of Tiffany Court and the hate blazing in that beautiful face. But there was another reason why Miranda cried today.

'I should have known that talk of Philip would upset you.' Contritely Dick took her hand.

'It isn't only Philip. My dog died yesterday.' Miranda gulped and managed a smile. 'I ought not to be sad, because Richie was fourteen and that is a good age. She was given to me by Rafe Deverill during the South African War.'

'Deverill!' Dick's face flushed angrily. 'Miranda, it is simply not done to mention that name. Even his mother forbids any reference to him.'

'I know. It all happened at Brightwell, remember? For months afterwards Papa snapped my head off if I mentioned him. "I forbid you to speak of that man in my presence" he would roar. Papa has an inordinate dislike of Captain Deverill.'

'He had good reason. But I would prefer not to discuss those reasons – they are not a suitable subject for you.'

Miranda laughed with genuine amusement. 'Don't be so stuffy and old-fashioned! I assure you there are certain circles where Rafe Deverill is discussed with great relish. I learned the gruesome details of his misdemeanour from the girls at my finishing school in Dresden when I was seventeen.'

'Good Lord, surely that scoundrel has not become some sort of schoolgirl's hero?'

'Far from it, not to me anyway,' Miranda retorted sharply. 'I detest him for causing Papa such distress – but all the same I cannot help remembering how kind he was to me and what pleasure Richie gave me over the years.'

With her family history, it was small wonder she preferred business to people! But Dick's mind went back to a phrase she had used earlier.

'You said that business is clean. Not always, surely?'

'Ours is,' Miranda asserted firmly.

After dinner Dick took her home to Park Lane,

accompanied her into the drawing-room and accepted her offer of a nightcap. Laura was staying at Brightwell and Matthew had gone down there for the night, so Dick had Miranda and the house to himself. He accepted the glass she handed to him, but did not sit down as he watched her move about the room. She was wearing a slim satin gown in a soft shade of pale old gold and over it a thigh-length tunic of matching georgette which was draped in delicate folds across her breasts. The deep oval neckline, long sleeves and flared hem of the tunic were edged with gold marabou and a narrow belt of gold velvet emphasised her slender waist. Her thick hair was swept slightly to one side, curving over her ears before being fastened into a roll at the back of her head, the luxuriant waves surmounted by a circlet of pale gold ribbon which bore a golden feather placed by the hair-parting to the right of her forehead. A single string of pearls decorated her creamy throat and diamond-and-pearl drop earrings sparkled at her ears. As she walked the sheath of her skirt swirled around her legs, providing the watcher with a tantalising hint of the beauty which lay beneath.

She had unbent to him tonight as never before, talking about herself with unusual frankness, and her comments about Rafe Deverill revealed a knowledge of affairs which proved she was no prude. Perhaps tonight was the time to try . . . perhaps this was the moment to find out if his touch could awaken her . . . After ensuring that the drawing-room door was closed, Dick set down his glass and took Miranda in his arms.

Miranda acquiesced to his kiss but did not return it with any degree of passion. His caresses were familiar to her, the days when a kiss was synonymous with a commitment being past, but then she sensed a new tension and purposefulness in his embrace. His mouth was hungrier and his arms held her more tightly than before, hands sliding over her body, trying to feel the flesh under the protective armour of her corsetry. Frustrated in these attempts by her complicated clothes but encouraged by her apparent compliance, he pulled her down on to a sofa and dared to place a hand on her ankle. Slowly he lifted her skirt, raising it higher and then higher still until he looked upon the longest, most perfectly-shaped legs he had ever seen, slim and beautiful in gold silk stockings. He felt Miranda stiffen slightly but when she uttered no protest Dick gave way to temptation and lowered his head to press his lips to the erotic patch of white thigh above the stocking top. And then suddenly he felt Miranda's hand on his hair and she was pressing his head hard against her so that briefly he was half-smothered in the soft silken skin and his head nestled in her crotch. When he kissed her again she responded so ardently that a few moments later he was murmuring breathlessly against her ear, 'Marry me, Miranda! Will you, please?'

He was disconcerted when she did not reply and raised his head so that he could look at her. 'Please!' he urged.

Miranda's eyes were half-closed, but now they blinked and their gaze cleared. 'Please what?' she asked.

She had not heard. He had spoken into her ear and she could not see his lips, so she had not heard. Dick knew a momentary qualm at the prospect of living with this for a lifetime and the responsibility and constant consideration it imposed. Was her condition hereditary? Firmly he squashed these unexpected doubts. 'Please marry me.'

A cautious, wary expression settled on her face, dispelling the desire which had been so evident a minute ago. 'I would like to think it over,' she said at last.

'How long must I wait for an answer?' He was not normally an impatient man, but instinctively felt that if this moment and this mood slipped away, he would lose her.

'Come to Brightwell for the weekend and I will give you an answer then.'

Next day in her office at Bright Diamonds, Miranda meticulously carried out her work and, as promised, considered marriage with Dick Latimer. The question of whether or not he was marrying her for her money did not enter into the deliberations because Miranda expected nothing else. What she did debate was the fact that she did not love him. However, she thought that she ought to love him and certainly should be flattered by his proposal. Dick was one of the most eligible bachelors in London, pursued by many a Mama of a debutante daughter. His lineage was impeccable, his features handsome, his intelligence undoubted and his character unblemished. Dick Latimer was perfect! But perhaps, queried a niggling demon in Miranda's mind, he was a little *too* perfect? He was a trifle dull, Miranda conceded, conforming exactly to the dictates of society with a brilliant career in the Diplomatic Service and the expectation of a safe Tory seat at the next election. However, against that she must weigh the advantages of his generosity, kindness and the certainty that he would not interfere with her career at Bright Diamonds. If she married him, she would remain Matthew Bright's daughter.

And gradually, during that day, Miranda faced and gave conscious voice to what she had always known – that it was Matthew who mattered, Matthew whom she wished to please, and that the only marriage she would contract was one he wanted. In no way had he tried to achieve this state of affairs; it was merely that Miranda loved him so much, was so proud of his magnificence and success, that she was sure she could not meet – and indeed had no wish to meet – a man who could supplant her father in her heart. She would have married anyone in the world if it brought Matthew some advantage. No, the debate was defined: Matthew approved of Dick Latimer, but would he approve of her *marriage* to Dick Latimer?

She had been staring blankly into space, her customary concentration broken by the importance of her decision, but now she turned her gaze to the parcel of diamonds on her desk. Slowly she picked up a stone and inspected it carefully, assessing its quality clinically, enjoying the confidence of knowing what was good or bad, right or wrong, in this context. She was unaffected by the beauty of the gem, she felt nothing. And there lay one of the chief differences between Tiffany and Miranda. Tiffany loved diamonds with a fierce, all-consuming passion – she and the gems were one, inseparable, immutable. Miranda loved Matthew and her interest in the diamond business was merely an extension of that intense affection – the diamonds were his obsession, not hers.

Miranda's reverie was broken by Matthew himself as he stormed into her office with a thundercloud on his brow and a letter in his hand. He was sixty-four years old, his waistline thickened and flecks of grey in his abundant hair, but there was still a spring in his step and his grasp of affairs was as incisive as ever.

'Ellenberger!' he roared, slamming down the letter on Miranda's desk. 'He's been to bloody South-West Africa again!'

Miranda grimaced and perused the letter which was written by an executive of the Diamond Company in Kimberley, reporting on Ellenberger's activities. Her father's agitation made her anxious; the diamond industry had been through turbulent times and Matthew had shouldered many burdens in recent years – too many burdens, in Miranda's opinion, for a man with a heart condition. The market had begun to weaken in 1907, forcing the Diamond Company to retrench until economic conditions improved again in 1910. Then diamonds were found in Angola – and another source of gems was the last thing the industry wanted. The Angolan mines were not yet in production, but diamonds were pouring in from the Diamond Company's South African mines, the Premier Mine and the German South-West African fields, forcing prices down relentlessly. Matthew's nightmare had come true: supply exceeded demand. Over-production was draining the resources of the Syndicate, so that its members were battling to maintain that adequate margin of liquidity which was vital to its ability to buy the entire diamond output. And only the Syndicate's purchasing power stood between the Diamond Company and a total collapse of the market.

314

As chairman, Matthew controlled the output of the Diamond Company's South African mines. Through Bright Diamonds' investment in the Premier Mine, he was exercising a delicate touch on that source, gradually coaxing the Premier into the fold of the cartel. But there remained one festering sore – the diamond production of German South-West Africa which Matthew, taking Philip's assessment at face value because of the alluvial nature of the fields, had discounted. By doing so, Matthew lost the initiative. It was his first mistake in forty years in the diamond business.

Not that he had sat back, impotently wringing his hands, when the true position was revealed. The Germans were selling their stones through their Berlin Regie to a combine in Antwerp which operated in direct competition with the London Syndicate. Over the years Matthew had made a number of attempts to instil into the Germans the necessity of maintaining prices by limiting production and now he seemed to be on the brink of success: he was finalising an agreement with the Regie whereby, in a complicated system of production quotas, their stones would be marketed through the Syndicate.

'Why would Anton go to South-West now?' Miranda queried. 'He has no part to play in the negotiations with the Regie.'

Matthew was pacing up and down, his face flushed and animated. 'It's obvious. Think, Miranda, *think!*'

It was always the same with Matthew. He refused to spoonfeed Miranda with information but forced her to think it through logically, step-by-step, for herself.

'Calm down, Papa,' she begged, 'and do *sit* down, you are becoming over-excited.' After Matthew had obediently thrown himself into the chair opposite her, she applied her brain to the problem. 'War,' she said slowly. 'It seems to be the general opinion that a European conflict is unavoidable. If we go to war with Germany, our agreement with the Regie would be worthless.'

Matthew applauded but did not prompt her.

'So the future of the South-West African diamonds will depend on who wins the war and certainly I will not contemplate any outcome but victory for *us!* One must assume that Anton, who is a naturalised British citizen, thinks the same.' Miranda paused, frowning deeply. 'Papa, he must have an alternative scheme – a way of acquiring control of the South-West fields if Germany loses the war – but I do not see how or why. Surely Anton would not dare to compete with the Company or the Syndicate?'

'Wouldn't he?' Matthew's tone left no doubt that he thought this was precisely what Ellenberger intended and also that he knew how it would be done.

Miranda knotted her brow into deeper furrows of concentration. 'He would have to buy out the rights of the German companies in the *Sperrgebiet* – the closed area. What would those rights be worth, with all the plant and equipment – £3 million?'

'Nearer to £4 million. Let's say £3½ million.'

'Where on earth would Anton lay his hands on that kind of money?' Miranda stared at her father in perplexity. 'He is a wealthy man – his company is flourishing and he has edged into the gold mines on the Reef – but apart from the initial investment he would need development capital as well. No one in London would back him because the Company and the Syndicate are too important to the financiers here and, at the moment, diamonds are a risky investment.'

'Let me give you a hint. You spoke to Anton during his last visit to Europe – where did he say he was going when he left London?'

'New York.' Miranda's eyes widened. '*New York!* Of course! Tiffany Court.'

'And, equally important, *Randolph* Court – head of the Court Bank and one of the shrewdest and wealthiest financiers in the United States. *Now*, do you still think Anton Ellenberger, with partners like the Courts, could not take on the Diamond Company?'

Matthew paused as he reflected grimly on his other

nightmare – that one day someone would try to topple the King of Diamonds from his throne. All his life Matthew had believed that the only salvation for the industry was the existence of one powerful man who could turn the tap of that sparkling stream on or off as market conditions dictated. He had achieved that position, but could he retain it? He was uncomfortably aware that a combination of Anton Ellenberger, Randolph Court and the South-West African diamonds could be sufficiently powerful to make a bid for control of the industry.

At this stage Miranda did not fully comprehend the threat. She was thinking purely in terms of diamond production.

'We must do something! Can we offer the Regie a better deal?'

'What we must do is perfectly clear. We must repeat my strategy with the Premier – Bright Diamonds must buy an interest in the South-West African fields in order to enable me to control the company from the inside and eventually bring it into line with the Diamond Company. Whether we can offer a *better* deal than Ellenberger remains to be seen.'

'We cannot make any outright overtures at present because war remains only a possibility – albeit a *distinct* possibility,' Miranda remarked. 'You will have to continue the negotiations with the Regie in the meantime.'

Matthew nodded. 'Yes, but I am *not* intending to miss out on South-West Africa for a second time! I cannot ask questions in Berlin, but I *can* try to find out what Ellenberger has been doing in South-West – to ascertain just what his position is and what kind of offer he is likely to make. You see,' and he paused again, 'I do not have unlimited finance at present. As you are aware, the responsibilities of the Syndicate have eaten deep into my reserves. I have to strike a balance between the importance of acquiring an interest in the South-West African fields while not over-committing myself. So,' and he stood up, 'that is why I shall be leaving for southern Africa next week.'

'No!' Miranda rose also. 'You are not well enough. I will go.'

'You will do no such thing!' They stood, glaring at each other across the desk.

'Why not? Because I'm a woman?'

'That is partly the reason.'

'Really, Papa, I expected better of you than that! You force me to remind you that you would have sent Philip had he been alive and therefore you must send me!'

Matthew winced and cast around for another argument. 'War could break out. This is no time for a young girl to be cavorting about the world, particularly as the job entails visiting German territory.'

'As I intend to leave immediately, it is extremely unlikely that war would be declared before I reach the Cape. But as you have brought it up, let us develop that contingency to its logical conclusion – war happens to be another reason why you must stay in London. You *are* the diamond industry and you represent a fair slice of the gold industry too. You would be needed here.'

'We would close down the diamond mines in the event of war. I shall go and that is final.'

'*I* will go. Afterwards, depending on the reception I receive in Luderitzbucht and the information I can gather, I may visit Anton in Kimberley.'

'Do you believe that the Germans will deal with a woman?'

'Are you trying to tell me that I am not sufficiently competent to handle it?' Miranda asked furiously.

'No, of course not,' Matthew assured her hastily, then his face hardened. 'Anyway, my question was purely rhetorical because *you are not going!*'

But in Miranda Matthew had met his match. She refused to give way and on Saturday, at Brightwell, there was a development which doubled her determination – she received a letter from Anton Ellenberger, announcing that he had been elected Mayor of Kimberley and inviting her to visit the city in order to participate in the civic

318

celebrations. The main social functions were planned for the beginning of June, giving her just enough time to sail to Cape Town and pay a swift visit to Luderitzbucht before travelling to Kimberley. The timing was absolutely perfect and Miranda was so delighted that she failed to detect the coincidence of Anton issuing the invitation at the precise moment when he must have known that both he and the South-West African diamond fields were very much on her mind.

Stubbornly Matthew continued to resist and was supported vigorously by Dick Latimer, who was utterly appalled at the prospect. At the outset Laura remained neutral, listening carefully to the opposing viewpoints. She had never regained the intimacy enjoyed when Miranda was a little girl, but the slight distance between them enabled her to take a more objective view of her stepdaughter, without the sentiment and fierce love which characterised Matthew's relationship with her. She understood the burden which had been imposed on Miranda – the strain of striving constantly for perfection, to be worthy of the father she adored – a burden made heavier during her youth by her handicap and increased in later years by the death of Philip. She realised that Miranda's hearing difficulties only served to drive the girl harder and faster, forcing her to prove that she was as competent as, indeed more competent than, people with perfect hearing. And, most of all, Laura comprehended that Miranda's emotional dependence on Matthew must be loosened.

'You must let her go.'

'Never! Damn it, Laura, I expected you to support me in this. What is it – jealousy, I suppose? You are jealous of my love for her and would prefer her to face the difficulties. You are jealous because the family trust arrangements give her some advantage over *your* children!'

Bright Diamonds was wholly-owned by the Bright family and, in turn, it held the largest shareholding in the Diamond Company – thirty per cent – as well as being an

319

important partner in the Syndicate. The terms of the family trust were intended to ensure that there was no possibility of an intrusion into Bright Diamonds by outside shareholders and that the Bright family maintained its influence in the Diamond Company.

Originally, the terms of the trust had allowed for each of Matthew's six children to receive equal shares in Bright Diamonds in the event of his death. However, although the childrens' financial position was the same, the voting rights of those shares were not inherited automatically. Matthew had stipulated that the firm's voting rights in his holdings were vested in the eldest child and that the eldest child had first option to buy out the shares of any sibling who wished to sell. On reaching the age of twenty-five, any of the younger children could make a challenge for power, but Matthew had ensured that any in-fighting was carried on within the confines of Bright Diamonds and that the family influence in the industry as a whole, through that thirty-per-cent shareholding in the Diamond Company, would remain intact.

It was the old system of primogeniture at work, ensuring that the family's wealth and power was perpetuated – but Matthew was forced to adapt it to allow continuation through the female line. Philip's death had been a mortal blow, not only to a father but to the founder of a dynasty. After careful deliberation Matthew had concluded that Miranda was his best hope to continue the family tradition – even if she was only a 'stop-gap' measure because he would prefer the name of Bright to remain in the forefront. It so happened that she was his favourite child, but he was influenced by more important considerations – at the time of Philip's death, Matthew was fifty-eight years old, with a weak heart, and Laura's eldest son was only seven. He dared not wait for that son to reach adulthood, but must groom Miranda as his successor. To help her he had transferred Philip's shares to her *in toto*, instead of dividing them into five equal lots. This gave her a decided advantage over her half-brothers and sisters, but it was done to increase her prestige and bargaining power in the industry *and* to create a highly desirable heiress who, although deaf, would experience no difficulty in finding a husband to assist her in fighting the battles which would rage after Matthew's death.

It had been the only move he could make, but Matthew felt guilty when he faced Laura and what he believed were her silent allegations of favouritism towards her predecessor's children.

Laura was staring at him steadily now with an almost amused contempt in her emerald eyes.

Matthew sighed and put his arms around her. 'No, it isn't that – you of all people would never react in that fashion. I know – you would do anything rather than have *me* go to South-West.'

'It would be suicide for you to go,' Laura replied calmly. 'You were very ill after Philip's death and no amount of protestations on your part will alter the doctor's verdict that you suffered a serious heart attack. Also, Miranda is quite right: you will be needed here.'

'Then I will send someone else – a young, healthy man from the office.'

'Miranda will say, and I agree with her, that young healthy men may be needed to fight for their country, not for the diamond industry. Anyway, the most important point is that it will do her the world of good to get away for a while – on her own.'

Deliberately Matthew was ignoring the implications. 'Miranda cannot achieve anything by going. The Germans will not take it, for a start.'

'She has the advantage of speaking perfect German,' Laura reminded him patiently.

'She cannot handle Ellenberger.'

'On the contrary, Miranda's influence with Anton Ellenberger is likely to be far greater than yours.'

Matthew's face turned purple and he spluttered incoherently at this outrage.

'Anton has paid attention to Miranda since she was a

little girl,' Laura continued imperturbably, 'and he seeks her out every time he comes to London. He is thirty-seven years old, wealthy and unmarried. Miranda is an extremely attractive heiress. I would say those facts are sufficient to establish that she is likely to make more headway with him than you are.'

'That is the most disgusting idea I have ever heard! You seem to be suggesting that Miranda should use her sex appeal to sway Ellenberger's judgment!'

'Of course, you never did anything like that,' Laura observed drily.

'Certainly not,' Matthew said virtuously, conveniently forgetting at least one episode on his climb to fame and fortune.

'Hm.' Laura was not deceived but effected what she deemed a fair compromise. 'There were very few women of consequence in Kimberley in the early days, so you did not have much scope.'

'It may be necessary for Miranda to use her charm from time to time,' Matthew averred, 'but not on Ellenberger. There is too much of the tradesman in him.'

'You are being rather unfair. Anton is astute, honest and likeable and his ambition carries him beyond the confines of mere trading.' Laura smiled and passed her hand caressingly over Matthew's thick hair. 'But he is not in the same class as you. He is a merchant while you are a merchant prince.'

Mollified, Matthew smiled back but only briefly. 'On the surface this affair appears a case for delicate negotiation, but it could degenerate into dirty dealing. I don't want Miranda hurt.'

'Matthew, understandably you are blind to some of your daughter's faults and virtues. Under that sweet exterior, Miranda is solid steel. She is not yet aware of her beauty and power, but when she awakes it is the Ellenbergers of this world who will deserve your sympathy, not her.'

'I don't see why she cannot stay at home and marry a man like Dick Latimer,' said Matthew fretfully.

'He wants to marry her but . . .' Laura did not complete the sentence. Again she was aware of her old fears – fears that Miranda would not find a lover who could outshine Matthew. Assuredly Dick Latimer, suitable though he might be, was not such a man. On the other hand, Laura fervently hoped that Miranda's exaggerated sense of duty to Matthew would not impel her into a marriage with Anton Ellenberger, contracted for business expediency!

Not even to Laura could Matthew voice the real reason for his opposition: that if Miranda went away, he would lose her – to the diamonds, to Africa, to another man . . . He played his trump card which he felt no one could refute. 'I am afraid she will come to some harm. I will not sacrifice another child for the diamonds of South-West Africa.' It was a cry of anguish for the daughter he loved and of guilt for the reparations to Philip which had been thwarted by death.

Laura's heart ached for him but she did not weaken. 'Miranda is a person, not a possession. You are thinking of *your* sacrifice and your pain, not hers. *You must let her go!*'

And now it was Matthew's turn to feel the wings of memory brushing his face. He was back in the library at Park Lane, saying to John Court, 'When the time comes for me to let her go, I pray I will remember what I am telling you today.'

With a groan Matthew buried his face in his hands and conceded defeat.

Accompanied only by her maid, Miranda boarded the next mailship for Cape Town. Matthew, Laura and Dick – who had been told he must wait for an answer to his proposal – came to see her off, but of course it was Matthew who experienced the most anguish. Looking at the eager expectancy on his daughter's face, he was inexorably assailed by memories of his own departure for the Cape forty-four years ago on the first stage of his journey to fame and fortune. He knew only too well how the diamonds could impose their will on people, how the ways of the

323

diamond world could change a personality, and he knew too how easily Miranda could slip from his influence. Yet, as he watched the ship sail, in his heart he could not deny her the opportunities and experiences he had grasped for himself.

The fourteen-day voyage aboard the Union Castle liner was irksome to Miranda, who was impatient to start on the next vital part of her mission. But even after so short an absence from her father, the girl who disembarked at Table Bay into lashing rain and a strong nor'-wester was not quite the same dutiful daughter who had left South-ampton. For the first time in her life Miranda was out in the world on her own and, despite her love for her father, she was conscious of a wonderful freedom of movement and expression. No longer need she glance constantly over her shoulder to assess his opinion or reaction to everything she said or did; Matthew was six thousand miles away, becoming more remote with every day which passed. Growing in self-confidence, stretching, flexing physical and mental muscle, Miranda felt capable of achieving any goal.

But disappointment was waiting. When the Diamond Company representative escorted her to the Mount Nelson Hotel, he informed Miranda that the next coastal steamer for South-West African ports would leave Cape Town ten days from now and, despite extensive inquiries, no other vessel had been found to take her to Luderitzbucht.

In disbelief Miranda gestured towards the harbour, which was packed with all manner of craft from tiny fishing vessels and pleasure boats to whalers, fine yachts and schooners, up to the largest category of all – the cargo ships. 'If I wait for ten days I will be late for Mr Ellenberger's functions and there are very important reasons why I do not wish to offend him. *Surely* there must be another boat I can charter!'

The man looked uncomfortable. 'There are a few trading vessels which sail up that coast, but I do assure you that they are dirty and uncomfortable and totally unsuitable for a lady such as yourself, Miss Bright.'

Miranda wondered how hard the man had tried and that thought led her to query the instructions which the Diamond Company had received from Matthew. Well, to hell with them! She was not a little deaf girl in need of paternalism and protection – she was Matthew Bright's daughter and she would bloody well prove it! Miranda was unaccustomed to using guile but it was astonishing how easily she discovered the knack, as though it had been lurking in her nature all along, together with certain of Matthew's other characteristics. She smiled innocently.

'I cannot pretend that I am anything other than extremely disappointed, but Mr Ellenberger will have made arrangements and I cannot possibly let him down.'

The Diamond Company representative positively slumped with relief.

'I will spend the time in Cape Town. I have friends here,' Miranda lied shamelessly, 'and will have plenty to do.'

When he had gone Miranda's expression changed from artlessness to determination. With luck her act had been sufficiently convincing to allay the suspicions of the Diamond Company while she made alternative arrangements.

She dressed for dinner in the same golden gown she had worn on the evening Dick Latimer proposed. As befitted her position she possessed an extensive wardrobe, but was not greatly interested in clothes and tended to dress demurely because she wished to avoid drawing attention to herself. However, like any woman she had made impulsive purchases which were later regretted and, in Miranda's case, never worn. Glancing in the closet in the bedroom of her hotel suite, she noticed that some of these 'mistakes' had been packed by her maid, presumably in the hope that one day Miranda would find the courage to put them on. Not tonight, however. It was enough of an ordeal for her to walk into the dining-room of the Mount Nelson and sit down at her single table. She was aware that people were staring at her but imagined they were pitying her – a young woman, dining alone – for she was too conscious of the flaw of her deafness to realise how her beauty drew all eyes.

Hesitantly, because she was unaccustomed to dining alone in public, Miranda ordered her meal. She sipped the wine, wishing fervently that she had obeyed her instincts and taken dinner in her suite, but knowing that she must emerge from her shell and speak to strangers if she was to find a solution to her present predicament. She raised her eyes and glanced round the room. The tables were full and the clientele comprised well-dressed sophisticates instead of the slightly inferior 'colonials' as she had expected. Nearby sat a group of men wearing immaculate dinner jackets. Briefly Miranda pondered on their bachelor status and decided that, entertainment in Cape Town being limited compared with London, they were dining together before an evening of cards.

Then she noticed that one of these men was staring at her fixedly. And Miranda froze as she gazed at the lean suntanned face and cold grey eyes of Rafe Deverill.

CHAPTER EIGHTEEN

Rafe walked across. 'May I join you?'

Miranda was too stunned to protest and besides she did not wish to make a scene in public. She nodded speechlessly and he drew up a chair.

'What are you doing here?' she managed to say at last.

'I live in Cape Town.'

'But . . . *here*!' and Miranda indicated the sedate grandeur of the dining-room at the Mount Nelson Hotel.

'Ah, you mean that I appear to be moving in polite circles in spite of . . . everything. It so happens that not everyone in South Africa is influenced by London opinion, but it may comfort you to know that I am not received by the upper echelons.'

'Your circumstances do not affect me one way or the other, Captain. I take no comfort in that information, but neither do I feel any sympathy for you.'

Rafe laughed. 'Sympathy! Good God, you surely do not imagine that I feel deprived by exclusion from the Governor-General's garden parties!' He looked at her, wondering how much she knew, wondering how much London remembered and whether society gossiped about him still. 'There are some of my acquaintances in South Africa who do not believe the stories spread about me,' he said slowly, 'but I am sure *you* believe every word. Or, of course, it could be that young ladies are sheltered from the unpleasant realities of life and you have no knowledge of my history.'

'You may rest assured, Captain, that your misdemeanours have been well-publicised and much discussed. Also, girls today are not so sheltered in the way you suggest – times have changed since you were young.'

His mouth tightened, but whether one or both barbs had struck home she could not tell. 'This may be a very stupid question but I shall risk it – why do you believe what they say about me, Miranda?'

Miranda hesitated, her eyes fixed on his face which, although deeply suntanned and a little lined, seemed virtually unchanged. She remembered how he had passed in and out of her life when she was a child, sometimes with Laura, sometimes with Julia but never, she realised with a sudden jolt of surprise, with Matthew. She had no quarrel with Rafe Deverill. He had always been kind, always courteous and thoughtful, treating her with a blend of gravity and humour which she had appreciated. Most important, he had given her the dog.

'Richie died,' she said.

He had been studying her with equal intensity and at these words his expression flickered, softened, but then hardened again almost immediately. He did not let her off the hook, but unyieldingly waited for an answer.

The only occasion on which she had seen Matthew and Rafe together was at Brightwell during that ghastly weekend. Not enlightened at the time about what had happened, the occasion had been imprinted indelibly on Miranda's mind because, being a sensitive child, she had been greatly affected by the force of adult emotions which buffeted the house. She had no quarrel with Rafe, but Matthew did and suddenly she was sure that whatever ill-feeling there was between them had started before that weekend.

'I believe it because my father said so.'

'And you always believe what your father says!'

'He has never lied to me. I don't believe he has ever lied to anyone!'

Rafe's eyebrows rose sardonically but at that moment a waiter appeared to replenish her wine-glass and hovered, obviously expecting instructions to pour a drink for Rafe. Manners cost nothing, Miranda thought and nodded.

'Thank you.' Rafe lifted the glass in salute. 'Welcome to Cape Town, Miranda.'

'I am surprised that you recognised me.'

'You are Matthew Bright's daughter and no one could mistake you for anything else. His likeness is stamped on your every feature.'

'I take that as a compliment, Captain, though I doubt you intended it as one.'

Rafe smiled. 'Is your character also moulded on his lines?'

'I hope so.'

'Matthew in female form. What a fascinating combination!'

It was one of those occasions when Miranda wished desperately that she could hear and so interpret his tone and inflections but as usual, lip-reading, she could only take his words at face value and try to gauge his meaning from his eyes. With Rafe Deverill this proved impossible. She did not reply.

'You asked me what I was doing here,' Rafe continued, 'and I ought to return the compliment. However, as you are a diamond heiress, the question is superfluous. Diamonds are bound to be the reason.'

'I was on my way to Luderitzbucht, but no ship is available to take me there.' Miranda paused, hating to ask him a favour but swiftly deciding that pride took second place to expediency in an emergency. 'I don't suppose you know of anyone who would provide me with a passage?'

'I'll take you there myself,' he said casually.

'That is out of the question! I could not possibly go with you!'

Rafe shrugged. 'Take it or leave it. The offer is there and I doubt you will obtain another.'

'Do you have your own boat?'

'I still sail my old schooner, the *Corsair*.'

'Do you sail for business or pleasure?'

'Business, of course. I have a living to make.'

'In what commodities do you trade?'

He smiled. 'Oh, a little bit of this and a little bit of that,' he replied enigmatically.

'How long would it take to reach Luderitzbucht?'

'Depends on the weather. It is winter and we would be beating into a north-west gale. I would estimate four days there and three days back, but I should warn you that the *Corsair* will pitch like hell in those waters, so you could be very seasick.'

'That is not the reason why I cannot go.'

'No, of course not. First of all, Daddy wouldn't like it. Well, Daddy wouldn't have to find out if you didn't tell him, because I do assure you that the secret would be safe with me. But the second reason is that you believe there are other things which would not be safe with me!' He grinned at her and rose to his feet. 'Think it over. I will send my mate, Sergeant King, to see you tomorrow – if you decide to come, be ready for him at ten in the evening. You have nearly twenty-four hours to balance the importance of your reputation against that of your mission.'

Miranda lay awake. Obviously acceptance of Rafe's offer was utterly impossible . . . and yet the arithmetic throbbed ceaselessly in her head. Four days there and three days back plus, say, two days in Luderitzbucht – nine days, allowing ample time to catch her scheduled train to Kimberley. It was essential to learn more about the attitude of the South-West African producers before she met Anton, for she could not walk into Kimberley 'cold'.

But Rafe was right: Matthew would have a blue fit if he heard about her enterprise. On the other hand she could cover her tracks carefully and be back in Cape Town before the news reached him. No, it was the risk to her reputation which constituted the real obstacle.

Perhaps she could locate another captain of another ship. But what sort of man was she likely to find – a shady skipper, as interested in her fortune as her virginity?

As the hours ticked slowly by, that sense of freedom she had experienced when she arrived in the Cape was replaced by the most empty, aching loneliness. There was no one with whom she could discuss her dilemma – she was completely alone. She longed for Matthew, for the love, protection and guidance he had always provided in such abundance, yet it was for his sake that she must take the risk. Besides, in her heart she did not believe that Rafe Deverill would do *that* to her. What's more, her problem with Rafe arose because she was a woman and therefore it must not be allowed to stand in her way.

In the grey dawn the scales tipped in favour of the importance of her mission.

During the morning she wrote a letter to Matthew announcing her safe arrival and informing him that unfortunately she had literally 'missed the boat' for South-West Africa. 'However,' she continued, 'I met some charming people on the voyage out who have offered to show me the sights and I may spend a few days with them in Constantia.'

She decided it was politic to take her maid into her confidence. The girl was loyal and could be trusted to guard the secret and throw inquisitive Diamond Company representatives off the scent. Together they packed a bag with a selection of serviceable clothes for the voyage and several smart dresses with which to impress the Germans. Miranda lodged her jewels in the hotel safe and then there was nothing she could do but wait, an uncomfortable period during which she was disconcerted to find that she dwelled more on Rafe Deverill than on her forthcoming meetings with the Germans in Luderitzbucht.

Miranda was ready in the foyer when Rafe's crewman, King, walked into the hotel. He did not inquire at the reception desk but walked straight up to her, evidently primed about the delicacy of her position and provided with a description of her appearance. She would have liked to use the journey in the hansom to find out more about Rafe and his life during the past six years, but was unable to do so because in the darkness of the cab she could not carry on a conversation. They travelled to the harbour in total silence and Miranda, straining to see where they were going, noticed that the cab was veering away from the quay where she had disembarked from the mailship. Alighting from the cab, she found herself on a wooden jetty. Behind her the massive bulk of Table Mountain with its cloth of cloud was faintly illumined by the glow of the city lights, while around her was a bobbing forest of masts for this was a corner of the old world of sail, in stark contrast to the new Victoria Basin alongside.

The wind had abated but nonetheless the water was choppy, the reflections of the harbour lights dancing crazily on its surface. As King helped her down into the dinghy which would take them to the *Corsair*'s moorings, Miranda became acutely aware of the chance she was taking. The little boat rocked alarmingly as he cast off the painter and Miranda, clinging to the sides, discovered that there was a great deal of difference between a small craft and an ocean liner. The old family stories about the Harcourt-Brights' fear of water no longer seemed so ridiculous. However, it was not fear which caused her discomfort but the unwelcome realisation that she had only just stepped off dry land and already was feeling most unwell. On the voyage out she had felt queasy once or twice, but had never been seasick. Now the unfamiliar and more violent motion of the dinghy made her distinctly nauseous.

At last the dark shape of the schooner loomed up out of the blackness and shakily Miranda clambered aboard. Clinging to a stay to help her balance on the deck, her first impression was one of surprise at its small size.

'The captain's below,' King informed her and preceded her into the doghouse and down the companionway to the saloon where Rafe was bending over a small table. He turned as she entered and they stared at each other in silence.

Miranda had been taken by surprise the previous evening, too bewildered to notice details of his personal appearance, and now she looked at him for the first time with a woman's eyes. She saw a tall man in his mid-thirties, very slim, the muscled hardness of his body accentuated by tight, hip-hugging trousers tucked into knee-length boots. His white open-necked shirt contrasted with the deep bronze of his face, neck and chest, but while Miranda appreciated the undeniable attraction of his face and figure, she also noticed that although his lips curved in welcome the smile did not reach his eyes. He was the man who had raped Tiffany Court, but in addition he was a man who had a quarrel with *her* father. Suddenly Miranda realised that she had overlooked one important factor – she had been so busy working out her response to his unexpected offer of a passage on the *Corsair* that she had omitted to ask herself why he had issued the invitation.

Yet, perversely, she also found herself wishing desperately that she had not put on her oldest skirt and coat and that her hair was not so hopelessly disarranged by the Cape Town winter weather. 'Are you surprised that I came?' she asked in a more aggressive tone than usual.

'Not in the least. I had no doubt whatsoever that you would put your business interests before everything else – diamond heiresses always do.'

'In that case I expect a cabin has been prepared for me,' Miranda said stiffly. 'We must come to an arrangement regarding the cost of my journey.'

'That will not be necessary.'

'I would prefer to pay my way.'

'In other words, you do not wish to be in my debt! Let's discuss it later, shall we? After all, money is no object to you and I am unlikely to overcharge for my services – *fleecing* young ladies is not what I am famous for!'

'Why did you offer to help me?'

'Still afraid that I might have designs on your virtue? Here, the key to your cabin.' He picked up a key from the table and held it out to her. 'It is yours and yours alone – protection against me and my rascally crew! By the way, you look a trifle pale. Did you have something to eat before you left the hotel?'

333

Miranda's stomach had not settled after the dinghy trip and nausea was nipping at her throat. However, the uncertain state of her health was not bad enough to prevent her noticing his neat evasion of her own question.

'I ate dinner. Why do you ask?'

'It is better to be seasick on a full stomach. Now, I have work to do so allow me to conduct you to your cabin, ma'am.' He picked up her valise, preceded her aft along a short corridor and threw open a door. 'Here you are! I doubt that the accommodation meets your usual high standards, but perhaps in the circumstances you will make allowances.'

'Captain Deverill, when my father first went to Kimberley he lived in a *tent*!' Miranda snapped. 'He slept on a rough mattress and suffered every kind of discomfort from rain, cold and flood to dust, heat and flies! This cabin has a bed, or bunk or whatever you call it, and I am not in the least dismayed by the absence of silken hangings or luxurious carpets!'

His expression changed subtly and he seemed to look at her more thoughtfully. 'As it happens, I doubt that the décor will matter very much,' he murmured after a moment's pause. 'Please remember, Miranda, that this really is the only key to this cabin.' He placed her bag on the bunk and left, closing the door behind him.

Miranda glanced round the tiny cabin. The sleeping berth, on the port side beneath a stern window, looked snug with its thick mattress and stout bunkboard which was hinged at the bottom so that it could be raised at night. There was a settee on the starboard side with lockers forming the back-rest, two hanging lockers beside the door and a small basin on gimbals let into the top of the table. A lantern, suspended from a hook in the cabin roof, swayed to the gentle motion of the boat. The fitments were spartan and Miranda's chief impression was one of extreme simplicity and shabbiness. Varnish had worn away on the hand-rails, the porcelain basin was chipped and the curtain was frayed. Whatever trading Rafe

Deverill was doing, it did not appear to be very profitable.

She unpacked her modest selection of clothes, stowed them in the lockers and then became aware that the boat was under way. Miranda looked at her nightgown and at the door, picked up the key and turned it firmly in the lock. Then she undressed and climbed into bed.

The squeamish sensation in her stomach was making her feel cold and lethargic. Shivering, she lay back in the bunk and tried to rest, but found herself watching the swinging lantern. Ever since the Siege of Kimberley Miranda had been afraid of the dark and therefore she had kept the lantern lit. At first its motion was soothing, but then the *Corsair* reached the open sea beyond the breakwater and began to dip and pitch. The lantern swung more violently, accentuating the movement of the boat . . . up and down . . . up and down . . . Miranda was hypnotised by the lantern and then her stomach heaved. Scrambling hurriedly out of the bunk, she vomited into the basin, sagging back weakly on to the bed as the pitching and rolling of the vessel threatened to fling her off balance. Again and again she vomited. Twice she managed to fall into an exhausted doze on top of the bunk, but frequent changes of course dragged her back to wakefulness and back to the basin.

She was growing weaker . . . she knew she needed help . . . pride would not permit her to unlock the door. But as the pale light of dawn seeped through the starboard porthole, Miranda surrendered and crawled to the door, turning the key before collapsing into unconsciousness on the floor.

There followed a series of blurred images, of light and dark, of knowing vaguely that she was in bed, of Rafe leaning over her, followed by a period of consciousness during which she had recovered sufficiently to feel embarrassed and humiliated by Rafe's presence and the fact that he was witnessing her sickness. She had a vague recollection of his forcing her to swallow some dry biscuits and at one stage during the nightmare she woke to the realisation

335

that the motion of the boat was different, calmer, almost as though it was at anchor, but perhaps that was only wishful thinking . . .

At last Miranda slept, a sleep of sickness and exhaustion but one from which she woke refreshed. She let the peace flood through her, feeling that she had returned, if not from death, at least from the gates of hell. Closing her eyes she lay quietly in bed, aware that the violent pitching of the ship continued unabated but that by some miracle her body had adjusted to it. Her repose and relief were complete and she was sinking back into the warm embrace of well-being when the touch of a hand on her shoulders startled her out of her tranquillity. Her eyes flew open again, but all she could see was a white shirt and the V of a bronzed chest as Rafe leaned over to lift her into a sitting position. Her head was against his shoulder and she was aware of the pressure of his hands on her bare flesh as he eased her up. Miranda was too weak and debilitated to feel any sexual excitement but she prolonged the moment by lying limply in his arms, savouring the strength and security he emanated. Abruptly she remembered who he was and where she was and jerked away, hastily drawing up the sheet to her chin.

'I think you are feeling better,' he remarked, perching on the edge of the bunk.

'I must look terrible,' she said lamely.

'Now I *know* you are feeling better!'

'I really do apologise for being such a nuisance.'

'Think nothing of it.'

'No, but really . . . you had to clean up and . . . everything.'

'Stop worrying about it. Everyone gets seasick at some time or another. Besides, I've known you since you were that high,' and he held out his hand several feet above the floor to indicate the size of a five-year-old child, 'and although I didn't exactly change your napkins I'm entitled to a bit more familiarity with you than most men.'

Rafe grinned at her cheerfully but his eyes lingered on

the white fingers which were clutching the sheet to her chin. He had found her spreadeagled on the floor, had gathered her up in his arms and carried her to the bed where he had nursed her for three days, permitting none of his crew to enter the cabin. He had seen what lay beneath the sheet – the diaphanous nightgown lavishly trimmed with lace which covered those long, lovely limbs – but had touched her no more than circumstances demanded. He could only guess at the beauty of her body when it was naked and the texture of that velvety skin . . . Matthew's skin, so it would turn gold in the sun . . . one could stretch Miranda out in the sunshine and watch her ripen like a peach. Once Rafe had told Matthew that Miranda's resemblance to her father guaranteed her safety with him, but now he rather thought that he might change his mind.

His casual dismissal of his ministrations helped Miranda to overcome her embarrassment. 'I am afraid I have lost track of time. When do we reach Luderitzbucht?'

'Early tomorrow morning.'

'So soon! But I must get up! I must be fit and well to face the Regie.'

'Good God, you have barely returned to the land of the living and the diamonds are the first thing you think about! Tell me one thing, Miranda – if this trip is so goddam important, why didn't Sir Matthew come himself?'

'His health is not good and he has a great many other worries. In fact he did not want me to come – my brother died in Luderitzbucht – but I insisted.'

'So Daddy's little girl does have a mind of her own occasionally,' Rafe murmured. 'I had best remember that.' He got off the bed. 'May I help you to dress?'

'Certainly not!'

He heaved a deep sigh of mock disappointment. 'Not even the teeniest bit of assistance with so much as a button or bow? No? Oh well, I'm sure it would be far more rewarding to *undo* your buttons anyway! Come up on deck when you are ready.'

Dressing took Miranda longer than expected. She was weak and her shaking limbs would not do what she wanted them to do, her fingers fumbling with the fastenings. She put on the simple skirt and blouse in which she had come aboard because these garments came easiest to hand, then pulled on her coat and tied a scarf over her hair. Very cautiously she ventured along the corridor, through the saloon, climbed the companionway into the doghouse, opened the door and paused as she met the full force of the wind. Clutching a hand-rail, she edged along the uneven deck.

The weather had improved while she was incapacitated and the *Corsair* was beating up the Atlantic coast of southern Africa. Although the sea breeze was strong and cold, the sun was shining and the rain-clouds of the Cape had been left far behind. The *Corsair* was under sail and the sensation was exhilarating – the billowing canvas overhead, the salt spray stinging her face, but most of all the wind which whipped skirts and hair and pumped lungfuls of fresh air into her. Revived, Miranda was even able to manage a smile as Rafe appeared at her side and propelled her into the wheelhouse.

'I'm rather surprised that the *Corsair* is under sail,' Miranda remarked breathlessly. 'Don't you have an engine?'

'Only a modest contraption, I fear, which is used as infrequently as possible. Engines cost money to run but the wind is free. I am only a poor tradesman, remember.'

Miranda nodded. 'I see. You know, you never did tell me about the business which takes you up this coast. You merely described it as "a little bit of this and a little bit of that".'

'Did I? Well, I don't think we need elaborate on the "this", but the "that" is guano.'

'What on earth is guano?'

'Bird shit.'

Miranda found the expression crude but declined to give him the satisfaction of shocking her. However, he read her thoughts.

'The language is less offensive than the actuality! Bird

338

droppings are rich in phosphates and make superb fertiliser. Millions of gannets, cormorants and penguins breed on the islands off the South-West African coast.' He pointed to a chart on the table. 'The islands are dotted along the coast in the vicinity of Luderitzbucht – Roast Beef Island, Plum Pudding, Albatross, Possession, Ichabo, Mercury . . .'

'They have very English names for islands which are so close to German territory,' Miranda remarked.

'They are British; they were annexed fifty years ago.'

Miranda stared thoughtfully at the tiny dots on the chart. 'The islands cannot be more than a couple of miles off-shore,' she said slowly, 'off a *diamond-bearing* shore! Surely there must be a possibility that they contain diamond deposits?'

'You really do have a one-track mind! The guano islands are mere specks of rock but, yes, I do know of at least one diamond discovery. However, it has not been developed.'

'Incredible.'

'No, merely sensible. The diamonds were not present in payable quantities and it was decided that the disruption to bird life was not worthwhile. No doubt this comes as a terrible shock to you, Miranda, but in this instance bird droppings were a better investment than diamonds.'

Miranda compressed her lips, uncertain whether he was mocking her or teasing her. She turned away and a movement in the corner of the wheelhouse caught her eye. 'While on the subject of birds,' she remarked sarcastically, 'what are those?'

'Pigeons.' Rafe bent down in front of the cage and clucked encouragingly at the birds.

'I can see that! What are they doing here?'

'Company for me.' He straightened up and smiled at her wickedly. 'Something for me to talk to in the long watches of the night when there is no raping or looting to be done.'

Now he was obviously making fun of her and yet he was a rapist . . . wasn't he?

'No,' she said, 'seriously, why have them aboard ship?'

339

'I am a pigeon fancier. In all modesty, I think I can claim to be a leading light of the Pigeon Union of the Western Province. The sport is becoming quite popular out here, the stock being improved considerably when birds were imported by the military authorities during the war.'

Miranda gaped at him in astonishment, trying to reconcile the image of a pigeon-fancier with that of this lean, intensely masculine swashbuckler of a man. However, her mind was still woolly after her sickness and she was saved from replying by the arrival in the wheelhouse of Sergeant King, bearing three mugs of tea. Miranda accepted the tea eagerly, actually wanting it, looking forward to refreshment for the first time in three days.

'Have you been back to England since . . . it happened?'

Rafe smiled thinly. 'You ought to know better than to ask a question like that. Surely you can picture the reception I would receive? No, Miranda, I can never go back.'

'But your crew – don't they wish to return home? Don't they have families?'

'They are all single men and are free to leave whenever they wish. So far all have stayed.'

Miranda was silent for a moment, trying to absorb this shadowy glimpse of a different Rafe Deverill, trying to imagine what inspired such loyalty.

'Did you sail straight to the Cape when you left England?' she inquired.

'I went first to the Caribbean and came to southern Africa towards the end of 1908.'

'Just after diamonds were discovered along this coast.'

'Precisely,' and his lips curved into a dry smile.

Miranda was too preoccupied to notice his reaction. 1908 was the year in which Philip had died and that recollection, plus the reference to diamonds, concentrated her mind on her mission. She finished her tea and went below to eat a substantial meal; she must build up her physical strength and gather her wits about her for the forthcoming confrontation.

*　　*　　*

When Miranda woke the next morning vibrations were throbbing through her and she knew that the *Corsair* was proceeding under engine. She jumped out of bed and ran to the porthole. The morning was clear and in a rose-pink dawn the *Corsair* was inching past a small island, threading her way through a mass of tiny fishing boats towards the jetty at the head of the bay. Beyond the harbour her sharp eyes could see a huddle of buildings nestling amid grey granite and red-gold dunes, a mass of peaked roofs, gables and dormer windows dominated by a tall church tower. Miranda's heart twisted. Had Philip seen it like this?

She did not linger at the porthole – she had not come to Luderitzbucht to look at the view or admire German colonial architecture – but turned her attention to the important matter of what she would wear. She chose a two-piece of pale blue cashmere, comprising a straight skirt and a high-waisted tunic with elbow-length sleeves and modest decolletage, and pinned up her hair under a wide-brimmed blue hat. Opening the cabin door, she started with surprise as she saw Rafe Deverill leaning against a bulkhead. In that unguarded moment there was no doubting the admiration which flared in his eyes.

'I do apologise for loitering outside your cabin, but your hearing difficulties make it impossible for one to knock on the door and naturally I should not wish to intrude at a delicate moment.'

People did not normally refer to her deafness so frankly. Either they ignored it or turned pink with embarrassment if the subject could not be overlooked. Miranda found Rafe's attitude remarkably refreshing. 'You are most considerate, Captain.'

'I merely wished to find out when you intended going ashore, but your appearance is answer enough.' He looked past her into the cabin and saw the valise, which Miranda had hurriedly packed with a change of clothes and toilet articles, lying on the bunk. 'Not leaving us permanently, I trust?'

'I thought I would spend the night at an hotel. I may be busy this evening.'

'With you looking like that, I imagine the Germans would like to keep you very busy this evening!'

He picked up her bag and followed her along the corridor. At the foot of the companionway Miranda paused.

'After you,' she said.

Rafe eyed the tight slim skirt which hampered her ankle movements. 'No, no, after *you*.'

Miranda glared at him. However, she seemed to have no option but to precede him up the steep and narrow stairway, even though her progress necessitated hitching up her skirt and giving him a generous glimpse of trim ankles and shapely calves.

'By Jove,' he said gaily when they reached the deck, 'but it's lucky for you that the *Corsair*'s draught is sufficiently shallow to allow entry to the harbour. The sight of you climbing down to the dinghy in that skirt would have been the talk of South-West for months!' He signalled to Sergeant King. 'Escort Miss Bright to Kapps Hotel, Sergeant. Miranda, don't go wandering off on your own, will you?'

'Is it likely, Captain, after what happened to my brother?'

'No, of course not.' He paused and, very lightly, stroked her cheek. 'Take care. Oh, and good luck with the Regie!'

Several hours later Miranda was kicking her heels in the office of the Regie, fuming because she was being kept waiting. The experience was annoying, humiliating and, to her, new. Usually the name of the Diamond Company opened every door and people fell over themselves in their efforts to please her. She had not expected red-carpet treatment out here, but this measured insult did not bode well for the relationship between the Regie and the Company.

When she was shown into the presence of the Regie representative, she concealed her annoyance. 'How kind of you to spare me your valuable time,' she said sweetly in her flawless German, 'particularly as I arrived without an appointment.'

Hugo Werth was staring at her, thunderstruck. He *had*

kept her waiting on purpose, but had not expected this gorgeous creature who addressed him in his own language.

'Not at all,' he stammered. 'What can I do for you?'

'I have business in South Africa, but decided to take this excellent opportunity to pay my respects to the Regie.' She smiled at him disarmingly. 'This is where the real work is done. I imagine that many of the Berlin staff have never even been here.'

She succeeded in striking a chord in Werth, who was frequently frustrated by the attitude of the Berlin bureaucracy which, in his opinion, was singularly ignorant of conditions in the field.

'I would like to say how happy we are that the Diamond Company and the Regie have been able to come to an agreement regarding the marketing of the stones,' Miranda continued, feeling her way cautiously. 'Certainly I am sure that the result will be beneficial to both our organisations. I do hope you agree.'

'I doubt whether my opinion matters very much. I am concerned with mining the gems, not selling them.'

'And very successful you have been! What was your production last year? About one-and-a-half million carats, wasn't it?'

'You are very well-informed, Miss Bright, so doubtless you are also cognisant with the profitability of our mining companies which have declared dividends ranging from 30 to *3800* per cent! Therefore it will not surprise you to know that there are those in Berlin who believe the agreement benefits the British-owned Diamond Company and the London Syndicate more than the German Regie.'

Again Miranda cursed the fact that she was unable to hear nuances and emphases in conversation but, despite this disadvantage, somehow she sensed an extra urgency in his phraseology.

'The agreement benefits the diamond industry,' she insisted, 'and as such it rises above international politics and nationalistic considerations.'

343

Silence. Each knew that the other was thinking about the possibility of war in Europe, but on such short acquaintance and in this office it was impossible to mention it.

'I wish we could pursue this discussion in less formal surroundings, Herr Werth. Perhaps you could join me for dinner this evening – with Frau Werth, of course.'

'I am not married and I should be delighted to accept your invitation.'

Back at the hotel Miranda threw off her hat and furiously tugged pins out of her hair. Britain versus Germany, was that the key? Well, she would damn well show them something, and in the process she would worm more information out of Herr Werth than either Matthew or Philip could have done. She sat down in front of the mirror to wrestle with her hair which was thick, wavy and possessed a decided will of its own. Moreover, Miranda was accustomed to having a maid take care of it. However, when it was finished she felt a glow of satisfaction.

The hair was parted in the centre, plaited into thick bands over her ears and caught up in a further coil of plaits at the back of her head. A few tendrils refused to cooperate and hung loosely at the nape of her neck, but the effect only enhanced the innocence and artlessness of her appearance. In her most simple evening gown, Miranda was the perfect blonde, fresh-faced *fraulein*, as Teutonic and wholesome as the middle-class ladies portrayed in Ludwig of Bavaria's 'Gallery of Beauties' at the Nymphenburg Schloss in Munich.

This time Herr Werth did not keep her waiting and Miranda set out to entertain him charmingly, speaking of her year at finishing school in Dresden, telling anecdotes about her German governess. He was enchanted, of that there was no doubt, and he began to relax visibly and to partake liberally of the excellent Riesling. Gradually Miranda guided the conversation towards diamonds, but instead of describing her father's tuition she dwelled on her association with Anton Ellenberger.

'Dear Anton,' she murmured, smiling at Hugo over the

344

rim of her glass as she took a sip of wine. 'He taught me so much. What he doesn't know about diamonds isn't worth knowing.'

'Our compatriot is indeed a remarkable man,' he agreed.

'He has been such a good friend to me over the years. Back in 1908 he made his first journey to South-West in order to investigate my brother's disappearance. Were you in Luderitzbucht at that time?'

'Yes, it was a great tragedy. My condolences, Miss Bright.'

'Did you meet Philip?' she asked eagerly.

'I did.' Hugo hesitated, not knowing quite what to say about that odd young man. 'You are not a bit like him.'

'In what way are we different?'

'Philip Bright was not . . . friendly. He seemed strangely alienated in some way. Also, he was not the least interested in diamonds. I took him to the diggings and explained the potential of our fields, but he did not ask any of the questions which I expected. Yet I am certain he understood the importance of the find.'

This statement was so much at variance with the report Philip had submitted that Miranda was bewildered. 'Did you take part in the search for him?'

'I organised that search and I really am so sorry that we failed to find him. I do assure you that we tried but in the desert . . . ' Hugo shrugged apologetically. 'Also, we questioned everyone who had spoken with him. Oh, there was one exception – a girl who was seen with him at this very hotel – but she was due to catch the Cape Town steamer and by the time the alarm was raised the ship had sailed.'

'My family is so grateful to you and all our German friends for your assistance at that terrible time.' Miranda laid a hand lightly on his arm. 'I do pray that we need never be enemies. However, if our two countries should go to war, we must remember that human relationships and commerce have a way of re-establishing themselves after the military have had their fling. The diamond industry has such world-wide importance that its future and its stability must not be jeopardised by one conflict.'

'I doubt that the politicians would agree with you.'

'Fortunately the politicians do not run the diamond industry.'

'No,' Hugo said quietly. 'The British run the diamond industry.'

It was there again. Miranda had not realised that the bitterness, the *envy* of the Diamond Company's control of the industry ran so deep.

'My only defence against that charge is that the British started the industry and placed it on a proper footing. But, please, don't let us spoil the evening by arguing. I am enjoying myself too much to quarrel! In fact, I do wish I could stay in South-West a little longer and see something of the mining operations. I would have liked to undertake the same journey that Anton made recently.'

'You would find it most interesting.' Hugo was relaxed but still sober. He had no intention of revealing secret information, but there was no harm in describing Ellenberger's journey. 'Anton visited Kolmanskop, Elizabeth Bay, Pomona and Bogenfels. Are you sure you could not prolong your visit? Unfortunately I could not accompany you myself, but I could arrange an escort.'

'I really cannot.' The mining operations were not helpful to Miranda in themselves. It was Regie policy and *thinking* which she was attempting to fathom. 'Did you escort Anton into the *Sperrgebiet?*'

'Oh, no. Anton knows all the producers and, besides, why should he require an escort into the "forbidden area"? He is one of us.'

Somehow Miranda maintained a calm expression, talking for a few minutes about her forthcoming visit to Kimberley and then asking Hugo about his own background. She appeared to listen intently while he talked about himself, but in reality her mind was far away. Unwittingly Hugo Werth had given her the information she required.

Whether Germany won or lost the war, the numerous small producers in the *Sperrgebiet* must be amalgamated, just as the small claimholders in Kimberley had been merged into the cohesive whole which was now the Diamond Company. But the German producers of South-West Africa disliked dealing with the British and resented the power wielded by the British-controlled Diamond Company. So to whom would they turn?

Miranda felt a hysterical laugh rising within her. She had gone to so much trouble to appear German tonight, but her efforts paled into insignificance beside those of Anton Ellenberger. For six years he had cultivated these people and this particular arm of the industry. Forget the fact that he was a naturalised British subject. Here he was German – a German based in South Africa where anti-British factions flourished. Here he was 'our compatriot', one of them. And he had tied up the future of the South-West African diamond fields. Bright Diamonds would not stand a chance of competing with him or outmanoeuvring him.

Well, Miranda thought grimly, if she could not beat him, she must join him.

CHAPTER NINETEEN

Before boarding the *Corsair* Miranda wandered slowly through the sandy streets of Luderitzbucht, her mind full of Philip. Although he was dead she found herself looking for him, searching for his face among the people on every street corner, at the shops or in the hotel. She even sought for any familiar face, anyone whom she knew or who might know her, in the vague hope that they might throw some light upon her brother's death. But of course there was no one. The mystery would remain unsolved but she was glad she had come, glad to have made this pilgrimage, even though it was irrelevant to anyone but herself and although there was nothing she could do to help Philip, save him or bring him peace.

Ignoring Rafe's warning, Miranda trudged to the out-skirts of the town and sat down, hugging her knees. Then, attuning herself to the desert, she listened to the silence. Instinctively she knew that the silence in her head was deep, fathomless, total. It was not that she was unable to hear sound, but there was no sound to hear. In this envi-ronment she was equal. For one crazy moment she was tempted to stay here in this savage land astride Capricorn, and to escape her responsibilities. Had Philip felt like this? She could not begin to divine his reaction to this or to anything else; she could not interpret his attitude to the diamond industry or even to a girl in an hotel. He had been her brother, but she had not known him. She understood nothing of his life, nothing of his loves and hates, hopes or fears. Today she had sought his face among strangers, but he was the most complete stranger of all.

Reluctantly Miranda turned her head and looked at the

massive dunes – hills of sand, sculpted by the wind into curving sharp-edged ridges, glowing red and gold, apricot and burgundy, plunging into deep purple valleys on their endless march to the horizon. The wind was rising, stirring her hair, sending smoky wisps of sand spiralling from the crests of the dunes . . . perhaps, somewhere beneath these mountains of sand, Philip's bones were whitening . . .

Miranda rose abruptly. Philip's death was the main reason why she must go back to London, why she must always go back, why she could never lead a life of her own. Matthew depended on her and she loved her father too much to leave him.

The news that Sir Matthew Bright's daughter was in Luderitzbucht had spread, but only one solitary figure watched the *Corsair* sail. Vaguely he wondered about the schooner's normal line of business and about the identity of her captain who had not set foot ashore, but mostly he speculated on the future movements of Miss Miranda Bright. He waited, watching, motionless on the quay, until the *Corsair* reached the open sea and then Danie Steyn set out for the offices of the Regie.

With the wind off her beam, the *Corsair* was on a broad reach and the motion of the boat was far more comfortable. This sort of sailing Miranda could enjoy. Her seasickness did not return but as a precaution she extinguished the lantern at night, even though this plunged her into the darkness she detested.

The return of her health enabled her acquaintance with Rafe to develop. One could not describe his manner towards her as gallant – it was too full of amusement and teasing for that – yet this badinage was in itself suggestive that he held her in some affection. It was suggestive in other ways, too . . . The chrysalis of Miranda's latent sexuality, briefly touched by Dick Latimer, was stirring within the shell of her shyness and constraint. She was intensely aware of his physical attraction and it dawned on her that not only was it difficult to imagine him raping a woman,

349

but it would be more difficult for a woman to resist him. Because Matthew had voiced that accusation, Miranda forced herself to believe it, but her doubts were reflected in the fact that she did not lock her cabin at night and left the key on the outside of the door.

Apart from Rafe's disturbing presence, only one incident interrupted Miranda's sleep. On the second night out of Luderitzbucht she awoke to that same realisation as before – that the motion of the boat had changed. To her the *Corsair* seemed to be rocking gently at anchor, but surely they could not have reached Cape Town by now! She peered through the portholes, but all that lay beyond was the blank blackness of the South Atlantic. Groping her way across the cabin, Miranda pulled at the door handle, but nothing happened. She tugged again, but still the door did not open. She was locked in.

Suddenly Miranda was terrified. Locked in darkness, unable to hear or see, not knowing what was going on outside, she was back in the Kimberley Mine during the Siege sheltering from the Boer bombardment. The dank atmosphere of the underground passages and caverns seemed to swirl around her, bringing back memories of the tension in Laura and the other adults, her own sensations of helplessness because she could not communicate. She had been terribly frightened – but of what?

Frantically Miranda fumbled for the matches to light the lantern. Beneath her feet vibrations told her that the boat's engine had been started but even these were stronger, more insistent, *louder* – if she could use that expression – than before. Not the note of a 'modest contraption' at all. Then Miranda tensed as the door opened to admit Rafe Deverill.

'Are you all right? I saw the light under your door.'

'What is happening? Why did we stop? Why did you lock me in?' she burst out.

'There was a bad squall, so we put in to the shelter of a small cove,' he said smoothly. 'I'm sorry you were disturbed.'

'That does not explain why you locked me in!'

'You are imagining things. The door must have jammed. It does that occasionally and merely requires an exceptionally strong heave to move it.'

His manner was so reassuring and normal that Miranda felt rather foolish. 'It was the dark,' she said slowly. 'It reminded me of the Kimberley Mine during the Siege. I cannot hear in the dark.'

He took a step forward and for a moment she thought he was going to touch her, then he turned abruptly on his heel.

'Try to sleep,' he said curtly. 'I will be in the cabin opposite if you need me.'

Miranda did not fall asleep for a long time. There was one certainty about her forthcoming visit to Kimberley: nothing would induce her to go down that mine!

Next morning the weather was grey and threatening so Miranda spent most of the day in her cabin, washing her hair and dozing. She did take one turn about the deck, peering into the wheelhouse in the hope of seeing Rafe, but he was not there. Neither were the pigeons. The cage was empty, so presumably the birds were winging their way to Cape Town. Would they reach their destination before the *Corsair* and if so who would receive them? Miranda's stomach knotted uncomfortably as she contemplated the very real possibility that Rafe Deverill could be married.

'Where do the pigeons go after you have released them?' she asked him that evening as they were dining together in the saloon.

'To my house in Cape Town.'

'Who looks after them for you?' she said carefully.

'I have a . . . housekeeper.'

Miranda felt a ridiculous sense of relief. They had finished their meal but to her pleasure Rafe showed no sign of leaving. They were sharing a jar of wine: good wine, deep, red and fragrant, from the lovely valleys of Tulbagh in the Cape and it tasted of sunshine and happiness. Miranda *was* happy – except for a peculiar ache whenever she remembered that this was their last evening together.

'Why did you offer to take me to Luderitzbucht?'

Rafe's face tautened. He had been as surprised as she by their unexpected meeting but had come to terms with it more quickly. In that moment he had realised that, after years of waiting, the time had come to reach back into the past, to find the answers to questions which haunted him and to even old scores. Miranda might not be able to throw any light on the actions of Tiffany Court, but she was a base from which he could work – through her lay the road to Matthew. It had occurred to Rafe that the most subtle retaliation against Matthew would be to win Miranda's heart and that is precisely what he had set out to do. He had not intended to carry the relationship to its ultimate conclusion, of course. Marriage formed no part of his plan. She is young, he had thought dispassionately at the Mount Nelson Hotel; she will get over it.

But that had been before he knew her, before he . . . Once Rafe had dreamed of finding a woman who combined the qualities of Laura and Tiffany and when he looked at Miranda he saw that very combination: beauty of face and figure; courage, determination and intelligence; the occasional flash of Tiffany's fire and independent spirit; a steadfastness in the eyes, a goodness and honesty, an air of tranquillity so reminiscent of Laura. Yet Miranda retained an intrinsic individuality: her composure, that self-containment and completeness, was very much her own. It set her apart, adding a mystery which a man longed to penetrate in order to discover the real Miranda within.

Rafe's hand clenched on his wine glass. Usually the wine gave him happiness of a kind, too, taking him back to a time when treachery and exile did not exist. But now he regretted seeking out Miranda. She reminded him too strongly of what had been and what could have been – of what he, disgraced, could never possess. The irony was that Matthew had been in disgrace at the outset of his glittering career – and it was the thought of Matthew which urged Rafe on to find the answers, to hit back. If hurting Miranda was the only way to achieve these aims, then hurt her he must.

'You are taking a long time to answer,' Miranda remarked.

'Only because I find the question superfluous. Why shouldn't I wish to assist you? Apart from our long friendship, any man would welcome the opportunity to help a woman as beautiful as you.'

He means 'as rich as me', thought Miranda, but all she said was, 'It is not "any man" who has a quarrel with my father.'

Rafe laughed lightly. 'Actually there may be more of us than you think! But I follow your line of reasoning and I am astonished – you are implying that I would seek revenge. Really, Miranda, the very idea!'

'But if you are innocent as you maintain, aren't you bitter? I'm sure I would be.'

'Bitter?' Rafe shrugged carelessly. 'Why should I be bitter? I was rejected by a society which I had myself rejected years ago.'

'Why did you reject that society?'

'That,' said Rafe slowly, 'is a very long story.'

For a moment he was tempted to tell her, to find out if she could offer forgiveness and if her forgiveness could lift the burden of guilt. But no, she would talk of 'duty' and he had discarded that excuse long ago.

In the ensuing silence, Miranda reflected that vengeance would be directed at Tiffany Court rather than Matthew. Her mind flinched from thoughts of Tiffany; her memories of the other woman were too painful and now there was another dimension to her disquiet – Rafe Deverill had been discovered in Tiffany's bedroom, so what had been their relationship? Had he been in love with her?

She glanced up to find him watching her. She had put on a simple evening gown of slithery satin, cut on the bias and

353

low at her breasts, and her freshly-washed hair was caught back with combs to hang loosely down her back. The informality of life aboard ship had prompted her to discard her corsetry and the only lingerie she was wearing comprised silk slip, knickers and stockings which were supported by garters. The sense of release was wonderful, like relaxing into the loose freedom of a nightgown, the silk and satin smooth and sensuous against her skin. She was surprised at her own daring and honest enough to wonder if shipboard informality was the only reason for it . . . she remembered Dick's hands feverishly trying to feel her flesh . . . remembered his head pressed against her thighs . . . Now she flushed at the expression in Rafe's eyes, afraid he might read her thoughts, certain he detected her lack of underwear.

'You must have had London at your feet,' he said huskily. 'Have there been many men in your life, Miranda?'

'My work comes first,' she said evasively.

'Naturally – in your position I took that for granted! But you find a little time to play? There must have been, or may still be, someone special?'

'Dick Latimer has asked me to marry him.'

Rafe was silent for a moment. 'I remember him as a very fine young man. Congratulations.'

'I have not accepted . . . yet.'

'Why not?'

It was on the tip of her tongue to tell him to mind his own business, but he was penetrating her defences as no one had done before. The absence of Matthew, her new awareness of Rafe's sexuality and her own, were prompting Miranda to throw off her inhibitions as well as her underclothes.

'I don't love him. Besides, I expect he is only after my money.'

Rafe rose, walked towards her and pulled her to her feet. Gently he cupped her face in his hands.

'Do you really believe that?' he asked incredulously.

Miranda did not reply but lowered her eyes and tried to turn her face away.

'You're crazy! Either there is something wrong with your eyes or something drastically wrong with your mirror! You are one of the most beautiful women I have ever seen.'

'As beautiful as my cousin Julia?' She could not resist the taunt. Or Tiffany? But no, no one was as beautiful as Tiffany.

He dropped his hands to her shoulders and caressed them softly. 'If I was to show an interest in you, I could not be accused of being after your money.'

'Why should you be any different?'

'Because if I married you, you wouldn't get the money.' One hand began stroking the back of her neck.

'My father would never disinherit me – *never!*'

'Your father hates my guts! I am the one man in the world he would never accept as your husband. You would have to choose and that choice could be too unkind, couldn't it, Miranda!'

She stared up at him, dizzy with desire, not wanting to think about her father or impossible choices, just wanting *him* . . . His arms were around her, his face was very close and then his mouth was on hers. One hand moved to her breasts, the intensity of his kiss deepening as he felt the taut erect nipples beneath the shiny satin. Miranda clung to him but was brought back sharply to reality when Rafe suddenly pushed her away.

'Go away, Miranda,' he said harshly. '*Go away!*'

'Why?' All she wanted was to be close to him, as close as a woman could be to a man.

'Because if I go on touching you, I will be unable to stop.'

'But I don't want you to stop.'

Rafe looked at her, her hair a bright aureole in the lamplight, the purity of her face and the innocence in her eyes which he longed to banish and replace with passion.

'In the morning you would think differently,' he said. 'In the morning you would remember that not only am I *persona non grata* with your father but that I am an exile – a disgraced man. If you become involved with me, you could not return to London. You might never see your father again.'

Her mind told her it was true . . . her body urged her not to care . . . 'You and I will not see each other again anyway,' she said slowly, 'because I am going to Kimberley for important discussions with Mr Ellenberger.'

'Lucky old Anton!'

She was surprised to hear him refer to Anton by his Christian name. 'Do you know Anton Ellenberger?'

'Oh, we bump into each other from time to time,' and his lips twitched slightly as he suppressed a smile.

Miranda was trying to collect herself for a dignified exit, but Rafe stepped forward and again cradled her face in his hands.

'I don't want you to go away, but it would be in your best interests. Also, I have vowed that I will not touch you aboard this ship, no matter the temptation, because if I did you might believe the lies which have been spread about me.' He bent his head and kissed her lightly on the lips. 'Go to Kimberley, Miranda, but do not be surprised if I follow you.'

When she returned to the hotel Miranda was relieved to find that no frantic cables from Matthew had been received and that although a representative of the Diamond Company had called, her maid had covered for her. She read the letters which had arrived from Matthew and replied immediately, enthusing about fictitious people and events. She was astonished – no, *horrified* at her duplicity – how could she have changed so soon? Absence from Matthew . . . the will of the diamonds . . . or Rafe? Miranda had no doubt as to the identity of the culprit.

She was due to leave Cape Town for Kimberley two days after her return from South-West and was glad of the period of grace in which to compose herself. However, she had to consciously resist the temptation to visit him and at dusk on the second evening she was standing at her bed-room window gazing up at the bulk of Table Mountain behind the hotel.

'Where do you live?' she had asked him as she disembarked.

'On the Mountain.'

'Whereabouts on the Mountain?'

'Devil's Peak, of course! Where else?'

Where else indeed! Miranda stared wistfully in the rough direction of the Peak. Then a flock of pigeons caught her eye, wheeling in the sky above her briefly before van-ishing from her line of vision. Pigeons . . . she still could not see Rafe as a pigeon fancier . . . those birds had been released from the *Corsair* after that strange stop on the homeward journey . . .

Suddenly Miranda stiffened, two bright spots of colour burned in her cheeks and her blue eyes blazed. She was angry – angrier than she had ever been. Grabbing a coat, she ran out of the hotel into the gathering darkness, called a cab and directed it to a certain house on Devil's Peak where she stormed up the path to the front step and pounded furiously on the door. Presumably the house-keeper would answer the knock. But when the door did open, Miranda's heart lurched.

Within stood a beautiful young girl. Her face was oval with perfect honey-gold skin, wide lips and almond-shaped eyes. Her straight black hair was wound into a thick coil at the nape of her neck, while her petite form made Miranda feel like an Amazon. She had inherited the very best char-acteristics of her mixed parentage and was a magical blend of European and Malay. Miranda knew that most Cape houses had Coloured servants, but this girl not only kept house for Rafe Deverill – she also kept his bed warm at night.

Icily Miranda extended her card and was shown into the plainly-furnished drawing-room which boasted few crea-ture comforts. She did not sit down. Neither did she have to wait long before Rafe entered.

357

'Miranda! What a pleasant surprise. Did you just happen to be passing or is my company irresistible after all?'

'Pigeon fancier,' she shouted. '*Pigeon fancier*! You're a bloody diamond smuggler, that's what you are!'

'Ah.' He folded his arms and stared at her and she waited for him to deny the charge, but he did not do so. 'You disapprove,' he observed with a charming unconcerned smile.

'That is a masterpiece of understatement!'

'You will need to modify your delicate sensibilities if you are to succeed in the business world, Miranda.'

'My father managed very well without sinking to such depths!'

'Did he? In the early days Kimberley was a jungle in which only the fittest survived – and "fittest" meant the most clever and cunning. I doubt very much whether Matthew Bright escaped unsullied. Mind you, they called it IDB – Illicit Diamond Buying – not smuggling, but it amounted to much the same thing.'

'My father would not do a thing like that,' Miranda insisted stubbornly.

How different she was from Tiffany! The situation of the two diamond heiresses was so similar that one was tempted to lump them together in one's mind, to see them as a type or entity, with only their nationalities and hair colour to tell them apart. However, Tiffany would seize eagerly on any profit-making enterprise and would sail as close to the wind as she dared. If Miranda held such scruples and maintained such a moral outlook, Tiffany would crush her easily in any head-on clash.

'They *all* did it,' Rafe said quietly. 'How do you think the titans of the industry got started? Sure, they were shrewd. Sure, they were clever. But so were a lot of other diamond diggers. What set the big boys apart from the rest? I'll tell you – determination, ruthlessness and IDB.'

'I came here to accuse you of a crime, not to defend my father against mythical misdemeanours in his past,' Miranda flashed. 'Smuggling is stealing!'

358

'I take diamonds from undeveloped diamond fields which are unknown to anyone but the natives of the country, who have no use for them. From whom am I stealing?'

She hesitated for the first time. 'Smuggling diamonds harms an entire industry.'

'Why the hell should I give a damn about the diamond industry? Just what did it, or its barons, ever do for me? You, of all people, know bloody well what it did to me! I see no reason whatsoever why I should not have the right to discover a diamond claim, dig up the stones and sell them. Why should a powerful cartel dictate to me?'

'You must know perfectly well that it is a matter of market stability, particularly in a luxury commodity like diamonds.'

'Unfortunately the value of the diamonds I produce is not in the least likely to affect the market price!'

'Where do you sell the stones?'

'Come, come, Miranda, you don't seriously expect me to answer that!'

'Then at least tell me how you found them,' she insisted.

'I listened, as all sailors do, to the stories which are told on the Cape Town waterfront – stories of buried treasure, gold and diamonds. There was a Hottentot, a native of South-West, who swore he knew a source of diamonds but refused to tell anyone where it was. After a while most people lost interest in him, deciding he was telling a fine tale in order to obtain money for his brandy ration. As it happened I was able to do him a favour and in return he agreed to guide me to the diamonds.'

'Why did you believe his story?' Miranda's anger was fading and she was feeling very tired.

'I was not absolutely sure, but it was worth a try. By God, was it worth a try! In fact my little friend revealed two sources of gems, the one we visited on this trip and another further up the coast where I buy stones from the Bushmen.'

'What price per carat do you pay?'

He laughed. 'Money is no use to a Bushman trying to

survive in the Namib Desert! I pay in blankets, water-bottles, penknives, food . . .'

'All of which is much cheaper than a diamond; your profit margin must be enormous.' Miranda's tone was scathing.

'Everything is relative. To a Bushman diamonds are pebbles, but water is the most valuable asset on earth.'

Miranda nodded, reluctantly acknowledging the logic of his argument. 'When we were in the Kimberley Mine during the Siege, Papa brought us some grapes and Laura said, "We are in the heart of a diamond mine, but these grapes are more precious than gems".'

'Laura is a very wise lady.'

They had not sat down but still stood, confronting each other. Miranda was growing more and more fatigued, worn out by the force of her emotions.

'Well,' she said wearily, 'the diamonds solve one problem. I wondered what prompted the peculiar loyalty of your crew. Now I realise their devotion is to the diamonds, not to you.'

He made no reply and his steady gaze did not waver.

'Don't you worry about being caught?' she asked.

'Constantly. The Germans patrol the coast in gunboats – the *Panther*, the *Habicht* and the *Condor* – which is why I have the Hotchkiss aboard.' He saw the surprise in her eyes. 'Did you not notice the gun? Well, I'm glad that at least some of my activities are well camouflaged. How did you find out about the operation?'

'It was quite easy once I put my mind to it. The *Corsair* stopped on the way out and on the way back, to put off and then take on the crewmen who dug for the diamonds while we sailed to Luderitzbucht. Then you sent the diamonds home by pigeon, because under South African law it is an offence for an unlicensed person to be in possession of uncut gems. Also, the *Corsair* has a better engine than you admit, presumably to make up time and so allay the suspicions of the Cape Town harbour authorities. Oh yes, it didn't take a genius to work out the details of your "little bit of this".'

Miranda paused. 'But I will tell you what really made me

angry, Captain,' she said softly. 'Not just the smuggling, despicable though it is, but the fact that you dared to do it while I was aboard. I may be deaf, Captain Deverill, but that does not make me stupid!'

Rafe stepped towards her but she recoiled, moving away to keep the same distance between them.

'I don't think you are stupid, but I do admit that I had not thought you would be aware of what was going on. I made a mistake and I apologise.'

Miranda's only reply was to throw a wad of banknotes on to a table. 'Payment for my passage, Captain! I hope you will agree that I have calculated a fair price.'

He ignored the money. 'Will you report me to the Diamond Detective Department?'

Miranda looked at him, painfully aware that she had not voiced all her emotions. The factors she had described were real enough, but in addition was the awful truth that she was hurt because she had begun to warm towards him, to trust him . . . to love him . . . and the presence of that *housekeeper* did not help!

'No, it isn't worth it,' she said wearily. '*You* are not worth the trouble.' She walked to the door and glanced back at him, at his faded clothes and the shabby room. 'As you so rightly say, the value of the diamonds you are smuggling could not possibly affect the industry in any way at all.'

He had not wanted her to find out about the smuggling but perhaps it was no bad thing. Her reaction was interesting . . . anything which cast some light on Miranda was interesting.

The thread of the diamonds had run through his life, implanted by Fate, chaining him against his will. The gems had touched him at every turn – Matthew and Laura, the role of the diamond magnates and Randlords in the Boer War, Tiffany and Philip, Miranda – and he had been so affected by the involvement of the Brights and the Courts with the stones that the deliberate, cynical smuggling of diamonds had begun as his own rude gesture at their obsession.

Also, Rafe was sufficiently self-aware to realise that his presence in this part of the world was no accident. He had unfinished business in southern Africa, stemming from the Boer War. Here he had lost his way and subconsciously he hoped that here he would find it – and himself – once more.

He decided he could not allow Miranda to depart for Kimberley without making a gesture of reconciliation and that he would go to the station tomorrow to see her off.

Cape Town station was crowded and Rafe had to fight his way across the concourse to the platform where the Kimberley-Johannesburg train was waiting. Fortunately it would be no trouble to find Miranda because she would be travelling in the distinctive, private and luxurious Diamond Company coach. But as Rafe reached the ticket barrier he became aware of a sudden hush, a stilling in the throng, and he turned his head curiously to discover the cause.

A woman was striding haughtily, disdainfully, towards the Kimberley train. She was tall, dressed all in black, her coat trimmed with sable and a sable hat upon her dark smooth hair. The station lights accentuated the sparkle of the diamonds at her ears as she walked swiftly and purposefully through the human corridor which had opened up naturally before her. She had several companions trailing in her wake but no one, including Rafe, noticed them. All eyes were fixed on that proud, beautiful face.

Hastily Rafe moved back to conceal himself in the crowd as Tiffany Court, looking neither to right nor left, swept past him, leaving a breath of expensive perfume lingering in the air. He stood motionless on the same spot for a long time. The wheel had come full circle. He would follow the diamond heiresses to Kimberley and when he came face-to-face with Tiffany he had one word only to say – *why?*

CHAPTER TWENTY

Tiffany had not wanted to visit Kimberley but the diamonds had compelled her to come. Against her will, inexorably, the gems had lured her to the Diamond City in which she had been conceived, drawing her into their very heart. But in those depths there was no longer any magic. The fire was cold, the spark faint, the light dimmed even though the spirit had not been crushed. Tiffany was cloaked in night, trapped in the evil grip of Randolph and the dark side of the diamonds.

Standing at the window, gazing sightlessly at the garden, she fingered the pear-shaped pendant with restless, fevered fingers. It blazed on the bodice of her black gown, for now Tiffany wore no sunlit shades, no soft cream or pure white; she dressed in black or strong harsh colours – scarlet, vermilion, purple and red – symbolic of the hell in which she lived.

There were no visible scars of seven years' marriage with Randolph Court. The legacy was in the coldness and hardness of her stare, in the bitter lines of the mouth – bitterness which bordered on cruelty – and in the implacable hatred within her soul. She was aware of the change in her, of the vile creeping corruption which Randolph cast over her, and knew that she must escape from his power. She had turned instinctively to the diamonds. Perhaps the gems which had enslaved her would set her free – and it was on the diamonds of South-West Africa that Tiffany was pinning all her hopes.

Anton Ellenberger had invited them to Kimberley for his inauguration as Mayor, but the real reason for the visit was to finalise terms for the partnership which would acquire the South-West diamond fields and form a base from which the challenge for ultimate control of the industry could be launched. Tiffany desired that control, she had always desired it, but now the implications went further than industrial influence; in this deal she saw a means of breaking Randolph's power over her and of regaining control over herself and her affairs.

Always Tiffany had possessed the body of a woman but the mind of a man. She had not the strength to break him physically, but if *she* could win the South-West African diamond fields she could prove her mental superiority.

Her fingers clenched on the diamond at her breast. How far down the evil road had Randolph driven her? How much further would he force her to travel? How far was she prepared to go to break him?

Kimberley held the answer. Here in the Diamond City she must find her destiny. This was no sentimental journey into the past – indeed, the past was the reason why she had not wanted to come. Tiffany recoiled from memories of her father. She had not forgiven him for Anne, for Alida or the chain of circumstances which had led to her tragedy. Most of all, she had not forgiven John Court for inflicting her with Randolph.

He walked into the room now, an envelope in his hand, and he was watching her like a sleek, smooth cat, eyes narrowed with lazy detachment but always holding that hint of menace. He had not had sex with her for more than a year, but the reason for his absence from her bed was more degrading than any assault.

After Benjamin was born, she had realised that he wanted her to fight him and to fight her repugnance of the acts they performed, so Tiffany began to conceal her abhorrence and to be passive in her reactions. She was assisted by two more pregnancies – contrived merely as a means of avoiding Randolph's attentions – and gradually his visits to her room became more infrequent. Then one night, when he entered her and moved within her, she achieved orgasm. It was completely involuntary, a purely muscular response, but to Tiffany it was the most humiliating and mortifying moment of her life.

For Randolph this was his greatest victory, his ultimate triumph, and afterwards he no longer felt the need for her physically. In truth he had begun to tire of her body, his sexual persuasions propelling him to a wider sphere of activities with a variety of women until even that stage passed and nowadays he obtained his pleasure from pornography and his satisfaction from masturbation. Having gained the ascendancy over Tiffany, his frenzy had abated but his sinister use of power remained unimpaired. Two years ago, on her twenty-fifth birthday, Tiffany had inherited Court Diamonds but Randolph retained control of the Bank and he had entangled their business affairs so thoroughly and intricately that the knots could never be undone. He was not sure which gave him the most satisfaction: his impregnable hold over her professional life, or the wary apprehension on her face which betrayed her fear that he might resume sexual relations with her.

'A letter from Anton,' he said, tapping the envelope, 'inviting us to dinner this evening. At least it atones, in part anyway, for his absence from the railway station when we arrived.'

Tiffany snatched the envelope from him, scrutinised it, saw that it was addressed to Mr Randolph Court and angrily flung it on the bed. Would Anton Ellenberger never learn whose diamond company he was dealing with?

A smile twitched at the corners of Randolph's mouth as he interpreted her action. 'However,' he continued, 'he does not explain why he rented this house instead of inviting us to stay with him or booking us into a hotel.'

Tiffany shrugged. 'What difference does it make? This entire town looks like a dump to me.'

He did not answer her directly. 'Normally one would rent a house for an extended visit, but I was planning to stay here for only a week at the most. After our discussions with Anton in New York, the negotiations should not take long.'

'I am surprised that you accepted Anton's invitation. Usually you cannot be prised away from your desk for more than two days at a time.'

'I need a holiday,' he replied smoothly. 'All those complicated, tedious moves towards banking reform were extremely exhausting and now that the Federal Reserve Act is safely on the statute books, I feel entitled to a rest.'

'Rest!' Tiffany snorted. 'Like hell you want a rest! You came to Kimberley because you dare not let me out of your sight. You will not concede that I could have handled this deal perfectly well by myself.'

'I dislike inflicting this blow to your self-esteem, my dear, but it is *I* who am important to Anton Ellenberger, not you. He requires finance. In other words he needs my bank, not your diamond company.'

'Really, Randolph, a child of Benjamin's age could see that the Court Bank must advance the money to Court Diamonds rather than invest in the diamond fields direct. *I* intend to be Anton's partner in gaining control of this industry. The diamonds are mine and don't you forget it!'

'Chance would be a fine thing. You mention it often enough.' He watched as she snapped open a jewelled cigarette case, lit a cigarette and dragged on it furiously to relieve her frustration. 'Why are you so upset that I accompanied you? Am I cramping your style?' And he glanced meaningfully at the bed.

He had kept his unspoken 'bargain' and ignored the casual affairs she conducted at her studio in Greenwich Village. Curiously, since he had ceased sexual relations with her, he had become increasingly fascinated by the idea of her in bed with another man. He would have liked to hear the most intimate details. Most of all, he would have liked to watch.

'God, Randolph, but you have an obscene mind – although I ought to be used to it by now! I am not ruled by sex and anyway I doubt whether Kimberley could offer

366

anything remotely beddable.' She was still standing, smoking the cigarette, unable to relax in his presence. 'Even if you considered yourself indispensable, I fail to see why we had to bring Pauline.'

'Pauline needed a change of scene.'

'She could have had a change of scene staying at our home, helping your mother to look after the children while we are away.'

'Pauline needed to get right away – she was extremely upset over Frank.'

Frank Whitney had been devastated by Tiffany's marriage. Against all the odds and every ounce of commonsense, he had continued to hope – utterly unable to escape from her spell. He began to drink even more heavily and when his work suffered, Tiffany fired him. To do her justice she did not stop his salary and continued to send him a handsome monthly cheque, but she refused to see him, being too impatient of human failings to extend a sympathetic or a helping hand. Frank had used the cheques to buy alcohol and had died of cirrhosis six months earlier. Tiffany had been on the receiving end of a few sharp, accusing glances which she considered totally unjustified – it was not her fault if the man behaved like a bloody fool.

'Pauline must pull herself together,' Tiffany announced briskly. 'Frank never had the slightest intention of marrying her, but then neither has anyone else. She should be grateful for what she has got – my father left her comfortably off, although why he should have bothered I really do not know.'

'Feeling the pinch, my dear? Has Pauline's modest bequest made you short of a dollar or two? If it has – which, of course, is absolute nonsense – bear in mind the profits which *I* am making. Soon I will have doubled your father's fortune.'

'And you are going to lend it to me for the South-West African investment.'

'I should not pursue this *personal* approach to the matter if I were you.'

367

'You are here as my banker – nothing else!'

Randolph remained calm, being confident of his supremacy over her. 'I do trust that you will maintain a united front with me at Anton's dinner party this evening. Your stridency and lack of acumen in this affair is unlikely to make a favourable impression.'

'Don't tell *me* how to handle myself in such circumstances! Of course I will keep up appearances in front of Anton.'

'Good! After all,' and he smiled, 'we are a team.'

'A team?' Only up to a point, Randolph, she thought, only up to a very clear breaking point. 'I do hope,' Tiffany said aloud, 'that no other guests will be present.'

The Bright house had been a palace amid a shanty town when Matthew built it in the mid-Seventies, but it was a far cry from Brightwell and the mansion in Park Lane. Indeed the rambling single-storey dwelling was modest by present-day Kimberley standards, but as Miranda wandered slowly from room to room, she was glad that it had been repaired after the Siege, not demolished and rebuilt. Here Matthew and Anne had lived during the early years of their marriage; here their baby daughter, Victoria, had been born and died; here Philip had been born and lived for the last year of his life before his fateful journey to South-West; and here Miranda herself had come at the age of five, only to be caught up in the dangers of the Siege.

Miranda sought memories, but only a few faint feelings of familiarity and recognition were aroused. She walked into the garden. Somewhere here Uncle Nicholas died after the house was shelled and nearby was the dug-out where we sheltered. Now the lawn was smooth and no physical trace of those days remained, but did any spiritual presence linger here? Had the events of those early pioneer days left an imprint on the fabric of the building or the still warm air? Had Matthew left his mark? Miranda stood in the garden, reliving her family's history, unaware that

John Court had shared this house with her parents or that in this house Tiffany had been conceived.

It was late afternoon when she received Anton's note, inviting her to dinner. She had expected him to meet her at the station but Mr Pemberton, the Secretary of the Diamond Company, had swept her swiftly from her private railway coach to a waiting car. No lack of red-carpet treatment *here*, she had thought wryly, as obsequious officials cleared a path for her. At the house a heap of envelopes and cards awaited her.

'It is not every day the Chairman's daughter comes to town,' observed Pemberton, smiling at her consternation. 'You will be inundated with invitations and offers of hospitality.'

'I had not realised . . .' She was so wrapped up in the real reason for her visit that she had overlooked the possibility of other commitments and responsibilities. More than anything, Miranda wanted to be left alone so that she could concentrate fully on Anton. 'The length of my stay is uncertain and my programme is in the hands of Mr Ellenberger. I do not wish to offend anyone, but I fear I may have to decline most of the invitations.'

'You will meet most of these people at the civic functions which Ellenberger is organising. However, naturally you will wish to visit the Mine and I shall be delighted to accompany you.'

'No, no . . . it is very kind of you, but I will not have time.'

'No time to visit the Mine?' Pemberton stared at her in astonishment. The Mine – the famous 'Big Hole' of Kimberley, the largest man-made hole in the world – was the sole reason most people visited the town.

Miranda could not explain her fear of the place. She realised that in a town as small as Kimberley she could not avoid the dominating presence of the Mine, but she could avoid the 'Big Hole' and the underground workings beneath.

'I have seen it before,' she said, rather abruptly. 'But perhaps I may let you know if I change my mind?'

That evening she dressed in a simple gown of cream

chiffon in the style of the French Empire, its high waist and the spirals of its layered skirt banded in silver. There was a tight knot of nervousness in her stomach. Don't be silly, she admonished herself, Anton is an old friend. But did the fact that he was an old friend render her task easier or more difficult? Miranda was not sure – she knew only that Matthew was depending on her. However, the evening would be made easier for her if she and Anton were dining alone: she did hate crowds.

But the windows of Anton's residence blazed with light, a motor car was parked outside and another carriage was driving away from the porch. While she took off her coat, Miranda resigned herself to the fact that this was a party, but the realisation was overshadowed by another factor: Anton lived in an extremely imposing house. She frowned thoughtfully. She knew that Anton had built up a sound business in Kimberley and had invested in the gold mines on the Reef but, brought face-to-face with the tangible evidence of his success, she wondered for the first time how he had accumulated the necessary capital. Either he must have been very thrifty during his years with Bright Diamonds, she decided, or had met with a stroke of immense good fortune.

It was not only Anton Ellenberger's financial status which had changed; the demeanour and bearing of the man who came to meet her was altogether different from that of the diffident clerk she had known in London. Even recently, despite his increasing wealth, there had been something about Anton which did not fit into the London social scene. He was not smart, witty, handsome or well-born and remained unacceptable to Britain's upper echelons. During his visits to London, he and Miranda had met over a succession of quiet dinners together and so she was astonished at the new air of confidence which he exuded. That pervasive aura of inferiority had vanished.

'Miranda!' He took her outstretched hand and held it between his own for slightly longer than was strictly necessary. 'I am greatly honoured that you should accept my

370

invitation.' As usual he spoke to her in German.

'Nonsense! I wouldn't have missed it for the world.' She smiled at him with genuine warmth, aware that she was sincerely glad to see a familiar and trustworthy face. 'Congratulations on your appointment.'

'Thank you. Unfortunately I had to lose a good friend before I was elected.'

'Oh?' Through the open doors Miranda could see several people standing in the drawing-room and deliberately she prolonged the personal moment with Anton, postponing the ordeal of conversing with strangers.

'Kimberley was raised to the status of a city at the end of 1912, when it merged with the township of Beaconsfield. I took an interest in local politics from the time I settled here and was elected to the council, but was surprised to be chosen as Mayor when the first holder of the office – as I say, he was a friend of mine – died suddenly a couple of months ago.'

'Will you find time to undertake the necessary duties?'

'I will make time,' Anton answered quietly. 'Kimberley has been good to me and I would like to give something in return.'

Miranda nodded and, reluctantly, allowed him to steer her gently into the drawing-room. She recognised none of the other guests, but noted the slight air of deference with which their entry was received and that it was not directed solely at herself. In Kimberley Anton Ellenberger was *somebody!*

'Once again, Miranda, thank you for coming. I must confess that I did not believe Sir Matthew would allow you to make the journey.'

'Why?'

'I have the impression that I am not popular with him.' Anton spread his hands in a slight gesture of apology. 'I feel he was displeased when I left his employ.'

'My father respected your ability and the contribution which you made to Bright Diamonds,' returned Miranda, 'but I am certain he is realistic enough to understand the position when someone wishes to set up in business on his own account. Besides, my father is . . .' She stopped abruptly, for she had been about to explain Matthew's obsession with his dynasty, that the family and its name must retain control of his empire, that an outsider like Anton could only act as caretaker for the family interests . . . No, she thought quickly, don't say it . . . don't say too much about anything.

'Will you excuse me for one moment? My final guests . . .'

Miranda walked towards the window, unconcerned about being left on her own temporarily, knowing full well that the dreaded round of introductions would start all too soon. It was not that she forgot names or faces but that in a crowd she had no means of telling who would talk next and therefore could not watch the speaker's lips. In a crowd Miranda lost the thread of conversation quickly.

She felt a touch on her arm and turned to see Anton say, 'I would like you to meet someone . . . but perhaps you two ladies remember each other?'

Miranda composed her lips into a smile and slowly her gaze left Anton's lips to travel towards the face of the new-comer . . . and then the smile froze as the room started to spin.

Tiffany had entered the house gaily, masking her disappointment that they were not to be *tête-à-tête* with Anton. She had greeted their host effusively and sailed into the drawing-room on his arm – very much the sophisticated American society woman about to bestow her favours and the honour of her company upon the inhabitants of this humble colonial outpost. Like Miranda she was wearing a Parisian gown, but Tiffany's was the latest fashion, its deep violet folds flowing sinuously from her shoulders, the loose light 'over-coat' of violet and crimson caught to black shoulder-straps with diamond clips and trailing into a short train. On her head she wore a chic black turban edged in violet and crimson. The effect was rich, exotic and dramatic.

When Anton guided her in the direction of the blonde girl

who stood with her back towards them, Tiffany automatically analysed the girl's dress. 'Good quality,' she thought with some surprise, 'but very dull!'

A second later Tiffany noticed nothing but the face, the blue eyes and golden hair which so exactly resembled those of Matthew Bright.

They were back in the hall at Park Lane, Tiffany in the first flush of her horror and hate, disgust and despair, her head whirling with images of Matthew, Anne, Philip and her father – and with Miranda and everything which Philip had told her about Miranda . . . as violet eyes locked into blue, they relived that moment again . . . Tiffany aggressive, Miranda defensive because she did not understand . . .

Tiffany saw Philip's sister, *her* sister, and could not come to terms with it. Philip was dead and, God help her, she had been *relieved* when he died because his permanent departure helped to relegate the entire ghastly affair to the mists of unreality. *It had never happened!* She had succeeded in banishing all thoughts and memories of Philip – if there was one good thing about Randolph, it was that he did take your mind off your other troubles! God, if Randolph should find out that she was illegitimate and that she had committed incest with her half-brother – then there would be no escape from his power! But he would not find out. Tiffany was certain that Matthew would tell no one, not even Miranda. Gradually the colour returned to her cheeks as she regained control of her emotions.

Miranda saw only a disturbing, disruptive influence, the perception of which was heightened by her extreme sensitivity. She was aware of feeling defenceless against such strength of character and inferior to such peerless beauty – for now she saw something of which she had been unaware at their last meeting: Miranda was certain she was looking at the woman whom Rafe Deverill loved.

The moment was over in seconds, unnoticed by anyone else – except Randolph.

'Of course we have met,' said Tiffany. 'What a pleasant surprise to meet you here, Miss Bright.'

The mouths of Anne's daughters curved into fixed, polite smiles but their eyes remained locked.

'What brings you to Kimberley, Mrs Court?' Miranda asked softly.

'Oh, I feel sure that the purpose of my visit is the same as yours!' Now Tiffany's lips curled. 'An invitation from Anton. What a charming gesture, Anton, to invite us both to your civic celebrations!'

'Not charming, merely logical and infinitely enjoyable,' Anton said smoothly. 'The two diamond heiresses – in Kimberley, the city which their fathers helped to found. Somehow the situation seemed exactly *right* – my inauguration as Mayor was merely a convenient excuse.'

'*That*,' said Tiffany crisply, 'is the truest statement you have made all evening!' And she winced as Randolph's hand gripped her arm tightly.

'Don't be a fool,' Randolph hissed as Anton led Miranda towards another group of guests. 'Keep a cool head. That is twice you have overreacted.'

'Twice?' She looked at him sharply.

'Your discomposure at meeting Miranda Bright was most marked. Could it be that you take your father's old feud with the Brights more seriously than I realised ? Or,' and he smiled, 'is there something I don't know?'

Tiffany's throat constricted. 'I was discomposed for only one reason! Anton has invited Miranda and me here because we are rivals! He possesses, or nearly possesses, something we both want – the diamond fields of South-West Africa – and he is cultivating our rivalry for a very good reason: when two people compete for the same thing, the price goes up!'

'Your argument is over-simplified. This development means only that there is a component missing from the offer we intended to make. We shall go ahead with that original offer and in the meantime you may leave it to me to locate the missing ingredient and rectify the matter.'

Tiffany bit her lip sharply to prevent the retort. Leave it to him? Under no circumstances did she intend to leave it to him! This development meant that she had to take on Randolph *and* Matthew – because Tiffany did not see Miranda as a threat in herself; she saw only the larger-than-life figure of Matthew Bright standing behind his daughter. For a moment Tiffany's courage wavered – could she out-manoeuvre these two brilliant men? Yes, she could because she *must!*

Facing each other on either side of Anton at the head of the dinner table, both Tiffany and Miranda were glad that he proved to be an excellent host and that he guided the conversation along lines which enabled them to avoid a direct exchange. The respite allowed time for adjustment to the changed circumstances and for mutual observation. Anton was describing the strata of Kimberley society with a wry humour.

'At the top are the Directors of the Diamond Company,' he announced, looking at Miranda, 'who rank next to God – whether above or below being uncertain!'

Miranda joined in the general laughter, grateful for an opportunity to ease some of her tension but wondering if she would ever dare to relate the joke to Matthew.

'Next come the senior executives of the Diamond Company, followed by the diamond dealers,' and here Anton bowed gravely. 'Then the doctors, lawyers and bank managers and finally *the rest* – unclassified, but young men are likely to rise in the ranks if they catch the eye of a senior lady.'

He smiled at Pauline Court in a conspiratorial fashion, conveying the impression that *she* would be besieged by such suitors and that the fortunate recipients of her favours would advance rapidly in the hierarchy.

Pauline smiled back shyly. She was still a plain little person, dressed in an unfortunate shade of pink, but the plumpness had gone, melting from her bones as she witnessed the destruction of Frank Whitney. She knew that Frank had not been a particularly worthy or sensible man, but had clung to her hopes of marrying him, not only out of genuine affection but also because he was her only chance. Now she was resigned to spinsterhood but sometimes, when she looked at Tiffany, Pauline wondered if she would ever be able to forgive her.

So Pauline watched with considerable satisfaction as this pleasant, courteous Mr Ellenberger snubbed Tiffany after dinner.

'Miranda, do come and look at an old photograph of Kimberley which I have acquired – it shows a glimpse of Sir Matthew's office in the main street. Perhaps the rest of you will be good enough to excuse us for ten minutes?'

Anton led Miranda to the door, leaving a seething Tiffany to notice the familiarity with which he held Miranda's arm and how intimately they conversed in German as they left the room.

The photograph was virtually identical to one Matthew displayed in his London office – a fact of which Anton must be well aware, having entered that room a thousand times. Miranda sat down beside his desk and sought an opening gambit. Blandly Anton solved the problem for her.

'Did you enjoy your trip to South-West?'

'Very much.' That the Regie had reported her visit underlined the closeness of the relationship between the German authorities and Anton Ellenberger. 'But what I saw and what I learned disturbed me, too. The potential of the South-West African diamond fields is unknown – at any rate, to anyone outside the Regie – but the production figures are staggering. If Britain goes to war with Germany, the agreement my father is negotiating with the Regie will be nullified, but it is vital that the diamond production of South-West is kept within reasonable limits.'

'A limit on production is vital to the Diamond Company and, in particular, to the Syndicate. Whether it is so important to everyone connected with the industry, I wouldn't be too sure.'

'But it is – of course, it is! Each arm of the industry must be affected – from the producers to the dealers, cutters, retailers, purchasers and investors – because the *price will fall*. Even the final purchaser of a cut gem would not want

376

that to happen, because where is the pleasure and prestige in owning a fine diamond if everyone, from the washerwoman to the street-walker, is festooned in the bloody things!'

Anton smiled at her vehemence and turn of phrase. 'The whole point is that the Syndicate would never allow that to happen. Miranda, when you and I used to sit in your schoolroom at Park Lane and talk about diamonds, how did I define the role of the Syndicate?'

'To have always sufficient capital on hand to buy the diamonds which are produced,' Miranda recited slowly. 'In times of over-production or recession the Syndicate must continue to buy in order to maintain market stability, even if that entails placing the diamonds in "cold storage".'

'Exactly – and that is precisely what has been happening. The producers have been digging the diamonds out of the ground while the Syndicate have been burying them again in London vaults! Now, do you still think that over-production harms the *producer*?'

Miranda did not reply. Her mind was edging slowly, painfully ahead to the logical end to this argument.

'Incidentally,' Anton went on with great delicacy, 'the purchases of the Syndicate in recent years must have . . . *stretched* its members' resources somewhat?'

A fire was burning brightly in the hearth a few feet away, but Miranda was seized by a sudden chill. All the owner of the South-West African diamond fields had to do was to go on producing, in the certain knowledge that his entire production must eventually be bought in by the Syndicate. An unscrupulous owner could virtually bankrupt the financiers behind the Syndicate and by this means make a bid for the Diamond Company itself, using the Company's own resources to buy its shares. It was a threat she had not fully comprehended before – a threat not merely to the Company and the industry but, most of all, to her father.

Anton was not unscrupulous, she thought doubtfully, but he possessed more ambition than she had realised.

And if he went into partnership with the Courts … Miranda shivered … 'Unscrupulous' did not seem a sufficiently strong term to describe Tiffany and Randolph.

'The cash resources of the Syndicate have been under some pressure,' she responded cautiously, 'but obviously there is sufficient liquidity to weather the storm. My father, for instance, would experience no difficulty in raising the necessary finance for the purchase and development of the South-West fields – if he found the right partner, of course.'

'Of course,' Anton agreed, smiling.

Miranda hesitated, unsure whether she dared to venture beyond the boundaries of her authority. Matthew expected her to report on the situation, not to initiate action, but the unexpected entry into the lists of Tiffany Court had surely changed all that.

'It seems to me,' she said slowly, 'that if Bright Diamonds entered into a partnership to obtain the franchise in South-West, the enterprise would result in an exchange of shares with the Diamond Company and a seat on the Board for that partner.' She stood up, opened the study door and, remembering the discussion at dinner, continued, 'A Director of the Diamond Company – a seat next to God in one simple step.'

Anton took hold of her hand and said softly in German, 'Without having to catch the eye of a senior lady?'

She smiled. 'Some men – but only a very few – might manage both.'

He raised her hand to his lips but then, after a brief hesitation, leaned across to kiss her lightly, in continental fashion, on both cheeks.

'It has been a most interesting discussion,' he said, 'and I look forward to seeing you again tomorrow.'

Miranda left without re-entering the drawing-room. At home she sank on to the floor in front of the fire. Her shock at seeing Tiffany had abated slightly and now it seemed impossible that the situation could ever have been other than it was – the two of them, heirs to the fortunes of the

378

early pioneers, competing for a stake in the new El Dorado, fighting it out in the very city where it had all begun. Or did the threat go further than the diamonds of South-West Africa . . .?

She stared into the heart of the fire. Whether Matthew liked it or not, she was on the spot and she must *do* something! She had placed an opening offer on the table which was based on her major advantage over the Courts – Matthew's influence and his 30 per cent holding in the Diamond Company. Doubtless it would be necessary to raise the bid, but there was no hurry, for Anton would be happy to milk the situation for all it was worth – that is why he had asked them here. Oh Philip, Miranda cried silently, how could you fail so completely to comprehend the potential of the South-West diamond discoveries! If you had not sent such misleading information to Papa, this need never have happened!

She rose and walked from room to room, seeking inspiration and reassurance, trying to breathe in any vestiges of her father's spirit and flair which might linger in the air. Tiffany had Randolph to help her and he looked exceedingly capable – in fact he looked capable of just about anything! But she had no one. Wandering through the empty house, Miranda felt lonely, very lonely indeed.

On the pretext of visiting the bathroom, Tiffany had positioned herself in the ante-room between the hall and the drawing-room from where she hoped to catch a glimpse of Anton and Miranda. She was watching when the study door opened and she witnessed their farewell. Her eyes narrowed thoughtfully, but she decided not to tell Randolph what she had seen – every bit of knowledge she acquired must be used to strengthen her own hand.

'One must admire Miranda Bright's command of language and speech,' Randolph remarked when she rejoined him, 'and, of course, her personal charms.'

'Oh, I'm certain that her personal charms would be right up your alley, Randolph!' Tiffany murmured in a low

voice. She had a sudden mental picture of Miranda enduring Randolph's assault and it was an image which she
found pleasing. Tiffany had not forgotten Miranda's youthful deceit in reading other people's letters. 'But she might
be too subdued for your liking. On the other hand, one
should not be misled by her air of innocence – once I
remarked that she did not look like competition, but now I
am not so sure.'

'Did you really say that? To whom, and on what
occasion?'

'It is not relevant,' Tiffany snapped, cursing herself for
the unguarded remark. 'What does matter is the indisputable fact that Anton is giving priority to her.'

'No. He is playing off one party against the other, which
is precisely what I would do in his position. Have patience,
my dear. Our turn is about to come.'

Sure enough, when the other guests drifted to the door,
Anton indicated to Randolph that the Courts should
remain behind. He came straight to the point.

'You examined the projections in my latest
memorandum?'

'In great detail. The potential of the South-West African
fields appears to be ... impressive.' Randolph chose his
words carefully and, as usual, verged on judicious understatement. 'Can we rely on your projected production
figures?'

'I carried out a personal survey during my recent visit to
the *Sperrgebiet* and I have discussed every aspect with my
consulting geologist and engineer. There can be no doubt
about it – the diamond fields of South-West Africa are ...'
Anton paused, then shrugged and shook his head, 'I was
going to say that they are inexhaustible, but obviously that
could not be strictly true! However, they will last our lifetime and beyond, well beyond.' He leaned forward. 'There
may be diamonds beneath the sea along that coast, and
one day we might possess the engineering expertise to
push back the waves in order to retrieve the gems from the
ocean bed itself.'

'But will the quality of the stones be maintained?'

'Undoubtedly. As you have seen from the specimens I showed you in New York, the quality is exceptional and the yield contains a particularly high proportion of fine gem stones.'

'Hm.' Randolph was leaning back in an upright chair, his elbows on the high wooden arms, hands held fingertip to fingertip. 'There is the political situation to consider. We discussed it at length when you were in New York but do you stand by your opinion that, if the British were to gain control of the territory after a war against Germany, the commercial producers could not be forced to sell to a government nominee?'

Anton hesitated. He did not wish to reveal the entire truth – to tell Randolph that the South African authorities were against a total British monopoly of the diamond industry. Randolph must believe that a deal with Matthew Bright was a very real possibility. 'I maintain that if the Germans were ousted from South-West, the territory would be administered from Pretoria, not from London,' he said at last. 'And it does so happen that the South African Minister of Mines is a very good friend of mine.'

Randolph's eyes gleamed appreciatively. 'I rather thought he might be.'

Randolph had made up his mind about the deal before leaving New York, but not even the unexpected presence of Miranda Bright would deter him from striking the best bargain he could. Competition might mean that Randolph had to *offer* more, but it did not mean that he must *receive* less.

'In themselves the diamonds might be too much of a gamble,' he said in his most precise voice. He glanced at Tiffany, expecting a protest, but she was gazing into space with a faraway look in her eyes. 'The deal must be tied to your other project – the gold mines of the East Rand. While the demand for diamonds is extremely sensitive to fluctuations in the world economy, there is an unlimited market for gold.'

'I intend to form a holding company for my gold-mining and diamond interests. One million shares will be issued, of which I and my South African associates would retain 51 per cent at par, while the remainder would be offered at a premium of £7 to investors like yourself. That would work out to approximately £3½ million. In addition we would need development capital in the form of a loan and I shall be seeking this in America.'

'It is surprising how little American investment has been made in southern Africa,' Randolph commented, 'considering the contribution made by our engineers. There has been personal investment on a small scale by men such as John Court, but nothing significant.'

'Surprising,' Anton agreed, 'but fortuitous. It leaves the field wide open for you, Randolph.'

Randolph's lips twitched. He was discovering what Miranda had found out an hour ago: that Anton Ellenberger had a way of presenting a proposal in a manner which depicted it as being more in his partner's interests than his own.

'So you would use your holding company as a spring-board for the diamond venture,' he observed. 'It would invest in the South-West African fields and from that base you would build up a network of interlocking companies – an Afro-American partnership which would be a new and powerful force in the mining world, challenging British supremacy.' Randolph nodded, suppressing a quiver of excitement at the prospect. 'I think it fair to say that the finance is available,' he said quietly.

He and Anton exchanged a smile. Each understood the other's position perfectly. Like Miranda, Randolph had made his opening offer. Now Anton would wait while both parties reviewed their own and their opponent's position and put in a higher bid.

Tiffany was very quiet – dangerously quiet. She had ignored the conversation. Let them fence with each other, she thought – or perhaps it was more like a bloody mating dance! The outcome of the discussion had never been in doubt, because the groundwork had been laid in New York. No, it was the next move which mattered. She could not erase the image of Anton kissing Miranda or the memory of their intimate conversation in German.

Suppose he married her?

Tiffany's glance flashed first at Randolph, full of venom because his existence precluded her from matching this card held by her rival. Oh, the vistas which could open up before her if she was not burdened with him . . .! Then she considered Anton. He was, she judged, a man who would make a marriage of convenience if the inducement was sufficient. In this instance Tiffany believed that the Courts' offer of finance would be more attractive than the Brights', *but* she was forced to concede that Miranda had a certain attraction of her own. Miranda could make all the difference.

She had been wrong to think in terms of Matthew; it was at Miranda that she must strike. In fact, although Miranda's challenge created difficulties, the situation had an advantage, too: Tiffany saw that it presented *her* with opportunities to prove her superiority over Randolph – to win the diamonds by her own initiative.

An idea was nagging at the back of her mind, trying to push its way through . . . but while she waited for that idea to be born, she must scotch any notion Anton might cherish of marrying Miranda. He was a practical man, with ambitions in both the political and industrial arenas, and he must be made to see that Miranda was totally unsuitable as a wife. That approach has the added advantage of enabling me to undermine her self-confidence, Tiffany reasoned, which in turn should weaken her bargaining prowess – if any!

Fortunately Miranda possessed the ideal Achilles heel at which to strike. She was deaf.

CHAPTER TWENTY-ONE

During the civic functions which took place over the next two days, Tiffany observed Miranda closely. She reviewed constantly the Brights' position, but that half-formed plan for countering their offer was hazy and would not crystallise. It felt strange not to discuss the matter openly with Randolph, because normally business was the only constituent which made the relationship tolerable, but now she must formulate her own strategy. In the meantime there was the other plan to consider . . . Tiffany watched how Miranda became confused in a crowd and how she relaxed visibly when talking *tête-à-tête*. Then, unwittingly, Anton Ellenberger provided the perfect opening.

'The people of Kimberley are notorious for their hospitality, but I do hope you are free on Wednesday night. June the tenth is Miranda's birthday and I am planning a small party for her.'

'*Small* party?'

'I thought that a dinner party of about a dozen guests would be suitable. One must remember that Miranda is . . .'

'Miranda is the daughter of the Diamond Company's chairman,' Tiffany cut in quickly, 'and that Company is the hub of this entire town. Kimberley will expect more of its Mayor than that! You ought to hire the Town Hall for the evening.'

Anton hesitated. Her suggestion was sound and yet . . . 'Not the Town Hall,' he said at last. 'The doors dividing my reception rooms fold back to create an area as big as a ballroom.'

'Excellent. You draw up a guest list of, say, sixty people and send out the invitations. You may leave the rest of the arrangements to me.'

Definitely she was up to no good and Anton felt a pang of concern for Miranda. However, he had brought them to Kimberley to fight it out and if Tiffany saw a way of gaining an advantage, so be it – and he had a shrewd suspicion that Miranda was tougher than she looked.

'Thank you,' he replied. 'You will find my housekeeper tolerably efficient.'

The ensuing forty-eight hours were a whirlwind of activity as Tiffany bullied and berated the servants into performing miracles. She supervised the preparation of the food, scoured the city for winter flowers and ensured that every piece of silver and furniture was polished to its brightest sheen. In particular she rearranged the furniture in the reception rooms, ordering the servants to move it first this way and then that until she was satisfied.

After opening the folding doors between the drawing-room and the dining-room, she had set the tables slightly to one end of the combined area, leaving a rough semi-circle of open floor by the doors into the ante-room which she kept closed. The main table was placed centrally, surrounded on three sides by clusters of smaller tables and on the fourth side by the empty space which provided a natural amphitheatre for the central characters in the drama Tiffany was composing.

'You look very pleased with yourself,' Randolph remarked when she arrived home. 'Have you set a sufficiently sticky trap for the poor little fly?'

'I don't know what you are talking about!'

'I am talking about the possibility that Anton might marry Miranda and the steps you are taking to prevent it.' He smiled at her expression. 'You see, my dear, I *know* you – very well indeed.'

A chill ran through her. How could she gain the advantage over him when apparently he was able to read her mind! 'Miranda is young and inexperienced,' she said

385

flatly. 'Also, she is very much "Daddy's little girl", but Daddy is thousands of miles away so she is on her own. Undermine her self-confidence and she will crack. Do it well enough and she might even cut and run. The key is Miranda's own character.'

'And we all know what a splendid judge of character you are, Tiffany,' Randolph murmured drily, 'particularly of the female character. But go ahead, my dear. It sounds a splendid scheme.'

Which probably meant that he really believed the whole idea stank, but that it was keeping her occupied while he made plans of his own! Come to think of it, he had been unusually reticent since the meeting with Anton but he was unlikely to have been idle and if he was not discussing his scheme with her, it was probable that the tactics centred on Court Diamonds. It might be worthwhile to pay a strictly secret visit to his study.

'We must hope,' Randolph was continuing, 'that Anton is not genuinely fond of the girl.'

'What a statement coming from you! Surely you believe he would marry for expediency, not for love? After all, wouldn't you? In fact, *didn't* you?'

He stroked her cheek with long cold fingers, sending a shiver of revulsion through her. 'I think you have more experience in that field than I do. If you had to choose between diamonds and love, I know very well what the outcome would be. You would not even find the choice difficult.'

Tiffany turned away and hurried upstairs to her room where she stood for a moment to calm herself. Such talk always reminded her of Philip and her design to gain control of Bright Diamonds. Sometimes it seemed as if Randolph *knew*, but perhaps her reaction was prompted by a guilty conscience . . . Love . . . Tiffany stared at herself in the mirror, admiring the beauty of face and figure which was reflected there. Why shouldn't she possess love? Why should all this be wasted on Randolph and a succession of ineffectual boring lovers! Somewhere there must be a man . . . and her heart twisted at the memory of the one man whom she had loved. But Tiffany was still a woman who lived for the present, not for the past. *Never regret* . . . She changed her clothes for the party but before leaving the house, unobtrusively tried the study door. It was locked.

The diamonds gleamed in the blue velvet depths of the casket. Slowly Miranda lifted out the necklace and draped it across her hands, moving her fingers so that the gems rippled like rivers of light: the Bright necklace, her childhood plaything, which she had inherited on her eighteenth birthday. Now the jewels were even less of a toy, not even a decoration, but a symbol of the burden which her inheritance placed upon her. The necklace represented the gems which aroused no passion in her but which were Matthew's obsession. It was a manifestation of the South-West African diamonds for which she cared nothing but which she must acquire for Matthew's sake.

Miranda disliked the necklace. It set too high a standard, demanding that her beauty should be as flawless as its own. It asked too much. But she did not need to wear the Bright jewels tonight – in Kimberley, of all places, she had no need to flaunt her wealth and status. She replaced the casket in the drawer and put on her pearls.

No one had told her any details of the evening's entertainment and it would be rude to ask in case it was supposed to be a surprise. Miranda groaned. Oh God, how she hated surprises! But on the other hand how completely *feeble* she was being, sitting here in a state of deep depression, dreading her own birthday party! The trouble with me, she thought, is that I am not any fun. People are kind to me because of *who* I am, not because of *what* I am – or should that be the other way round? And just as she was beginning to believe that there might be one man who was interested in her, and not in her father or her father's money, he had turned out to be . . .

Angrily Miranda directed her thoughts back to Tiffany

but found no comfort. Inevitably everyone would draw comparisons between the two diamond heiresses and, as Pauline had found years ago, Miranda felt it was impossible to compete. Tiffany was cracking the mask of Miranda's composure, exposing the weaknesses which Miranda had fought so gallantly over the years, her absolute perfection impressing upon Miranda that people only courted *her* out of duty, avarice or pity for her deafness.

In the ante-room at Anton's house Miranda stood woodenly, knowing that although this was her birthday party she was not the chief attraction. Everyone was watching the door, waiting for Tiffany to make her entrance. Then there she was, sweeping into the room in a low-cut black evening gown whose full skirt was fully fifteen inches from the ground, and with diamonds sparkling in her dark hair and at her ears, throat and wrist. The guests stared, hypnotised by the creamy breasts which swelled beneath the daring neckline, by the tantalising ankles and calves in black silk stockings – and by the diamonds.

In that moment, lowering her eyes to her own traditional attire of white chiffon and lace, Miranda was overwhelmed by her own inadequacy. It was not enough to be a diamond heiress – you had to *look* like one! The public wanted its heroines to be glamorous and controversial; it wanted them to wear diamonds because it wanted to gossip about them, envy them and emulate them. Oh why, oh why, had she left the Bright Diamonds at home!

At dinner she was seated at the main table, flanked by Anton and Randolph, with her back to the open area of floor behind. Her demoralisation was nearly complete and she was withdrawing into herself, making less than her customary effort to communicate. But even if she had tried, Tiffany was ensuring that she would not succeed.

Tiffany had seated herself at Anton's other hand, on the same side of the table as Miranda, knowing that the deaf girl could not see her face. And she was dominating that table, tossing the conversation like a brilliantly jewelled ball from person to person, conquering by the force of her wit, the subtle nuances of her voice and the animation on that exquisite face.

The more Tiffany talked, the more isolated Miranda became. She had a clear impression of waiting for something dreadful to happen – but what? That 'surprise'? Gratefully she relaxed for a few minutes while Anton rose to make a warm polite speech in her honour. She could follow snatches of it when he turned in her direction, but then she noticed that Tiffany's seat was empty. Where was she? Miranda stared at the blurred sea of faces around her and then became aware that Anton had sat down again and that everyone was staring at her expectantly. But why?

Tiffany was standing behind Miranda in the empty space which provided a natural stage, beside a trolley bearing a large birthday cake. She was holding that stage magnificently, knowing full well the effect of her black-gowned figure with the diamonds dancing in her hair, as compared with her pale blank-eyed rival.

'Miranda,' she called for the second time. 'Come and cut the cake!'

Now there was a stir in the room. No one else intended to be discourteous, but ironically Miranda was the victim of her own brave endeavours – most people had genuinely forgotten that she was deaf, so natural had she seemed when speaking to them. In the embarrassed silence no one noticed a side door open and a man step quietly into the room. He leaned against the wall, folding his arms across his elegantly cut tailcoat, and watched.

Anton shook Miranda's arm. 'The cake,' he said clearly.

Stumbling to her feet, Miranda turned to look behind her. She felt confused, her head full of strange discordant noises and a tension as if a tight band was bound around her brow. Tiffany was holding the cake knife and Miranda stretched out her hand to take it. But Tiffany was holding the knife by the handle and before she could turn it round, Miranda's hand brushed clumsily against the blade. The point pressed into her palm and a drop of bright red blood dripped on to the white icing of the cake.

Their eyes met. To Miranda that knife was a dagger, aimed not at her heart but at the diamond industry and at her father. To Tiffany that spot of blood was a terrifying revelation: she was enjoying this, was revelling in her victim's struggles. Her own actions reminded her of someone – Randolph! She was becoming more and more like Randolph. It was revolting and yet it was fascinating. He *was* driving her further down the evil road . . . Thrusting the handle of the knife into Miranda's hand, Tiffany remembered that today was also the twentieth anniversary of their mother's death. The thought was so disturbing that she could virtually watch herself take another step into darkness. She waited for Miranda to resume her seat while the servants completed cutting the cake. Then Tiffany clapped her hands.

'Surprise!' she cried.

At the signal the folding doors opened, revealing the presence in the ante-room of Herr Rybnakir's famed dance band. They struck up a merry polka as servants hurried forward to roll back the carpet from that empty area which, with the ante-room, now provided a spacious dance floor.

'Anton, will you open the dancing with Miranda?' Tiffany asked, smiling angelically.

He looked at her but he looked also at the happy faces of his other guests, the women in particular delighted at the prospect of an informal dance. Tiffany Court was a bitch, but she was a beautiful bitch and therefore he could forgive her. She was establishing his reputation in Kimberley: people would remember Miranda Bright's birthday party.

Then Tiffany's expression changed and Sarah Bernhardt could not have done it better. 'Oh my God, I forgot,' she said loudly, staring hard at Miranda so that of course everyone else did the same. 'You poor dear, I am *so* sorry!'

Miranda flushed scarlet but pride came to her rescue. 'I do not dance but enjoy watching. Please, Anton, do dance.'

He hesitated, not wanting to give Tiffany total victory, and then effected a compromise. 'Pauline, will you do me the honour?'

Pauline felt real sympathy for Miranda but had been too long in the wilderness herself to forgo this moment of pleasure. Besides, Miranda Bright did not look as though she wanted to talk. Pauline gave her hand to Anton, Tiffany sulkily accompanied Randolph, gradually the table emptied and Miranda was left on her own.

She had her back to the dance floor but did not change her position or turn her head, visualising only too well how marvellously those black-stockinged feet in their black satin shoes would be spinning round the room. She felt utterly humiliated, for if there was one thing she could not stand it was *pity*. She sensed that pity all around her, coupled with embarrassment and with guilt because people felt that they ought to be sitting with her instead of enjoying themselves. I might as well go home, Miranda thought, right home to London, because I haven't a hope against Tiffany.

In the shadows on the far side of the room the man was still leaning against the wall, but now he walked over to the table and sat down beside her, laying his hand on her arm to attract her attention.

'Dance with me,' said Rafe Deverill.

She stared at him in bewilderment, wondering how he had managed to gatecrash the party and what he was doing in Kimberley. Had he really followed her, as he said he would?

'Impossible,' she said.

'Nothing is impossible. Try!'

'I cannot hear the music.'

'No, but I can. They are playing a waltz and I will count the beats. You have watched others waltz?'

'Yes . . . but only watched.'

'*Feel* the music through me . . . Don't panic if you stumble – just look as though you are enjoying yourself.'

'People will laugh at me.'

'Courage is more likely to evoke a tear than a laugh. Trust me – I will not let you fall.'

'Trust *you*?' Her eyes were wide with wistfulness and disbelief.

'There does not appear to be anyone else upon whom you can rely – except yourself.' He stood up, but when Miranda did not move he took her hands and pulled her to her feet. 'Tiffany is doing it on purpose,' he whispered. '*Do not let her win!*'

Damn it, what did she have to lose! Miranda allowed him to lead her on to the floor.

'Forget that anyone else is here. Concentrate on me.'

When his arms were around her, his face and body so close to hers, it was not difficult to obey. Miranda watched his lips.

'One, two, three,' he counted rhythmically. '*Now.*'

Miranda stumbled over the first few steps but she did know the movements of a waltz and he supported her easily, half-carrying her across the floor. The rhythm *did* seem to flow from his body into hers . . . she was floating . . . she was *dancing!* Suddenly her face lit up and she smiled so spontaneously and joyously that it brought a lump to the throats of the onlookers. Because the other guests were watching. At first they had gaped in astonishment at the sight of Rafe Deverill with Sir Matthew's deaf daughter, but now they stood against the walls and applauded. Alone on the floor, Rafe and Miranda circled until at last he led her back to her seat.

'The best way to hit back at Tiffany is to go on dancing. Herr Rybnakir will play waltzes all night if you want him to – it is *your* party!' In front of everyone, he kissed her hand. 'But you must be on your guard,' he said softly, 'and in this you must trust me, because no one knows better than I just what an inventive mind Tiffany Court possesses!'

He turned and his gaze swept lazily over the crowd until it alighted on a deathly-white face and a pair of blazing violet eyes. Rafe Deverill smiled, bowed ironically and left the room.

At the sight of Rafe Tiffany had jerked to an abrupt standstill, frozen with horror, the colour draining from her face. The shock was stunning but it must be concealed – at all costs it must be concealed from Randolph! Tiffany fought one of the hardest battles of her life to maintain that cold, proud expression. In the midst of her own raging emotions she was very aware of what other people would be thinking – that here in the same room was the man who had 'raped' her. She must brazen it out. People would gossip – but they would not gossip behind the back of Tiffany Court!

Tiffany danced on, trying not to meet Randolph's eyes, trying not to watch Miranda's triumphant progress. If I ever hear another waltz, Tiffany thought hysterically, I shall scream.

'Tiffany, I do apologise,' Anton said sincerely. 'Needless to say, Captain Deverill was not invited but as he seemed to be a friend of Miranda's, I could hardly throw him out.'

'It was a shock to me, but I am perfectly all right now so there is no need to make a fuss.' She, Anton and Randolph were sitting alone at the table while the others danced. Tiffany took a long gulp of wine to steady herself. 'So this is the hole he hid in! You might have warned me.'

'I understand that Deverill lives in Cape Town, but he has friends in Kimberley whom he visits from time to time. I had no idea that he was here – perhaps he came to see Miranda.'

This possibility did nothing to improve Tiffany's state of mind. 'His effrontery is amazing,' she said, with an attempt at a laugh. 'To dare to show his face in society – invited or not!'

'Kimberley is far removed from London and the distance is not only geographical. I hate to say this to you, but half-remembered gossip only adds a certain spice to the Captain's character! After all, no one knows quite what happened ...' Anton coughed apologetically. 'Under-standably, the details of the affair always were a trifle vague.'

'Yes, they were, weren't they,' murmured Randolph.

'However,' Anton continued, 'naturally I shall let it be known that his company is unwelcome to you.'

'No, don't do that.' Tiffany was thinking quickly. If peo-ple here had forgotten the affair, then it was best not to stir it up again. She needed to sort out her whirling thoughts and until that was achieved doors ought to be left ajar. 'As long as I don't have to speak to him, it doesn't matter.'

'Randolph?'

Randolph had been watching every flicker of expres-sion on Tiffany's face. 'All things considered, I would pre-fer to have Captain Deverill out in the open where I can keep an eye on him.'

Tiffany hung on to her self-control until she reached home and the privacy of her bedroom. Then, as she had done when she heard the truth about Philip, she allowed the torment to wash over her. She had learned what it took John Court a lifetime to discover: that your sins will find you out, that your lies will follow you across oceans and pursue you across continents. Bad enough to be faced with Miranda, but to have Rafe resurrected before her eyes ...! What was his relationship with Miranda? And Randolph ... Randolph would not sit back and let this pass ... Oh, why all these complications when she needed a sharp clear mind for the most important manoeuvres of her life! Tiffany could feel the pressure building up inside her head and she leaned back on the bed, pressing her hands to her throbbing temples.

She had come to Kimberley determined to avoid her father's past, but it was the ghosts of her own past which were haunting her! At least the cast must be complete – there could not possibly be anyone else to rise from the graves she had dug in her mind.

Outside in the passage a floorboard creaked. Randolph? Hardly daring to breathe, Tiffany watched the door. He had not spoken to her about Rafe during the journey home, but Pauline had been in the carriage and suddenly Tiffany was glad of her presence, grateful that her sister-in-law was asleep in the room across the landing because surely that fact imposed certain limitations upon Randolph. She heard a door close and her breath exhaled in a long sigh of relief. It would be more like Randolph to play cat-and-mouse with her, keep her wondering what he would say and when he would say it, what he would do and when he would do it.

But an interview with Randolph was not the only prospect which awaited her, for surely Rafe Deverill would seek her out. As dawn broke Tiffany still lay awake, contemplating a confrontation which she both dreaded and desired.

When the last guest had departed, Anton strode purposefully to his study and flung open the door. As he had expected, his chair was occupied and a large pair of well-shod feet rested on the desk beside a half-empty whisky bottle.

'As Tiffany so aptly remarked, you might have warned me!'

'Is that what she said?' Rafe swung his long legs off the desk, stood up and stretched. 'I could not tell you in advance because I only heard about the party today and my decision was made rather on the spur of the moment. Anyway, you might not have wanted me to come.'

'*Might* not have wanted . . . Christ, Rafe, you could have ruined everything!' Then Anton smiled. 'Mind you, the look on Tiffany's face when she saw you – waltzing with Miranda . . . Oh God, it was wonderful!'

'I do wish I could have seen it, but one cannot have everything.'

Anton looked at him curiously. 'I was not aware that you were so friendly with Miranda.'

'Surely your spies in the Regie told you that I took her to Luderitzbucht?'

'No, they made no mention of it and I did not think to

395

inquire into her means of transport. Rafe, what the hell are you up to?'

Rafe's only reply was to adopt an expression of bewilderment and injured innocence.

Anton made a gesture of despair. 'Perhaps it is just as well if I don't know – life is complicated enough already! But do me one favour – refrain from rocking the boat again.'

'How on earth would I do that, even if I wanted to?'

'I have the feeling that your mere presence might be enough! Seriously, Rafe, it isn't only Tiffany and Miranda – I thought we had agreed that your visits to my house would be distinctly unpublicised.'

'We did, but this might be my last visit of this nature anyway.'

'Why?'

'That coast could become pretty uncomfortable if war breaks out, and besides there is a chance that my lifestyle may change.' Rafe's smile was enigmatic but, after ensuring that doors and curtains were closed, he produced a small leather bag from his pocket. 'The latest shipment,' he said as he poured the diamonds on to the desk.

Anton picked up several stones at random, examined them and then scooped all the gems back into the bag. 'I will value them as soon as possible. In the meantime, I expect you would like the usual cash on account?'

Without waiting for a reply he opened a safe, placed the diamonds inside and took out a large wad of banknotes which he handed to Rafe.

'You must have built up a tidy nest-egg,' he remarked.

'My dear Anton, if only that were true!'

'A great deal of money has passed across this desk in the past five years. What do you do with it? Obviously you keep the house and the *Corsair* looking shabby in order to avert suspicion, but you never seem to spend anything.'

'My crew receive a percentage and I have other overheads. As for the rest,' Rafe shrugged carelessly, 'I play a rotten hand of cards, my friend, and am an even worse judge of horseflesh. Would that I had been like you, Anton, and invested wisely.'

Anton stared at him sceptically. 'Whatever the case, it has been a profitable partnership and actually I think you may be right – the time may have come to stop. Smuggling is like gambling: the temptation is to carry on while one is winning. But that is the greedy way. The wise course is to set a limit upon one's profits and pull out of the game before one's luck runs out.'

'And before someone starts wondering where and how *you* acquired your stake money,' Rafe remarked. He sat down and poured himself another whisky. 'Drink?'

'Please.' Anton sank down into a chair, picked up the glass and sighed luxuriously. 'Best bloody drink of the entire evening. Diamond heiresses can be damn hard work.'

'Don't tell me – I know! But I must congratulate you on your scheme. If I have worked out the moves correctly, you appear to have covered every contingency. You ought to take up chess – your performance would be masterly.'

'Why play with pieces of ivory when one can manipulate real people?'

'Which king are you trying to checkmate, Anton – or need I ask!'

'The King of Diamonds, of course – Matthew Bright.'

'And which girl offers you the best path to that king?' asked Rafe softly. 'The white queen or the black?'

'The black,' Anton replied instantly. 'The Courts can offer by far the strongest financial backing, because they enable me to link the diamonds to my plans for the gold mines of the East Rand. Also, I like the idea of involving Americans in South African investment – it is a move which would appeal to the authorities here – and Randolph Court is the ideal partner.' He saw Rafe's expression and smiled. 'Oh, Randolph is an unpleasant character in many ways, but he is a very good man to have on one's side! Yes, the Courts are the best bet financially speaking because, whatever Miranda says, I am sure that Matthew is stretched for money right now.'

'Is that so?' Rafe's eyes narrowed thoughtfully.

'Don't forget that I worked with Matthew for years and possess an intimate knowledge of his resources.'

'Then it seems as if it is all over bar the shouting.'

'No, not quite.' Anton hesitated. 'Originally, I thought that too. I only asked Miranda here to give the Courts a fright and squeeze a bit more out of them! But Miranda can offer two things which the Courts cannot match – at the moment, anyway. Through the Brights' immensely powerful shareholding, she can offer a seat on the Board of the Diamond Company, *and* she can offer . . .'

'. . . herself,' Rafe supplied grimly.

'Yes.' There was a long pause. 'She is very lovely,' Anton murmured, half to himself.

Rafe said nothing.

'So,' Anton continued more briskly, 'I have the option between an inside or an outside track. I must decide whether I use the white queen to check the king – which means waiting in the wings to succeed him. Or I can use the black queen to topple him from his throne and remove him from the game altogether.'

'Matthew Bright's health is not good.'

'He could live for another thirty years – that sort of man *does*!'

Rafe smiled faintly. 'I tend to agree with you. Well, whichever path you choose, you are a certain winner.'

'The *only* certain winner.'

Rafe drained his glass and stood up. 'Not necessarily the *only* one,' he said softly. 'There might be others who can benefit from this contest.'

CHAPTER TWENTY-TWO

No matter how hard she deliberated, or from how many angles she examined the situation, Miranda always came up with the same answer: she had only one card to play. And it happened to be the one card which she did not wish to play, because between her and her exaggerated sense of duty there would intrude a pair of grey eyes and a hard mouth which, for all their coldness, warmed her more than any diamond mine.

But marriage with Rafe Deverill was impossible while marriage with Anton Ellenberger was the obvious solution because, particularly after the birthday party last night, Tiffany must not be allowed to win!

'Over my dead body!' Miranda said aloud.

'I do hope that it will not come to that!' and he was standing only a yard away from her in the dining-room, grinning with disarming cheerfulness.

Miranda's heart was pounding from shock. 'One of the worst aspects of being deaf is that people can creep up on me!' she said breathlessly. 'Also, I instructed the servants that I was not at home to visitors.'

'Ah, but I let myself in through the garden door. Is there any tea left in the pot?'

She was sitting over the breakfast table and now rang for fresh tea and another cup. 'You appear to be well-acquainted with the geography of this house?'

'Only from the outside. When I visit Kimberley, I stay with an old army friend who lives only a few minutes away – you can see the house from here,' and Rafe indicated a roof which was just discernible through the trees. 'So I often pass by and naturally I take a special interest in this house. It is almost a place of pilgrimage, as you might say!'

'I can imagine,' Miranda said drily. 'I take it that you walked across this morning?'

'Through the garden,' he agreed, 'which affords easy access. If you wish to keep out intruders, you really ought to borrow a guard-dog from the Mine.'

They were silent for a moment, remembering Richie and how the Great Dane had been intended to prevent anyone from creeping up on her. Rafe felt again that chill of concern for her vulnerability.

'Mind you,' he continued with forced cheerfulness, 'I don't think that lurking in the bushes is quite Tiffany's style!'

She stared at him thoughtfully. 'Thank you for helping me last night,' she said slowly, 'but why did you do it?'

'That is a very silly question. Whose side am I likely to be on in this contest?'

'How do you know about a contest?'

Rafe collected himself quickly. 'You told me why you were visiting Kimberley. It seems logical to assume that Tiffany is here for the same reason.'

Miranda nodded. She wanted to believe that he was on her side, but could not help doubting it. Somehow, when she thought of Rafe and Tiffany, she could easily – too easily – envisage them . . . together.

She was standing in front of the fire and he walked across to her, resting his hands on her shoulders.

'It was *you* whom I followed to Kimberley,' he pointed out, 'just as I said I would. Does last night make amends for our quarrel? Am I forgiven for being a smuggler?'

Miranda hesitated.

'I tell you what,' he continued. 'You shall reform me! I will give you a solemn promise that I will never smuggle diamonds again.'

'You are giving me your word as a *gentleman*?' Miranda's tone was sceptical but her eyes smiled.

He laughed. 'Friends?'

She nodded.

'In fact, perhaps rather more than friends.'

His hands tightened on her shoulders and for a moment she thought he was going to kiss her, but to her disappointment he released her and walked back to his chair. He lit a cigarette with fingers which trembled slightly.

'There was enmity between you and my father before that weekend at Brightwell,' Miranda said suddenly. 'Why?'

'I can give you only my side of the story, not his!' He drew thoughtfully on the cigarette and then nodded. 'But yes, I think you ought to know. First of all, your father told me in no uncertain terms to keep away from his womenfolk.'

'Julia?' queried Miranda unsteadily.

'The name was mentioned,' he agreed drily, 'but in a minor capacity. No, it was Laura he feared losing to my fatal charm, although why I cannot imagine – there is no more faithful wife in all England and I have a shrewd suspicion that Matthew Bright is a pretty hard act to follow! However, he also referred to you – most specifically.'

She had not believed her feelings for Rafe could become more impossible, but they just had. 'Is that all?' she asked desolately.

'No, there is my quarrel with him to consider. It is less personal but equally sincere. To me, Matthew Bright is the embodiment of the diamond magnates and Randlords in whose interests the Boer War was fought and in whose name the sins of that war were committed.'

'What sins did you commit?'

'You have heard of the concentration camps?'

She nodded. 'Julia talked about them a lot. What happened there seemed . . . a shame.' And Miranda grimaced at the inadequacy of the expression.

He laughed harshly. 'That is what Sergeant King said: "The whole thing seems a shame, sir," he said when we burned the first farm – a conflagration caused by the shooting of three of my finest troopers by the occupants of the farmhouse. So I asked the good Sergeant if he had

401

another suggestion, an alternative method of preventing the Boers from using the farms as supply depots so that they could continue the war indefinitely and go on killing men like those three lying in the mud. Lord Kitchener, I said, would be delighted to be acquainted with an alternative.'

Miranda said nothing, but stood watching his face.

'Naturally the Sergeant could not suggest an alternative – no one could! The Boers had chosen guerrilla warfare and our only retaliation was a scorched earth policy. So my troopers slaughtered the livestock and in the yard they piled the contents of the house. There was an attempt at looting because it was considered "commandeering" when an officer was present. "Not when this officer is present," I declaimed in the true traditions of the British cavalry.' His lips curled as he stubbed out the cigarette. 'We burned the lot – even the baby's cradle.'

'And afterwards you sent the homeless women and children to the concentration camp?'

'Yes. The concentration camps – where more than twenty thousand of those women and children *died*.'

She could not hear the expression in his voice but she could see and sense his torment.

'For me there was one who came to represent all the others. There was a girl called Marianna.'

'With you there would always be a girl.'

'Perhaps . . . but this girl was six years old and she looked exactly like you.'

Miranda's eyes widened.

'She had a pet calf which she adored. I can still see her, clinging to its neck while one of my men stood by with a bayonet ready to cut its throat. She reminded me so much of you and that damn Great Dane!'

'You saved it?'

'Oh yes, I saved it – temporarily. I sent both Marianna and the calf to the concentration camp. What happened to the animal, I don't know. But Marianna died. I watched her die. So, coincidentally, did your cousin Julia.'

There was a long silence.

'I cannot help you,' she said. 'You need forgiveness – but not mine. I do hope that you find it.'

'For thirteen years I have searched for that forgiveness – I am beginning to give up hope because I don't know where to look.' Then suddenly he smiled. 'But those thirteen years have not been all doom and disaster. I have lived . . .'

'. . . and loved.'

He did not reply.

'If Marianna was symbolic of the women and children who died, don't I represent the other side of the coin?' she asked.

'At one time – but not any more. Nothing is your fault.'

He crossed the room, caught her in his arms and kissed her. And as she clung to him, pressing her body against his, there was such a stirring, such a melting within her, such an opening up and reaching out towards him, that Miranda felt she could die of it . . .

'Matthew's daughter,' he whispered at last, cradling her face in his hands. 'My God, but you are Matthew's daughter! It makes what I have to do easier and yet more difficult! Please remember that whatever I do and whatever I say, I *am* on your side! *Trust me!*'

And then he was gone, leaving Miranda to sink down in front of the fire and re-enter the real world – the world of Matthew and Anton Ellenberger, the diamonds and Tiffany Court, a world where Rafe Deverill was only the impossible dream. She was aware of the heat within her and the empty ache . . . but in this harsh world of reality her body was for sale, not for giving away. She must procrastinate no longer, yet part of her prayed for a miracle. Trust him? If only she could . . . if only she could . . .

Tiffany had lain awake all night, but dawn cast a shaft of light through her confused jumble of thoughts and she remembered that Randolph had not come straight to bed after the party. The chances were tha⁺ he had sat in his study and he might, just might, have left the door unlocked. Silently she crept downstairs and tried the door-handle. It turned. Either Randolph believed she was a weak-willed woman who would be so overcome with emotion after the party that his secret was safe tonight – or there was no secret.

The desk was covered with papers, meticulously sorted into neat piles, relating to the business of the Court Bank. Randolph was a born manager and one of the chief reasons for his success was his excellent choice of subordinates to whom he could delegate responsibility, but nonetheless he was keeping in daily touch with New York by cable. Carefully Tiffany examined each heap of documents, but found no hint of Randolph's plans, no mention of the diamond industry.

Then she noticed a copy of the local newspaper, the *Diamond Fields Advertiser*, lying on a table, folded back to an inside sheet. Tiffany picked up the paper and glanced idly at the page, but as her eyes alighted on a particular paragraph she stiffened. She read that paragraph several times before replacing the newspaper on the table. And then Tiffany smiled triumphantly. Of course! *This* was the factor which had been bubbling at the back of her brain – *this* was what she must do. It was the card which would beat Miranda and it would break Randolph, too.

At the writing desk in her bedroom, Tiffany composed a long and detailed cable. She placed the message on the dressing-table where her maid would see it, together with a short note of instructions and some cash. Then she went back to bed and slept until noon.

As she expected, the copy cable was lying on the bed-side table when she awoke, stamped with the date and time of despatch, beside the paper-knife and the morning mail. Tiffany thrust the cable into the pocket of her black fur-trimmed robe and then went downstairs without dressing, knowing how much this gesture would annoy Randolph. She intended to throw down as many challenges as possible – if Randolph expected her to be cowed after last night's fiasco, he was very much mistaken! In the dining-room she rang the bell.

'Champagne,' she commanded crisply. 'And ask Mr Court to come here.'

The champagne arrived before he did and when he entered the room, Tiffany interpreted his mood exactly – irritation at her summons, tempered with anticipation of making her squirm.

'Is this a liquid lunch or a champagne breakfast?' he inquired.

'Neither, as I have no intention of eating anything.' She handed him a glass of champagne and flashed him a brilliant smile. 'I am not feeling well.' Tiffany was planning ahead.

Undeceived, Randolph raised his glass ironically. 'In that case – your health, my dear! But perhaps we ought to toast the astounding success of your enterprise last night.'

'It would have worked had it not been for *him*!' Tiffany stared at him defiantly, denying him the advantage of raising the subject of Rafe.

'Quite. Captain the Honourable Rafe Deverill.' Randolph drew slowly on every syllable. 'Except that he turned out to be dishonourable – or did he?'

Tiffany tensed, but her courage did not waver. 'Why do you say that?'

'You are forgetting my basic bankers' code – I judge a man's capital, capacity and *character*. I have only met Deverill socially, but even so I was able to form an opinion of his character. In short, Tiffany, I would lend money to Captain Deverill.'

'We can all make mistakes – even you!'

'A mistake has been made,' Randolph agreed, 'but it remains to be seen by whom. Naturally, when his or her identity becomes known, steps will be taken . . .'

Always the veiled threat. Tiffany knew – how she knew! – that Randolph was capable of violence, but instinctively she felt that this side of his nature was for female consumption while his approach to men would be more subtle. Physically faced with an angry man, Randolph would deflate like a pricked balloon.

'Miranda is your only target. Wouldn't you like to see her stretched out helpless before you while you lift the whip to strike?'

'That is a very accurate description of her present position – figuratively speaking.'

Tiffany smiled. She had confronted the matter of Rafe and got it out of the way. Now for the real business of the day. 'Correction. Miranda is at my mercy, not yours.'

He sat down opposite her and they stared at each other across the table. 'What gives you that idea?'

'I will start at the beginning.' Tiffany's tone was faintly patronising. 'We believe that we can offer Anton more favourable terms financially than the Brights, *but* Miranda has one advantage over us – apart from her marriage prospects, that is – in that she can offer Anton a seat on the Board of the Diamond Company. Just refresh my memory about the shareholdings, will you?' she added sarcastically.

'Over the years Matthew has built up his shareholding to 30 per cent. In the present context one should take into account that Anton owns 5 per cent. We have 15 per cent.'

'Not *we* – *me*! *Court Diamonds* owns 15 per cent of Diamond Company shares. As a client speaking to her banker, I might reasonably ask why, if you are the financial genius you pretend to be, you have not increased that holding!'

'Diamonds have not been a good investment in recent years.' He was watching her, eyes glittering, fingers coiled round the stem of the glass which he twirled ceaselessly.

'Alternatively, it might be that you did not wish Court Diamonds to acquire greater influence in the industry – you did not wish *me* to acquire that power!' Tiffany leaned back in her chair. 'Whatever the reason, some shares are available. The tight grip which the pioneers exerted on the Diamond Company is loosening as the founders die and their heirs seek greater returns on their capital in more profitable avenues. Not everyone in the diamond world founded a dynasty.'

'Matthew Bright has founded a dynasty,' Randolph reminded her grimly. 'And he is still there – the last of the titans, the final representative of the old order.'

'It is the name of another pioneer which is on my mind at the moment – Julius Wernher. He died in 1912 and his parcel of shares is for sale.' Tiffany smiled at Randolph's suddenly savage expression. 'Did you think I was unaware of the fact? That parcel comprises 10 per cent of the Company shares; when added to my holding and to Anton's, it will enable us to match Matthew Bright. The Company could not avoid offering us a seat on the Board and we can appoint Anton as our nominee.'

Tiffany paused. In fact she had every intention of trying to take that seat herself, but it would be unwise to give that impression now.

'With the weight of the South-West African diamonds in his favour,' she continued, 'Anton would possess considerable influence and would stand an excellent chance of gaining support from other shareholders. One doesn't get into Matthew Bright's position of power without making enemies – there must be others who want the King dethroned!'

Randolph had been taken by surprise, but was collecting his thoughts quickly. 'Those shares feature largely in my plans,' he said evenly, trying to conceal his fury. 'But the purchase must be handled with tact and diplomacy. It is my suggestion that we should buy the shares through one of my other companies in order to . . .'

'Too late.' Tiffany stood up. 'I have already instructed my broker to approach the Executors of the Wernher Estate and put in a bid for those shares on behalf of Court Diamonds.' And she threw down the copy of the cable.

'You meddling *bitch!*' White-faced he snatched the cable and read the first few lines of the message which verified her statement. 'You have ruined everything!'

'Not everything – just your plan to control those shares instead of passing the purchase through Court Diamonds.'

Randolph's hand was clenched on the piece of paper,

crushing it just as he wanted to crush her. He could feel the frenzy rising within him again for the first time in months. Tiffany was right, that was exactly what he had intended to do. Now she had outwitted him and he was as angry as he had ever been in his life. But there had been another reason for an oblique approach.

'You have ruined *everything*!' he repeated icily. 'The Executors must consider the following factors: availability of cash, the price offered and the *suitability of the bidder*! In that respect they are likely to be influenced by the Diamond Company, who wish to ensure that the Company remains in British hands and who would not welcome additional American investment.'

'If you would read that cable properly, Randolph,' said Tiffany sweetly, 'instead of trying to squeeze it to death, you would discover that I thought of that. I instructed my broker to make the bid through nominees – the name of Court Diamonds will not be mentioned.' She paused and smiled thoughtfully. 'Doubtless legislation will be introduced one day to prevent such secrecy but until then we may as well take advantage of the situation.'

He did not read the message but very slowly placed the crumpled paper on the table. 'How very clever you are, my dear,' he said silkily. 'Just how did you anticipate financing this little venture?'

'That is why I wanted to speak to you.' Tiffany flashed him another charming smile. 'Or did you think I desired the pleasure of your company? This is a professional meeting, Randolph – I wanted to speak to my banker.'

His lips compressed into a thin white line.

'*You* will supply the finance – as you intended to buy the shares anyway, I am sure you have the details worked out. As I see it, a readjustment of our personal portfolio would be sufficient. Of course it means putting more of our eggs into one basket than you would advocate normally, but I am sure you will concede that the circumstances are exceptional.'

'Have you considered that the cash outflow will place

limitations on the capital we can supply to Anton for development purposes?'

'Oh, I'm certain the Board of the Court Bank will look favourably on an application for a loan – especially if you speak to them nicely!'

That infuriating smile seemed to be fixed permanently on her face and it was driving him mad. 'Suppose I do not recommend such a loan?'

'But you will – you want that deal with Anton as much as I do because you want the gold mines of the East Rand. I am even prepared to let you have those gold mines – as long as you confirm that the diamonds are mine.'

'We shall see.'

'But in the meantime you will arrange the finance?'

'Yes,' he muttered from between clenched teeth. At the door he turned. 'I do hope you succeed in acquiring those shares, Tiffany – because if you fail . . .' He left the sentence hanging in the air as he closed the door behind him.

Alone, Tiffany refilled her champagne glass and drank to her success. She felt wonderful – the joy of outsmarting Randolph was indescribable. Of course she would not fail! Lovingly she smoothed out the crumpled cable – it would look good on her office wall, she decided, as a reminder of the occasion.

Maintaining the pretence of feeling unwell, Tiffany stayed in her room and excused herself from the evening's dinner engagement.

'I am sure I can rely on you to compensate for my absence,' she said sweetly to Pauline.

Her cousin's face remained expressionless. 'I really do not know why you bother to be so catty when there is no one else to hear. It so happens that I find the people of Kimberley remarkably friendly.'

'I *am* glad.'

'In fact I have little doubt that I will enjoy tonight's dinner as much as I enjoyed my luncheon appointment.'

Pauline waited for Tiffany to inquire where and with

whom she had lunched, but Tiffany's mind was elsewhere.

'*Lunch*!' remarked Tiffany absently. 'You must take care, dear, or you will be getting fat again.'

Randolph entered the room quietly and stood behind his sister, looking at Tiffany lying languidly in the chair. 'I shall present your apologies to our hostess,' he said softly. 'However, I need hardly tell you to go to bed early because of course that is precisely your intention.'

She laughed recklessly, not caring if he guessed what was on her mind so confident of her power did she feel. After Randolph and Pauline had gone, she crossed the room and, framed in the lighted window, stared down into the darkness of the garden. Would Rafe Deverill come – and if so, what would he do to her?

Why was he in Kimberley? Coincidence . . . had he followed her . . . or had he followed Miranda? A frown creased Tiffany's lovely brow as she contemplated the possible variations of that relationship. At least Miranda could not marry Anton *and* Rafe, but it was becoming intensely, painfully, clear to Tiffany that Miranda must not possess *either* because she herself wanted *both*. Yet it was equally clear that Miranda might have a choice which Tiffany as a married woman could not challenge. As usual in moments of stress, Tiffany's fingers played with the diamond pendant . . . to win a bout with Randolph was satisfying, even heady, but to be rid of him completely would be . . . But she was running ahead of the game – Rafe had not yet arrived.

She was hoping that he would have located the house, would have ascertained that the others were out and pinpointed her room. She stood in the full glow of the light a little longer to give him every opportunity, before opening the window which abutted a sturdy tree outside. Then she closed the curtains, told the servants to take the night off and changed into her most becoming nightgown – of black silk edged with swansdown.

Champagne . . . she *must* have champagne. Not bothering to switch on the passage lights, she ran lightly down the stairs to the kitchen. She collected a bottle of champagne and two glasses – then, thoughtfully, she replaced one of the glasses and started back up the stairs. The house was silent and in the darkness Tiffany paused: she was not of a nervous disposition, but the combination of quiet and blackness was eerie. Was this what it was like for Miranda – deaf and alone at night?

A shaft of light illuminated the passage outside her bedroom and Tiffany pushed open the door a little wider with one foot. Then she froze. Straight ahead of her the curtain was blowing gently in the breeze – the window was wide open. Before she swivelled her gaze to the other side of the room she knew what she would see . . .

He was sitting in the chair, smoking a cigarette, wearing a dinner jacket and a white tie, his long legs stretched out in front of him and – unusual for a man of his manners and breeding – he did not stand up when she entered. His face was dark and brooding, his eyes hard and his mouth savage.

'You can scream all you like this time, Tiffany, because before I entered the house I ensured that there was no one to hear.'

Tiffany walked across the room, placed the champagne and the glass on the dressing-table and turned to face him. She leaned one hand on the dressing-table and the other on her right hip, aware of the alluring picture she made.

Now he did stand up. After stubbing out the cigarette viciously, he walked a couple of paces towards her, put his hand under her chin and jerked her towards him.

'*Why?*'

'I cannot tell you. I can only say that there was a reason – and it was a very good one.'

'You must tell me. For Christ's sake, Matthew Bright obviously knew what was going on. You owe me an explanation.' His grip on her chin tightened.

Tiffany did not answer.

'I have a right to know,' Rafe insisted. '*I* paid the price for your play-acting. The least you can do is tell me the plot.'

411

She stared up at him. He was hurting her but it did not matter. She was not afraid of him; the only person whom Tiffany feared was Randolph.

'I cannot tell you,' she repeated. 'I cannot tell anyone, now or ever. But,' and her eyes flickered slightly, 'you would be wrong to think that you were the only one who suffered – very wrong.'

He released her and took a step back. Tiffany could feel his gaze burning through the thin black silk to the pale gleaming flesh beneath. She waited. She would not explain or apologise or plead. She waited while he threw his jacket on to the chair, then his tie and white shirt, waited until his bronzed chest was inches away from the pointed mounds of her breasts and he was drawing the nightgown over her unresisting head. Rafe did not rip the silk from her body; he removed it slowly and with great deliberation, but when he cupped her breasts in his hands his touch was rough and without tenderness and he did not kiss her.

'More than anything I wanted an explanation,' he said in his low beautiful voice. 'Perhaps I even expected an apology. In the absence of either, *I* shall act. I have nothing to lose by committing the crime of which I was falsely accused and found guilty.' Suddenly his left hand clamped across her mouth, pushing her back across the dressing-table so that her head was pressed against the mirror on the wall. Perhaps he had forgotten they could not be overheard, or perhaps he needed a touch of violence to exorcise the devils within him – perhaps, over the years, he had imagined it this way. 'Your eyes and your body convey compliance, but I have trodden that path with you before. This time there will be no backing out at the last moment and no shout of rape – even though rape is exactly what I intend to do.'

With his right hand he began to fumble for the fastenings of his trousers but Tiffany's fingers were there before him. Deftly she unbuttoned his trousers and released his penis, caressing it provocatively. Then she arched her back and, still pinned against the dressing-table, guided him into her. The act was crude and brutal for their emotions were intense and raw. Tiffany's hands clasped the edge of the table, bracing herself against the impact of his repeated thrusts, but her eyes stayed open, locked into his. Only once did his gaze tear away from hers – for one brief moment he raised his eyes and stared into the mirror, as if imprinting its image on his mind forever.

Suddenly Tiffany's eyes closed and she was loose and shuddering beneath him as orgasm engulfed her. Only then did Rafe remove his hand and he remained leaning over her, supporting himself with both hands flat against the wall. Slowly his limp body slid from hers and their breathing steadied. Then with a deep sigh he straightened up and turned away, removing his trousers and reaching for a towel.

'Was that why you came to Kimberley?'

'That – and an explanation. I saw you in Cape Town and I followed you here.'

Tiffany's lips curved in triumph. So he had followed *her*, not Miranda. He was gazing at her fixedly and she knew that he was feasting his eyes on her body – on Nature's miracle. 'And how do you feel now? Satisfied? Was your revenge sweet?'

'Revenge? Yes, I thought of revenge. But you are so beautiful, Tiffany, that a man can forgive you anything.'

She believed him, but she must ask one more question. 'In that case, why did you dance with Miranda last night?'

'Miranda!' He shrugged carelessly. 'You, of all people, need not fear competition from Miranda! I have plans for her – but not pleasant plans. Do you really think that I blame *you* for what happened that night? No, that was Matthew's work – and Miranda is the path to Matthew.'

He stood behind her and pivoted her towards the mirror. 'Look at yourself – if it came to a contest between you and Miranda, who would a man choose? On whose side am I likely to be?'

He smiled at her and she reached for the champagne,

uncorking it expertly . . . barmaid at her own parties . . . the thought was unexpressed but completely shared. She held the bottle closer to her and let the froth bubble over her naked body so that her flesh glistened and shone in the muted light of the lamp. She filled the glass and raised it to his lips, tipping it carefully into his mouth. Then she raised the glass to her own lips, drinking from the same spot as he.

Rafe had been gazing at the diamond which blazed in the cleft between her breasts, trying to remember where he had seen it – or one very like it – before. But now he saw a Tiffany transformed – a Tiffany with eyes glowing and luminous, a face softened and fulfilled. Still she did not explain, still she did not apologise, but she said something which was nearly as difficult for her to express.

'I love you,' she said with simple sincerity. 'I have always loved you. Even *then*, in the old days, I loved you, but I was too young and foolish to know it.'

Very slightly she tipped the glass, careless of the carpet, dripping the champagne on to his lower body. She was aware of him taking the glass from her and placing it on the dressing-table while she sank to her knees. Clasping his buttocks with her hands, she began licking the champagne from his groin, working her way up gradually, tantalisingly but inexorably towards his penis. She took it in her mouth, feeling it stiffen at her tongue's insistence, feeling his fingers stroking her neck and hugging her head towards him.

Then he pulled her to her feet and held her close, running his hands over the slim perfection of her body. He lifted her and carried her to the bed, but this time he closed her mouth with his kiss . . .

CHAPTER TWENTY-THREE

Tiffany's expression was that of the cat which had stolen the cream. On Saturday, attending a meeting at the Kimberley racecourse organised by Anton in honour of the two diamond heiresses, Miranda watched Tiffany presenting the prize to the winning owner of the specially-staged Court Stakes. Tiffany was dressed in a slim black sheath with a black over-tunic which had one white shoulder and sleeve and a hem stiffened in the 'lamp-shade' style, the outfit topped by a large black and white hat. As usual the effect was superb but Miranda was aware of the beautiful face, not the dress – the glorious skin, the sensual mouth, the patrician nose and those vivid violet eyes. Philip's eyes, Miranda realised with a sudden shock.

Had Philip ever come to this racecourse? How had Philip passed his leisure hours here, deprived of his beloved motor cars? Drinking, she thought dully. Everyone who mentioned Philip drew attention to his drinking. Had he been unhappy and if so why? Standing quietly in the crowd, Miranda regretted deeply that she had not known her brother better but was conscious, too, that if there had been a grave to visit, his death might be easier to bear. Guiltily she remembered that there were two graves in the Kimberley cemetery which must be visited before she left the town.

However, her departure was not imminent. She looked again at the smug satisfaction and anticipation on Tiffany's face and seethed. Damn Tiffany Court – and damn Rafe Deverill because, but for him, she would have played that crucial card.

Was he here? For at least the tenth time Miranda's eyes

roved round the Stewards' Enclosure in search of him and on this occasion she located his tall figure and dark well-groomed head. Her knees trembled slightly as she absorbed the fact that Rafe was the only man in the vicinity who was not watching Tiffany. He was looking at *her* and as their eyes met he smiled – a lazy intimate smile full of admiration, memories of shared experience and suggestive of further experiences which could be mutually enjoyed. Miranda smiled back, even though she recognised the futility of a relationship which could lead nowhere except to heartbreak.

'It is your turn now, Miranda.' Anton stood beside her with the Courts. 'The next race is the Bright Handicap.'

'How extremely apt,' Tiffany murmured, so quietly that no one but a lip-reader would know.

Confident though she was, Tiffany was irritated by the vision of virginal loveliness Miranda presented this afternoon in a layered gown of old-rose, with romantic full frilled sleeves and a feathered hat curling over her thick blonde hair. However, it was more than irritating to intercept that smile which had passed between her sister and Rafe. Her *sister* . . . it still did not seem possible. My God, thought Tiffany as she walked with Anton and Miranda to the paddock, but I could wipe that look of *innocence* from her face . . . I could tell her a few facts about Kimberley and her mother and that bloody brilliant father of hers . . .

The wind was rising, fluttering the feathers on Miranda's hat and stirring the dust from Kimberley's dry earth. The winter afternoon was warm and sunny, the racecourse pleasant and the meeting well-organised, but nothing could gild the distant head-gear and tin-roofed houses into splendour. By no stretch of the imagination could Kimberley be deemed picturesque or even pretty. It was too dry and dusty, its street pattern too disorderly having evolved from the old shanty town of tents and cabins, its surface too red, brown and blue with few green 'lung' patches to let the city breathe – even on the golf course the 'greens' were blue. It was a small, rather ugly, functional town dominated by its creator and sole reason for its existence – the Kimberley Mine.

Anton took Miranda's arm, trying to envisage her loveliness and elegance in these humble surroundings, trying to visualise her outside her Park Lane milieu or himself *in* it, trying to gauge how she would divide her loyalties between a husband and a father.

'Would you ever be able to consider living in Kimberley?' he asked Miranda, after ensuring that Tiffany was within earshot.

There was an almost imperceptible pause before Miranda replied, 'Certainly, for part of the year anyway. Obviously I would need to spend some months in London to attend to business matters and to see my father.'

Anton nodded. 'Of course. Do you think that the climate would suit you? I recall Sir Matthew mentioning that your mother, Lady Anne, ailed here.'

'I never knew my mother, but I am told that I do not resemble her at all!' Miranda laughed. 'I am sure I would do very well here.'

Tiffany bit her lip, seeing in her mind's eye the portrait on Matthew's drawing-room wall, visualising those delicate fragile features in the context of the raw red dustbowl which was Kimberley. For the first time Tiffany wondered what her mother's life had been, what she had thought and felt ... but of course Lady Anne had gorgeous golden Matthew for a husband – and John Court to help pass the time. Her mouth tightened again into bitterness.

'We must talk about this more fully, Miranda,' Anton said, pitching his voice low so that Tiffany could hear but would believe she was not meant to do so. 'Perhaps we could dine together one evening next week, say Wednesday? Just the two of us ...'

She must make up her mind by Wednesday ... Her throat dry, Miranda accepted the invitation and then stepped forward to present the prize.

The same thought was in Anton's mind. He had judged that it was time to nudge the negotiations along a little.

417

Neither party would have been idle in the interim, but it would be no bad thing for them to be given a deadline, however vague. The Courts must make another bid before Wednesday and then he must decide what to do about Miranda. He contemplated her for a few more minutes before turning aside to speak to Pauline, who was standing alone several yards away.

'With the others I always feel that I must apologise for Kimberley's parochial and provincial aspect,' he said, 'but not with you.'

'I love it here.' Pauline's dark eyes shone with warmth and sincerity. 'I have never been happier in my life.'

'You don't find us boring after the glitter of New York society?'

She smiled. 'That glitter can be very tarnished at times! Here the task for someone like myself is less daunting. Everything is on a smaller scale and the people are more friendly.' She hesitated. 'They even seem to look *up* to me and that gives me confidence.'

'I understand perfectly.' Unobtrusively Anton rested a hand on her arm. 'I, too, prefer to be a big fish in a little pond.' There was a brief pause, but the silence was relaxed and comfortable. 'Thank you for a most enjoyable lunch on Thursday. Could you join me again tomorrow?'

Pauline nodded. Following the diamond negotiations from the sidelines, she knew that she had no hope of competing with Miranda Bright but there was no reason why she should not enjoy a few days of happiness with this man. However, she had every intention of concealing the relationship from Tiffany, because undoubtedly Tiffany would spoil it.

At that moment Tiffany, having ascertained that Randolph was safely occupied elsewhere, was walking directly towards Rafe Deverill. She dared not speak to him openly in public but as she drew level with him she said one word, looking straight ahead and without hesitating in her stride. Only Miranda, having completed the prize-giving, noticed. Tiffany was facing her and Miranda's sharp eyes and lip-reading ability enabled her to know precisely what had been said. The word Tiffany had spoken was 'Tonight'.

Desolation engulfed her. Rafe Deverill was making love to her, but was he making love – *really* making love – to Tiffany as well? Damn it, whose side was he on?

Tiffany's path brought her into direct confrontation with Miranda. Before either could turn away, an earnest young man approached them ingratiatingly.

'Ladies, a photograph please – for the *Diamond Fields Advertiser.*'

The crowd was forming a semi-circle round them at a respectful distance, forcing them into an isolation from which there was no escape. Tiffany and Miranda waited for the young man to prepare the camera.

'You cannot possibly win,' Tiffany said suddenly. 'Not all your youthful cunning and deceit can help you now.'

'What cunning and deceit?'

'You don't fool me with that air of innocence – Philip told me how you inveigled your way into your father's affections so that Philip was neglected *and* he told me how you used to read his private letters.'

'I never read anyone's private letters in my life,' Miranda retorted furiously and then, remembering that people were watching, tried to fix a smile on her face.

'No? What about the letter you showed to your father, when he fell into the fire?'

'I have not the faintest idea what you are talking about! Henriette handed me some documents to give to my father that night, but they were burned.'

Her bewilderment seemed genuine. 'Henriette?' Tiffany queried.

'The housekeeper. She was my mother's maid. And just what the hell has it got to do with you?'

Tiffany smiled, satisfied that Miranda knew nothing of the incident and that she was a simple naïve little girl after all. She had been right at the start: Miranda was no competition.

419

The photographer was taking his time. It was a very important picture: the two beautiful diamond heiresses, of equal height and slim figure, the one dark-haired and magnolia pale, the other tawny-blonde with a warm bloom on her skin. He wanted it to be perfect.

'As for my relationship with my father,' Miranda continued slowly, 'I never intended to hurt Philip.'

'His death was very convenient for you. His absence strengthens your hand.'

'You wouldn't speak like that if *you* had lost a brother!'

The retort nearly escaped Tiffany's lips, but she succeeded in restraining it. With sudden detachment, it occurred to her that this contest would have been simpler had Philip lived – he had been unaware that they were brother and sister and she could have manipulated him more easily.

'But you are correct in assuming the relevancy of my standing as my father's favourite and eldest child,' Miranda said softly. 'He strengthened my personal position in ways which are of great interest to Anton Ellenberger and I shall not hesitate to fight you with any means at my disposal.'

Tiffany laughed, intoxicated by the strength of her own position: with the superior financial offer she could make to Anton, with the shares she was buying, with her ascendancy over Randolph and her love affair with Rafe.

'Don't place any faith in your tryst with Anton next Wednesday – I shall have won by then.'

The photographer was apologising for the delay. 'It is a wonderful story,' he was saying, 'you two ladies here in Kimberley together, where your fathers met and became friends, where it all started. Smile, please . . .'

Lady Anne's daughters smiled at the camera and were recorded for the *Diamond Fields Advertiser* and for a picture which was published round the world.

Where it all started . . . In the public enclosure someone else was thinking the same. Instead of watching the horses, Danie Steyn lifted his field-glasses – a relic of the Boer

War – and trained them on Kimberley's high society.

There she was . . . unmistakable. Danie's hands shook. It was eerie to stand here, in Kimberley in 1914, and see such a perfect replica of the young Matthew . . . Matthew as he had been at twenty years old when Danie met him for the first time. The face, hair, eyes and skin, the carriage of the head – all were exactly the same. Only the facial expression was different, hers being reserved whereas Matthew's had been bold, but as Danie watched her, framed in the lens of his field-glasses, he could almost sense the mask of shyness slipping from her in order to let Matthew's indomitable spirit shine through.

Until this moment Danie had wondered if he could go through with it. To kill a man . . . the brother – was one thing, but to kill a girl was another matter entirely. The irony was that after his unsuccessful attempt to murder Matthew, he had saved this girl's life – because no Afrikaner, not even one as unstable as Danie Steyn, could stand by and watch a child die.

But now that he had seen her, it was all right. Killing Miranda would be nearly as good as killing Matthew himself, as well as striking again at the Bright family so that in the end all Matthew's endeavours on the diamond fields were worthless. Moreoever, killing the girl compensated in some small measure for the women and children who had died in the concentration camps, because in his heart Danie blamed Matthew – the diamond magnate, the Randlord, the *uitlander* – for the atrocities of the Boer War. But then Danie blamed Matthew for everything.

Talking about the Boer War . . . Danie stared intently for a long moment and then lowered the glasses. Deverill . . . Deverill who had burned the Grobler farm, sentenced the women and children to the concentration camp, executed Paul de Villiers and smashed Steyn's Commando. He had not seen Deverill since that final battle, so his presence in Kimberley was the answer to another prayer. Could he take two birds with one stone? Steady, Danie cautioned. This is Kimberley, not the desert. Here it is more difficult to commit murder and get away with it. Matthew first ... he could deal with Deverill afterwards. He would be visiting the Union more frequently in the future, fermenting rebellion among the diehards who, like him, dreamed of a Republic. A war between Britain and Germany would provide the perfect opportunity to challenge Botha's leadership and Danie was the ideal emissary between the German authorities in South-West and the embittered Afrikaners. Indeed this mission was his 'official' reason for being in South Africa – not even his wife, Susannah, knew about Miranda.

Yes, Deverill could wait. In fact it might be wise to avoid him altogether in case he remembered some talk of Danie's feud with Matthew. With his mind on the Boer War again, Danie's thoughts strayed to Helena. Had fate brought *her* to Kimberley as well? Danie's eyes roved restlessly around the racecourse, seeking his sister-in-law's face among the crowds as was his habit when he visited the Union. Where was she? She had vanished after their meeting in Luderitzbucht and although she must have boarded that steamer for Cape Town, her brothers on the farm denied all knowledge of her. Perhaps she was dead. Danie shrugged and returned his attention to the present.

Miranda was posing for a photograph with the other girl, John Court's daughter. He had no quarrel with John Court ... But that picture would become a collector's item. It would be published over and over again in every newspaper in the world – because it was going to be the last photograph taken of Miranda Bright while she was alive.

It was too early to leave for her luncheon engagement with that incredibly boring banker, but how did one occupy a Sunday morning in this dump? Tiffany knew what she would like to do during this spare hour – she would like to see Rafe. Pauline had gone to church and had a separate luncheon engagement, while Randolph was at the Club and would meet her at the banker's home.

Tiffany ordered the carriage to drive to the house where

Rafe was staying. The route took her past the Bright residence and as usual she averted her eyes. However, further along the road towards the town she saw a figure dressed in sober grey, holding an armful of flowers . . . Miranda . . . Tiffany drove on but she frowned: a grey dress, flowers, Sunday morning – the cemetery, she decided – family graves. The thought was disturbing, so she pushed it aside and concentrated on Rafe instead.

To her relief and pleasure he was in the driveway but he was dressed in riding clothes and a groom was holding two horses. He hurried across to the carriage and climbed in.

'I am so sorry about last night,' he said, 'but I could not get away. The friend with whom I am staying is leaving for the coast and we held a farewell party.' He smiled. 'The guests were all male, I assure you.'

'I waited the entire evening because Randolph was out.'

'It is so difficult to send a message,' he pointed out gently. 'If you had paused for one second in your imperious stride at the racecourse, I could have told you the meeting was impossible.'

'You know perfectly well that I cannot be seen talking to you in public.' She sighed, the acute disappointment of the previous night fading slightly in the reality of his presence. 'And I take it that you are going out now?'

'I am afraid so . . . such a waste of time when it could be spent with you.' He took her in her arms and kissed her lingeringly. 'Come here tomorrow evening,' he whispered. 'My friend will have gone and I shall have the house to myself.'

'I'll think about it,' she said lightly, but as she drove away Tiffany knew she would move heaven and earth to be there.

She was still left with the problem of an hour to kill – and the memory of Miranda kept returning. Perhaps she might as well find out if her guess was correct.

'The cemetery,' she told the driver.

'The old one or the new?'

'Heavens, I don't know – the old one, I suppose.'

423

This really was ridiculous, Tiffany told herself as she walked through the gate. Her boredom threshold might be low, but to be driven to such a depressing place . . .! She shivered slightly. She certainly did not want to wander among the graves, and in particular she had no wish to come across any family associations. But for some reason she continued her slow progress, glancing reluctantly at the tombstones. A large proportion of the graves bore no inscription, only a number, but the headstones which did exist revealed that this was the Pioneers' Cemetery which had been used between 1871 and 1905. Men, women and children, who died of fever, smallpox, mining accidents . . . So many of them were so *young* . . . Tiffany's face remained impassive but even she lingered for a moment beside the graves of seven members of the same family who had died within a two-year period. Those early days were hard, Tiffany thought dispassionately, and the diamonds demanded a high price. They were demanding a high price from her, too.

Ah, there was Miranda, kneeling on the ground. She had her back to Tiffany and was intent on arranging the flowers. Except for the two of them, the cemetery seemed deserted and, not wishing Miranda to see her, Tiffany crouched by a large headstone which afforded some cover. She risked a glance in Miranda's direction and suddenly her heart lurched as she thought she saw a shadow move among a group of graves nearby. God, this place gives me the creeps, she said to herself, and what I am doing here I really do not know! When she glanced round again, Miranda was walking away. Tiffany waited until she was out of sight and then slowly approached the spot where Miranda had been kneeling.

The two graves were neat and well-tended. Possibly Matthew paid someone to look after them. The larger of the two bore an inscription to 'Nicholas Grafton, dearly loved friend and brother-in-law of Matthew Bright, died during the Siege of Kimberley, February 1900'. Her mother's brother . . . The knot inside Tiffany's stomach tightened. She ought not to have come . . . Abruptly she turned her head and almost glared at the second headstone. She did not read every word but what she saw was enough: 'Victoria, beloved daughter of Anne and Matthew Bright, died June 1884 aged one year'. Oh God, another little sister! For some unaccountable reason Tiffany's legs began to tremble. Suddenly she had a clear picture of Matthew and the woman in that portrait standing on this very spot exactly thirty years ago, burying the tiny coffin. Her hands clenched as she tried to get a grip on herself. Our mother, she thought with an attempt at her old mocking style, did not have much luck with her daughters: one died in infancy, the second was taken from her at birth and she died when the third was . . .

A shadow appeared beside hers, looming over the grave, and as a hand touched her arm Tiffany uttered an involuntary scream . . .

'We meet again, Mrs Court.'

She was so relieved that he was flesh and blood that she rounded on him furiously. 'What the hell do you mean by creeping up on me like that!'

'I did not creep up on you, Tiffany – *you* are not deaf.'

Was that an intentional reference to Miranda? And what did he mean by 'we meet *again*'?

'I do not know you.' Yet there was something faintly familiar about him.

'Danie Steyn.'

She remembered now. He was the man she had met in Pretoria when she was ten years old, the man who had taken her to his farm to show her a picture of his sister, Alida. Since then his name had cropped up in conversations between her father and Frank Whitney and she seemed to recall Rafe mentioning him. She stared at him curiously but without presentiment, her only doubts stirring over the name Alida.

'What a coincidence that you should be in Kimberley.'

'In a way it is a coincidence. I came to see the other one – Matthew's daughter.'

'Yet you did not speak to her a moment ago?'

'I do not want her to know that I am here – not until it is too late.'

The man was talking riddles. 'In that case,' Tiffany said impatiently, 'I do hope that you did not travel far.'

'I came from South-West Africa. I was in Luderitzbucht in 1908,' he added reflectively, 'in *August* 1908.'

Tiffany's throat constricted. 'That date and place mean nothing to me – except the discovery of diamonds, of course.'

'I think they mean much more than that.' Deliberately he stared at the tombstones.

A silence seemed to descend over the deserted cemetery, a hush during which no breeze stirred and no bird sang. Tiffany stood frozen, gripped by an icy chill, aware only of the awful certainty that he *knew*.

'Come with me,' he said. 'There is another grave you ought to visit.'

'I have seen more than enough graves for one day, thank you!'

She began to walk towards the gate but he caught hold of her arm, dragging her resisting body towards a nearby grave. He was shorter than she, but his grip was strong and he forced her to stand in front of the tombstone. Tiffany read the name and then closed her eyes . . . Alida.

'My sister,' he said, 'but of course you know that. Did you find out about *your* Alida?'

'No!'

'Your eyes say that you did – *her* eyes . . . I must admit that I do take off my hat to John Court – it is not every man who could cuckold Matthew.'

'You possess an excellent command of the English language, Mr Steyn, but regrettably I have not the faintest idea what you are talking about.'

'It was your father who taught me English – he was always kind to me and to my sister. So you need not look so frightened – I intend *you* no harm.'

'I am not frightened.' But she was – desperately.

Irrationally, she wished Matthew was here. Matthew would know what to do about this madman.

'Her eyes,' Danie repeated. '*He* had them, too.'

He seemed to be implying that he had ... Speechlessly Tiffany stared at him.

'You must understand that I had to deal with your brother,' he said gently. 'You see, I assured Matthew that I would carry the quarrel into the next generation.'

And Miranda was next ... Tiffany's skin crawled but she seemed trapped in a web of fascinated horror. 'Why?' she managed to croak. 'What is your quarrel with Matthew?'

'So many things ... ' He released her arm and laid his hand tenderly on the tombstone. 'But Alida mattered most. She died giving birth to his baby – and yet she was the only real family I had and she promised never to leave me!' Briefly there was an anguish and a vulnerability in those unusual grey-green eyes, but a second later they were glittering with hate. 'I was only a child, but later I realised that he had never intended to marry her – a respectable Boer girl was not good enough for him.'

He paused. 'You won't tell Deverill that I am here, will you? And you will not warn Miranda? But no, of course you will not do that – because Matthew rejected you too. You were not good enough for him either.'

Tiffany turned and ran, out of the cemetery to the safety and privacy of her closed carriage. He was crazy ... he had to be crazy ... She ought to warn Miranda – but did not Danie also pose a threat to *her*? He *knew*. Suppose he told Randolph? Just as she had been about to step into the sunlight, the darkness gathered round her again. But she would win! Tomorrow she should receive a cable from London confirming the purchase of the shares, and then she could escape from Kimberley.

Huddled in the corner of the carriage, she could feel the weight of the diamond pendant pressing into her breast and she held her hand against the dress beneath which it lay. She was wearing that diamond more frequently, despite its association with Philip, fascinated by it . . . possessed by it. She knew that she would not warn Miranda but, growing within her, was the most deep and terrible desire to be rid of this nightmare: which death would benefit her most – Miranda, Randolph or Danie?

CHAPTER TWENTY-FOUR

At noon on Monday Miranda entered the offices of the Diamond Company. She was anxious, for the tone of Mr Pemberton's summons had been urgent and she was worried that there might be bad news of her father. Reassured on this point by the Company Secretary, she sat down in his office, but his next words caused her relief to be short-lived.

'Sir Matthew has asked me to convey to you some information concerning Company affairs.'

He studied the sheet of paper on the desk and then considered the girl sitting opposite him. Naturally he was aware of his Chairman's concern over Anton Ellenberger's connection with the South-West African fields, but was puzzled by the girl's role in the affair. The only answer seemed to be that Sir Matthew was playing some private game. If this was the case, Pemberton was content. He was a 'Bright man' and trusted Matthew to do what was right for the industry as a whole.

'You will recall that Julius Wernher died two years ago and that his holding in the Company amounted to approximately ten per cent. You may have seen notices to the effect that his Executors have offered the parcel for sale.'

Miranda's throat was dry as comprehension of Tiffany's strategy began to dawn. 'Yes, I did see a piece in the newspaper. Are the shares being offered on the open market?'

'Oh no, such a move would depress the price and Wernher's estate would not benefit. The sale is being conducted privately by the Executors. We have just received a statement from them to the effect that an offer has been made and is under consideration.'

'By whom?' Please, let there be another explanation! Please let the buyer be someone else!

'We do not know,' Pemberton replied shortly. 'The Executors inform us that the bid has been made by nominees and, of course, they are not revealing the identity of their client. It is a mystery and needless to say speculation in London – and now here – is rife.'

'But surely, as the Company Secretary, you ought to be informed? Surely the Diamond Company has a right to know?'

'The Company cannot dictate who buys its shares. We can only request the Wernher Executors to behave in a responsible fashion, bearing in mind the implications for the industry.'

It does not matter anyway, Miranda thought bitterly, because I know the identity of the buyer. And so does Papa.

She rose and walked to the window, where she stood staring down at the quiet street and the little town of Kimberley which her father had helped to found. She did not see the dust and shabbiness, the iron-roofed houses and ugly skyline. Miranda saw an industry, people and jobs and, in particular, she had a vision of one man and his life's work.

While she had dreamed away the days, reflecting only on marriage contracts, Tiffany had acted like a true professional. Or, of course, it might have been Randolph's idea – how comforting it must be to have a husband and a colleague with whom to discuss such matters. Again Miranda was engulfed in loneliness – if only she could speak to Matthew, if only the voyage on the mailship did not take two whole weeks! Her mind went back to the birthday party and the cake knife – but now that knife was a dagger aimed straight at the throat of her father. The battle for the South-West African diamond fields had evolved into a fight for control of the Diamond Company and the entire industry.

The shock might kill Matthew . . . that power was his life-blood.

'Mr Pemberton, I should be grateful if you could place an

officer at my disposal for half-an-hour. Also, be good enough to bring me the Company code book – I have a message to send to my father which is strictly private.'

The message was short and succinct, simply confirming to Matthew that the 'mystery buyer' must be Tiffany Court and that at all costs Matthew must put in a bid for the Wernher shares.

But if he was able to buy the shares, Miranda asked silently as she walked to the Telegraph Office, would Matthew not have done so already?

In this pensive frame of mind, she turned into the Telegraph Office – and bumped straight into him.

'Rafe!'

Her face lit up and it struck her immediately that he was precisely the person she wanted to see. He *had* said that he was on her side and she needed so desperately to talk to someone. But her smile faded as she noted the preoccupied expression on his face.

He raised his hat, but paused in his stride only long enough to smile and say, 'Darling girl, I cannot stop now.'

'But I wanted to ask . . .'

'Another time,' he called over his shoulder and then he was hurrying away.

Unsure whether to be angry or upset, Miranda despatched her cable and returned home. Had he brushed her aside because he could not be bothered with her – because, in fact, he was really in love with Tiffany – or had he just been busy? What could possibly have been so important? 'Darling girl' he had said and for the umpteenth time Miranda cursed the fact that she could interpret only words, not nuances.

She paced restlessly round the house, wanting to speak to him but fighting an old-fashioned disinclination to take the initiative or foist her company upon him. However, as the afternoon drew into evening, she admitted that a desire for his advice and guidance was not the only factor: she wished to clarify his feelings for her, and hers for him, before Wednesday's dinner engagement with Anton.

Miranda pulled on a coat and, leaving by the back door, headed across the garden to the street on the other side of the house. It was growing dark and she walked briskly, but the house where Rafe was staying was only a short distance away. In the drive she stopped abruptly, for a carriage was standing in front of the door. It could mean nothing . . . perhaps the visitor was talking to Rafe's host . . . on the other hand . . . Take no notice, she told herself firmly; just walk up to the door, ring the bell and find out if he is at home. But instead she was drawn irresistibly to the back of the house where the light from a downstairs window streamed across the lawn. Feeling intolerably foolish and guilty, Miranda cautiously peered inside.

Rafe was standing by the fireplace, talking. His head was turned away from the window so Miranda could not see what he was saying. Carefully Miranda craned forward and there, reclining full-length on a sofa facing her, was Tiffany. She was wearing a pair of black harem trousers and a black tunic. One elbow was propped on the arm of the sofa while the other hand raised a cigarette in a long black holder to her lips. Miranda watched as Rafe crossed the room and sat down on the sofa, watched as he removed the cigarette from Tiffany's hand and stubbed it out, watched as he took Tiffany in his arms and kissed her.

Miranda fled, down the drive and along the street, until she reached the garden gate. Closing the gate behind her, she leaned against it for a moment to catch her breath and close her eyes in anguish. When she opened her eyes again she was assailed by the peculiar impression that she was not alone. She stiffened slightly and glanced around the tall trees and thick shrubs but could see nothing. Suddenly nervous, she picked up her skirts and ran towards the house, crashing shut the garden door behind her. As soon as she was inside, her fear evaporated and she was left with an empty ache of misery. She had achieved her object, but the outcome was the opposite of what she had wished: she loved Rafe but he loved Tiffany.

*　　*　　*

432

Tiffany lay on her back in Rafe's bed, warm, glowing and satisfied. He was leaning over her, fingers playing lazily with the pendant.

'I have seen a diamond resembling this before,' he murmured, 'but I cannot remember where.'

'Not in circumstances like this, I hope!'

He laughed. 'If that was the case, how could I possibly forget! Besides,' and he pressed his mouth into the curve of her neck, 'in the whole history of the world, there never was a woman as beautiful as you.'

Tiffany caressed his back, trailing her fingers delicately but sensually over his skin, luxuriating in the feel, the smell and the sound of him. She had made love with a hitherto unknown frenzy, as if orgasm would vanquish the devils within her. Although she had not found complete peace, in his arms she was resting temporarily in a calm haven – and it did not occur to her that this might be the eye of the hurricane. With her cheek against his hair, Tiffany knew that she loved him, possessed him and that this time – no matter the danger, no matter the sacrifice – she was determined to *keep* him.

'You always had a superb eye for jewellery,' he was saying.

'You weren't so bad yourself,' she replied. 'You picked up some fine pieces during our professional associaton. I still think you were mad not to accept your share of the proceeds.'

'The partnership has had its compensations.' He cupped a breast in one hand and laid his head against her shoulders. 'Do you still keep a certain page open in that large ledger?'

'Of course.'

'It must show quite a healthy balance.'

'A *very* healthy balance – particularly after compound interest is added.'

'Compound interest! Good Lord, do you mean to say there is an honest little soul lurking beneath that seductive exterior?'

'Certainly,' she said indignantly. 'I do wish you would take that bloody money!'

'Persuade me.'

Her kiss was passionate and prolonged and when Rafe emerged from its depths, he heaved a long sigh.

'Very well, you win. It goes against the grain to admit it, but I do find myself a little short of cash at present. You may settle the debt.'

'Shall I remit the funds to you in Cape Town?'

'No, to my bank in London. I will give you the details . . . afterwards,' and he reached for her hungrily again. 'I hope that you will not live to regret your honesty.'

Never regret, never explain, never apologise . . . 'I shall not regret it any more than I regret *this*.' She gasped and clutched him fiercely as he entered her. 'But,' she whispered, 'I *do* regret what happened that night – darling Rafe, I *do* regret that . . .'

Tiffany arrived home before Randolph returned from the Club. A cable was lying on the hall table. She stared at it – the cable which ought to confirm the purchase of the shares, the message which would release her from Randolph and bring victory over Miranda. With hands which shook slightly, Tiffany opened the envelope . . .

Wednesday – and obviously Tiffany had won.

The message had just come through from Matthew: the Wernher shares had been sold to the 'mystery buyer'.

In forthright language which expressed his intense anxiety and frustration, he had explained to Miranda that he had been unable to put in a rival bid. His commitments to the Syndicate had stretched his resources as the stockpile of diamonds mounted and, in fact, he was finding it difficult to raise the finance for the South-West African deal without the burden of other expenditure. He could not borrow the money, because the bulk of the collateral he could offer was Diamond Company shares and no bank would lend money on that basis.

Miranda opened the casket containing the Bright jewels and lifted out the necklace. The stones gleamed dully, their mysterious magic muted in the shadows of the room. What was it worth – this necklace which was one of the most valuable and the most beautiful in the world? It was impossible to say, but one thing was very clear – that a fortune in diamonds was no help at all when it came to raising ready cash! And yet this was what she was fighting for – these damn useless pebbles! In an uncharacteristic fit of fury, Miranda flung the necklace across the room. It landed on the bed where it lay in a tangled heap, taunting her.

Her mind went back to the conclusion of Matthew's message. 'Speak to Anton again. Use what influence you can.' But what did Papa mean by 'influence' or was he, as seemed likely, leaving it to her judgment?

She had learned enough in recent weeks to realise that Matthew was not the perfect gentleman she had imagined him to be. He was a hard-headed and ruthless businessman who would stop at nothing to achieve his ends – but he would not sacrifice his daughter willingly: he had left the choice to her. However, Matthew was unaware of the real choice which had faced her, for he did not know that she had fallen in love with Rafe Deverill. For most people that choice might have been straightforward – the diamonds or the man – but for Miranda the matter was more complex: not the diamonds or the man, but Matthew or Rafe.

That had been the situation until Monday evening. Now she had no choice. Rafe was in love with Tiffany, while Matthew was depending on her. It was her destiny to make the marriage which would please her father. Everything pointed to the fact that she was good for nothing else.

Her thoughts strayed to Philip who had implanted this sense of inferiority in her mind. How friendly had he been with Tiffany? Had Tiffany's destructive force been at work on him and was she the reason he had turned to drink? Or was it *her* fault – had she taken all Papa's love and left none for her brother, as Tiffany had suggested?

Wearily Miranda picked up the necklace and threw it back into the casket. Then she opened the closet and took out the dress which she would wear to dinner with Anton tonight – one of the so-called 'mistakes' which she had never dared to wear before, a dress straight out of *Sheherazade*, more a stage-costume than an evening gown. Its silk folds rippled, floated, clung. In style it was not unlike the violet and red gown which Tiffany had worn at their first meeting, but Miranda's was blue, green and turquoise, shimmering like the sea in sunshine. Her maid brushed her hair high and away from her face so that it hung loosely down her back in waves which blended with the sensuous curves of body and gown, but Miranda obtained no pleasure from the beauty reflected in the mirror – she saw only a pathetic parody of the virgin on the sacrificial table.

Then they brought her a card and told her that he was in the drawing-room. My God, but he really could pick his moments!

He took in every detail of her appearance and one eyebrow rose in appreciation.

'You wanted to see me,' he said.

'Not any more.'

'But at the Telegraph Office . . . I could have sworn . . .'

'That was two days ago, Captain. Circumstances have changed.'

'I have been working.'

'You call that *work*?' She could not suppress the retort. 'Let me not detain you further.'

'Aren't you going to ask me to stay to dinner?'

'I am dining with Anton.'

'Don't go, Miranda! Talk to me instead. You might hear something to your advantage.'

'My time will be more profitably spent with Anton. Tiffany thinks she has won but I am not finished yet!'

He grinned. 'Are you going to take off the gloves and fight?'

Miranda stared at him coolly. 'As a matter of fact,

Captain, I thought it might be more effective if I took off my dress!'

His eyebrows shot up, but whether in genuine or merely mock alarm she could not tell. 'Hey, don't go that far!'

'You disapprove.' Deliberately she used the phrase he had uttered when she confronted him over the smuggling. 'Ladies ought not to misbehave. *Tiffany* would never do a thing like that!'

'On the contrary, of course she would – but you are not Tiffany.' He moved closer. 'The two of you are so different – it is like comparing fire and water. Tiffany is all heat and light; she blazes, sparkles and burns. But you – you are like a mermaid in that dress . . .' Gently he stroked the sea-green gown. '. . . like the ocean, soothing and calm but with a turbulence beneath the surface which is not immediately apparent. Your waters are cloudy and opaque, so that a man cannot see into your heart.' Rafe paused. 'Bear in mind, Miranda, if fire and water come into conflict, which element conquers the other!'

Was he referring to the diamonds or to himself? Whatever his meaning, it made no difference for she had made her decision. She picked up the white velvet cloak which was lying on a chair and swung it round her shoulders. He opened the door for her.

'As your father would say regarding his big business deals in the City, don't over-commit yourself,' he said softly.

Miranda did not reply. She walked out to the waiting carriage, leaving him standing there, staring after her.

How she wished that she could modulate her voice to just the right pitch of intimacy! As it was she must be grateful that she could speak and concentrate on picking her words with the utmost accuracy in order to achieve the maximum effect. Talking in German, Miranda proceeded to reminisce and to emphasise their long-standing friendship. Gently but relentlessly she referred to Anton's years with Bright Diamonds, to the apprenticeship he had served with Matthew, to all that Matthew had taught him . . . and delicately Miranda hinted at a debt which was owed.

'You were with Bright Diamonds when my brother died,' she said when dinner was over. 'Are you aware of the arrangements my father made for the future of the company?'

Anton was feeling profoundly uncomfortable. He had precipitated this meeting, but had expected to hear from the Courts before it took place. The identity of the 'mystery buyer' of the Wernher shares was no more a mystery to him than it was to Miranda, and he was disconcerted that Randolph had not approached him. What was he going to do? The prospect of Randolph's finance plus that shareholding was dazzling; the sight of that lovely face and body only a yard away was irresistible. Anton averted his eyes and tried to concentrate.

'I understand your basic position, Miranda. Lady Bright's eldest child is only thirteen years old, so control of your father's empire would lie with you for the foreseeable future. However,' he paused, 'you are extremely capable and in the unfortunate event of Sir Matthew's death, ought to find no difficulty in managing his affairs.'

'Wrong. Oh, I could manage Bright Diamonds but can you really see a *woman* running the Diamond Company? This is 1914 and the women of Britain do not even possess the franchise as yet – despite the efforts of my cousin Julia! No, Anton, the gentlemen of the City of London would never countenance it.'

It made sense, Anton reflected. What Miranda was really saying was that she would appoint her husband to the Board of the Diamond Company and vest in him the voting power of Bright Diamonds, but . . . 'Sir Matthew sets great store by the family name. He wishes the name of Bright to be perpetuated in the diamond industry, not . . .' He stopped.

'It did occur to me that my husband might be willing to change his name to Bright, but if such an idea is unacceptable then my father must accept the position as it is.'

438

'Don't *you* care about the family name?'

Miranda gazed into the fire so that he could not see the expression in her eyes. She could hardly tell him that she did not care about the family name or the diamonds. She could not say that her only concern was to protect Matthew's position in the Diamond Company during his lifetime: their own shareholding of 30 per cent plus Anton's 5 per cent and the South-West African diamond fields easily outgunned Tiffany's 25 per cent – automatically Miranda added the newly acquired percentage to Tiffany's previous holding.

'No, I don't mind about the name.'

'But what would your attitude be when Lady Bright's children are of age? Laura's sons might find your position and that of your . . . nominee unacceptable.'

'Obviously it is too early to say how much interest any of them will evince in the business,' she answered, 'but certainly none is forthcoming at the moment and neither are any manifestations of sibling loyalty! I start with the advantage of possessing a shareholding double each of theirs, and ought to have a chance of gaining the support of at least two of them. Whichever way it was to turn out, my husband has a good few years in which to establish himself and his power base.'

That was the second time she had said it – *husband*. But what was he to do? Accept the position of Crown Prince or go along with Randolph the Kingmaker? Even without the Wernher shares, financially his preference was for Randolph – but Miranda was so very beautiful.

She was sitting very close, almost touching him, leaning forward slightly so that the low-cut gown gaped over her breasts, the turquoise silk rising and falling to the thud of her heart. Anton desired her as he had never desired any woman in his life – but would he ever dare to touch her? He had dreamed of marrying her since she was a little girl, but he was in awe of her beauty and her station in life. Now that the moment had come when the unattainable was within reach, something was terribly wrong. Was it just the

439

financial arrangements? Was it merely that he wanted a placid, happy background to his working life, a wife who would look up to him and make him feel ten feet tall? Perhaps that was asking too much, along with his other ambitions, yet there was a woman who made him feel like that, a woman with whom he felt ... *comfortable*. The realisation came with a jolt but no, it was still not the reason ...

'In addition,' Miranda continued slowly, 'I can offer a five per cent ...'

Suddenly something snapped inside him and he leaned over and pressed a finger against her lips. 'No,' he said in anguish, 'no, *stop it*! Miranda, you don't have to *sell* yourself to me!'

With a movement which was not of his own volition, his arms went round her and he held her close. What had he been thinking of? How could he have done this to her? Had he sunk so low – or had the diamonds dragged him down – to depths where he must subject her to this? He was too fond of her to humiliate her or to condemn her to a loveless marriage.

'Please,' he said as he released her, 'forgive me. I never intended this to happen! The situation has gone out of control. I am not sure exactly why – except that I think it has a lot to do with the efforts of Randolph and Tiffany Court!'

Her expression remained the same, serious and determined.

'Miranda, I have loved you since you were a little girl. Marriage is not only a question of business expediency – I would wish you to be happy, for both our sakes.'

'We have always been happy in each other's company,' she replied calmly.

'Perhaps we could start again,' he suggested desperately, 'on a new footing, and find out how we feel about each other. Miranda, I can discuss finance and shares in connection with the South-West African diamonds, but I cannot haggle over you!'

440

Miranda smiled. She did feel more relaxed and was warmed by his sincerity and concern but equally, with that dogged determination, she intended to succeed in her mission. Only marriage with Anton could save Matthew now and so she had played her last card – the card placed in her hands by the death of Philip: the promise that Anton would succeed to her father's throne.

'We will do what you think is best but I have made a commitment, Anton, and I shall stand by it.'

Earlier that same day, in Cape Town, Helena had stood for a long time with the newspaper in her hands before placing it on the table, folded back at the page which bore the photograph. Her attention was distracted momentarily by the sight of her small daughter making a determined dash, on all fours, for the door. She caught the child up in her arms and sat down, grateful that her son was with her husband in the workshop. It was the nanny's day off and Helena had been harassed even before she saw the picture but now . . . Should she tell her husband immediately or wait until he came into the house for lunch?

She waited, greeting him with her gentle smile and ruffling her son's bright, fair hair. While her husband washed the grease from his hands, she fetched the newspaper and silently pointed to the photograph. He looked at it, towelling dry his hands, but did not take the paper from her.

'So? What has it to do with me?'

'Danie. That photograph will have been widely circulated. Even without it, he would know she was in Kimberley – Danie has a way of knowing things like that!'

'Leave it alone, Helena. There may be undercurrents in the situation that you know nothing about.' Deliberately he averted his eyes from the two women in the picture.

'I cannot leave it alone! Danie vowed constantly to carry his quarrel "into the next generation" as he put it. He threatened all Matthew Bright's children. Danie is insane – and if he was mad enough to do it once, he is mad enough to do it again!'

'Old family feuds are no concern of ours. We have avoided contact with all our relatives and most especially we have avoided Danie Steyn!' Wearily he sat down, but raised his eyes to her face and smiled tenderly. 'In a moment you will say that if I do not try to save Miranda, I will never forgive myself.'

'No,' said Helena, stroking his hair as she had ruffled the child's. 'I was going to say that *I* would never forgive you.'

'At this moment Miranda Bright is dining with Anton and doubtless is offering her lovely self to him on a plate while Anton wonders why we have not raised *our* bid!' Randolph's face, always pale, was the colour of parchment. His hand snaked out and grasped Tiffany's wrist. 'Who has bought those shares – because it certainly wasn't *you*, was it!'

CHAPTER TWENTY-FIVE

She knew that expression on his face and dreaded it. Not only was he drawing her back into his power, but he was reaching that pitch of fury and frenzy which forced him to exert his power over her – physically and mentally. Through his own grip on her arms he would sense her body's rigidity, but she would allow nothing else to betray her fear.

'I thought that perhaps the buyer might be you,' she said, staring him straight in the eyes. 'No? Anton then, or Matthew?'

'Don't be ridiculous! Anton is fully committed and I do not believe Matthew Bright could raise the necessary finance at the present time either. Added to which, neither of them would have reason to buy the shares anonymously.' He twisted her wrist upward, wrenching her towards him so that she was pinned against him. 'You failed, didn't you!'

Her face was drawn and tense, but her eyes still blazed defiance. 'You would not have succeeded in my place! On Monday I heard that another bidder had offered a higher price. Accordingly I raised my offer. Today the message was that the other buyer had raised his price and that his – or her – offer had been accepted. What the hell could I, or you or anyone, do about that?'

Randolph pushed her away violently and walked to the window.

Feeling that she had regained a slight advantage, Tiffany continued, 'Is the existence of a real "mystery buyer" a coincidence?'

'I do not believe in coincidences. However, I am satisfied

that the buyer is not involved directly with the negotiations for the South-West African fields. If Anton was in touch with another financier, he would have invited him here to take his seat at the poker table along with the rest of us.'

'Then I must discover the identity of his buyer and ascertain if he will re-sell. Will my banker permit me to raise my price again?'

'No – your "banker" will conduct the inquiries and negotiations himself! You have done enough damage!' Randolph was motionless by the window, but Tiffany could feel the frustrated energy swirling out of him. 'The Wernher executors must know the person's identity,' he said, half to himself, 'and deemed him a suitable buyer. For some reason either he, or they, do not want the name revealed immediately.'

'In that case Anton and Miranda will be in ignorance also. If this is a poker game, we could try to bluff it out – there may be some advantage in their thinking we do possess the shares.'

'We? Did I hear you say "we"?' He smiled at her coldly. 'Are we a team again, my dear?'

Tiffany did not reply.

'I am allocating the duties of that team,' he said, 'and for you there is woman's work to be done.'

'What!'

'Matchmaking. You might have been on the right track at Miranda's birthday party, after all. We must find another wife for Anton.'

'Oh, brilliant!' Tiffany scoffed. 'And where do you suggest I start looking? I imagine he has exhausted the local talent – and anyway I don't know any of the Kimberley ladies sufficiently well to choose a candidate.'

'You ought to cultivate your own sex rather more – you might be surprised at the advantages such a move would bring.'

'Any advantages would be more than offset by the intolerable tedium of their company,' she snapped. 'And you didn't answer my question.'

Randolph beckoned. Tiffany was raging at his condescension – woman's work indeed! – but she had to walk to the window. Outside Pauline was strolling in the garden.

'You must be joking!'

'On the contrary, I am perfectly serious.'

'But . . . *Pauline!*'

'Take another look. My little sister is not bad looking now that she has lost weight.'

It was true, Tiffany noted reluctantly, that Pauline could make more of herself.

'A new hairstyle,' Randolph continued, 'and some new clothes – any colour except pink! You must take her under your wing, my dear, and give her the benefit of your excellent taste.'

To Tiffany the task of beautifying Pauline was utterly demeaning and abhorrent, but Randolph's stare was hypnotic, compelling her to obey, surrounding her with the sinister, seeping aura of evil which he exuded. She could not resist, not even though she knew this scheme was Randolph's counter-attack – Pauline's marriage would strengthen *his* position, not hers!

With an apparently indifferent shrug, Tiffany turned away.

'In addition, we must find another husband for Miranda,' Randolph said softly. 'I believe there is one name which springs immediately to mind, don't you?'

She tensed, wanting to run out of the room, but Randolph was standing behind her and he clasped her breasts in his hands.

'You do not care for the idea,' he murmured into her ear. 'Are you thinking of keeping him for yourself, my dear? Tell me, what makes Rafe Deverill such a good lover? What does he do that is so special?'

Tiffany closed her eyes but was incapable of other movement. Her legs and her tongue were petrified. Randolph's mouth was touching her ear.

'I know precisely what has been going on. How do I

know? Because I know *you*! But do not contemplate keeping Deverill. I will acquiesce to your casual *affaires* but I will not tolerate *anything else!*'

Suddenly he squeezed her breasts and his teeth bit into her ear-lobe, so hard that Tiffany had to restrain a cry of pain and revulsion. He is going to hit me, she thought, and braced herself for the blow – but at that moment footsteps sounded in the hall and reluctantly he let her go.

'We must take the initiative,' he said calmly, as if nothing had happened. 'The time has come for all the poker players to sit down at the same table. You and I are going to give a dinner party.'

Stiffly she turned to face him.

'We owe Anton hospitality,' he said, 'and naturally Pauline will attend. It would be ... friendly to invite Miranda – and fitting to invite Deverill.'

Tiffany clutched the table for support. 'Impossible,' she choked. 'All of us together . . . and *he* wouldn't come.'

'I disagree. As we decided the other day, Captain Deverill is a man of character. Besides, curiosity would drive him here if nothing else.'

'How could he come? What would people say? What could *you* possibly say to him?'

'I could always pretend that the rape never happened – which should not tax my theatrical talents unduly.'

'You bastard!' Tiffany turned on him, her lovely face contorted into ugliness and murder blazing in her eyes. Her detestation of him, her fear and frustration, her longing for freedom from him – all were printed plainly on every feature. 'Oh God, I wish you were dead! What a widow I would make – what a very merry widow!'

'Fortunately I am in excellent health and you would be wise to ensure that I stay that way.' Randolph's precise tone did not waver. 'Remember that Anton needs the bank for his finance. Remember that he needs *me*, not you. Also, intelligent though you are, Tiffany, it is beyond your capabilities to guide one of America's premier banks through the turbulent times which lie ahead, and to train our sons for the parts they will play.'

At the door he paused. 'You will do exactly what I have told you to do – no more or no less. I intend to finalise this deal with Anton if it is the last thing I do, because *I will not be beaten* – not by anyone!' He stared at her meaningfully and left the room.

Tiffany sank on to a chair, her legs trembling and her forehead beaded with perspiration. Oh God, how she hated being a woman – loathed the weakness of her woman's body which betrayed her in times of stress and which lacked the physical ability to retaliate against Randolph. The only occasions on which she had been glad to be a woman, she reflected bitterly, were the brief hours she had spent in the arms of Rafe Deverill.

She lifted her head and watched Randolph cross the garden to speak to Pauline. After only a few seconds, the contamination of his presence seemed to ebb slightly and with a supreme effort of will Tiffany fought to regain her own sense of direction. She must win her freedom! She would pay any price for those shares – any price at all!

Randolph had delivered a verbal dinner invitation to Anton. At last, thought Anton – the shares! But his eager expectancy was distinctly dimmed when Randolph mentioned casually that Miranda and Rafe Deverill were also invited. The Courts want to gloat, Anton said to himself on Friday evening as he prepared for the party. He did wish that Tiffany would not be so dramatic. Personally he had not the slightest desire to gloat in front of Miranda, neither was he keen to attend such a small party with both Miranda and Pauline. The entire situation had become extremely complicated and was way outside his usual territory. In future, Anton decided, he would deal with men wherever possible and ensure that the bedroom and the board-room were kept strictly apart.

And there was one other problem to ponder. Why was Rafe included in the gathering?

Mentally Anton reviewed the chessboard which he had set up so cleverly and he concluded that the pieces were in violent disarray. Rules were being broken and the pieces were not moving in their preordained pattern. It is because of the black queen, he thought suddenly. She is the strongest influence – the desire to defeat her or win her is dictating all the moves. It is a destructive influence, but she is the most exciting player in the game.

Rafe had received a written invitation and had not the remotest idea why he had been asked. What was Randolph trying to achieve? But during the twenty-four hours which elapsed between receipt of the invitation and the party itself, he worked his way towards some understanding of Randolph's strategy. It was a bold tactic, he conceded, to gather all the participants together and to see what sparks were struck.

His reluctant admiration for Randolph's ability was blended with an intense distaste for the man. Try as he would, Rafe could not fathom the relationship between Randolph and Tiffany. Try as he would, he could not visualise the conception of those three children. Tiffany had changed and it was a difference which penetrated to the depths of her heart and soul. That clear bell-like quality had gone from her voice and there was a harshness and discordance in her nature which was new – and profoundly disturbing.

But as Rafe adjusted his white tie in front of the mirror, he was smiling. Tonight was the night he had waited for and it was exceedingly agreeable of Randolph to have set the scene so perfectly!

Miranda's first reaction had been to decline the invitation. She sensed a trap – a drama which she could not handle. But then she learned from Anton that he and Rafe would also be present and she knew that she could not leave the field wide open to Tiffany.

From the closet Miranda lifted her most daring and

glamorous gown. From the dressing-table she removed the jewel casket. Tonight she would show them who was the true diamond heiress!

Once she had thought that nothing could make her beautiful, but the reflection in the mirror proved to Pauline that a miracle had been wrought. The skin was clear if a little sallow, the bone structure delicate and the dark hair glossy. The resemblance to Randolph was marked, but Pauline's brown eyes were liquid shining pools which contained none of Randolph's sinister intent. However, she was aware that the change was not entirely due to Tiffany's transformation work – it was the admiration in a man's eyes which had brought about the blossoming.

Tiffany came into the room and stood behind her.

'Just casting a critical eye over my protégée. Hm, passable, I suppose, *but* will you outshine Miranda Bright?' Tiffany's smile was sarcastic.

'It is not only *I* who must compete with Miranda.'

Tiffany laughed, confident that her beauty was incomparable, that the cut of her black velvet gown was faultless and that nothing could outshine the pear-shaped diamond at her breast.

'I admire Miranda,' Pauline continued thoughtfully. 'Other people ought to overcome their character defects in the same way that she has conquered her physical handicap.'

'And you ought to address that remark to your brother!'

Pauline rose from the dressing-stool, smoothing the folds of the topaz silk gown. 'I would like to make one thing quite clear, Tiffany – that my loyalty is to my brother. If by any remote chance I should marry Anton, do not count on my using my influence with him on *your* account!' And she swept out of the room.

White-faced, Tiffany stared at herself in the mirror, disturbed not by Pauline's impertinence but by the voicing of another reason why she must remain married to Randolph. She dreamed of divorce – but he would never let her go!

449

No, it was still a struggle between her mind and his . . . Or could she be driven further? Suddenly the face in the mirror was not her own, but was a chalky mask superimposed over the flesh-and-blood features beneath as Tiffany battled with the unspeakable . . . Then she wrenched herself free and went downstairs.

'I understand your tactics,' she said softly to Randolph as he handed her a drink in the drawing-room. 'I do realise that one of the reasons for this gathering tonight is to put me at a personal disadvantage. But you will not succeed. Nothing will discompose me – nothing at all.'

Anton was the first to arrive and he noticed the difference in Pauline – very definitely he noticed. He sat down beside her but although he talked amiably, his gaze returned constantly to Randolph. He is waiting for us to mention the shares, Tiffany thought – but he must wait a little longer! Her own attention was fixed on the door as, despite her brave face, the tension within her increased. Who would be the next to arrive? Her heart lurched as the door opened and Rafe was ushered into the room.

Randolph rose and for a moment the two men stared at each other expressionlessly. Then both bowed, but neither made any attempt to shake hands.

'May I offer you a drink, Deverill?' Randolph inquired.

'The Captain will have a whisky, won't you, Rafe? You usually do.' Tiffany held out her hand and smiled brilliantly.

The corners of Rafe's mouth twitched appreciatively as he took her hand.

'I have not seen you since the race meeting,' she lied coolly. 'I trust you enjoyed the occasion?'

'I not only enjoyed it – I made a profit out of it.'

'You are a betting man?'

'I fear so. Actually, I am rather good at it.'

A spluttering sound attracted everyone's attention: Anton was choking, none too quietly, over his drink. 'You told me that you were a rotten judge of horseflesh,' he said accusingly to Rafe when he had caught his breath.

'Did I? That must have been years ago, my friend. My luck has changed since then.' Rafe smiled engagingly at Anton, who returned his gaze suspiciously. 'Which is just as well, because I gamble frequently. A man in my position must do something to pass the time – I do not receive many invitations into polite society.'

Rafe spoke as if the circumstances had nothing whatsoever to do with them! He seemed completely unconcerned and thoroughly at ease. Added to which, he was looking impossibly handsome in his evening clothes. When Tiffany took out a cigarette, he rose to offer her a light and, as he turned his back on the others, he winked at her. A flood of wonderful warmth went through her – he was the only man who understood her and she loved him for it. In fact she loved him for a great many reasons. With Rafe beside her, she could conquer the world. Not even the sight of Randolph, coiled on his chair like a serpent waiting to strike, could spoil that moment of deep and intense joy.

'We are glad you accepted this invitation into society, Deverill,' Randolph said silkily. 'Perhaps you hope that it will set you on the road to some sort of rehabilitation?'

'I am not a man who lives in *hope*,' Rafe replied, 'but you are correct in assuming that this evening will alter my circumstances.'

The faintest trace of a frown flickered across Randolph's face, only to be exorcised in an instant. 'Possibly you refer to the charming Miss Bright,' he remarked. 'She should be here at any moment.'

Rafe smiled. 'I imagine that Miranda features largely in the hopes – or fears – of us all.'

There was a brief lull and in the silence voices were heard in the hall. Slowly they turned their heads as the door swung open and Miranda walked into the room.

The ivory silk was a web of gossamer which floated and shimmered, the simplicity of its lines emphasising every curve, the bodice clinging precariously to slender shoulder straps and plunging low over her breasts. The creamy translucent skin of face, shoulders, breasts and arms

451

gleamed in the soft lights, but tonight its perfection was eclipsed . . . because Miranda wore the Bright diamonds. The tiara sparkled in her golden crown of hair, the bracelet shone at her wrist, on her right hand flashed Lady Anne's massive engagement ring while at her throat was the Bright necklace.

It was that necklace which riveted Tiffany's attention. Her connoisseur's eye dissected it, her professionalism analysed it and she could find no flaw. Every stone had been chosen and matched by a master and its peerless magic tore at Tiffany's heart. Her love of diamonds told her that this necklace was their ultimate expression and it galled her beyond belief that it did not belong to her.

For once Tiffany had nothing to say. Miranda greeted Randolph courteously, crossed the room to kiss Anton possessively on each cheek and then sat down. The atmosphere subsided slightly with her. It was Rafe who leaned across and raised her right hand to the light so that the rays from the huge solitaire diamond dazzled their eyes.

'Pretty,' he murmured with quiet understatement. 'Are these the Bright diamonds?'

Miranda nodded. 'They were my father's wedding present to my mother. Papa selected every stone himself here in Kimberley, took them to London and directed the design. After my mother died they were kept for me – because I am her only daughter.'

Bile was rising in Tiffany's throat and the agony was twisting stomach, heart and mind. Oh Matthew, she cried silently, why did you reject me, why did you send me away! You created that necklace and I could have worn it – if you had brought me up as your daughter, how different *everything* would be!

Rejection reminded her of Danie Steyn. Was he still following Miranda? She could warn her sister now . . . but her lips would not shape the words . . .

At dinner Miranda was seated at Randolph's right hand. 'You will be leaving Kimberley soon, I assume, Miss Bright?'

'Whatever gives you that idea, Mr Court?'

'As I have completed – or virtually completed – my business here, I thought you might have completed yours.'

'Oh no, Mr Court, I am by no means finished yet!'

Ensuring that Anton was listening, Randolph continued, 'Perhaps you have personal reasons for prolonging your stay?' and he glanced meaningfully at Rafe.

Miranda flushed, while Rafe leaned back in his chair and smiled.

'But of course there are obstacles . . . the little matter of Captain Deverill's reputation . . .' Randolph looked at Tiffany. 'Would it not be magnanimous, my dear, to let bygones be bygones and clear the Captain's name?'

Tiffany's hands were clenched in her lap, but she had vowed that he would not disturb her composure! 'No,' she said flatly.

Hurriedly Anton tried to change the subject. 'Before any of you leave, you must visit the Mine,' he said.

Tiffany shook her head. 'The mechanics of the operation do not attract me. I love the finished product, not dark tunnels and truckloads of dirt.'

'Miranda?'

She made no reply and Rafe, sitting at her other side, touched her arm to prompt her to speak.

'Dark tunnels do not interest me much, either.'

No, of course not . . . Tiffany remembered the sensation on the stairs the other evening – no sight and no sound. Below ground in the Mine, Miranda would be very vulnerable.

'The Kimberley Mine has been in existence for only forty years,' Rafe remarked, 'and yet what changes it has witnessed during that time.'

Anton agreed. 'From a kopje to the largest man-made hole in the world, and from open-cast mining to a sophisticated system of underground working.'

'Production methods are not the only aspects of the industry which have altered.' Rafe lifted his wine glass. 'I imagine the early pioneers indulged in all manner of skulduggery – claim-jumping, IDB, even murder – but these days the battles are confined to the board-room.' He drank the wine and slowly replaced the glass on the table.

No one spoke.

'Kimberley abounds with rumours of a "mystery buyer" of Diamond Company shares, so it seems that just such a battle is being fought now.' Rafe paused, watching the white wary faces around him. 'Hasn't it all gone far enough? Hasn't the time come to end the charade?'

'How dare you presume to interfere in our affairs?' Randolph hissed.

'Mind you, Tiffany likes charades.' Rafe smiled reminiscently. 'Come on, Tiffany, put everyone out of their misery – offer Anton the shares.'

'No!'

'If you don't, he might think you haven't got them.'

'I will offer them when I am good and ready to do so!'

'You will never be good, Tiffany, and as far as the shares are concerned, you will never be ready – because you have not got them.'

Rafe stood up.

'You did not buy the shares. *I did.*'

His grey eyes were splinters of ice in his lean, taut face. 'I do not need to tell anyone at this table that I want no part of the diamond industry. I do not need to dilate upon what that industry has done to me! The shares in the Diamond Company are for sale, but they are for sale to only two people: Tiffany and Miranda.'

Rafe stared steadily at each beautiful face in turn, at each pair of agonised blue eyes. 'You will want to know the price,' he said softly. 'The financial outlay is the same for both of you: the price I paid for the shares, because commercial profit is not my aim. But for each of you there is an extra forfeit. To you, Tiffany, the price is an answer to a certain question and the clearance of my name. To you, Miranda, the price is your hand in marriage.'

CHAPTER TWENTY-SIX

The door had slammed behind him.

They were all on their feet but no one else moved. Miranda and Tiffany stared at each other across the table.

Miranda had won – and the agony was greater than anything Tiffany had ever known. She had vowed that she would pay any price for those shares – but Rafe Deverill had asked the one price in the world which she could not pay. Whereas Miranda's price . . . Tiffany was swamped in an almost uncontrollable tide of anger and despair; she had lost everything – the diamonds, the man and her bid for freedom. And God only knew what Randolph would do to her now!

Then Miranda's mouth curved, not gently and sweetly as was her custom but into a mocking smile of triumph which would have been more at home on her rival's features than her own. Without speaking she walked out of the room but Tiffany ran after her, catching up with her at the front door.

'He loves me, not you!'

'After what you did to him!'

'It was what *your father* did to him! Rafe didn't rape me . . . Matthew set up the entire incident. Rafe Deverill's marriage proposal is revenge on Matthew Bright, not love for you!'

Miranda had worked that out for herself. She had been right in the first place when she raised the subject aboard the *Corsair* . . .

'Why should that matter to me? I don't love him – and I am as capable of making a marriage of convenience as anyone else.' Miranda paused. 'Any kind of marriage with

Rafe Deverill would bring its compensations, don't you think?'

The urge to strike her was overwhelming and Tiffany struggled to keep her hands by her sides. 'You cannot marry Rafe *and* Anton. I suppose you have been hopping in and out of bed with both of them, while maintaining an expression of innocence which would deceive the Virgin Mary! It's disgusting!'

'It is *business*,' Miranda retorted crisply, 'and you would do the same in my position. Your problem is that you are not in my position and you wish like hell that you were.'

'You cannot marry Rafe and return to London – because I swear that if you do marry him I will never clear his name.'

'I shall manage. It cannot have escaped your notice that I find a way around most problems in the end. Anyway, I gather that you are conceding defeat; you cannot pay the price.'

'Of course I can.'

'In that case, please excuse me because there is a call I must make. After all, Rafe did not make the position perfectly clear. It might be a matter of first come, first served – if you will pardon the expression.'

Haughtily Miranda turned on her heel and swept out of the house, but she did not direct her carriage to Rafe's residence. Instead she went straight home and as soon as she was inside the door, that air of confidence crumpled. Marry Rafe Deverill? She would not marry him if he was the last man on earth!

It was impossible for three reasons: first, she would not be able to return to Matthew; secondly, Matthew did not have the money to buy the shares; and, thirdly . . . it was the third reason which hurt most of all – she loved him and she was sure he knew it, yet every time he had taken her in his arms he had been using her for revenge; every time he whispered, 'Trust me,' he was only making a fool of a stupid little deaf girl . . .

Part of her wanted to cry, part of her wanted to scream,

but another – and the strongest – part vowed that she would still win, even though she now had to take on Rafe as well as Anton and Tiffany.

Seeking inspiration, Miranda went to Matthew's old study and sat in the chair by the desk where he had formulated so many of his plans in the old days. What would Matthew do now? *Think it through logically, Miranda, step by step*. She closed her eyes and then something began to stir at the back of her mind until suddenly it burst upon her so clearly that she could almost hear Matthew's voice saying *where did he get the money, Miranda?* And everything fell into place.

Casting aside any moral qualms, together with her customary consideration for staff, Miranda ordered the driver to bring round the carriage and convey her immediately to the home of Anton Ellenberger.

Lights were burning and Miranda brushed impatiently past the housekeeper, entering the drawing-room unannounced.

'I thought it was the black queen who was destroying the game, but now I see it is the damn white knight,' Anton was saying. 'For God's sake, Rafe, I told you to keep out of this . . .' He stopped when he saw her.

In a swirl of silk and a blaze of diamonds, Miranda advanced into the room. Ignoring Rafe, she addressed Anton.

'I do not know how or when you went into partnership with Captain Deverill, Anton, but the other details of your operation are quite clear. Until tonight I had made two mistakes: I omitted to investigate where the Captain sold his diamonds, and I believed that the value of those stones was insufficient to affect the industry. Now I shall ensure that his enterprise has a beneficial effect on that industry and, in particular, benefits *me*!'

Anton started to speak but angrily Miranda continued: 'Both of you will do exactly what I tell you, otherwise I shall report your illegal dealings.'

'But that is blackmail, Miranda,' protested Rafe, who had

457

risen to stand beside Anton and had the most maddening smile on his face.

'If you don't like it, lay a charge against me for extortion,' Miranda retorted. 'Yes, it is blackmail – and why not? Why shouldn't I use the situation to my advantage? Everyone else has been using *me*.'

Rafe shook his head sorrowfully. 'I would not have believed you could do a thing like this.'

'It should not surprise you – it was you who called me "Matthew's daughter".'

'Are you actually admitting that Daddy might have strayed from the straight and narrow in his time?'

'Yes,' shouted Miranda. '*Yes*! Only now I do not think the less of him for it. *Now* I understand the penalties for success. Because,' and she turned back to Anton, 'I hate doing this. I looked upon you as a friend, but if you do not accept Bright Diamonds as your partner in South-West Africa, I will reveal where and how you obtained the necessary finance to place your business on a sound footing.'

'Even if it were true, Miranda, you could not prove anything,' Anton pointed out uncertainly.

'*Even* if . . . Oh, for heaven's sake, can we please stop side-stepping the issues! Every conversation we have had in Kimberley has been "if this" or "perhaps that". It *is* true and you cannot have covered every inch of your tracks. Moreover, the origins of stones can be traced and at least one *Corsair* crewman might crack under interrogation.'

Miranda paused and then added gently. 'Apart from which, I could spread some very nasty rumours which, coming from sweet little Miranda Bright batting her eyelashes in innocent dismay, might be extremely convincing. Distinctly damaging to Kimberley's first citizen, wouldn't you say?'

Anton could not answer. There were aspects to his position in Kimberley which as yet had crossed no one's mind but his own. He was a German and he bore a German name; if war broke out, there were anti-German factions in Kimberley who would do their utmost to ensure that the

458

repercussions rebounded on to him. He dared not risk a scandal.

'By the way,' Miranda continued crisply, 'the validity of my statements the other night still stands – a husband would be useful to guard my interests in the Diamond Company if my father dies. We will discuss the possibility of our marriage when the atmosphere has cooled.'

'But darling Miranda,' Rafe remonstrated, 'you are marrying me for the shares. I thought it was rather neat that you should marry me for my money instead of vice versa.'

Miranda ignored him. 'I am aware,' she said to Anton, 'that Captain Deverill has less to fear from any revelations of smuggling activities than you – his "good name" went down the drain years ago, although the prospect of a prison sentence might give him pause. I trust you will use your influence with him to sell me the shares at *less* than the price he paid – payment to be spread over a period to be mutually agreed between you and my father.'

'Darling, if you accept my marriage proposal you can have the shares for nothing,' Rafe protested.

Miranda swung round, the diamonds flashing in the light but blazing no brighter than her eyes. 'You can *stuff* your marriage proposal, Captain, and if I stay another second I shall be so unladylike as to describe most precisely *where* you can stuff it!'

When she reached home Miranda was exhausted, but it was a mental tiredness and so she paced slowly through the house before resting for a while at the dining-room window, gazing out at the darkness of the garden. Suddenly her heart missed a beat as she thought she saw a shadow move, as if someone was out there watching her at the window. She felt a moment's fear but then remembered Rafe saying, in this very room, 'lurking in the bushes is not Tiffany's style'. A smile tugged at the corners of her mouth, but it was bittersweet. She had won but felt no pleasure in her victory. Papa, did you suffer like this . . . did you *hurt* like this? Somehow Miranda was sure that for Matthew the sacrifice had been less and the treachery had been easier. But instead of censure, she felt only envy of her father's good fortune.

After Miranda had left, Tiffany went straight to her own room where she dismissed the maid and undressed herself, taking her time over it, wondering what she could do . . . wondering what Randolph would do . . . It was nearly an hour later when the door opened and he walked in; he was carrying the silver-topped cane.

'You wouldn't *dare!* Pauline . . .'

'. . . is fast asleep. I took the precaution of administering a sleeping draught. My sister needed to relax after such an upsetting evening.'

Tiffany shrank back against the wall. 'My maid . . .'

'. . . has sneaked out of the house to meet a lover. It really would pay you to take an interest in affairs other than your own.'

He padded softly towards her, holding the cane by its tip, swinging it so that the heavy silver head gleamed menacingly. Then he raised it, cracking it across her hip so violently that she staggered and fell across the bed. He hit her again and again across the back, buttocks and thighs, while in a daze of pain she tried frantically to twist away from him. The cane was not breaking her skin, not even tearing her nightgown, but was bruising her, raising livid crimson welts on that tender pearly flesh. Randolph did not strike her head but the battering of her body, the throbbing agony of every blow caused her brain to reel until she was nearly senseless with pain. But she was not totally beaten into submission yet . . . She managed to roll on to her back, looking up into his face – a cruel face which poured perspiration, eyes glittering and mouth set in a snarl.

'We will not worry about the marks on your body this time, Tiffany. We will say you have suffered a nasty fall – because you have, haven't you! You have suffered a *very* nasty fall!'

She could endure it no longer – his physical abuse, his

financial and mental stranglehold and his suppression of her own individual self. She would, she could, she *must* be free of him! As he bent over her Tiffany stretched out an arm to grope desperately for the paper-knife on the bedside table. She knew it was there – she had used it to open Aunt Sarah's latest bulletin on the children. Her fingers closed on the knife, but she was conscious of no relief as she grasped the cold blade. Driven only by blind desperation, she gathered all her strength and thrust up the knife towards Randolph's chest.

But he sensed danger and moved so that she caught him merely a glancing blow on the arm. It was enough for the blood to spurt and for him to drop the cane, but not enough to prevent him grabbing her wrist and forcing it backwards, harder and harder until the awkward angle of her arm and the intensity of his grip compelled her to let the knife fall. Then he picked it up and held the point against her throat.

'Don't *ever* try anything like that again!'

And then his free hand was pulling up her nightgown, wrenching aside the belt of his robe and he was lying on top of her, thrusting into her with a violence which was unbearable.

However, she *had* to bear it. Not only was the knife still in his hand, but her female body was too weak to fight him. God, if she possessed a man's strength, *what* she would do to him! Tiffany adopted the only possible attitude. She closed her eyes, went limp and suffered the assault, uncertain which hurt most – the odious, disgusting intrusion of his body inside hers or the physical pain as his weight and repeated thrusts pushed her bruised back against the bed.

'Tomorrow,' she heard him say, 'you will go to Deverill and meet his terms. Because *I will not be beaten*!'

Next morning Tiffany was up and dressed before her maid entered the bedroom. Slowly and painfully she drew the garments over her bruised flesh, choosing a light gown with a high neck and long sleeves. Her body was stiff and aching, but she displayed no outward sign of discomfort or discomposure when she confronted Rafe Deverill.

'Congratulations on a very shrewd move,' she said lightly, kissing him on the cheek, 'and on a very dramatic moment.'

'Not quite up to your standards, I'm afraid.'

'You flatter me!'

'Not intentionally,' he said drily.

'Where did you get the money?'

'I told you last night that I was a gambler – but at the beginning of this week I did find myself a little short. Fortunately a lady of my acquaintance settled an old debt.'

Tiffany stared at him, wide-eyed. 'You mean that it was the money *I* paid for the jewellery which enabled you to raise the price?'

He nodded. 'I told you that you might regret your honesty.'

Tiffany threw back her head and laughed. Her amusement was genuine – even in the midst of her blackness and despair, the irony was irresistible.

'Oh well,' she said, 'it only means that the cost of the shares goes up by that amount. Because you do intend to let *me* have those shares, don't you, my darling? After all, you are seeking revenge on Matthew, not me.'

'The shares are yours – if you pay the full price.'

She hesitated for the first time. 'I had hoped that we could come to a private arrangement . . .'

'Private it must certainly be,' he agreed, 'because I will not deal with Randolph. You will give me the explanation now, then you will clear my name publicly and after that I will transfer the shares.'

'You must transfer the shares *first!*'

He shook his head sorrowfully. 'I do dislike saying this but . . . how do I know that I could trust you?'

'How do *I* know that I could trust *you*?'

Sitting down beside her on the sofa, he took her hand. 'Quite easily. You know how I feel about you . . . how every man feels about you. Would a man double-cross the woman he loves?'

She smiled but did not reply. He raised her hand to his lips and began covering the palm with kisses, but then the sleeve of her dress slid back to reveal the ugly abrasions on her wrist. Hurriedly Tiffany withdrew her hand and pulled down the sleeve, but she had noticed the expression on Rafe's face change from tenderness to thoughtfulness.

'So,' he continued, 'give me the explanation – now.'

'Surely there is something else which would benefit you more than that? Name anything – anything at all – anything but that!'

'No, Tiffany. The explanation.'

Never regret, never explain, never apologise . . . 'I have already said that I regret the incident. I am prepared to go a step further – I apologise, most sincerely. But I *cannot explain*!'

'Then it's no deal,' he said apologetically. 'Surely you can tell me! Surely you don't want me to accept Miranda's offer?'

'I will clear your name,' Tiffany said desperately. 'If we are seen together publicly here, that would be enough to tell the world that all is forgiven. I will even say that the whole affair was a misunderstanding!'

'That is not enough. I must know *why*!'

She was tortured by the prospect of returning to Randolph empty-handed, tormented by the vision of Rafe and Miranda . . . but she could *not* . . . It was not only that she could not bring herself to tell him the truth, but that if Randolph knew she had explained to Rafe he would give her no peace until she had told him, too . . . Tiffany shook her head.

'Then I must accept Miranda.'

Tiffany stood up. She had lost but she did not lose easily, not without one final flare of defiance. 'In that case I will never clear your name – *never*!'

Randolph was waiting for her.

'I went to see Anton,' he said. 'The atmosphere was distinctly cool and he says he needs time to consider his

463

position. I could almost believe that he no longer favours our partnership.'

The words were ordinary enough but his tone, expression and bearing conveyed the measure of the fury within him which must find an outlet or consume him completely.

'Did you meet Deverill's terms?' he asked softly.

'It was too late. He has already accepted Miranda's offer.'

Randolph stepped forward and hit her across the face, sending her reeling against the wall.

Tiffany closed her eyes, seeing only too clearly the hell of her future, seeing a vivid picture of Miranda's blonde beauty, of her little sister's golden childhood and of the sunshine in which she would walk . . .

'Damn Miranda,' she screamed suddenly. 'Damn her! I could bloody well kill her for what she has done to me!'

Randolph turned to face her. 'You know, my dear,' he said slowly, 'that might just be the best idea you have ever had.'

CHAPTER TWENTY-SEVEN

Tiffany leaned against the wall for support. The room was reeling and her mind was dull and confused. Randolph's eyes were fathomless black pools, drawing her deeper into their depths.

'It was not a serious suggestion ... merely an expression.'

'Obviously it must appear to be an accident – a very carefully contrived accident, because not only must the police be convinced of the circumstances but Anton and Deverill must be equally unsuspecting of foul play.'

'Not *murder* . . .!'

'You tried to kill me – why not her?'

She could not explain that her clumsy attempt on his life had been incited by heat, passion, desperation. It had not been cold . . . not premeditated.

'You concede that the removal of Miranda would clear our path to the South-West African fields and to the shares?' he asked.

She nodded.

'It would also clear your path to other things.' Randolph paused. 'I will strike a bargain with you. If we achieve our goal, I will not touch you again. Also, I would be prepared to turn a blind eye to your relationship with Deverill. Keep him in America if you like. In view of his position as the shareholder, I will be civil to him – what better way to clear his name than welcome him as an honoured guest in our home?'

Tiffany stared at him, still struggling feebly against the encroaching tentacles of evil which were coiling round her.

'You are concealing some secret over that alleged rape,' Randolph continued slowly. 'My final concession is this: it can remain your secret. I will ask no further questions.'

Randolph had never reneged on his word to her. She pressed a hand against her breast in an attempt to steady the violent thudding of her heart and to alleviate a strange burning sensation which seemed to emanate from the diamond. Murder – she flinched from it, recoiled from it . . . but even more powerful than the bargain he offered was the fear of what he would do to her if she demurred . . .

'I could not actually kill her myself.' She heard her voice from a long way off. She had wondered how far down the evil road Randolph would drag her – now she knew.

'We must do it alone. Accomplices are too dangerous and there is no time to find one.'

'I know a man who would help.' She was terrified of the two men talking alone, but it was the only course she could take.

Tiffany walked to a chair and sat down shakily. She gave Randolph an edited version of the story of Danie Steyn, but when she had finished she said sharply, 'But you must let me handle him! He trusts *me* and it is better that both of us should not be seen with him.'

'From what you say it seems likely that he killed Philip Bright, so he must be capable of killing again.' Randolph fell silent and to Tiffany's raw nerves it seemed an eternity until he spoke again. 'Very well, speak to him, but the plan must be ours. I will trust no one's brains but my own.'

'Miranda is deaf. The *place* is obvious.'

'Yes, but will she agree to go?'

'She must be placed in a position where she cannot possibly refuse.'

The following day was Sunday, but this time Tiffany was first at the old cemetery and it was she who caught Danie Steyn unawares as he watched Miranda lay fresh flowers on the graves.

'You are still here, Mr Steyn – and so is she.'

He was disconcerted by her appearance and looked at her warily.

'Do you lack the resolution or merely the opportunity?' she asked softly.

'I have been watching the house, but always there is a factor which prevents my entry. It was easier in the desert . . .'

'Yes, I am sure it was.' Tiffany's skin crawled. Was it only a week ago that he had approached her here? What she would give to turn back the clock and re-arrange events . . .

'I think I can help you.'

'Why?' But he was not surprised – nothing connected with Matthew surprised Danie.

'The quarrel between the Courts and the Brights goes much deeper than the fantasies you have created. My father taught you English, but he also taught Matthew Bright everything he knew about diamonds – and I do not have to tell you who filched the major portion of the fruits of that partnership.' She paused. 'You maintain that Matthew was responsible for the death of your sister. In 1907 my father committed suicide only hours after his first meeting with Matthew Bright in twenty years. I trust you would agree that my cause is as just as yours.'

Danie's emotions towards the Bright family were beyond logic, had grown beyond explanations and expanded beyond justification. His feud with Matthew was an intrinsic part of himself; he queried it no more than he questioned his possession of arms and legs.

'Maybe . . . but I do not need a partner,' he said.

'The plan I propose would appeal to a man of your sophistication, Mr Steyn. It possesses a certain roundness, a completeness, a poetic justice.' She smiled as she saw the quickening of interest. 'First, it is necessary to establish if Miranda knows you and would recognise you as an enemy.'

'I met her once – I saved her life when she was a child.'

'You *what!*'

'She fell over the edge of a steep kopje, so I climbed down and lifted her from the ledge.'

'Good God – what a deal of trouble you would have

467

saved if only you had let her fall!' Again Tiffany felt that it was not she who spoke, that another spirit present within her was uttering such cruel and callous words.

'She was only a child,' Danie said quietly. 'It is not likely she will recognise me and as your brother had not heard my name, I feel sure she will not know it either.'

Philip . . . what a difference it would have made if he could have benefited from Miranda's early death instead of the other way round! Swiftly Tiffany outlined the rough plan and Danie nodded in agreement.

'My husband will obtain the necessary information tomorrow morning. Meet me here by Alida's grave at two o'clock, when we can finalise arrangements.'

'Can you do it?' she asked at that next meeting, after she had shown him Randolph's meticulous drawings.

'Will the area be empty except for the official party?'

'Yes,' Tiffany answered confidently. 'No actual work will be going on – the whole affair will be a demonstration, "stage-managed" to give us the feel and atmosphere of the place.'

'Then it is merely a matter of ensuring that the girl is in the right place at the right time – alone.'

'That is my responsibility, but it will not be a problem. If I interpret her correctly, she will not be able to endure the demonstration for very long.'

'Where shall I meet you tomorrow?'

'At the offices of the Diamond Company. I have obtained permission for you to accompany us as my guest – "my father's old friend from the early days", "sentimental journey" and all that sort of thing! Incidentally,' and Tiffany glanced at his threadbare clothes, 'you must buy a new suit. Overalls will be provided, but it would be more convincing if you looked respectable. Here . . .' and she held out a bundle of banknotes.

'I do not need your money – even for a suit!'

Replacing the notes in her bag, Tiffany smiled placatingly. 'I was not offering you money for the dastardly deed, Mr Steyn. I do appreciate that it is a matter of principle, not profit.'

'I will fetch the suit now.' He stared at her, a sudden flare of disquiet in his eyes. 'I have been avoiding the town centre because I do not want to run into Deverill. He will not be in the party tomorrow, will he?'

'Of course not. I have issued the invitations and Captain Deverill is certainly not included among my guests.'

'It is just that nothing must go wrong – you see, she is the closest I can come to Matthew.'

'Oh, I think it goes further than that. I am reliably informed that Matthew adores her – and he has a bad heart. By killing Miranda, Mr Steyn, you stand an excellent chance of finishing him off at the same time!'

Helena had not been to Kimberley before and she looked around her with curiosity as she strolled across the market square, past the law courts, the post and telegraph offices and the Town Hall. But she also looked around cautiously, for although she was seeking Danie she did not wish him to observe her. She would have preferred to watch Miranda, who could not recognise her, but the residential area near the Bright house was exposed and, particularly in daylight, there was no point in guarding Miranda if Danie was not in town. No, they must locate Danie and then they would know if danger did exist. Her husband could not walk the streets of Kimberley during the day so Helena ventured out, concentrating her search on the town centre, praying that she saw him before he saw her.

'Still no luck,' she reported on Sunday evening. 'If I do not find him tomorrow, I may have to risk inquiring at the hotels.'

'Probably he is not here and this affair will turn out to be a wretched waste of time.'

But Helena looked at him and shook her head. She knew Danie better than anyone. He was here, she was sure of it.

'If he is here,' her husband continued, 'and he leaves without harming Miranda, then we leave too. We do not speak to anyone.'

Helena sat down on the arm of the chair and put her arms round him, holding his head against her breast. 'If that is what you want, then that is what we will do.'

But on Monday, at about noon, Helena did see a familiar figure in the street. Rafe Deverill was walking towards her. After her initial surprise, her immediate instinct was to turn away but instead she found herself approaching him, suddenly certain that he would be an ally.

'Helena! Good Lord, what are you doing here? Do you live in Kimberley?'

'No, in Cape Town.'

'But so do I.'

'Yes, I know. I have often seen you in Adderley Street – but I always crossed the road so that we should not meet.'

'Why on earth would you do that!'

'It is a very long story.'

'Have you time to tell it to me? Come to lunch – talk to me.'

She hesitated, wondering if her husband would worry if she did not return to the hotel for lunch but, deciding that he would not, agreed to the suggestion.

'Before I start,' she said when they reached the house, 'have you seen Danie?'

'No. Is he in Kimberley?'

'That is what I am trying to find out.' Helena grimaced, feeling that she could not explain further.

'I'm surprised you don't know his whereabouts.'

'I have not spoken to Danie for nearly six years. You see, I married an Englishman.'

He had noticed the ring on her finger. 'And in Danie's estimation, you are a traitor! Have you been happy, Helena?'

'Very happy, thank you.' She talked for a few minutes about the children who had stayed in Cape Town with the nanny and some neighbours, but was aware that he was watching her intently. 'My husband is with me, but he is not feeling well today,' she ended lamely.

'Is that it? Is that your *long* story? You have not explained why you avoided me in Adderley Street.'

'I cannot explain.'

He laughed harshly. 'Women dressing up as men – and feminine secrets which cannot be divulged. It is the story of my life!'

'It is not my secret, otherwise I would tell you.'

Rafe stared at her reflectively across the table. 'There is a quality about you which makes me believe that. I take comfort from one thing – you married an Englishman and therefore you must have forgotten the war.'

'Not forgotten. But I have forgiven.'

At that word his head jerked up and his eyes beseeched her to continue.

'You have not forgotten,' she said steadily. 'It is written all over your face. What is your trouble? Is it Paul?'

'Partly.'

'But you warned him – I heard you. It was the night when Danie shot the Zulu and Japie Malan. Paul was standing beside Frank and you, knowing that Frank had led you into the trap, said, "Having a nice day, Mr Whitney? Are you proud of your valuable contribution to the success of this operation? Do you still think it will make good copy for the New York press?" Frank did not reply but Paul defended him . . .'

'That was the trouble. Paul was so gentle, so kind . . . he was the only one who comforted Japie at the moment of death. If I had been forced to execute Danie, it would have been easier.'

'Paul told you that he was from the Cape and that made him a traitor, too. You said, "And yet you compound your invidious position by wearing a British uniform – don't you know that the penalty is death?" And Paul replied, "I can only hang once".'

'He didn't hang – he was shot. I tried to save him, Helena. I went to Graaff-Reinet and pleaded for clemency at the Standing Court Martial. But I failed. The commander-in-chief was displeased by my action and it

471

was no coincidence that I was ordered to carry out the execution. I protested, saying that I was a soldier and not an executioner. Then I was told that I would carry out my duties as directed by the General in accordance with my allegiance to the Crown and the law of the land.'

He twirled the stem of the wine glass, gazing into its depths. 'I won two concessions: first, that the execution should take place in private outside the town, on a hillside of Paul's choosing; and, secondly, that the *dominee* should be present. I mustered the entire regiment of Deverill's Horse and asked for five volunteers to form a firing party – and I am not ashamed to admit that I fought for composure as every man stepped forward, although they liked the task no more than I did.'

'Paul would have forgiven you.'

'Yes, he did. As I lifted the blindfold, he offered his forgiveness and even regretted that it was I who was burdened with the task. That helped ... but to look into a man's eyes at such a moment ... a man whom you respect for the sincerity of his beliefs ... to take a life like that and snuff it out ...!'

'You warned him,' Helena repeated. 'Paul was a man and knew the danger. He had a choice.'

'Marianna did not have a choice!'

The anguish in that cry tore at her heart, for Helena remembered her little golden-haired niece who had died in the concentration camp.

'Tell me,' she said quietly. 'about Marianna.'

'It was the day we parted, on our way to the Middelburg Camp ...'

' ... It was the day you *let me go*,' she emphasised.

Rafe made a deprecating gesture. 'Whatever ... The delivery of one Helena Grobler was not the only reason I was going there. I had received a message that a friend of mine, Lady Julia Fortescue, was visiting the camp as a member of the Ladies' Committee and wished to see me. The irony was that I could hardly wait! You would have to know Julia to understand. She is so beautiful, so impeccably groomed, so malicious, so . . . *predatory*! But I found her pleading for a cup of milk for a sick child – no, not pleading, *demanding*! Stamping her foot and demanding! She got that cup of milk and a group of horrified, guilty khaki-clad soldiers followed her and watched her give it to a little boy of about six years old; he was so emaciated that his eyes were enormous in his wasted face, his legs and arms spindly beyond belief, and his lips so thin that they would not meet but were pulled back in a grotesque grin over his face.

'Then she conducted us – she had not seen me at this juncture – to two small white coffins which were open, two tiny faces visible among the folds of the shrouds. "They photographed them this morning" she said, "to show to their fathers – if their fathers are still alive, that is." She walked to the hospital, berating men and their wars, and there she knelt by the bed of Marianna. "The child is dying," she said, "but I want to show you the manner of her death." She lifted the child and underneath was a bedpan, full and stinking and her hand trembled so violently that she spilled the contents over herself just at the same moment as Marianna vomited weakly down the front of Julia's dress. "The orderlies forget to remove the bedpans" Julia said, "or else they are too lazy to bother and the patients are far too ill to complain. The children have to lie in their own filth and their skin becomes raw . . .".

'The other men fled. But I could not leave – *I* had sent Marianna to her death. A large fly crawled down her nose, but she was too weak to brush it away . . . Marianna died, and I killed her . . . She was so like Miranda and perhaps that is partly why I love Miranda to distraction and am trying to win her, to help her . . . if she would let me – but she won't.'

Miranda . . . Helena was tempted to tell him the whole story, but loyalty to her husband prevented it. Instead she stayed with the subject of the war.

'Japie Malan's family were in the Middelburg Camp,' she

said slowly, 'because they had been driven off their land by Danie. It was for people like the Malans that the camps were established, but then the burnings began so the numbers of homeless families increased.'

'Surely you, as a Boer, cannot defend the burnings!'

'At first I could not, but as time went on I began to see both points of view. Take the burning of our farm, for example.' Rafe winced, but she went on, 'Danie, Frank and two other men were in the farmhouse, collecting supplies for the commando. They saw you coming and hung out a white flag. When your three troopers rode up to take the surrender, Danie, Frank and Susannah fired the shots which killed them. Susannah was very proud of that, but I was ashamed of my family who sullied the white flag of surrender. Anyway, as you know, Danie and the others escaped – and that is a point to which I will return in a moment.'

Silently Rafe waited for her to continue, the hope growing within him that Helena was his deliverance.

'Undoubtedly the British did make mistakes in the administration of the camps, but my people made their own contribution to the tragedies. Train-wrecking by commandos hindered delivery of supplies and there was a policy of non-cooperation by the women. They preferred their own remedies for illnesses – cow-dung baths for rheumatism, a coat of varnish on the chest for double pneumonia, roasted cat's fur on a child's chest as a cure for bronchitis. And many of those "lazy orderlies" were Boers.'

Rafe got up and walked to the window. Helena watched every flicker of emotion on his face as she spoke.

'It was Japie Malan who opened my eyes to the futility of that war,' she said. 'Marianna died, but who killed her? British or Boer? You or Danie? Because Danie *knew* you would burn the farm, yet he escaped and left his women and children to face that fate. I suppose we could describe the attitude of the *bittereinders* as a kind of emotional blackmail – they expected *you* to capitulate because of the sufferings of the women and children, but refused to do so themselves. They knew they could never win that war, but their pride was more important than lives.'

She followed him to the window and looked up into his face. 'Murder or suicide?' she said softly. 'We will never know. But if it is forgiveness you are seeking, Rafe, I can offer mine.'

He remembered how, on that ride through the Transvaal all those years ago, Helena had symbolised the Boer woman. And now he knew what he had sought, what it was that could lift the burden of guilt – the forgiveness of the Boer woman. He was aware that Susannah Steyn would never forgive him, but Helena's absolution had made him whole again. The earth-mother, the essence of Nature, had granted him re-birth. Silently Rafe put his arms around her and held her close.

She refused his offer to escort her back to the hotel because his tall figure would attract Danie's attention, and it was as she returned to the town centre that she caught a glimpse of a stocky man crossing the main street and disappearing into a men's outfitters. Was it Danie? Helena dawdled unobtrusively, inspecting shop windows, until he re-emerged carrying a large parcel. Her heart quickened when her suspicions were confirmed and she hurried after him at a safe distance until again he vanished, this time through the doorway of a small hotel. Helena ran all the way back to her own lodgings.

'Now do you believe me!'

'Yes,' said her husband. 'As a matter of fact, I do.'

'We must watch him twenty-four hours a day. You will have to help me – I cannot undertake it alone.'

'Of course I will help.' He laid a reassuring arm round her shoulders. 'He is unlikely to attack her in daylight. Miranda is deaf and darkness is Danie's ally. Rather than loiter outside the hotel, I will go to the house tonight and keep watch from the garden. You get some sleep – if nothing happens this evening you can return to the hotel in the morning.'

'Rafe Deverill would help. He says he is in love with Miranda.'

'Really?' He hesitated, but shook his head. 'Not yet. I do not want to meet anyone unless it is absolutely necessary.'

'If Danie does try to harm Miranda, how will we stop him?'

But until Danie made his move, there was no answer to that.

Miranda was trying to come to terms with the forthcoming ordeal.

'Mrs Court has requested a trip down the Mine,' Mr Pemberton had informed her, 'and has asked that you should be included in the party. I should point out that in the event of war the diamond mines would close and the condition of the Kimberley Mine is such that it might never re-open. This could be your last chance to see the rock face below ground and, with your fathers being such respected founders of the industry, it would be fitting for you and Mrs Court to view the Mine together.'

No, no, not under any circumstances . . . Rather walk into a snake pit, venture into a room crawling with spiders, climb the highest mountain with a sheer drop on all sides, than descend into the darkness and claustrophobia of that diamond mine. She remembered how as a child she had fallen down a cliff and balanced perilously on a narrow ledge until rescued by a stranger, but the incident had not left her with a fear of heights. It had not scarred her in any way – probably, Miranda thought, because she had been able to *see*.

But it was her duty to go down the Mine. Not only would she appear foolish and ungracious if she refused, but her churlishness would reflect badly on Matthew. She would never win the support and allegiance of the workforce in the diamond industry by displaying disinterest in conditions underground. A man would go, a hearing person would go, therefore she must go.

'Thank you,' she said, 'I shall be delighted to attend.'

The Company sent a carriage to collect her, but at the offices in Stockdale Street Miranda descended politely to greet the officials, the Courts and Anton Ellenberger. They were divided into two groups for the short journey to the Mine – Tiffany, Randolph and a short dark man who was evidently an old acquaintance of John Court's in one carriage; herself, Anton and Pauline in the other, both parties being accompanied by a Company representative. A small crowd had gathered to stare at the two diamond heiresses and there, standing slightly to one side, was Rafe Deverill. Suddenly, with all her heart, Miranda wished that he was coming with them, conscious of the security he exuded, aware that his mere presence beside her and the touch of his hand on hers would carry her through the ordeal ahead. Never had she been so tempted to push aside her pride, to admit that she was frightened, that she was deaf and needed help.

But at that moment Rafe was watching Tiffany, Randolph and the stranger and with a small sad sigh Miranda climbed into the carriage. Perhaps Anton would understand . . . Out of the corner of her eye she saw his hand brush accidentally against Pauline's and saw the glance which they exchanged. That hurt – realistically she could not expect him to like her, let alone love her, not after the way she had spoken to him, but all the same it hurt. Everyone seemed to have someone – everyone except her. How did this development affect the South-West African diamond deal? Miranda's mind could not assimilate the implications, not right now.

The carriages halted at the gates in the high barbed-wire fence which surrounded the Mine while armed guards checked the credentials of every visitor. Miranda could see other guards with dogs patrolling the perimeter fence and when the carriages moved forward again she did not share the general excitement but felt as if prison gates were closing behind her.

At the mine manager's office Miranda was ushered into a room where, with Tiffany and Pauline, she changed into a pair of overalls. They were to go underground first, then inspect the treatment, washing and sorting plants, and finally be escorted to the rim of the 'Big Hole' itself as the climax to the great day. Miranda did not speak but withdrew into herself, building a wall around her which she hoped would stave off the memories and behind which she could maintain a kind of calm.

The cage was waiting at the black, gaping hole of the shaft, beneath the towering head-gear. Rough benches had been placed in the cage and Miranda sat down, glancing up at the thick cables and big winding wheels overhead. The rest of the group crowded in, the mining officials wearing helmets which bore little brass lamps, then the doors of the cage closed and the descent began.

Miranda sat rigid as the cage plummeted down the vertical shaft, her eyes wide open and watching a blur of wet timbers. Occasionally a light flashed and she knew enough about the mine to realise this indicated they had passed another 'level'. Warm damp air was rushing past her face, the sensation in her stomach was sickening, but at last the rapid downward plunge was over and the cage shuddered to a halt in a well-lit chamber approximately half a mile below the surface. A tunnel stretched away to their right and on its track stood a line of small cars loaded with 'blueground'.

Normally this area would have been alive with activity, but now it was quiet because the Diamond Company were not taking any risks with their important guests. An official was explaining the principle of the 'chambering' method of mining which was in operation at Kimberley. From the vertical shaft, layers of horizontal tunnels were driven into the diamond pipe at 40-foot intervals. At each of these working levels, another series of tunnels was set out which opened into large chambers separated by 10-foot-wide pillars. The chambers were positioned so that they were under the pillars on the level above, thus allowing the pillars to collapse into the chambers beneath. The blocks of blueground mined from the chambers and caved from the pillars were transported in trucks through a network of loading tunnels and ore-passes to the main haulage tunnel from where it was hoisted to the surface.

At this point the light was sufficient to enable Miranda to lip-read but she was not listening anyway, having learned the rudiments of chambering from Matthew years ago. Her gaze would insist on wandering towards the tunnel down which they must walk and when they did set out along it, her heart began to thud uncomfortably. She could not remember its physical characteristics, but the atmosphere was hauntingly familiar – the oppressive, humid air, a stillness which she was sure was silence and that terrifying claustrophobic sensation of being completely cut off from the outside world.

This was a haulage tunnel, a thousand feet long through worthless rock, but then they reached the low narrow passage in the pipe itself with a single line of track on the ground, the roof and sides supported by dripping timbers which were covered in fungus. At several points the tunnel widened slightly and at each spot a loaded truck stood under a chute, or ore-pass, down which the rock was dumped from the sub-levels above. Now the only illumination was the yellow, flickering light cast by the lamps on the helmets of the mine officials – and it was not enough for Miranda to 'hear'. She was vaguely aware that everyone else – and Tiffany in particular – was asking questions and talking animatedly, but she was alone in a dark, silent world with only rising panic for company. She pushed back tendrils of wet hair from her perspiring forehead and stumbled, clutching at the nearest person for support without even realising that it was Tiffany and that the other woman glanced at her oddly.

The group stopped, Miranda cannoning into Tiffany again because she did not hear the instruction. They had reached the end of the drift and suddenly Miranda felt a strong blast of hot air and smelled the sharpness of acrid smoke which poured from a hole in the wall. Her numbed brain registered what had happened – a small charge of dynamite had been set off in the chamber above, all part of the 'demonstration' – but in the smoke and darkness Miranda could just make out the wooden ladder which led to that chamber. The 'pole-road', that ladder was called, and vaguely Miranda could remember being lifted up . . . She closed her eyes as the mine officials walked forward to ensure that all was safe above them and no one but Randolph and Tiffany noticed Danie Steyn slip away.

Miranda forced her shaking legs to carry her up the pole-road into the chamber. In just such a cavern as this she had sheltered with Laura during the Siege, huddled on a blanket, her deafness undiagnosed, waiting and afraid. But waiting for what? And afraid of what? She had been too young to comprehend the dangers of the Siege bombardment, but had realised that Uncle Nicholas had 'gone away' and he would not be coming back, and had sensed the tension in Laura. Now Miranda was desperate for sunshine, the open air and to see the sky above her, but what had she waited for then, when she was five years old? Standing motionless among the milling group which peered at the broken rubble in front of the solid rock face, realisation dawned. She had waited for Matthew. She had been afraid that he too would 'go away' and not come back, afraid that he would not fetch her from this terrible place, that she would stay here for ever and never see him again.

With a choking gasp, Miranda could bear it no longer. The darkness, the silence and the dank air were so heavy that the breath seemed to be squeezed out of her. She must get out of here! Blindly she turned, groping her way to the hole in the floor, sliding and scrambling down the pole-road. In the tunnel she did not pause for breath but set off at a stumbling run, intent only on reaching the lights in the chamber at the end of the main haulage tunnel and the cage which would lift her to the surface. In the inky blackness only the raised track along which the trucks were 'trammed' provided a guideline and she slowed to a walk, feeling the timbered wall with one hand. Suddenly

480

she let out a cry of pain and fright as she bumped into a solid object – but half-sobbed with relief as she realised it was only one of the heavy cars loaded with rock.

Miranda manoeuvred her way around it, but her footsteps were faltering. The initial impulse which had propelled her from the chamber was waning, leaving her heavy-legged, breathless and perspiring. She stopped, staring ahead into the blackness . . .

Behind her Danie crept from his hiding place by the chute. He fumbled for the brake on the truck, released it and began pushing the heavy vehicle down the slight incline. He pushed harder and faster until the truck gathered momentum and then pulled himself up, clinging to the rim, finding a flimsy foothold on a tiny platform at the back. The lurching load of metal and solid rock began to bear down on Miranda, clanking and rumbling along the track, but Danie knew that in the darkness she would not hear its approach . . .

She wanted to walk on but her legs refused to obey her. Then she thought that she saw a wavering light . . . three lights . . . growing larger by the second. Three figures were running towards her down the tunnel. As they came closer she could see that they were shouting at her, gesticulating wildly and somehow she managed to take one step forward. For a moment she thought the first man was Rafe, then her eyes rested on the face of the second man, weirdly illumined by the lamp in his miner's helmet . . . and Miranda froze. She was simply unable to move.

Philip!

Behind her motionless body the truck thundered on and Danie braced himself for the impact . . .

CHAPTER TWENTY-EIGHT

Tiffany was in hell, in an underworld of dark airless passages where the menacing shape of Randolph was that of Satan himself. Somehow she walked and talked, but again and again she glanced at Miranda. Once she steadied her sister as the girl stumbled and Tiffany felt her hand, cold and clammy with sweat.

It was in the chamber that the struggle reached a crescendo, that the sensation fermented within her and her nerves began to scream. Tiffany stood in the heart of the diamond mine . . . the mine from which she had been born . . . and knew that she had reached the end of the evil road. After this she would belong to Randolph for ever, because after this she was as vile as he. Her throat was constricted, strangulated, as if the golden chain which bore the diamond was drawing tighter and the heavy, cold burning of the gem was more noticeable. Miranda's face was a pale blur of terror in the shadows.

Then she saw Miranda flee.

In that moment Tiffany did not think of Matthew or even Miranda, not as an individual. She saw the fragile loveliness of Lady Anne; she saw Philip; and she saw the grave of Victoria. Two of her mother's children were dead and Tiffany knew that she could not kill the third. With a choking gasp she tugged at the gold chain, felt it break and the diamond fall. It was as if a weight had been lifted from her. Suddenly she could breathe and with a piercing cry of 'Miranda!', Tiffany ran after her sister.

The passage was dark, but to Tiffany it resounded and echoed with noise – footsteps and voices as her companions followed her, but above all the clanking and grinding of the truck. Desperately she called out to both Danie and Miranda and at every moment she expected to hear the scream which would announce that she was too late.

But the scream was her own as, ahead, she saw the truck and beyond it: Philip!

Opposite the offices of the Diamond Company, Helena had threaded her way through the crowd of onlookers and tugged urgently at Rafe's sleeve.

'*Where are they going?*'

'Down the mine.'

'We must stop them.' But the carriages were already moving away. 'Danie will try to kill Miranda.'

'That's crazy!'

'He killed Philip – or tried to.'

Rafe was bewildered, but through the confusion there surfaced the most overwhelming fear for Miranda as he visualised her vulnerability in those subterranean passages. 'He seems to be with Tiffany – we cannot make wild allegations against him. But neither can we stop him, because we shall not be allowed past the security gates at the Mine.'

'We *can* gain entry to the Mine. Come with me!'

She took him by the hand, pulling him towards the hotel where they burst into the room and Rafe stood in stunned silence, staring at Philip Bright who was undeniably back from the dead.

'There is only one way to get into the Mine – you must tell them who you are!' Helena begged.

For a moment Philip hesitated. 'I would have preferred to stay dead,' he murmured. 'I was much happier being dead, being anonymous, being *me*! But . . .' He tipped Helena's face up towards him. 'Promise me one thing – that no matter what happens, no matter what my father says or does, you will never leave me! Promise!'

'Of course.' The whisper of wistfulness in her tone betrayed her own fear that it would be *he* who left *her*.

'Never,' he said, reading her thoughts. 'Never!'

And then they were sprinting through the streets, up to the gates of the Mine where guards gaped at this ghost from the past and his insistence that he must see his sister *now*! But there were several men who had been in Kimberley during Philip's stay there and who could vouch for his identity. The gates swung open and, borrowing miners' helmets from a group of black workers at the pithead, they summoned the cage from below and were soon hurtling down the shaft.

Philip had been underground many times and led the way along the haulage tunnel confidently, but Rafe's superior strength and his greater anxiety for Miranda forced him past the younger man. It was a ghastly, nightmare journey – not knowing what to expect, their footsteps echoing eerily in the passage, dreading what they might find. Then there she was, a shadowy figure in the tunnel but her mane of blonde hair unmistakable, while from the other end of the tunnel came that rumbling, roaring noise.

'A haulage truck,' shouted Philip. 'It will hit her from behind!'

And all three were consumed with fear and helplessness as they realised that Miranda could not hear their warnings or the sound of approaching disaster.

Miranda's legs were still frozen but, wrenching her eyes from Philip, she managed to stretch out leaden arms towards Rafe who was closer to her. She just had time to register the desperation on his face before he lunged at her, knocking her bodily off the track against the wooden timbers lining the wall. A second later she was aware of a rush of air and the sensation of something moving past her, but its significance did not strike her. At that moment she believed she had seen a ghost and was aware only that Rafe had come to take her out of the Mine. And, wrapped in the enveloping security of his arms, she was also aware that he was holding her tightly, covering her hot dirty face with kisses which were entirely superfluous to any plans of revenge.

As Rafe flung himself at Miranda, Philip concentrated his attention on the truck. He had seen these cars hundreds of times and could visualise Danie's position. Sure enough, as the vehicle thundered past the beam from the lamp in Philip's helmet illuminated the figure which crouched monkey-like on the back of the truck. Philip jumped, his hands clinging to the coarse material of Danie's loose overall. Danie's body jerked back, but he maintained his hold on the rim while Philip's feet scraped awkwardly along the ground, braking the vehicle slightly but not sufficiently to stop it. Frantically Philip sought a foothold, finding it just as Danie wrenched free and began crawling forward over the piles of rock. Philip heaved himself up to follow and at that moment Danie turned his head.

The lamp in Philip's helmet cast an unearthly glow over the pale face beneath and Danie gazed in horror on the ghost of the man he had murdered in the desert of South-West Africa.

The shock caused Danie to lose his balance and, with a terrible cry, he fell, landing under the left front wheel of the car which shuddered and jolted as it struck him. The sickening thud was followed by a screech of metal and in a shower of sparks the container tipped sideways. A ton of blueground, with its hidden hoard of diamonds, emptied in a crushing cascade over the inert body.

As the truck began to tip Philip managed to jump free but then, for Helena's sake, he attacked the mound of rock, heaving with his hands and pushing with his feet until he bared Danie's head. One glance was enough: the skull was crushed and the neck broken. When Danie was a little boy, Matthew had saved him from suffocation in a claim at the old river diggings, but the diamondiferous earth of Kimberley had won him in the end.

Philip turned and walked back, emerging into the glow of light as the group from the chamber caught up with Tiffany. He was limping slightly and his face was scarred and bleeding, but at exactly the same moment Tiffany and Miranda realised that he was not a ghost . . . realised that Philip was alive. Tiffany swayed but willed herself to keep control. Miranda flung herself into her brother's arms.

He held her gently but then walked towards Helena. 'I am sorry.'

Helena's eyes filled with tears and she could think only of her widowed sister and of Danie's children. 'It was an accident,' she declared fiercely. 'Danie was trying to stop the truck.'

'Of course it was an accident,' said Randolph smoothly. 'Mr Steyn displayed great heroism.'

Both Philip and Rafe hesitated, but inexorably their eyes dwelled on the stiff, motionless figure of Tiffany . . . the possibilities were too awful to contemplate . . .

'Great heroism,' Philip agreed quietly.

There would always be those who doubted it, those who remembered Philip's headlong dash down the mine, but Danie Steyn was dead and it was much easier to let it lie. And in the turmoil of emotions, in the aftermath of Miranda's rescue, Danie's death and Philip's resurrection, no one noticed the fear on Tiffany's face or the venom in Randolph's eyes.

Philip did not notice because he was comforting Helena, whose head was buried against his chest.

'I wonder if your father will comprehend the irony,' she said in a muffled voice. 'Danie had many grudges against him, but the real foundation for that bitter hatred was the death of his sister. Danie truly believed that Matthew never cared for her, that to him Alida was a "simple Boer girl" who was not worthy of him. Now you, Philip, are married to just such a girl!'

He understood her dread of meeting his family and his arms folded around her protectively. 'We will go to London to see my father, but we shall return to South Africa,' he whispered. 'I promise.'

Anton and Pauline did not notice Tiffany because they were watching Miranda. Then, slowly, they turned their heads towards each other and smiled – mature, comfortable and very happy smiles. As Anton took hold of Pauline's hand the Afro-American Corporation was born, but neither of them was thinking about that aspect of their relationship.

Rafe did not notice Tiffany because he was taking Miranda out of the mine. He led her to the cage at the bottom of the shaft and they travelled to the surface alone, his arm gripping her as if to reassure himself that she was real, warm and alive. They stepped out into the open air and Miranda lifted her face to the sunshine but otherwise she seemed calm and it was Rafe's voice which shook.

'I nearly lost you. Please don't let me lose you again!'

'You only want me for revenge on my father.' But she was no longer so sure about that.

'It began as revenge, but I started loving you when we were aboard the *Corsair*. Everything I have done in Kimberley was aimed at helping you to defeat Tiffany and winning you as my wife.'

'Your "price" for the shares did not sound in the least like love,' she pointed out relentlessly.

'I told you to trust me! I had to state that "price" in front of everyone – it was important that Tiffany heard! And I could not warn you in advance because, my darling Miranda, you are essentially and wonderfully honest. I did not believe your acting skills would be sufficient to fool her! I thought that the prospect of our marriage would push Tiffany into giving me what I wanted.'

'I saw you with her,' Miranda said flatly. 'I am sure you love her more than me.'

'*No*! I pretended to love her because I intended to trick her into clearing my name so that I could marry you – she takes a man's devotion as her rightful due and was quite ready to believe that I loved her in spite of everything! If the plan did not work, I was hoping that you might marry me anyway.' He watched her steadily. 'I hoped that I might prise you away from your father.'

The choice was stark, agonising, but so very different from the other occasions on which it had been contemplated because now she trusted him and believed that he loved her. She saw that Rafe had been faced with a choice, too. He could have sided with Tiffany, let her have the shares and gone to New York. Instead he had chosen *her*, Miranda.

She smiled and let her kiss give him her answer.

'It looks as if Papa has regained one child but lost the other,' she said when he released her. 'Philip will go back to London in my place – and Papa will forgive me one day.'

'Fortunately for me, Helena followed Danie into the desert.'

Philip was speaking to Miranda alone in the drawing-room at the Bright house.

'When Danie did not return home, she became increasingly concerned that he might intend to do me harm, so she went to the hotel and was just in time to see Danie setting off, with me laid across the spare horse. She raced home, changed into her old commando clothes, packed the rest of her belongings, food and water and came after us.'

'How did she follow you through the fog?'

'The fog slowed her down, but luckily that night it lifted early. Even so, it was only the training Helena had been given during the war on commando which enabled her to find me – that, and her courage.'

'But if *she* could find you, why didn't the Germans succeed?'

'The alarm would not have been raised until well into the next day and by then the wind had dissipated the tracks. In the meantime Helena had helped me to a disused prospector's hut where we holed up while I recovered my strength.'

'But, Philip, why didn't you let us know you were safe?'

Philip leaned back in his chair and was a long time in answering. 'At first it was not my intention to "disappear",' he said slowly. 'The idea came to me gradually during those days with Helena. I fell in love with her. She is everything to me – wife, mother and friend – and gives me more love than any man has a right to expect. She would never fit into a London life and I could never leave her. But there were other reasons, too . . .' His voice trailed away.

'How long did you stay in the desert?'

'Nearly two weeks. We were lucky – just as we were running short of food and water, a couple of prospectors arrived at the hut. They agreed to sell us supplies, to provide me with a change of clothing and to keep their mouths shut in exchange for a considerable proportion of the contents of my wallet. Fortunately I was fairly flush – I was on Diamond Company expenses and was not stinting myself for cash! Then we realised that the next steamer for Cape Town would be due. We simply returned to Luderitzbucht and went aboard the boat – two unkempt, unsuccessful prospectors.'

Philip paused. 'Still I had not decided to disappear. I treated that return to the town as a kind of test. If someone had challenged me, I would have admitted my identity, but no one did. The longer I was with Helena, the more I knew I could not leave her. Besides, it was so wonderful to be free!'

'Free of what?'

'Of Papa and the diamonds, the weight of expectations and responsibilities. Oh, I was not bound to the business as others might be – as, possibly, you are. To my eternal discredit, I used the business to serve my own ends but even so, when I realised that I need not go back, the feeling of *lightness* was incredible.'

'I understand,' and Miranda recalled her own unexpected longing for freedom, experienced among the dunes at Luderitzbucht.

'I suppose I really made the decision when so much time had passed that I was presumed to be dead and the news would have made its impact. Would it surprise you to know that I believed that impact would not be very great?'

'Philip, Papa was *devastated* – he suffered a heart attack and his health has never been the same since!'

'Papa and I were never close,' Philip said slowly, 'although now I understand the reason why.'

'*We* were never close either.'

It was a strange sensation for brother and sister to be reunited, for the pattern of their lives was such that this was more akin to a first meeting. They were both slightly shy, reaching out tentatively to each other, but the path had been smoothed by Miranda's spontaneous joy at her first sight of him and a comforting warmth was spreading through them.

'Your cars,' Miranda said. 'You loved them so much!'

'That was the greatest sacrifice,' Philip admitted, 'but ironically my knowledge of cars, their manufacture and mechanisms enabled me to stay in South Africa and earn a living. I run a garage and taxi service in Cape Town.'

'A *garage* . . . oh, *Philip!*'

'Don't look so horrified. I enjoy it, honestly I do.'

His sincerity was touching and Miranda felt a pang of regret for all he had given up by coming to her aid. 'It was very good of you to sacrifice your privacy for my sake.'

'Thank Helena – I might not have been so public-spirited or put on such a display of brotherly love if she had not persuaded me.' A shadow passed over Philip's face as he spoke the words 'brotherly love', but it cleared again as he looked at Miranda. 'Helena is the reason why we must pretend it was an accident. How could she face her sister if the true circumstances were revealed?'

'Accusations would help no one.' But, like Philip, Miranda was wondering what those 'true circumstances' had been.

'Tell me about Tiffany Court and the diamonds,' Philip suggested.

He listened with growing astonishment to Miranda's story and when she had finished he chuckled. 'Good Lord, but you are much better at this sort of thing than I was!' Then his expression sobered. 'My gallant little sister – you go to all this trouble, only for me to come back to life and spoil your entire strategy.'

'I am sure that Papa would prefer to regain his eldest child rather than possess the South-West African diamonds.'

Philip's smile was crooked. 'I am by no means certain that Papa will consider it a fair exchange. Besides, he is not fully regaining his eldest child because I am not returning to London.'

'But you must! You must go back and take up your rightful place!'

'I could not take Helena to London and I will not leave her,' Philip repeated.

'But one of us must go back and I . . .'

'. . . want to marry the handsome Captain! That would not appear to be an insurmountable obstacle to doing your daughterly duty in the diamond market.'

'Philip, if I marry him Tiffany will not clear his name and therefore he cannot return to London,' Miranda reminded him patiently.

'I guarantee that Tiffany will clear his name if you offer her the South-West African diamond deal.'

Miranda stared at him in horror. 'But that is the reason I came here in the first place,' she wailed, clutching her head in frustration.

'Actually you have no option but to relinquish the diamonds. First, Anton Ellenberger would prefer a partnership with the Americans, particularly if he is interested in Pauline as you suggest. Secondly, if you marry Deverill you cannot carry out your threat to reveal the smuggling activities. However, it is my reappearance which is the crucial factor. You know, and I know, that I will never return to London but Anton would never be sure that I might not change my mind –that I might oust him from the position of heir apparent.'

'I must not fail Papa!'

'You are not failing him.' Philip seized her by both arms. 'Rafe Deverill's shares will safeguard Papa's position in the Diamond Company for the foreseeable future and I certainly do not call that *failing*! Besides, you deserve your own happiness.'

Miranda thought of Rafe and she nodded.

'Good girl! Now, you run along and tell Anton that you are withdrawing your offer of finance for the South-West fields.'

'Wouldn't it be better to speak to Tiffany first?'

'*I* shall speak to Tiffany.' Philip smiled. 'I rather want a word with her anyway.'

* * *

'Pauline, don't leave me!' Tiffany's hand clamped hard across her sister-in-law's arm. 'I don't want to be alone.'

'I have to go out but Randolph will sit with you.'

'*No* ... I am not feeling well and I want a woman's company.'

Pauline looked at Tiffany suspiciously but she was deathly pale and unusually agitated. 'Very well, but I do not intend to miss my appointment with Anton. I will ask your maid to take my place later on.'

They were in Tiffany's bedroom, Pauline sitting in the chair while Tiffany prowled restlessly round the room. Tiffany's head was swimming, throbbing, bursting ... but through the maze of confused emotions and images, one picture stood out more clearly than the rest – Randolph, downstairs in the study, waiting ...

'What are you holding in your hand?' Pauline asked.

Tiffany extended her palm in which the pear-shaped pendant gleamed. 'It fell off in the Mine, but fortunately it got caught up in my clothes ... the chain broke ...'

But the chains around her had not broken. What on earth was she going to *do*! She clutched the diamond, rubbing it frenziedly through her fingers.

Then Philip's note was delivered. To Tiffany, the prospect of an interview with Philip and of entering that house was nearly as formidable as the Mine had been to Miranda. She had avoided the Bright home throughout her stay in Kimberley because of its associations, but she was discovering yet again that the past could not be escaped. Philip ... what could she say to him? What attitude ought she to adopt? And then slowly her mind began to clear and in Philip's reappearance she divined a way of winning ... the crux of the matter was – *did he know*?

She managed to escape without meeting Randolph and when she alighted from the carriage in the driveway of the Bright home, walked briskly to the door. It was a house, only a house, and Philip was merely a man she had known. He was waiting in the drawing-room.

'Philip!' She swept towards him, arms outstretched. 'It is

492

too wonderful ... You gave me the most ghastly shock when you staggered out of that tunnel and the reality is only just beginning to sink in! If you knew the torment I suffered when I heard of your death! This is the happiest day of my life.'

'I can imagine.'

'And you are married! I do hope that you are happy – she has such a ... *kind* face.'

'Helena is very kind – among other things.'

'What I cannot understand,' Tiffany continued, settling down on a sofa, 'is why you pretended to be dead.'

'You, of all people, should understand the answer.' He smiled at her charmingly. 'My dislike of my father and sister was no secret to you.'

Sister – in the singular. Tiffany took heart. 'I expect Miranda has explained the situation. You do realise, of course, that you possess the means to best Matthew and Miranda once and for all?'

'Do I? How?'

He sat down beside her, smiling, around him that feckless air of irresponsibility and youth which she remembered so well from their days in Paris.

'You will be returning to London to take over Bright Diamonds instead of Miranda. But you never cared for the diamonds, Philip! You could go into secret partnership with me – with your voting rights in the Diamond Company and my own, I could run the diamond industry while you resume your interest in racing cars.'

'Good heavens, Tiffany, but you are always a step ahead of the game, aren't you?' he said admiringly.

'You always enjoyed hurting your father – do you remember Lemoine and his wretched formula for manufacturing diamonds?'

'Oh, I carried it a lot further than Lemoine.' Philip laughed easily. 'This entire situation over the South-West fields only arose because I fooled Papa into believing the finds were not important.'

'Marvellous,' exclaimed Tiffany in delight. 'With you

493

back in London, it will be child's play to topple the King of Diamonds from his throne. In fact, your reappearance may enable me to win the South-West African deal – Anton will not be interested in a Bright partnership *now*! And surely you can use your influence to prevent Miranda's marriage to Rafe Deverill?'

'There is just one difficulty.' Philip's tone was faintly apologetic. 'I am not returning to London.'

'Not . . .?' Tiffany did not believe her ears, but then she was appalled. He must be persuaded – but how far dare she go? 'You hate your father and sister. Why refuse this opportunity?'

'Because I don't hate them any longer. I have had six years in which to reflect on certain matters and, trite though this might sound, it is astonishing what changes in a man can be wrought by the love of a good woman.'

'But, Philip, what a team we would make.' Tiffany leaned close to him, laying a hand on his arm and gazing up at him out of those vivid violet eyes. 'Please do this for me – for the sake of what we once were to each other . . . for the sake of any future relationship we might share.'

'What sort of relationship did you have in mind?'

What indeed! At that moment Tiffany was so desperate that she felt capable of doing anything, being anything to anyone. Even so, there were limits . . . As she swayed closer to him, her only thought was to bluff her way through this in order to win his support.

'That depends on what feelings you have towards me after our last meeting,' she said softly. 'I am afraid that perhaps I was unkind.'

She lifted a hand to stroke his cheek, but Philip brushed it away with a gesture of violence and revulsion.

'It was fate which was unkind! Don't ever touch me like that again, *little sister*!'

Tiffany went white. 'Who told you?'

'Danie Steyn, before he tried to kill me.' Philip smiled grimly. 'Don't worry – I am not intending to ask any questions about Danie because I do not wish to know the

494

answers. What I do want to know is why you did not reveal the position to me at the time.'

'Your father wished to protect you from the truth. And I loved you so much that I tried to prevent you from suffering as I was suffering.'

'Like hell! The only truthful statement you ever made to me was when you said that you were interested in Bright Diamonds, not in me! You kept me in ignorance because you could not be bothered with me any more – I was no use to you! Now I am useful again, so you are reversing your tactics!'

'It wasn't like that at all! God, I *cannot* talk about it. Don't you understand – it never happened! You and I are not related.'

'Come with me.'

Philip seized hold of Tiffany and dragged her down the pasage to the other end of the house, where he threw open a door.

'This was our mother's bedroom. *That* is the very bed in which she slept. In all probability that is the bed in which you and I were conceived, albeit by different fathers, although,' and Philip smiled humourlessly, 'we cannot be sure about that.'

He was still holding her wrists. Tiffany tried to turn away, averting her eyes from the bed, wincing as his grasp aggravated the bruises on her flesh.

'Look at the bed, Tiffany! Face the facts – you have courage and you can do it! I remember how fascinated you were by your mysterious mother – don't you want to hear about her?'

'No.' Her lips felt strangely immobile and it was an effort to even whisper one word.

'There is little I could tell you about her anyway. That is one factor which you, I and Miranda have in common – none of us knew our mother. The difference between us lies in our relationships with our fathers. I hated mine, you despised yours but Miranda adores hers – you must clear Rafe Deverill's name of this ridiculous charge, allowing Miranda to marry him and so return to her father.'

'Never.' Tiffany fought to find a voice and some kind of mobility. 'Whatever the circumstances, there is not the slightest reason why I should do that. I still don't understand why you have changed your attitude towards her.'

'I was so intensely jealous of her! Neither of us had a mother, but she did have a father – a big, golden glorious god of a father who openly adored her while he ignored me. In some childish fashion I blamed Miranda for my exclusion, but of course it wasn't her fault. I look so like our mother that Matthew Bright must always have wondered . . . while who could doubt Miranda's parentage?'

'Very well, I'll buy that touching little tale but I am not persuaded to clear the aisle for Miranda's marriage to Rafe Deverill – and don't appeal to my submerged sense of sisterly love, because I still feel like an only child!'

'Clear that aisle and Miranda will withdraw her offer of finance for the South-West African fields – then Anton Ellenberger and the diamonds are all yours.'

Her heart leaped with a renaissance of hope – but the offer was not enough. 'I love him,' she said clearly. 'I want Rafe *and* the diamonds.'

Philip shook his head. 'Miranda is relinquishing the diamonds for love. You will relinquish love for the diamonds. Like it or not, neither of you can have both – and *you* will find that Rafe Deverill would not accept any other outcome.'

She closed her eyes in torment, consumed with longing for his face, his body and his touch – the only man who had ever been able to *bend* her to his will. 'Why shouldn't I find love – and keep it? Everyone else does. Everyone but me!'

'And yet you are the girl who has "everything" – beauty, wealth, status and power! You cannot have *everything*, Tiffany. No one can. No amount of money can buy that right. You and love do not go together – and I don't think you ever will!'

The sense of loss and loneliness was devastating because she knew that he was right. That utter trust and complete union of mind and body would never be hers. She would always be alone, deprived of communion with a husband, lover, brother or sister on whom she could rely or who would accept and love her for what she was. But sadness and self-pity were not Tiffany's style. Love or the diamonds? There was no choice. The diamonds were Tiffany and she was the diamonds: they were one, not merely bound together by history and heritage but immutable. Without her diamonds, Tiffany would wither and die, a fairy without a wand, a plant without sunshine or water, for the gems were the source of her magic and the foundation of her whole existence.

He thought she was hesitating. 'If you do not agree, I will tell . . . about us.'

'You couldn't . . . people saw us together at that party . . . you couldn't tell the whole world we are brother and sister!'

'Not the whole world, only Rafe – and Randolph.'

Again Philip grasped her wrist but this time he saw the bruises. Tiffany remembered the change in Rafe's expression at a similar moment and suddenly saw the bargain she must strike – the bargain which would neutralise Randolph and free her from threats.

'Where is Rafe?'

'In the dining-room with Helena.'

'Fetch him here.'

When Rafe entered the room, Tiffany met his stare steadily but then she held out her hand to Philip.

'The South-West African diamonds in exchange for Rafe Deverill's good name.' She turned to Rafe. 'If those fields live up to expectations, this could prove to be the most expensive wedding in history! I trust that you are flattered?'

'*Humbled* would be more accurate,' Rafe replied. 'However, Miranda will acquire the Diamond Company shares, so honours in the power struggle could be said to be even.'

'I am prepared to go further. Once I believed that I need "never regret, never explain, never apologise" ...' Tiffany looked at Philip and briefly they were transported to a sunny quadrangle in Oxford ... 'but I was wrong. I have already regretted my conduct towards you and I have apologised for it. Now I am prepared to explain – but I want to something in return.'

'I thought you might! Not the shares, Tiffany – it is too late for that.'

'I know.'

'Then what – or whose – powers of persuasion were greater than the shares?' Rafe queried in astonishment.

'My brother's,' and calmly Tiffany indicated Philip.

Rafe's face was ashen as he looked from one to the other.

'My mother was Lady Anne Bright, but I only found out after my father ...'

In one swift stride Rafe was beside her and holding her close. 'It's all right,' he murmured. 'I understand everything ... your father's suicide, Matthew, everything ... But why didn't you tell me?'

She pulled back slightly within his embrace and gazed up at him. 'Tell you that I was pregnant with my brother's child?'

Rafe's only reply was to pin her more tightly against his chest and to bury his face in her hair.

'Would you have married me if I had told you?' she whispered.

'Yes!'

'Did you love me?'

'*Yes!*' He would not hurt her by explaining that his love had been born of fascination, that it had been founded on physical attraction rather than affection. Perhaps a breath of that fascination still lingered, but he would not be ensnared by it again because now there was someone else whom he loved more.

'Tiffany.' It was Philip's voice, cracked and strange. 'I believed that you were mistaken about the baby. God help me, but I had forgotten . . . what happened to it?'

'I had a miscarriage.' Tiffany stepped back, taking up a position equidistant between the two men. 'Miscarriages are simple when Randolph is around.'

Slowly she lifted her arms and deliberately began to unbutton her gown. Wrenching off the bodice with a swift dramatic gesture she turned her back on the two men so that they received the full impact of the ugly bruises and abrasions. Then, very calmly and matter-of-factly, she described her wedding night with Randolph – and the manner of all the other nights thereafter. When she had finished, she whipped round and her tone changed.

'*Break him for me!* The acquisition of the South-West fields will give me mental superiority over him, but it needs a man's strength to break him physically. *Do it for me!*'

During their initial meeting in Kimberley, Rafe had told Tiffany that a man could forgive her anything because she was so beautiful. It had not been true and at that time he had not forgiven. Now both Rafe and Philip could look at her, and think of her, with compassion – moved, not by her beauty but by her spiritual scars and bodily bruises.

'He's mine,' said Rafe quietly. 'Tiffany, will he be alone at the house?'

'Except for the servants.'

'Give me half-an-hour. Then you can go home.' At the door Rafe paused. 'By the way,' he said. 'I have remembered where I saw that diamond pendant and how its previous owner described it. Do not wear it again.'

Rafe closed the door behind him but before leaving the house he spoke to Helena who, with a troubled look, handed him one of Danie's few possessions which Rafe concealed under his jacket.

In Anne's bedroom brother and sister were silent.

'I was just thinking about Oxford,' Philip said at last. 'We jumped off that bridge, Tiffany, but we did not soar into the air – we fell.'

Her face softened, then grew sad as she remembered

the gaiety, the happiness, the innocence of those days. 'You picked yourself up . . . you found Helena. You won the game of love in the end.'

'I hope I am wrong about you. I hope you find love, too.'

She pretended not to hear. 'You won't tell Miranda – about me being your sister – will you?'

'Of course not,' but he showed his surprise at her concern.

'Oh, don't worry,' Tiffany assured him with an attempt at her old careless scorn, 'I am not trying to protect her from the unpleasant facts of life. I am not overcome by sisterly affection – I haven't changed! I simply feel that the fewer people who know about it the better.'

Philip smiled. 'Don't ever change, little sister.' He kissed her gently on the cheek. 'Rafe was right about the diamond – throw it away.'

Rafe ascertained that only the Coloured servants were at the house and that they had retired to their separate quarters adjacent to the backyard. Entering the drawing-room, he noted with satisfaction that the curtains were drawn against the gathering darkness and that the door was stout. Coupled with the comparative seclusion of the house within its large garden, these factors should ensure the utmost privacy for the retribution he was intending to mete out.

'Ah, Deverill,' Randolph went so far as to smile and to offer his hand. 'I have been hoping that you and I could talk. I would like to come to an arrangement with you about those shares.'

Rafe ignored the greeting. Instead he slid his hand beneath his jacket and when it reappeared he was holding Danie's sjambok . . .

Randolph was still lying on the floor when Tiffany came home. She helped him up the stairs but after he had collapsed on the bed, she stood back and stared down at him.

'You broke my body, Randolph, but you never succeeded

500

in breaking my spirit,' she said, her voice hard and clear. 'I am delighted to see that, between us, Rafe Deverill and I broke both your body and your mind. I have not acquired the shares, but I have won the South-West African diamond deal and therefore I intend to hold you to the bargain which you made. Publicly I will continue to be your wife, but my private life is my own. If you touch me again, Rafe will pay you another visit – but I will play fair with you: I will tell him only the truth.'

She watched him without pity. 'Furthermore *I* will liaise with Anton over the diamonds and *I* will be his partner in continuing the fight for control of the industry. You will provide the finance as and when I require it. *Do you understand?*'

He lay inert, not answering.

'*Say it*, Randolph! Say that in future you are merely my banker. Say that I have won!'

'You have won,' he muttered into the pillow.

The sensation was not one of triumph but of peace . . . Swiftly Tiffany washed his back, applied the ointment which Helena had provided and then ran to her room to luxuriate in the inner calm which flowed through her. The diamond lay on the dressing-table where she had left it – coldly gleaming, its gold chain coiled like a snake, reminding her of Randolph. Hastily Tiffany pushed it into her bag – she would keep it, but she would not wear it again.

As usual she walked to the window, but now the Diamond City held no terrors for her – she had come to terms with her past and was herself again. She could confront the memory of her mother, her brother and sister and even make peace with the restless ghost of her father. She had been drawn into the heart of the diamond but its heat had purified, not destroyed her.

Now she was free of Randolph, free of the evil, but in complete freedom lay loneliness and it was with that loneliness and the future that she must fight now. Philip and Helena . . . Rafe and Miranda . . . Anton and Pauline . . .

Tiffany and – no one. But Tiffany did not flinch. She was the daughter of the diamonds and from them she drew her strength. Cold and hard but incomparably beautiful – like the diamond, this was the face which she showed to the world but, like the diamond, she would survive. There would be no shortage of men to be attracted by her fatal fascination – until she grew old.

Tiffany's face tautened at the very real anguish. But then, with a dawning sense of joy, she realised that she was not alone. There was love to be received – and given. Her children. She had not cared for them because they were Randolph's. Because they had been conceived in such misery, she had relegated them to obscurity. Now she dwelled on each little face in turn. Surely *one* of them must take after her!

Please, prayed Tiffany, let it be Benjamin!